THE ALIEN WITHIN—

He'd had so many names over the centuries, so many new identities that he could scarcely remember who he had originally been. Now his name was Daetrin, a name given by the alien conquerors of humankind, the Tyr.

Three hundred years had passed since the Tyr conquered the people of Earth as they had previously overcome numerous races throughout the galaxy. In their victory they had taken the very heart out of the human race, isolating the true individualists, the geniuses, all the people who represented the hopes, dreams, and discoveries of the future, and imprisoning them in dome colonies on planets hostile to human life. There the Tyr, a race which itself shared a unified gestalt mind, had left these gifted individuals to work on projects which would, the conquerors hoped, reveal all of human kind's secrets to them.

Yet Daetrin's secret was one no scientist had ever uncovered, for down through the years he had succeeding in burying it so well that he had even hidden his real nature from himself. But, taken into custody by the Tyr, there was no longer any place left for Daetrin to run, no new name and life for him to assume. Now he would at last be forced to confront the truth about himself—and if he failed, not just Daetrin but all humans would pay the price. . . .

**Novels by
C.S. FRIEDMAN
available from DAW Books**

IN CONQUEST BORN
THE MADNESS SEASON

THE
MADNESS
SEASON

C.S. FRIEDMAN

DAW BOOKS, INC.
DONALD A. WOLLHEIM, PUBLISHER

375 Hudson Street, New York, NY 10014

First Printing, October 1990
1 2 3 4 5 6 7 8 9
PRINTED IN THE U.S.A.

To the memory of Herbert Friedman,
1931–1988
Writer, Editor, Teacher, Square Dancer Extraordinaire,
and beloved father.

PART ONE:
EXILE

EARTH

When the series of images ended I reached out and flicked the projector switch off, sending the last holo spiraling down into darkness. That was when the years suddenly seemed to bleed one into another; past, present, and future so lacking in definition that for a moment I couldn't tell them apart. I couldn't remember how many names I had worn, or where in my life each one belonged. It was the darkness that triggered it, the absolute darkness of a moonless night, on a campus that had long since let its street lights fall into disrepair. Total blackness, within the classroom and without. And in that utter darkness, silence. Not the relative quiet of a handful of students who had other things to do, other places to be—that would have been reassuringly familiar, a restless silence filled with guarded whispers, the rustling of papers and tapes and clothing, and the barely audible shifting of flesh as one student stretched, another yawned, a third dared to turn off his recorder. But instead, nothing. An absolute silence, the sound of a dozen people who felt more comfortable with stillness than with life. An inhuman silence that had existed on Earth for so long that I could no longer count its years, or separate them in my mind.

A touch to the control plate brought up the lights, an unhealthy green to illuminate empty, purposeless faces. For a moment I was angry, and dared to hate the creatures that had brought us to this pass. But anger of any kind is a dangerous emotion, it eats at the nerves and eventually makes you careless. And care-

9

lessness was a luxury my kind couldn't afford. I took a deep breath to steady myself, and recited once more the litany of my post-Conquest existence: *You swore you would accept this. You have no other choice.*

"That's all for now," I announced. Bodies stirred, moving from lethargy to life without obvious reluctance. Why did they come here? What did they want? A comfortable ritual, perhaps, or a taste of the past. It didn't really matter. They came, and I taught them; the ritual exchange permitted us some illusion of purpose, so I encouraged it. At heart it was just another lie, another emptiness . . . but we must hold on to some illusions, and so they learned—or played at learning—and the ancient ritual held sway. *Education.* Without free thought, it had no meaning; without creativity, it had no purpose. Why did they bother? Why did I?

They filed out in silence, leaving me alone in the classroom, with only the projector for company. After a moment I turned its motor off. The pockets were in need of repair—had been, for some time now—and one of them jammed when I tried to open it to retrieve my holodisks. Just my luck. I pried back the lip to get the disk out, careful not to do any permanent damage. There were fewer and fewer people to repair such things, in the world that the Tyr had left us, and I hadn't worked in holography for . . . well, for long enough. I couldn't have repaired it.

At last I had them all, three matched disks in their labeled cases. ART OF THE SUBJUGATION, PARTS I, II, AND III. Holding them brought to mind images from our most recent lesson: an earthenware vase supported by ten identical figures, a sculpture of steel and plastic which was tedious in its symmetry, a computer generated light-sculpture too balanced to be dynamic. Disk after disk, holo after holo, the message of the Tyr was driven home: *In unity there is strength. Diversity breeds chaos.*

We've learned our lesson well, I thought grimly.

My image, seen in the shimmer of a plastic window,

against the backdrop of the Georgian night: A middle-aged man, well-schooled, retiring, an instructor of night courses in post-Conquest art in one of Northamerica's few remaining colleges. My age had always been difficult to judge (thirty-five? forty? perhaps a well-preserved fifty?) and now a touch of gray at my temples, artificial, added to the uncertainty. Hair a sandy color, not unappealing, body neither fat nor scrawny, but comfortably lean. Once I was considered tall, as the standards of men were measured, then average in height as man's fortune increased, now tall again by comparison. But not excessively so. *Averageness* was important, it was my only armor against discovery, and so I was carefully, studiously, *average*. What nature had not provided, cosmetics and tailoring did; my appearance should inspire no curiosity in either human or Tyr.

But when I looked at my reflection for more than a moment, when I allowed myself to *see* . . . ah, then the ghosts were visible. Visions arose from the past, images displaced from their natural timeframe, wrapped around my current visage like a mask. What I had been. The things I had failed to do. What I had chosen to accept. If it was true that the coward died a thousand deaths, then I died each time I looked at my reflection. And so I chose the easiest course: to look quickly and then turn away, lest I render myself incapable of maintaining that lie which was now a necessity of my life.

Mine was the last of the late-night classes, so I locked the building when I left. Coarse steel bars had been placed on the windows, ironic in light of the fact that theft was almost nonexistent. What was the point of accumulating wealth in a world that no longer had purpose? But what little thievery there was, was focused upon the few items of real value—such as sophisticated electronic equipment in working order—so I took the time to check the double doors when I was done, pulling hard at the two of them until I was sure that the ancient locks had caught.

Don't dwell on the past, I cautioned myself, but the
ghosts of memory were legion tonight. The spirit of
Earth had been destroyed, but what right did I have to
complain? The current world was no threat to me or
my kind; how often had I dreamed of that coming to
pass? What price would I not have paid, in my youth,
to purchase a lifetime of peace?

Not this, a voice whispered, couched in the cadence
of recall. *Never this . . .*

Memories: I felt them rising within me, tried not to
let them overwhelm me. Of all my unique weaknesses,
this was the worst—and the only one which I had not,
to some degree, mastered. My brain seemed loath to
distinguish between sleeping and waking, and plagued
my conscious hours with images that rightly belonged
in dreams. Pre-Conquest science had verified the
problem—electromagnetic patterns occurred in my
waking brain which should only appear during sleep—
but had offered no salvation; my own experiments, so
successful in every other regard, had failed to provide
a solution. All I could do was concentrate on the present, observe my surroundings—

And stop suddenly, alert. Something was wrong; I
knew it, but couldn't say how. I listened: no sound
existed that was any more or less than ordinary. I
looked, deep into the shadows of night, my vision adequate even in the relative darkness: I saw no shapes
or movement which any such night might not contain.
The air? I tested it: warm Georgian moisture, rich with
the smells of autumn.

And then the breeze shifted direction and suddenly
there was something else—horrible, stifling—that
awakened memories so intense that they struck like a
fist straight into my gullet, driving the breath from my
body in a sudden eruption of fear.

I ran. *Tried* to run. The past overlapped the present,
raining images down upon me as I dodged that hated
smell. But a hand shot out of darkness and grabbed
me by the lapel of my coat as I passed the corner of
the building. I was swung back, into the brickwork,

and there was blinding pain—but that wasn't what terrified me most. It was that smell: a thick, acrid odor, the stink of Earth's defeat.

Honn-Tyr.

There were six of them—at least, six that I could see—and they were all heavily armed. Taller than I. was by a handswidth, with black and mottled green and a dozen other shades of almost-black covering their bodies in random splotches. Identical, all of them, with an absoluteness that bore chilling witness to the unity of their nature. Six armed extensions of a single will, gathered about me like the fingers of a hand, poised to crush. And willing to crush, should I dare to defy them. But there was nothing to be gained by fighting them, I knew that from past experience. No hope of escape, on any terms. I knew that all too well.

The dark claws reached for me and I held myself still, despite my revulsion—submitted to the odor of their presence as they searched my person, tearing my clothing, discarding their finds—and tried to forget that once, in the distant past, I had dared to fight them. My current identity was passive, nonthreatening; I couldn't afford to lose control of that.

At last they finished. My disks were scattered, and I saw a clawed foot crush one of them as my assailant shifted his weight. My other possessions were scattered as well, lost in the thick summer grass. And the pills on which I depended—my God, if *those* were lost—

"Daetrin Ungashak To-Alym Haal."

My current name, a Tyrran number; voiced in the harsh, staccato whisper of the Honn-Tyr, it was a comment as well as a question.

I barely managed to get my voice to work. "What do you—"

"Tiye Kuolqa," my assailant announced. *It is the Will.* "You will come with us."

I considered running. Better in some ways to be shot down now, than to face whatever fate the Tyr might have in store for me. But there was, as always, a shadow of cowardice resident within me—and it was

this that won out, whispering, *Maybe they don't know
the truth yet. Maybe there's some other reason they
want you. Maybe, if you cooperate, you can talk your
way out of this.* And so, clinging to that fragile hope,
I moved away from the wall—slowly, making no sudden movements—and allowed them to drive me south-
ward, toward the bulk of the campus.

How had they found me out? Certainly not through
any outstanding display of intelligence on my part, or
any hint of a rebellious nature. Those things would
have stood out like armor-spikes on a human, and I
had been careful to suppress them. Since the time of
the Conquest, the Tyr had devoted itself to redesigning
the human species. From the wholesale slaughter that
took place during the Subjugation, to the current system of transportation, it had worked at weeding out
all seeds of possible insurrection, removing men of
intelligence and spirit from Earth's gene pool in the
hope of rendering the human race more tractable. And
it appeared that it had succeeded—not for genetic reasons, I suspected, so much as for psychological ones.
When any act of unusual intelligence might cause a
man to be taken from his native planet, geniuses were
loath to advertise their talents. As for whether the spirit
of revolution was hereditary, and could thus be erad-
icated, or whether it was latent in all human beings,
ready to spark to life in response to the proper stimulus . . . we hardly understood that ourselves, in the
years before the Tyr came. How could our conqueror
have gained any better comprehension?

By those standards, I should never have been discovered. With my averageness wrapped around me like
a concealing cloak, I should have slipped through the
years unnoticed, unharassed. So what had gone
wrong? Why had they taken me? Where had I miscal-
culated?

"There." A captor nudged me with the point of his
weapon. We had reached the concrete bridge that had
once spanned a football stadium. They herded me toward the bleacher stairs, and flanked me like hunting

dogs, driving me downward. Toward the nightmare vision of a Subjugated landscape. Transports had blasted the field clear of grass long ago, fusing the sod and clay beneath into a black, glasslike expanse. The surface was marked with a spiderweb of thin, jagged fissures, some barely discernible and others, which time and ice had widened, of treacherous proportion. The bleachers themselves had long since rotted away, leaving metal struts sticking out of the concrete like twisted knives, red with decay. And in the center of it all—

A skimship. But not the common, suborbital type which the Tyr often used to patrol its conquered territory. This was clearly an intership shuttle, capable of maneuvering in the dark, empty spaces which lay between the planets.

My heart nearly stopped as I realized what that meant. I had always known that I might be taken from Earth—that was a possibility we all lived with, subject as we were to the whims of our alien oppressor—but I had stored that knowledge in the dark back rooms of my mind, where such things can be deliberately forgotten. The thought that it might happen *here* and *now* was suddenly more than I could handle. My body froze in mid-step, and I felt incapable of moving it.

No one who leaves the Earth may ever return. That was the conqueror's law; it had never, to my knowledge, been compromised. To lose Earth now meant losing it forever.

What was the ancient belief, about leaving one's native soil?

They forced me across the cracked-glass surface, using the points of their weapons to drive me forward, and into the skimship. There, in the dimly lit interior, one of them shoved me down into an aircushioned plastichair. Not designed for human comfort. Another strapped me into it. With sharp, alien gestures they made their intentions clear. *Say nothing. Be still. We will kill you if you try to defy us.* Trembling, I sank back into the cold plastic seat, wondering where in this conquered universe they were taking me. In the skimship's claustrophobic confines the smell of Honn-Tyr was nigh on overwhelming, awakening memories that were better off forgotten. I fought them for a while, hanging on to the present moment as though it were a lifeline—but then, as the skimship blasted the field yet again, and lifted me from my native soil for the first and probably the last time, despair possessed me utterly and I slid coldly down into memory.

Icy. Mud. Beneath my fingers, nearly frozen. Pain.

I drag myself a few inches farther. And farther. Important to get away. The ship is burning, might explode when fire hits a fuel line. I dig my few functional fingers down into the frozen soil an inch, two inches, then hit slick ice beneath; my hands scrape back without finding traction. No farther, then. I lack the strength. I pray that this is far enough. All about me are greater and lesser bonfires, spurting orange and blue sparks into ebony blackness. Pyres of the dead, monuments to our last warplanes' final effort. I lower my head in sorrow and exhaustion; tears, like bits of ice, work their way slowly down my cheek.

We failed, my world, we failed!

I try to draw one arm up under me, to raise myself up a bit more, but sudden darting pain from forearm to elbow causes me to drop, gasping, to the ground. Broken, then—or worse. That sleeve of my uniform is still intact, preventing me from assessing the extent of the damage. As for my other arm . . . that, and the whole left side of my body, is a mess of blood and burns. Am I dying? Is this what dying is?

Forgive me, my world. I did what I could. Forgive me that it wasn't enough.

Footsteps. I feel them first, through the ground against my face: alien footsteps, a horribly familiar rhythm. Tyr. The sharp odor of burning flesh assails my nostrils, and I hear the sizzle of their weaponry as it turns our few survivors into so much roasted meat. Killing those remaining few who risked all for freedom, and lost; cleansing the Earth of its rebellious vermin, once and for all.

Including me.

The footsteps approach. I become aware of the sound of my breathing, the blood welling up from one lacerated lung. I don't dare cough, though the sticky fluid fills my mouth and throat, and threatens to choke me. Because then the enemy will know that I live. Death in battle is one thing, and I had been willing to risk it in order to save my people. But to be fried to a crisp by the Tyr's cleanup crew offers neither honor nor purpose, and so I lie as still as possible upon the cold, wet earth, and try to minimize the roar of my breathing. My body is cold, my blood pressure minimal, my heartbeat slow under the best circumstances. Perhaps they will mistake me for one of the dead; if so, it won't be the first time it's happened.

The footsteps surround me, stop. A scanner purrs—then silence. They have no need to speak, these alien warriors, but share each thought and purpose in a kind of species unity that we, being individuals, can't begin to comprehend. But apparently they have judged me dead—or dying— for they move on wordlessly, seeking out another wounded shadow to receive their judgment.

I live.

That thought takes form slowly, almost reluctantly. I live. Will live. *Want* to live, despite all that the Subjugation will mean. My powers of healing are excellent. I know; if I can survive the next few hours—and find shelter before daylight—I have no doubt that I can and will recover. Surely I can learn to play the game that the Subjugation will require, and adapt to the Tyrran will.

To survive. Is there shame in that? I did what I could to save my planet, risked giving up a longer life than most men even dream of. But that war is over now. And the need to survive is a powerful master. A jealous god. Is there such defeat, in bowing to his dictates?

I wonder what time of night is passing. How long the battle lasted, after I was struck down. The darkness of the sky is absolute, shrouded in cloudcover, unblemished by the light of day. Except . . . I catch sight of a narrow band of gray rising almost lazily from the far horizon, and I feel my body shiver in pain and fear as I know myself far from any hope of shelter.

I look around, desperately. There is no possible source of shade, not anywhere. And even if there were, I couldn't get to it. Not like this. I must face this first day unprotected, offer up my blood to that vicious, hungry star. . . .

I did fly into sunlight during battle, I remind myself, although the heavily tinted glass surrounding my cockpit protected me from the worst of the radiation. I seem to remember that the sun can't kill me. Burn me, yes, in the course of a long day's passage, and evoke a defensive reaction from my radiation-sensitive body . . . but it cannot, in and of itself, kill. I remember that, somehow. And try to believe it, as the sun rises into the heavens.

I feel it first on my outstretched hand.

. . . *my outstretched hand* . . .

Burning away the timefugue

. . . *sunlight?* . . .

Into a fever that is even more painful: reality.

I looked down at my hand, at the beam of light that had fallen across it, and moved it out of harm's way. It took me a moment to remember where I was, and then a moment longer to realize what was happening.

We were flying through a sunlit sky. Which meant that we hadn't left Earth yet. I felt a lurch of wild hope within me; was it possible we weren't going to leave Earth after all? I leaned toward the window, and dared to look outside. A calculated risk. I saw a field of brilliant white, seething with deadly radiation; it was too painful to look at for more than a moment, and as I fell back into my seat, shielding my eyes against the glare, I could feel the fever starting. *My own fault,* I thought. *I should have stayed in shadow.*

"Be still," a captor warned. A little late.

"Where are we going?" I didn't expect to be answered. But to my surprise, the Honn-Tyr seated opposite me spoke. "Ustralya. The Kuolqa-Angdatwa."

Through the thickness of his accent I made out the remnants of a familiar label: Australia. A land bathed in sunlight, when much of Northamerica was clothed in darkness. That prompted a new, and much more immediate fear: did they know the advantage it gave them, to bring me here?

No, I told myself. They couldn't possibly. The Tyr's ruling palace—the Kuolqa-Angdatwa—had been erected amidst the ruins of Sydney as a gesture of contempt for the soldiers Down Under, who had persisted in fighting long after the rest of us had accepted defeat. That's all. That it was daylight there so soon after I was taken prisoner was . . . well, bad luck. Damned rotten luck, to be blunt about it. But that was the extent of it. Surely.

We dove through the cloudcover with a suddenness that left my stomach in midair. Damned Tyrran pilots! I was only just recovering from that when we pulled into a tight circling pattern. I glanced out the window again, squinting against the glare. There: the Kuolqa-Angdatwa. Like a fat, stone spider it sprawled amidst the ruins, embracing fragments of buildings and pavement as though it had itself wreaked the destruction. A few bits of buildings remained intact, impressive in their decay. Like the Romans, who left the last wall of the Temple standing as a witness to the magnitude of what they had destroyed, the angdatwa squatted amidst the ruins of free Earth smugly, contentedly, its very position saying: *Here. See what I have conquered. See what I chose to destroy.*

I closed my eyes, but it was long before the vision faded.

We landed.

There was a jerk as the skimship was secured—to what, I couldn't say—and then the portal split open, and sunlight poured in. They unstrapped me and made me stand, and instinctively I reached into my pockets—for my sunshades, my cap, my thin cotton gloves, the dozen and one bits of clothing that would protect me from the worst of the radiation—but those things had been left on the ground in Northamerica, where my captors had strewn them. Along with my pills.

"Move!" I was struck in the back, forced to march forward. It was a choice between the sunlight and their wrath, and of the two, Tyr anger was infinitely more lethal. *Daylight can't kill me,* I told myself, reassured by my memories. I stepped into the puddle of light—like walking into fire, but I managed it—and then, reluctantly, stepped outside.

—And I had remembered the particulars, what it would do to me and why, but Christ, I had forgotten the *pain!* It hit me in the face like a panful of burning coals, and air like molten glass seared my throat and lungs with every breath I took. I could feel the fever rising as my body fought to adapt, and I was glad that my temperature had begun to rise on board the skimship; I could never have faced this, cold.

Had it hurt this much on that terrible day when I lay cold and bleeding on an exposed plain of mud? Or had I simply lived such a sheltered life since then that what little tolerance I'd once possessed had faded away? I could hardly move, couldn't see at all, just staggered forward when the point of a Tyrran weapon forced me to go: one step, two, then countless numbers—an endless march through the center of Hell, with my body racing to adapt. Blood pressure up, heartbeat pounding, all my vital signals readjusting themselves according to those terrible, alien instructions. Eyes readjusting as I walked. I could almost see my sur-

roundings by the time the thrust of a Tyrran handgun
sent me through a doorway, and into shadow.

I leaned, gasping, against the nearest wall. A big
risk, not to keep moving; angering the Honn-Tyr meant
courting death. But my body was in shock from adapting so quickly; I needed a minute to pull myself together.

To my surprise, no one disturbed me. I waited for
the fever to peak—it did so quickly—and then tested
my vision. A little blurry, but functional. The fever
would make terrible demands later, exacting a high
price for its alteration of my metabolism, but for now
it accomplished what it had to. My senses were altered, my muscles stiff with pain, my heartbeat pounding within my ears so loudly that it took effort to
concentrate on anything outside my body—but there
was a purpose in all of that, and I knew it would be
futile to fight it.

Honn-Tyr surrounded me: a dozen in all, waiting
with the stillness that was the hallmark of their species. And another creature, far more imposing. A Tyr,
I guessed, but not a Honn; taller and more deadly,
with sharp spikes jutting out of its bony plates at stra-
tegic points, and gleaming scales on its torso that made
its belly resemble that of a snake. Where the Honn
had two small arms, nearly vestigial, tucked beneath
their major pair, this creature had four taut, sinewy
limbs wrapped in serviceable muscle; where the Honn
had a minimal tail that served them merely for balance, this creature had a length of chiton and muscle
that culminated in a spear point of sharpened bone.
All of it guarded by bone plates, and bits of bone
plates, that slid over each other as it shifted its weight
in much the same way that medieval armor had done,
steel glistening on steel as it moved.

Raayat-Tyr, I guessed. One of the Unstable Ones. I
had heard rumors of them—all violent—but what unnerved me more than anything else was the extent of
its natural armory. The Honn were the Tyr's bred warrior caste, and they weren't nearly so well protected.

What role had nature cast this creature in, that it made its martial cousins look so vulnerable by comparison?

"You are ready?" it asked me. Its voice was more fluid than that of its shorter companions, its palate kinder to English phonemes. Surprised by that question, I nodded and pushed myself away from the wall, into the pooling of sunlight. There was no pain this time, aside from that of the fever itself. I had adapted, at last.

It indicated a somewhat circular tunnel, then entered. I followed. Six of the Honn-Tyr accompanied us. The interior of the angdatwa was dimly lit, and formed more like a rabbit warren than anything else. Twisting tunnels cut their way through miles of mortared stone, floors and walls varying in height, width, and texture as we progressed. Halls twisted chaotically, turned back on themselves, and merged by the dozens in intersections that were no more than rough-ceilinged caverns. There was no regular pattern that I could discern, nor any doors or other openings that might lead to adjoining chambers. Small patches of something green—perhaps some alien life-form, or maybe a synthetic substance—glowed dully, stuck to the ceiling at random intervals to serve as a minimal light source. The resulting semidarkness was soothing, but powerless to blunt the edge of my fever. It was too late for that, now; I was fully adapted, and must wait for the proper biochemical triggers before the process could begin to reverse itself.

Just when I began to think that we were going to walk this labyrinth forever, my guide halted. The Unstable One touched the wall to one side of him, just so and in a certain spot. I saw no markings. Barely a moment after he had touched the wall it split open, and a doorway the width of a Honn-Tyr was revealed.

He gestured toward the opening and I passed through, expecting him to follow. But the door closed behind me, so quickly that I felt it brush my clothes as I entered the chamber it guarded. I found myself in a dark room, almost but not entirely without light.

While I waited nervously for my eyes to adjust, I strained my other senses to the utmost, anxious to gain some clue as to where I was, or what was going to happen to me. My capacity for smell had been damaged by the sunlight, but it was still acute enough to tell me that I was not alone. One, maybe two different kinds of creatures were with me; as for just how many of them there were, I couldn't tell. The first smell was somewhat familiar, and might be Tyr; mercifully, the fever had made me much less sensitive to its fetid power. As for the second . . .

I sought its source, as my eyes adjusted to the darkness, and slowly a crouching form became distinct from the shadows surrounding it. Like a panther it was, but an alien version—more graceful in line than its Earth-brethren, more upright in posture, with taloned claws resting where a panther's shoulders would be; vestigial wings, which nature had redesigned for combat. Even if I had not known what it was, I would have recognized it as a hunting animal; its form, its poise, its aura of tense alertness, everything about it identified it as a predator of formidable capacity. A potentially deadly adversary, whose dark-colored fur was marked with random daggers of black, whose muscles rippled purposefully beneath the sheen of its alien coat. Its eyes fixed upon mine and held me, entranced, until I forced myself to look away.

A hraas. I had never seen one before, and hoped never to again. The sight of it awakened fear within me on a level so deep within, so primitive, that I could do nothing to control it. I could read its purpose—its only purpose—in the set of its body. It wanted to hunt. It wanted, more than anything, to hunt *me*. I wondered what contract the Tyr might have made with its bloodthirsty intelligence that managed to keep it under control; it did not strike me as a creature that would tame easily.

As if sensing my fear, it rose slightly from where it sat; delicately curved talons flexed beneath the smooth fur of its paws as those gleaming eyes fixed on me, colorless jewels set in a bed of ebony velvet; its hunger was palpable. Only when the figure beside it rasped a command did it settle, with a growl, into its former stance. Tensely. Waiting.

Seated beside it, behind a human-style desk, was a Tyr. But neither Raayat nor Honn, in size or in structure. If the Raayat's body had expressed the promise of power, this Tyr was its culmination. Fully armored, it appeared more insectoid than mammalian, and its spikes and crests were strongly, powerfully built. I realized, with a sinking sensation, just what it was—and *who*.

"Kuol-Tyr," I said, bowing. The Governor of Earth—or its Tyrran equivalent. Progenitor of Earth's conquerors, and the focus of the planet's alien consciousness. Too important a personage to be bothered with unimportant business; that it had seen fit to meet with me personally boded ill for my eventual fate.

Its two forward eyes, surrounded by rings of sharpened bone, were fixed upon me. When it spoke its voice was steady, not the hesitant whisper of the Honn-Tyr, but the full-bodied, rasping voice of Earth's ruler.

"You have come willingly."

"Tiye Kuolqa," I answered, and bowed my head submissively.

"I have questions. You will answer."

A tightness was growing inside me. I managed to nod.

"You will answer completely, and without deception. Your alternative is death. There is no other. Do you understand?"

"Yes," I whispered. Aware that if the Kuol were to permit it, the hraas could have me rendered down to a pile of tasty tidbits before I could move to defend myself. My eyes were adjusted to the darkness now, and as the Kuol-Tyr stood I could see just how tall it truly was. And how well armed. If the hraas didn't do me in, the Kuol-Tyr certainly could.

"How long have you lived on this planet?" it demanded.

The abruptness of the question threw me. Not that I was surprised to hear it. I had dreamed those very words in a thousand nightmares, said in every place and by every being that the Conquest might make possible. But in each of those dreams, no matter what my response, I failed to save myself. I died. Because there was no magic number that the Tyr would find acceptable; if it knew to ask the question, it knew too much already for any answer to be safe.

What could I say? To be caught in a lie would mean certain execution; to tell them the whole truth, if they didn't already know it, might be even more damning. I dared not speak.

"How old are you?" it asked me—and then, coldly, "How many Earth-years have you seen? Answer me, if you value your life!"

Silence was not the most intelligent refuge. But it was, I discovered, the best that I could manage.

It snorted; whether in disgust or anger, I couldn't tell. At last it drew a flat, printed sheet from out of its baldric and held it out to me. After a moment I stepped forward and took it. A list was inscribed on it, in bold black print. Seventeen items. I squinted, trying to read in the darkness.

They were names. My names. Identities I had designed, entering them into the census net in order to disguise my longevity. *All* of them. If there had been even a single one missing, or one here that was not mine . . . but there wasn't. I'd been found out.

"You are not human," it told me.

I looked up from the list, to meet its hooded gaze. "That's not true," I said quietly.

"You read the names. Yes?"

I brandished the paper. "These are human names, Tyrran numbers, in accordance with census custom—"

"The names are human, yes. And the writing is in your current tongue. But the light by which you read it"—and here it paused, letting the full impact of its words hit home—"is not sufficient for human vision. It is according to that, that I judge you."

Christ. Trapped by the spectrum. It would do no
good to explain that my vision was unusually sensitive,
capable of interpreting frequencies that were normally
invisible to the human eye, because that would lead to
other questions. Ones which I dared not answer. I
cursed myself for being careless, even as I felt a cold
knot of dread forming in my stomach. How could I
have dreamed this confrontation so many times, without ever finding a means of controlling it?

"Your age, now." Its voice was unforgiving; if I
stalled too long, it would kill me for my silence. "Tell
me."

I stiffened, and did some quick arithmetic. Even a
lie was damning, but the truth would be far worse.
"Five centuries."

"Your birth-year?"

"Eighteen forty-two," I answered, quickly enough
to make it sound genuine. "Old calendar. Pre-
Conquest."

It stared at me for a long, long while, and then said
coldly, "Humans do not live for five centuries."

"Some do," I retorted.

"How many?"

The fever was numbing my brain, making it hard to
answer. Hard to evaluate all the truths and half-truths
at my disposal, or choose an appropriate lie. If I told
the Kuol that there were no others, and it had found
others, I was in serious trouble. But if I told it how
many there really might be, might it not see fit to hunt
them down?

"I can only answer for my family," I replied. A
hedge.

"All alive?"

"All dead," I answered, and I repressed a shudder
as the memories came. "All killed, except for me."
And not pleasantly.

"You do not die naturally?"

"We age, but more slowly." A half-lie. "If one
were to live long enough, one would die of natural
causes."

Or so I was told. Who really knows? How many of us lasted that long?

"So. There are others alive today? Like yourself?"

Were there? I had known some once, many years ago, and my father had spoken of a time when we had gathered freely in the great cities, honored by our short-lived brethren for the knowledge that we accumulated. That was before my time, and long before the Tyr came. I had kept a low profile since the Conquest, haunted by the specter of the census computers; if others of my kind were still in existence, they had probably done the same. I could not say with certainty that any others had survived the Subjugation. But if they had . . . the wrong words now, I realized, would betray them. Would make them even more vulnerable.

"None that I know of," I told it. Hoping that would be enough.

It considered, its upper eyes fixed on me. "So," it said at last. "You witnessed the Conquest."

There it was. The one vital question, to which all others were mere introduction. It hung in the air between us like a knife, poised to strike. But I had already committed myself.

"Yes," I whispered.

"You fought us."

Did they know that I had volunteered, in those last desperate hours? Did the Tyr-memory recall a man of my features passing for dead on the plain of our defeat? It was dangerous ground, and I trod it carefully. "We all fought you, in our ways. I'm no hero," I added miserably. That, at least, was the truth.

"But you remember."

"Some of it." I shut my eyes, and fought back images from the past. "I would rather forget."

For a long time there was silence.

"You understand," it said at last. "Human or nothuman, Subjugated or enemy: you must be removed from Earth."

I had known it was coming—but it was still a shock,

to hear the words. *Removed from Earth. Forever.* The
fear was a hard knot inside me. Panic was seeping in.

"I accepted the Subjugation—" I began.

"You *remember.* That is enough. The purpose of the
Subjugation was to cleanse Earth of its past. You *are*
that past. To leave you here is to fail in our purpose."

"I would never interfere—"

"Of your seventeen lives since the Conquest, ten
have been spent as a teacher. The pattern is obvious.
When left to your own devices, you choose to direct
the thoughts of the young—you, who are a contami-
nation in the heart of our dominance. And you promise not to interfere? It is too late, Daetrin Ungashak
To-Alym Haal. The decision was made, centuries ago.
By you."

I felt the last of my fragile hopes leaving me, and
in their absence the first burning touch of hunger. My
fevered body would demand sustenance, frequently
and in quantity. Without my pills I was helpless to
sustain it.

"I want only to survive," I whispered. A question.

Again the silence. For the first time it occurred to
me that the Kuol-Tyr was not merely thinking; it was
submerged in the greater Tyr-consciousness, drawing
on that species' wealth of experience in order to evaluate the present circumstances. "Cooperate," it said
at last.

"How?"

"Explain. Your longevity. You claim to be human,
but humans are mortal; death is a constant of human
biology. Life expectancy can be increased, but only
within limits. You defy those limits, yet claim to be
human. Explain."

I had spent a lifetime struggling to understand just
that, and had only partial answers, hopelessly insuffi-
cient. Nevertheless, I offered them. "Our bodies are
the same, but they function at a different pace." Mnemonic overlap: I could hear my father's voice speaking
to me, as though he were in the room. *Understand the
differences in how we function, and you will compre-*

hend the differences in our souls. . . . "Colder overall, with a slower metabolism—"

"The human brain would not function well under
the circumstances you describe."

I laughed bitterly, remembering the timefugue. "It
doesn't."

The Kuol paused, shifting its attention to some other
focus. To the source of analytic machinery, it seemed,
for it then told me "Untrue. Or at least, unsupported.
Your internal temperature is 96.8 Farenheit, practically human-normal. Your other bodily processes are
similarly near-standard. Such minute differences could
not possibly affect the process of cell regeneration. I
reject your explanation."

It's the fever! I thought, but I dared not say anything. It was the greatest weakness of my kind, and it
could be used to drive us out of hiding. To explain the
fever to the Tyr would be to betray those few others
who might have survived the Subjugation. Though it
meant my life, I couldn't do it.

"Arrangements are now made," it told me. "You
will be sent to Kygattra, where you will be studied."

The words escaped me before I could stop them.
"Not killed?"

"The Honn-Tyr kill. Always. The Kuol-Tyr can
choose. I choose. The Tyr will understand you, not-
human that you are, and determine if you are a threat
to our stability." It paused, studying me. "You will
never come back here, Daetrin Ungashak To-Alym
Haal. That is the Will."

I shut my eyes in pain. The Earth cried out to me
and I reached for it within my heart, only to have its
essence slip through my fingers. The emptiness, the
fear . . . could I survive, once removed from my native world? Tradition said no.

"I understand," I whispered.

"There is a longship passing this system soon; you
will be taken to it immediately. You will not be mal-
treated," it assured me, "as long as you cooperate."

Suddenly I remembered the pills, and my hunger. "I have needs—" I began.

"They will be seen to."

I hesitated. "There are problems . . ."

The Kuol-Tyr waited.

How much should I say, and how should I word it? *An enzymatic deficiency, requiring certain formulae . . .* If they knew my background then they were aware of the years I had spent in biochemical research, and it was reasonable. But what if that led to other questions? *You were born in the nineteenth century. What did you do for sustenance then, before the molecular structure of proteins was understood?*

With a sinking feeling, I knew I dared not speak. Even if it meant my death—and it would—that was preferable to the death of all my kind. The others might never have analyzed their weakness; they might still be surviving the old way. If so, they were vulnerable; I dared not betray them.

"Nothing," I said miserably. *We die slowly, my kind.* "Nothing you can help me with."

My world, I will come back to you. Somehow.

The Kuol nodded, and the door behind me split open. Two Honn guards grabbed me by the arms; I did not resist them, in words or in action. The time for that was long past.

Wordlessly, in perfect unity, they led me into exile.

SHIAN

She loved to fly. She loved the challenge of it. Flying, and also gliding. She loved the play of her wings against the wind, the effort that it took to locate thermals—or in this case, magnetic currents—and master them. Which meant that she *should* have been enjoying herself on Shian, where flying was both difficult and dangerous. Only she wasn't. Not any more. The first thrill of creating a new body had passed long ago, and the challenge of the windworld had been muted by time into dull familiarity. And now she was worried, too, which was all the more disturbing because it was a new concept to her, and she didn't know how to deal with it.

Where were the Saudar?

Why hadn't they come for her?

What if they never came?

She unfurled a sail and caught hold of an updraft, angling herself into the upperwinds. Her sith-fibers were curled tightly against her torso, their magnetic sensitivity tuned to a minimum. All about her stormwinds raged, gusts of methane that could (and often did) rend a traveler's sails to shreds; navigating them was a challenge, and she should have enjoyed it. But her growing certainty that something had gone wrong made travel into no more than a bleak necessity.

If I'm left here . . . She didn't complete the thought. Surely she wouldn't be abandoned! As a Marra, she was too valuable to be left behind; the Saudar were experienced in dealing with her kind, and would understand the risk which that entailed. Already her most distant memories were beginning to slip away from her, in a process as predictable as it was inexorable. Eventually, the past she had shared with the Saudar would be lost to her forever. She would have no knowledge of the services she had rendered, as First Contact Ambassador for the Saudar Unity, or of that special symbiosis which enabled the Marra to interact with embodied life-forms. If she stayed on Shian long enough, she might even lose sight of what she was, and consider herself a native. Identity was no more than a function of memory, after all—and Marra memory was notoriously fallible.

It was vitally important to get home before that happened.

She extended a sith-fiber and touched the nearest magnetic Current. It was stronger than usual, and its force nearly yanked the fiber out of its socket. Good. The planet's magnetism should remain constant; that it had suddenly intensified, hinted at outside interference. Which meant . . .

She stifled that hope, as she had previously stifled her concern. Yes, it *might* mean that a science probe had entered the gas giant's magnetosphere, with enough ferrous matter in its structure to intensify the Currents. Then again, it might not. More likely, the magnetic disturbance was simply the result of some natural phenomenon she didn't yet comprehend. For if it was a ship—if the Saudar had returned to Shian— wouldn't they have contacted her by now?

There was only one way to find out. Carefully, she extended her sith and affixed them to the Current. With sudden force she was thrust northward, her velocity so great that a gust of wind, crossing her path, tore her mainsail at the base. She didn't bother to repair it. The flesh was inconsequential, save that it anchored her in time and allowed her to interact with her physical environment. Mere winds couldn't hurt a Marra. But there was a real danger in that the natives, unable to navigate the newly violent Currents, had abandoned this area; there would be no living creatures between

her and her goal, and therefore no way for her to re-
new her strength.

She settled for sealing her wound so that she lost no
more ichor, and fastened her wounded sail tight against
her torso. If her calculations were correct, she wouldn't
need to use her sails again; the Current she was riding
should take her directly to the disturbance's source.
And then, if there was indeed a ship—

One thing at a time! She wrapped her sails around
her small, compact body until the winds could strike
at nothing but her torso; that way, she would not be
swept from her mount. Soon—if her calculations were
correct—she would reach the heart of the disturbance.
Soon she would know if she was truly rescued.

And if not?

* * *

*Remembering: A Saudar scientist rich in dignity,
pacing as he spoke; with even, measured steps he
crossed in front of the projected image of Shian. His
eyes were wide, a sure sign of excitement, and his
kangi were erect, alert. Briefly he outlined his plan to
search for life in previously unexplored environments.*

"The Marra are vital to this project," he concluded. *"Their ability to locate and identify new biotypes is what makes such an undertaking possible."*

*She let the scent of her amusement fill the room.
"You need a volunteer?"*

"Your masters told me you might be interested."

"I might be." She indicated the projection. *"Tell
me more. Why this particular planet?"*

"Coloration." He stepped to the control console
and made a few adjustments. The first projection of
Shian gave way to another, slightly different, and then
to still more: a chronological series. Bands of red and
green moved across the gas giant's surface like ripples
across an immense ocean. "The seasonal pattern implies a biological origin. If so—"*

She understood, and was intrigued by the prospect.

Those worlds which had no life of their own, the Saudar colonized; where life already existed, Marra such as herself were sent to establish First Contact. But that happened only on free-water worlds: small, solid planets huddling close about their mother suns. What of the other planets, the gas-worlds, whose environments were so hostile that no one save a Marra could even think of exploring them? If life did indeed exist in such places, it would open up whole new vistas of exploration—and she would be at the forefront of discovery, her Marra skills challenged as never before.

The Saudar body which she wore reflected her thoughts, mottling with the pink of comprehension. "I understand."

His eyes, kangi, earchannels, all focused upon her. "Then you'll go?" he asked.

"I'll go." But she added, "A few conditions."

She would design her own body. She would choose her own support personnel. The Saudar must trust her Marra instinct, and let her choose the initial landing site. And they must make absolutely certain that no matter what happened, they would be there on time to pick her up. Because only if there was life on Shian would she be able to get home on her own—and then not in the proper timeframe, and not without killing.

A thousand points remained to be negotiated, but the most important one had been settled; she would go.

His kangi curled, a Saudar smile. "I believe you will enjoy it."

* * *

It was a ship, all right.

But it wasn't Saudar.

She flew around it, close enough that her undersail brushed its pitted surface. There were no markings to indicate its planet of origin, and its substructures were unfamiliar to her; she had no inkling of its purpose.

She was sure that it wasn't Saudar, though—she knew the masters' ship-plans, from probe to scout, and this didn't match any pattern of theirs. Was it alien, then? Truly alien?

An ambassador's excitement burned to fresh life within her, the hunger to learn, to communicate. What was this new civilization, which the Saudar had brought under their wing? What technology had the newcomers brought with them, what formulae and gadgets and systems of thought to enrich the whole of the Unity? What did they look like, and (most important of all) how did they interact?

Careful, Marra, she chided herself. *You're not out of the methane yet.*

First things first: she had to make contact. Skimming the strange ship's surface, she soon found its sensory access. Visual; that was good. She positioned herself in front of the proper screens and began to fly the Yull configuration. Three circles clockwise, three opposing. Then two. Then one. A simple pattern, designed to communicate species identity despite boundaries of form and language. Regardless of what type of body she was in, she could manage to display that sequence; the ship's inhabitants would respond with another Yull pattern, whose form would dictate the mode for future communication.

She waited. A long, long time.

There was no response.

She repeated the pattern, then waited again. Still no response. Perhaps she had mistaken the nature of the outlet . . . but no, an analysis of its form according to the generalities of ship design indicated that some sort of visual scanner was focused outward at this point.

So what was the problem? No alien ship could have reached this planet without first passing through Unity space; wouldn't the Saudar have told them about her kind, about *her,* before giving them free access to this star system? And while it might be true that there was no one watching the ship's exterior right now, through this outlet, it was inconceivable that a computer wouldn't have been assigned to the post, capable of recognizing meaningful data patterns and alerting the occupants when something important occurred.

Something was wrong. Very wrong. Could she have been away from the Saudar long enough that things had . . . *changed*, somehow? She was poor at judging time—all her people were—but it seemed to her that if she had been gone that long she would have noticed it. Noticed the erosion of her memory, the gradual loss of her memory, the gradual loss of her Saudar identity. Wouldn't she?

A strange emotion began to stir within her—dark, foreboding, non-Marra. As uncomfortable *something* that left in its wake uncomfortable questions, which she couldn't begin to answer. It seemed to have no constructive purpose, this emotion, but arose from the depths of her psyche like a drug-induced dream—or so it seemed to her, though she had never personally experienced either drugs or dreams.

Was it fear? she wondered suddenly. Was this what fear was? The possibility filled her with wonder. Fear was a survival-emotion, induced by biochemical changes—a primitive function of the brain, designed to ensure the body's survival. What was fear doing in a Marra psyche?

Uneasy, she settled to the ship's surface and affixed herself there. She needed to get inside the strange vessel, to see for herself what was going on. To make contact with whoever—or *what*ever—had come here. This ship might well be her only ticket home; she dared not fail to communicate.

She studied its surface, circling it nearly three times before she found what she wanted: the seal of an air lock. She settled down beside it, a tiny figure huddled against the great ship's surface. Stormwinds whipped by her, nearly tearing her free from her mount, but she was loath to adjust her body while still in the windsea. Then, when a sudden gust ripped the sith-fibers from forebody, she compromised by exchanging her undersail for suction cups, and affixed herself anew. It was a small Change—but it cost her in strength, which she could not easily replenish.

She waited.

A minor eternity passed, in which the air lock did not open. But she had faith in her reasoning, and remained where she was. Eventually, her patience was rewarded. A small metallic probe, self-propelled, approached the air lock and hovered there. In an instant she was upon it, clasped tightly to its surface. She damaged a sail in the process, but what did that matter now? She couldn't afford to waste her time making a patchwork repair of her flesh, when within minutes she might have to transform the whole of it. Drops of her ichor sprayed the wind as slowly, smoothly, the air lock opened. Darkness gleamed within. She shifted slightly so that the walls of the passageway wouldn't crush her, held tight as the probe approached its mothership, and then—

—she was inside. She let herself fall to the floor of the air lock as its outer portal was resealed, and prepared herself for Changing. Precision was required, or much of her strength would be wasted. She braced herself as Shian's atmosphere was pumped from the chamber—

—which left her in vacuum, and killed her current flesh. By an effort of will she managed to keep her body's cells intact, despite the drop in pressure. So far, so good. New air was beginning to seep in—an oxygen mixture!—and then suddenly the inner portal opened and the lock was filled with it, sweet nitrogen and oxygen and just a hint of carbon dioxide. She was home, by the Unity—she was home! The inhabitants of this ship might not be Saudar, but they were biochemical relatives. The worst was over.

She rearranged her mass into a comfortable and versatile form—four-legged, with bifocal vision and an acute sense of smell—and crept toward the lip of the airlock. Carefully. Discreetly. If there were live beings out there, she wanted to observe them without being noticed; it would give her time to plan.

She slipped her head around the ridge of the portal, and observed her saviors' form.

Tall they were, and brightly marked. They stood at least as high as the Saudar, and although it was hard to make an accurate comparison without the latter being present, she thought they might have been taller. They had jointed, symmetrical bodies, apparently mammalian. Though once the species might have crawled on all fours—all sixes?—now it stood upright, not unlike the Saudar, and one pair of upper arms had shrunk to a vestigial shadow of their original form. Long legs flanked the lower torso, which ended in a short jointed tail. At the tip of that . . . she waited for a clear view of it, got one at last. A daggerlike bone, apparently hollow. Poisonous? That, and the sharpened talons on both hands and feet, implied a warrior identity.

She watched them unload canisters from within the probe; they were too intent upon their work to notice her. Oddly enough they were neither clothed nor painted, and wore no ornaments save one simple baldric on which various tools—and possibly weapons—were hung. Most unusual. One thing which all advanced intelligences had in common was a love of ornamentation; whether they donned cloth or metal, or painted or deformed their own bodies, all advanced life-forms tried to improve upon nature by dictating some change in their basic appearance. Indeed, that was one of the simplest ways to recognize a full-reasoning intelligence. Perhaps these beings weren't permitted adornment while on duty. . . .

But social criticism could wait. She needed an impression of one of these creatures' organizing centers—the brain, or its equivalent—in order to unlock its secrets. There seemed to be little difference between the objects of her scrutiny, so she chose one at random and took an impression of its mass . . . Yes, that would do. A bizarre structure, but it had all the necessary components. All she needed now was privacy, and she could get to work.

She had it soon enough. When they were done un-
loading the canisters—some four dozen of those, she
estimated—they left, sealing the far wall behind them
so that no hint of a doorway or control panel remained.

Gingerly she stepped over the airlock threshold,
testing the floor with her paw. She half expected there
to be some kind of alarm, but nothing responded to
her presence. Nothing that she could observe, that was.

Good enough, she thought. *To work.*

She altered her mass until she had a fair approxi-
mation of the alien's brain to work with, then proceeded to analyze it. Once, in the distant past, such a
process had been both time consuming and difficult,
requiring endless study to produce the most basic of
language-analogs; now, after eons of practice, she approached the job with a speed and efficiency that would
have stunned her former selves.

She located the fight-or-flight response center and
stimulated it. Neural associations fell into place like
dominoes, each one branching out into a thousand
more, and a thousand more again; she mapped their
purpose with practiced Marra efficiency. Here was the
primitive brain, pure in its survival instinct, unclut-
tered by intellect or emotion. Here was the motor response center, and there that vast expanse of cells
whose only job was to keep the body breathing, the
heart beating, and the metabolism functioning at
something akin to an efficient rate. It was familiar territory, and she mapped it quickly. On to the language
complex, which should be—

She stopped, uncertain.

Here?

All the neural patterns pointed to it, the associations
demanded it, and yet . . . it wasn't there. Did that
mean these creatures had no language?—no language
at *all?* It seemed incredible. True, in all the time she
had watched them she hadn't observed them communicating, but any number of things might be responsible for that. To not be *able* to communicate . . . how

was that possible? She checked the olfactory centers, followed each smell-association to its destination, and found nothing that looked like language. She checked hearing, and vision, and every other sense that these creatures were capable of, but the result of all her searching was the same. No language center—of any kind.

What now? she thought, puzzled.

She waded through the ganglia, noting other anomalies. *I must be misinterpreting something,* she told herself. The structure of the creature's brain followed the standard pattern, but as for its functioning . . . she found herself lost, confused, for the first time in memory.

Had her Marra skills left her? Had all her experience been lost, somehow, in that gradual exchange of memories which was the very definition of her people? How long *had* she been on that damned planet?

She needed the Saudar—their calmness, their solidity—anything familiar to hold on to, to assure her that no, she hadn't changed, or at least not too drastically, and she hadn't in fact lost touch with her world. Hadn't lost hold of her chosen Identity, somewhere in the windstorms of Shian.

Get hold of yourself. The darkness that might be fear was distracting, and it took effort to think clearly, to plan. *Proceed without language. You can do it.*

She created a new body, not without effort. Her strength was beginning to run out. One more Change— two at the most—and then she would have to replenish herself. At least there were living beings here. She might not understand them, but life was life, and feed-or-be-fed-upon was the most basic of languages.

She checked out her new body's reproductive options and made her usual choice. The Nurturer: sometimes enslaved, often abused, but never perceived as hostile. It was the sexual role with which she was most comfortable, and the one (she believed) which best supported peaceable communication. In this case the role manifested itself in a small, compact body with no natural weaponry—little more than a womb on feet.

With no reproductive apparatus of its own, she noted. That was interesting. A true Nurturer, whose only purpose was to play host to the young while they developed. Most unusual.

She practiced with the body until she had sufficient motor control—or the illusion of it—to walk. Ran through the spectrum until her new eyes were adjusted properly, and guessed at the sensitivity required by all her other senses. She could fine-tune as she went. Now, to make contact.

She studied the room she was in, a large, irregular chamber shaped somewhat like a teardrop. The ceiling and walls were uneven, and reminded her more of a cavern than of a starship. Bands of color marked the walls and floor, and splotches of luminescent green on the ceiling supplied a reasonable amount of light. Chromatic chaos; was there a pattern to it?

She walked to where the alien door had been, and considered. Four bands of color crossed here, further accented by a whirlpool of reds and golds. She touched the chromatic intersection—

—and a section of the wall drew back. Excellent. She passed through the opening, into the corridor beyond, and stopped. Adjusted her hearing to maximum sensitivity, and listened to the sounds of the alien vessel. The thrumming of engines, the gentle hiss of ventilators, the occasional shudder of a navigational adjustment . . . they were all familiar, and their presence reassured her. And there, in the distance: a heartbeat that was not her own, and the rhythmic whisper of alien respiration.

She hurried down the corridor, anxious to make contact. One, two, three doors blocked her way, but now that she knew how to read the walls, she knew how to make them open. She caught glimpses of laboratories, storage rooms, chambers filled with alien equipment, but there was no time to stop. Making contact was the most important thing, finding that lone alien whose heartbeat was like a song of welcome. . . .

She turned a corner, and there he was. Warrior stock,

like the others. She waited until he turned and saw
her, gave him a moment to absorb the fact of her presence, and proceeded to indicate her harmlessness. A
lessening of height, a lowering of the head, the opening of hands which held no weapons, she tried it all—
everything listed in the Marra kinesic thesaurus under
nonaggression, and even a few things from *overtures
of friendship.* They were all gestures based upon universal concepts, and it was a sure bet that one of them,
if not all, would communicate her passivity.

Then she added, "Y'lo Marra"—*I am Marra*—just
in case these aliens could recognize that one Saudar
phrase.

He looked at her—just that, for a moment—and then,
without warning or hesitation, pulled a weapon and
fired. A beam of red light split the murky air and hit
her torso, burning where it struck. In an instant that
part of her flesh was converted to ash and heat; half
of her torso and two of her arms had been charred to
cinders, and several vital organs were inoperative.

She was stunned. In Saudar, she told him, "Listen,
I don't think you understand—"

Another shot. More damage. She had to repair it if
she was to have a self-sustaining body. She quickly
rebuilt her neck and upper torso, was working on her
arms when her assailant suddenly stiffened.

And dropped.

Dead?

She came to where he lay, and knelt by his side, shaken.
She had never seen a sentient act like this. Was it her fault?
Had she entered a starship manned entirely by warriors,
to whom her Nurturer-self was an unwelcome intruder?
Would they have been more tolerant of a member of their
own subtype? Cursing herself for failing to foresee such a
possibility, she adjusted her body once more, and became
a warrior. And though she knew the danger involved, she
took the exact shape of the alien who lay before her. It
might help her to get information. Once she figured out
how to communicate she could explain her presence, and
the warrior's death, and make her peace with his fellows.

She hoped.

She had weakened considerably, and didn't know how much longer she could control her mass without absorbing more energy. Stubbornly, however, she resisted the obvious solution. *First* she would make successful contact, *then* she would feed. Marra custom dictated that it was the height of bad form to drain something of its life before you even knew its name; she was damned if she'd be impolite just because she was hungry.

She hid the warrior's body behind a nearby computer console, so that she might have time to explore. Then she focused on the nearest source of life—hungry as she was, that was easy—and started toward it.

Have I lost my skill? Has it been that long? Would she have to go all the way back to the beginning, and do as the early Marra had done—feel her way through her communications step by step, gesture by gesture, robbed of that instinct for social intercourse which had once made her such a valuable diplomat?

No. Her instinct was sound. These biotypes were simply . . . different. Somehow. She would figure it out.

(Inside, the darkness whispered: *What if you don't?*)

Storage area. She walked down aisles marked in bright green, flanked by walls of stacked crates which seemed ostentatiously plain by comparison. A cargo center, of some kind. She could hear the object of her attention just one turn away, a short distance beyond the nearest wall . . . She tried to walk naturally, so that her footsteps would sound proper to him. No need to raise an alarm, at this point.

And then she was there. He looked at her for a moment and then, without question, he too chose a weapon from the assortment of items on his baldric and fired, point blank, at her vital center.

She was aghast. Amazed. How did he know she was anything other than what she appeared to be, another member of his crew? His brain had no special program for identifying her kind. How had he known?

She began to restore her body—and stopped, as her

weakness made it impossible. Alien blood spilled out of her wound, leaving her with less and less mass. *All right*, she thought angrily. He had hurt her, without even giving her the chance to communicate. Let him pay the price for her healing.

She reached out to him because that was the easiest way. He burned away the flesh of her arm, but the bone remained and that was enough—anything that let her make physical contact, so that she need not separate herself from her mass in order to reach him.

She touched him.

And grasped him. Not his flesh, but the energy that burned within: the essence of life, which gave his flesh vitality. It was the substance of which the Marra were made, and the fuel they needed to alter mass. Like all embodied beings he had enough to spare, could squander it wastefully and then feed her besides, but there was something more—something richer and more powerful, which lay coiled at the heart of him, tempting her. Because she was hungry—and frustrated, and perhaps foolish—she dared to taste it

—and she was lost, sucked into a whirlwind of alien substance, her consciousness a tiny mote in a measureless sea of *other*

—and there was too much life! Too much even for her, even for her hunger, too much to taste it without being dragged down into it, out into it forever, absorbed into something so vast that she could barely comprehend its existence

—could not interpret its form. What was happening? She fought back the chaos that was rising within her, the darkness that might be fear, the hunger that was clouding her judgment. Her hand fell away from the alien, and as her Marra soul slid back into its borrowed shell she could feel the last of her vital organs burned to ash, her blood a dried crust on a charred, broken skeleton. She let herself die—had no strength to do otherwise—and fell where she had stood, the baked remains of an alien corpse.

Lost.

She had been gone too long. Someone had changed the rules on her—had altered the very laws of her existence!—and then not told her of it. Or else these aliens were some new kind of life, neither embodied nor unembodied, but something entirely different. Something that didn't play by quite the same rules . . .

Her assailant had left her. Slowly, torturously, she dragged what was left of her body to a crevice between the crates. She was loath to abandon it, for doing so would sever her contact with the physical universe; nevertheless, she might have to. As it was she nearly lacked the strength to move, could hardly manage to drive off the bacteria which were gathering to feast upon her death. Something jammed against the edge of a crate, and she had to work it loose before she could continue. A weapon, which her body had worn— a duplicate of that which her first assailant had carried, marked with the same alien symbols.

It was then that the darkness became a cold, crawling parasite, that worked its way deep into the heart of her being. It drained her of the last of her strength to read those symbols, now that her eyes were gone. It took so much out of her that when she was done she was nearly massless, the barest strand of self-control attaching her to what once had been her body. But it had to be managed. Because she knew that alphabet. She *knew*.

It was Saudar.

And the coldness became a certainty, became her universe: became a lesson, in that which she had never understood before.

So this is fear, she thought.

LONGSHIP TALGUTH

I stood on the deck of an alien skimship, gazing out at the stars. Weak and fevered, yes, and filled with a despair greater than any I had ever known—but no less awed, because of it. I had been born in a time when the world was considered flat, had lived through a period when the stars were believed to be ghosts, or angels, or drops of the Holy Spirit . . . and now I was here, among those celestial bodies, and it was almost too much to contemplate; I could only stand in silence as we approached the longship, stunned by the raw power of the experience.

I had dreamed of the stars. We all had, at one time. But then science came and proved to us that the stars were not to be possessed—not by us, not in a single lifetime. Einstein had demonstrated that nothing could be accelerated up to the speed of light—much less past it—and his mathematical genius dictated the conditions of our bondage. Our children might reach the stars, immured in great ships that could span the generations, but never ourselves. That dream had died.

Or so we thought.

I gazed out at the massive longship, a black void outlined by a field of blazing stars, and mourned the coming of Truth to my people. For there *was* a way to break the bonds of lightspeed—a system developed by alien mathematicians, based upon concepts that the human mind could barely grasp—but rather than giving us our freedom, it had only exacerbated our bondage. For the stars could be reached, but only by the Tyr. The very conditions which made that species a

threat to us also decreed, with cosmic irony, that only
they could close the gap between the stars. Only as
their passengers could we set foot on foreign worlds,
and stand beneath the light of alien suns. This was our
true Subjugation: not the battles, not the Conquest,
not even the undermining of our spirit which was the
heart of Subjugation politics. This bondage upheld by
the very laws of nature, which had smothered our
dreams and taught us the meaning of humility. Only
as slaves might we conquer the universe. What more
total Subjugation was there than that?

The journey was long, and I had spent most of it in
a webwork cradle. They had tried to feed me, and I
had tried to eat. Fortunately, my illness was apparent
enough that they took it in stride when my body rejected the attempt; they cleaned the floor, and left me
to face my fears in solitude.

It was slowly sinking in, now: I was going to die.
Not suddenly, in the manner of a human soldier shot
down by Tyrran weaponry, but with the agonizing
slowness of starvation. True, I had known that my actions might lead to this—but words are one thing, experience quite another. Now I could feel the dread
certainty of death coursing through my veins, along
with sharp acid pinpricks as my body tried to digest
its own muscle tissue for nutrients—and failed. How
bitterly ironic that I, who had risked death often
enough in the past, should face such an end now—
after years of selling my soul for peace. Perhaps fate
was punishing me, for trying to hide my head in the
sand. Or was that my own guilt speaking? Using the
cover of fever and despair to remind me of all the reasons I hated myself?

I had no choice, I told myself, my inner voice shaking. *What more could I have done?*

The longship's bulk loomed before us, blotting out
hundreds of stars. It was like no spaceship I had ever
imagined—and I had imagined much, living through
the times I had. To say that it was large would not do
it justice. The longship's core was an immense sphere,

pitch-black, whose surface was split with a jagged tapestry of craters and fissures. Light swept across its
surface at regular intervals, and like a radar display it
revealed isolated details one after the other, leaving to
the human eye the task of combining it all into one
cohesive image. Craters and crevices loomed before
us, then were as suddenly gone. Had the Tyr started
with some natural satellite, already pitted by ages of
wear, or built themselves a massive sphere and let interstellar grit carve it up for them? Given the speed at
which most longships traveled, a single grain of sand
impacting against the surface could do considerable
damage.

With a sudden jerk, we began our approach. I cursed
the skill of Tyrran pilots under my breath as I grabbed
a cradle frame for support. As we came in closer,
approaching from the rear, it was possible to see that
the surface was covered with all manner of debris,
from cracked plastic shielding to animal waste. I supposed there was no real reason not to use the surface
of one's ship for waste disposal . . . but damned sloppy
housekeepers, my captors. Earth would have done at
least marginally better.

I found myself holding my breath as the landing bay
opened to receive us, praying that my captors would
be visited with a sudden improvement in their piloting
skills, before they tried to get us into that narrow stone
mouth.

A tunnel of stone engulfed us; there was the screech
of two rigid surfaces fighting for dominance, a brief
but ominous period of vibration, and then all motion
ceased. My captors stirred, assigning themselves duties as the Tyrran overmind dictated, some going below to fetch their supplies and two of them, their
clawed hands grasping my upper arms, leading me
forcibly out of the skimship.

The landing bay was an immense stone cavern,
crudely carved from the longship's substance by tools
that had left random gouges in the floor, walls, and
ceiling. It smelled like an Earth cave—cold and damp,

with an occasional whiff of mold, and the passing scent
of animal inhabitants. There was evidently some sort
of ventilation system at work, and I could feel its
breezy produce on the back of my neck, but it wasn't
quite up to the challenge of the Tyr; the sharp odor of
that species clung to walls and ceiling, a musty, fetid
scent that invaded my lungs with every breath I took.
Thank heaven the fever had dulled my senses, or it
might have overwhelmed me. Overhead, there was
more of the green fungus that I had noticed in the
angdatwa, only this was clearly healthier; solid clumps
of it hung down from the ceiling, and when a breeze
happened to disturb them they sprayed sticky spores
into the dank cavern air. Intertwined with that glowing
green stuff were black tentacles of what I sincerely
hoped was plant life. Its slimy lengths were knotted
and wrapped in a complicated webwork that clung to
the ceiling, with ends that hung down at random intervals, down about face level. Waiting for something
to walk into it, no doubt. I imagined the caress of
those slimy lengths upon my face, and shuddered; that
something would not be me, I swore.

My guards allowed me perhaps five seconds to get
my bearings, then parted one section of wall with a
touch and pushed me through. On Earth I would have
fallen, but here the gravity was less; I managed somehow to stay on my feet, and followed my captors into
the heart of the longship. Walking took all the concentration I could muster, and left me little for external
observation. I was dimly aware of us passing through
a labyrinth of intersecting corridors, tracing a complex
path that I knew I couldn't have remembered even
without the fever to dull my thoughts. Everywhere the
fungus glowed, and the webwork of moist dark tentacles hung overhead; the emotive effect seemed almost
too grotesque to be real. By the end of our journey my
legs were numb, and the Honn were more than half-
carrying me by the time we reached our destination.

Here, in this one place, the omnipresent tentacles
had been cleared away; the rough rock walls gave

way to reveal a tracery door—crudely carved, with irregular holes allowing for the passage of air and the
accommodation of eavesdroppers, but a door nonetheless. One of my Honn let go of me—I leaned
against the nearest wall—and reached to the wall
beside this portal. A touch activated some unseen
control, and the stonework slab was drawn aside. Revealing—

Jesus.

I pushed myself away from my supporting wall, and
managed somehow to step over the threshold. The door
slid shut again behind me. I leaned against it, shaking
my head in amazement.

The Tyr had tried. It had really tried. It must have
gone over every element of human psychology, tried
desperately to understand the nature of human aesthetic sense . . . and then failed, miserably, in every
regard.

In the irregular, L-shaped chamber, the Tyr had attempted to create a human-compatible living space; in
doing so it had tried to apply numerous elements of
environmental psychology, without ever once considering the total effect of all those elements *together.*
The walls—coarse, and varying in height—were an in-
stitutional greenish gray that would have done a mid-
twentieth-century factory proud. The floor was brown
and fairly smooth, although the scuff marks of former
inhabitants had scratched the paint and revealed the
longship's native stone. I supposed that the Tyr intended it to remind us of Earth. The bedding, which
lay in a niche in the far wall and seemed to be made
up mostly of synthetics, was a restful pastel blue, and
both the sanitary outlet and nutritive access had been
painted an aggressive orange. A battered mirror and
portable cleanser had been added, no doubt to humor
one's individual vanity; their placement and condition
reminded me more than anything else of an old, run-
down motel.

But be grateful for small things, I reminded myself.
There were no black tentacles here, and the lighting

was reassuringly bright. And there was a place to sit, if one hunched over a bit. I managed to get over to the bed-shelf and eased myself down onto it, grateful to be off my feet at last.

My captors were waiting, watching me through the holes in the tracery door. Reminding me of how little privacy I had, if the Tyr should want to observe me.

"When all the prisoners are secured," a Honn voice rasped, "and when the stores have been distributed, the Kuol will send for you."

They left me then, to contemplate my surroundings and my fate. Too sick to do either, I simply lay down to wait for them; contemplation took strength, and I had none left.

So this was outer space.

* * *

Sometime in the night—call it night, because sometime earlier I had fallen asleep—I awoke. My clothing was soaked with sweat, and my limbs felt heavy and swollen. I was sick with hunger—not as men normally know the sensation, but as only my kind can experience it. It was a desperate, cloying hunger which was half as much fear as starvation; a dreadful certainty that I would never be anything but hungry, from now until the minute I died.

I swung my feet down to the floor of my prison; the room circled dizzily about me. Carefully, I tried to stand up. And managed it—barely. Christ, I was in bad shape.

How many more "nights" before my condition confined me to bed? How long before the cold hibernation which was my kind's last refuge took hold of me, and I must die with that agonizing slowness which was the bane of my people's courage? I staggered over to the hole in the wall whose labeling promised refreshment, and found myself praying. To whom? For what? We make our own fate, and must deal like adults with the consequences of our actions. I read the instructions,

in English and five other languages, but was too
numbed by fever to make any sense out of them. At
last I set the control dial to a hopeful designation and
depressed the stud beside it. *Staple nourishment/ solid,*
it said. And I hoped. God, how I hoped!

What the longship delivered was a rectangular cake,
moist and grainy, with a bitter odor that was far from
reassuring. I knew what must happen if I ate it—but
what did I have to lose by trying? Maybe four centuries
of chemical sustenance had prompted my body to produce the enzymes that once were lacking; maybe the
Tyr had perfected the art of human nutrition, and had
placed everything in this cake in the form that I needed
it, so that it wouldn't tax my system. Maybe. I chewed
off a bit of it, managed to swallow. Then more. Its
substance filled me, gave me temporary respite; if I
managed to digest it I would still have to deal with the
fever, but at least I would have purchased some time.
If only . . .

It happened. About ten minutes later, right on
schedule. Humans fuss and rant about regurgitation,
but in the animal kingdom it's the simplest and most
effective means of ridding the body of something it
can't digest. The cake left my body the way it had
come, with little of its substance missing. Some sugar,
perhaps, and perhaps a few simple carbohydrates. Not
enough.

I leaned against the wall, exhausted. Defeated. And
I waited for the Kuol to call me, or for death. Which-
ever came first.

I no longer had the strength to care.

* * *

The Kuol of the longship looked surprisingly little
like its Earth counterpart; all the important elements
of Tyr anatomy were where they should be, but the
crests and plating hinted at a very different origin. As
for its raspy command of English, that was identical

to the Governor's. Which was only to be expected; they shared the same mental source, after all.

"You are not a prisoner," it informed me.

I refrained from saying the obvious: that our definitions of "prisoner" clearly differed. It didn't seem the time or place to argue.

"We consider that you are not human. We wish to know what you are. We transport you to Kygattra, where the Tyr will discover your true nature. In the meantime . . ." It paused meaningfully. (A very human touch, I thought.) "You are not considered an active threat to the Will. Although that assessment can be changed," it warned me. "You are therefore acknowledged as a guest at this time, rather than as prisoner. You will be treated accordingly."

Normally I would have been afraid to speak at all, wary of angering it. Perhaps it was the hunger that made me reckless. "What does that mean?"

"First, that surveillance will be minimal. Second, that you may have access to those areas of the longship which are set aside for your kind. —This is a long journey, not-human Daetrin Ungashak To-Alym Haal, and your wholeness of mind may well depend upon this privilege. Do not abuse it."

I blinked; my eyes were painfully dry. It was hard to understand what it was saying, much less respond to it properly. "I can go to these places whenever I want?"

"You may go with escort only. That is the Law. For your own protection," it clarified. "The hraas patrol our halls, and they kill any unaccompanied humans. Therefore your chamber will be locked while you are within. Within reason, you may bring back entertainment materials with you, as this is considered necessary for the emotional stability of individualized species." *But not for the Tyr,* its tone clearly said. *We're beyond all that.* "The nutritive outlet will supply you with a variety of sustenance forms, in accordance with Earth generalities. You may experiment, or question the Honn. They will come for you peri-

odically, to discover your will. You may request anything you need, from them.''

An effective system. Anyone without escort was automatically hraas-fodder—and I had no doubt that those
killers could handle the challenge. The Tyr was incor-
ruptible, hence escort guaranteed propriety. Neat, very
neat. If it was trying to let me know that escape was
impossible, it had managed it admirably.

"Any questions?" it asked me.

I felt their eyes upon me—Kuol-eyes, Honn-eyes, all
of them leading back to the same unhuman source. It
was far easier to be silent than to address that alien
consciousness. But that would mean dying. And while
speaking openly might not save me, it was my only
possible hope.

"You indicated special needs," it prompted.

I hesitated, at last decided to hedge. "You have a
chemistry lab? Nutritional facilities?" No more precise than that; let it make of that what it would.

The Kuol regarded me in silence. Perhaps it was
reviewing my file, somehow. Perhaps it was merely
considering.

At last it stirred, and said, by way of a question,
"You are always interested in such things."

Stalemate. I wouldn't specify what my need was
without getting a commitment regarding lab access,
and the Kuol wouldn't give away any information about
the longship's facilities. Game and set.

But then it added, "You understand the consequences of defying the Will."

An opening. I bowed my head, trying to look as
subservient as possible. Years of past practice made it
easy. "Of course, Kuol-Tyr."

Another period of silence, even longer than the first.
I sensed that something was amiss.

Its head jerked awkwardly, a motion that might have
been intended as a nod. "The Raayat will decide," it
announced. Was I imagining things, or did it seem
unhappy with that prospect? "You deal with that kind

at your own risk. The rest of the Tyr will not help you. Do you understand?''

I said yes, and nodded. In the name of laboratory access, I would have agreed to anything.

It moved on to another subject, informing me of the essentials of our journey. There were three stops we had to make before Kygattra, all of them human-colony planets. Three translations, then, before we reached our final nexus. It would mean nearly two years (as Earth measured time) before we reached my destination; even allowing for temporal distortion due to our considerable speed, that would mean months of subjective time spent within the longship. No wonder they took such care to see to our comfort! A man could go mad in that long a time, if isolated from his own kind— and from hope. Yes, I was grateful for my relative freedom. But even more grateful for the possibility of laboratory access.

As the Honn guards marched me back the way I had come, I wondered at the Kuol's demeanor. If it had been human, I would have suspected a backlog of bitterness between it and the Raayat, a history of unpleasant interaction: jealousy, rivalry, perhaps even actual combat. But the Tyr was one creature, unified, and to attribute Earth-emotions to its various parts would be like imagining that one's right hand hated, or was jealous of, one's feet. Ridiculous, right?

I wondered, if I ever had the chance to observe the Tyr's Achille's heel, whether I would recognize it as such.

* * *

My image in the mirror: a much younger man than I was accustomed to seeing, the dirt and grime and cosmetic art all stripped from my skin by a sonic/vacuum cleaner. A good length of hair removed, too. No gray at the temples, no collodian-induced crow's feet guarding the eyes—not a single mark to indicate that once, mere minutes ago, I could have passed for fifty.

The youth was an illusion. The weight of wasted centuries was heavy on my shoulders, and I could see the long years of failure framing my face like a dank cloud, giving lie to any appearance of youth which the mirror might otherwise reflect. How many years had I seen myself thus, and then chosen to turn away? How much of my life had I wasted, without the courage to acknowledge my own weakness?

As I lay back on the narrow bed-shelf I could feel exhaustion tightening my chest, making it hard to breathe. Would that it could stop me from thinking, too.

You knew what the situation was. You made your choice. What point does it serve to regret what you did? It kept you alive, didn't it? Isn't that all you cared about?

Self-accusation is a cold bedmate.

* * *

The Raayat came to me early in the morning—which is to say, it woke me up. I was deeply involved in a nightmare at the time, which was marginally worse than my current waking reality, and I willingly exchanged the one for the other.

It touched the wall to one side of my portal, and the thick pierceworked stone split down the middle to admit it.

It waited.

I could hear my heart pounding loudly in my ears as I struggled sleepily to a sitting position, and then to my feet. The mind can overcome great obstacles, and in this case mine overruled my body's preference, which was to simply lie down and wait for death. The Raayat's presence meant hope, albeit a faint one—but faint hopes were all I had left, now.

I managed to stand and confront it. It was shorter than its Earth kin, perhaps seven feet from toe to skull; the spiked plate which crested the central ridge of its skull added half a foot to its apparent height, its largest horn canted upward from the center of its forehead, like a unicorn's. Its upper eyes were set far to the side, in the manner of a browsing animal, but the lower pair and its protective ridges were so human in placement and purpose that its alien nature was made doubly disturbing by contrast.

"You have curiosity," it said to me.

A question? I dared a nod, wondering what it would read into that.

It turned, and indicated for me to follow. Its legs were long and its stride a brisk one, but I managed somehow to keep up. For a while. Then, when the strength left my legs, I inspired myself to further endurance by thoughts of the hraas, and what it would mean to be left behind in these tunnels, should one come by. It kept me moving.

When its step slowed at last, I fell in alongside it, grateful to have a chance to breathe again.

"You have curiosity," it said. A question? Those bright lower eyes were upon me, taking my measure—and for a moment their searching gaze was so hostile, so *human*, that memories shivered unbidden into my mind and I nearly lost my grasp on the present moment. Then it made a strange nodding gesture, which I couldn't interpret. Perhaps answering itself? "And you also have need."

I hesitated, then answered: "Yes."

We had come to a chamber where six corridors met; without hesitation it chose one path from among them—the narrowest, and the darkest—and led me down it. Spikes from its head-crest brushed the low ceiling as we walked, and bits of dislodged fungus splattered to the floor behind us. Not on us, thank God.

Several corridors later it stopped, without warning, and announced "I, too, have curiosity. You will serve."

Before I had a chance to respond, it touched the wall to the right of it, and a stone door slid open to admit us. I tried to see what manner of sensor it had touched,

58   C.S. Friedman

or how its presence was marked, but the wall was
wholly blank to my eyes; whatever cues the Raayat
obeyed must come from Tyr-memory, not observation.

It motioned for me to proceed it. I did. No sooner
did I cross the threshold than rich, familiar air filled
my nostrils; the scent of plant life in abundance, the
heady power of an oxygen-rich atmosphere. And
something more.

Man.

I entered an enormous cavern, noted the Honn
guards flanking the entrance while my ears picked up
the distant note of human voices. I looked at the
Raayat, confused, but it offered no explanation. *Go
on,* its expression seemed to say. I did. Wide, shallow
steps led down to the floor of a spacious arena, whose
confines had been filled with all manner of Earth flora.
Paths twined carefully between stunted trees and
dense, unyielding bushes, and led to a central area
bordered by a circle of rectangular stones. The green-
ery was so thick that once I stepped past its boundaries
I could no longer see the walls, nor hope to judge the
chamber's size; hundreds of sun lamps peeked through
the tree tops, casting green shadows, but the fever that
had acclimated me to sunlight rendered their radiation
harmless. There were some benefits to be had from
making that adjustment.

In the center of this bizarrely forested domain a
dozen humans huddled near to each other, speaking in
voices so low that my sun-adapted ears could barely
hear them. As soon as I saw them I stopped walking,
then fell back into a dark, man-sized shadow. *Observe
before you are observed,* my survival instinct cautioned. What humans would be here in such a place,
and what special risks were involved in joining them?
Snippets of conversation fell my way, voiced in tones
that varied from wild hope to despair. At least three
different languages. But I could make out few words,
not nearly enough to reassure myself.

The Raayat stepped behind me and whispered, in

that harsh but insightful voice, "They are your own kind. You do not want their company?"

For a moment I did. These were human beings like myself, taken from the Earth for reasons they could hardly begin to comprehend, facing an unknown and infinitely threatening fate. I felt a kinship with them which was greater than any I had previously known, for any people save my own. For many long minutes I watched them in silence, wondering just why I didn't go out and stand among them. Snatches of their muffled conversation gave me hints of their identities: A young man of unusual intellect, called Nogyat, was being transferred to some place called the Domes; a woman of outstanding technical skill was to be transferred to another ship, so that she could share her knowledge with its Tekk; other humans, who spoke a wide variety of tongues and were here for various reasons, all humbled by the one thing they had in common: that they would never see Earth again. Never. That was the Law.

I felt myself drawn to them, to the comfort of their company, but held back. Why? Like them, I must have some human contact in order to maintain my spirit; that was surely the reasoning behind this place, where the more harmless prisoners might congregate. Why then was I hesitant to join them?

Intimacy. I had always feared it, had stood aloof from other humans even while I walked among them. There was too much danger involved in closeness, for my kind; an unaging nature is difficult to disguise, when one is too close to one's neighbors. Such a threat was irrelevant here, but the instinct was too deeply ingrained; I couldn't fight it. I had settled down in the American southeast for just that reason; southern culture offered the trappings of intimacy without its substance, the geniality of polite social intercourse without any emotional contact. Likewise I had eventually drifted into teaching, a profession which enabled me to spend time with other human beings, while still maintaining my emotional distance. I had built

my house on the borders of a wilderness and I enter-
tained little company; the wild cats that I fed were wary
of strangers, which made them perfect companions.
Under such controlled circumstances, it was possible
to interact with human beings—occasionally—without
risk, and with only marginal awkwardness. But here,
where shock and uncertainty had dismantled all social
barriers, where fear of the Tyr had rendered a dozen
strangers desperate for human contact . . . here there
would be more closeness than I dared tolerate. My
soul hungered for human contact, but my instinct cautioned: *No.* And it was an instinct compounded by
centuries of experience; I didn't have the strength to
fight it.

I turned back to look at the Raayat, found its upper
eyes half-lidded in thought. It occurred to me suddenly
that it might have brought me here to test my humanity, and that by choosing to avoid my own kind I had
only made myself appear even more extraterrestrial
. . . but it was too late now. I had made my choice,
and it read it in the set of my body, the clutch of my
hands upon the rough tree bark at my side.

"Come," it said, and the experiment was done. I
could not tell if it was satisfied.

At the door I stopped, and turned to it. Fear caught
in my throat, but I managed to master it; it might play
with me indefinitely if I allowed it to. I would tolerate
anything it cared to put me through, if survival was
the end result, but I must have that hope to bolster my
strength. The Unstable Ones were too much of a mystery for me to try to second-guess this one's intentions.

"I requested access to a lab," I reminded it.

A pause, in which expressions that I could not read
moved across its face in rapid succession. Its features seemed much more expressive than that of the
other Tyr, but the forms it adopted were alien to my
experience; I was acutely aware of my inability to anticipate it.

"Come," it said at last—and surely it was my own paranoia that told me I had amused it.

More corridors, wider and better lit than those which we had previously traveled. I was dimly aware that my last strength was leaving me; even fear of the hraas was barely sufficient to keep me on my feet. How much longer could I keep up with it, playing this awful game?

Then: "The laboratory complex," it announced, and it touched open yet another door.

I knew at once from the smell of it that we were in the right place; there is a distinctive odor to biochemical research, a mixture of disinfectant and tissue preservatives, the molecular vestiges of a hundred experiments. . . . The ventilation was no better here than elsewhere in the longship, so I was welcomed to a catalog of smells that must have spanned weeks in the making. Not all of them were aesthetically pleasant, but every single one was gloriously familiar.

Hope. I grasped at it with all the strength left to me. Used it to hold my legs steady, as I entered.

The place was a vision of paradox, from start to finish. Gleaming white tables set against rough stone walls—glass implements side by side with primitive steel, and plastic—the paraphernalia of several centuries, mixed indiscriminately on shelves carved from the longship's stone. But everything was there, in one form or another; the Tyr labs were primitive, yes, but fully equipped. In this complex, perhaps even in this very room, the key to my survival might be reforged.

If the Raayat would permit me to do so, I reminded myself.

A sudden wave of hunger weakened my legs beneath me, and I caught at the edge of a worktable in an effort to keep myself standing. The Raayat looked at me impatiently, then gestured for me to follow. With a sinking feeling in the pit of my stomach, I realized that it was only giving me a sort of Grand Tour, and wasn't willing to be interrupted. I fought back despair as I pushed myself forward, as I left behind the equipment which promised my salvation, but I sensed that I must time this right—must satisfy the Raayat's curiosity now if I meant to have access to this place later. I would make it till then, somehow. Would convince it to bring me here again, and let me work. Somehow.

Onward. We passed another Raayat, hard at work—the two looked very different, almost as though they might have come from different species—and my guide explained, "That is work on Meyaga."

"Meyaga?"

"A human colony, in the Tyr's domain. Its biosphere is imbalanced, we move to correct. Come," it said, opening a side door. "I show you."

We were out of the laboratory complex, back into the major labyrinth. As we passed under a particularly thick clump of tentacular growth, I shuddered and dared to ask, "What is that stuff?"

It followed my gaze upward and answered, "That is *seyga*. A plant form from the Tyr-home that converts waste air to oxygen. Don't worry," it said, and it gestured me past it. "Only in summer-phase is it carnivorous."

If there was ever an award for understatement, I thought, the Tyr would trounce all competition.

Eventually we reached our destination, an area surprisingly free of seyga, and unusually well lit. A portal opened before my companion's touch, and—

Earth-smells, horribly familiar. I froze before the doorway, overwhelmed by memories. Too many and too uncertain to identify: a mental morass of animal recall, with no specific names or dates attached.

The Raayat prodded me forward, but there was no need; I was drawn forward by curiosity, and by a terrible need that I could sense but only half define. Slowly I entered a vast storage chamber, its mildewed ceiling easily forty feet above my head. Walls of stacked cartons flanked me as I walked, light and dark boxes making checkerboards from floor to ceiling, on both sides of me. Those smells! They gave me strength, where I had had none; gave me purpose, where I had lost it. What instinct were they triggering, and how?

Then I came to the center of that enormous cavern, and saw. Cages upon cages, stacked in rows and up ramps and above and below one another, a veritable sea of superplastic bars. And behind those bars, their souls fuming against the indignity of their captivity, Earth animals. Predators. Magnificent beasts, though the harshness of their imprisonment had dulled their coats, and confinement made them reek with sour parodies of their usual scents. Wolves. Lynxes. Wolverines. A dozen species at least, pacing their cages with anxious stride, their eyes hungering for freedom. Earth life. And memories. . . .

"Why?" I whispered.

"Meyaga is a cold world," the Raayat told me. "The Tyr anticipated that weather would keep some species in check. This was incorrect. Excess population of herbivorous species threatens planetary environment, hence the Tyr imports natural balance from Earth."

"But there are so many. . . ."

"It is a whole continent which we mean to seed. Also, many of these will die, some even before we reach there. Ultimately, there will be balance."

Half-entranced, I was about to step forward; there was no sense of purpose in my conscious mind, but raw survival instinct moved my limbs in a parody of rational intention. But wherever I meant to go, I didn't make it. A sudden wave of weakness came over me, and because there was nothing to hold onto but the bars themselves, and I didn't welcome the thought of making my flesh available to these angry predators, I fell.

And was stopped from falling, as the taloned hands of the Raayat gripped my shoulders.

"You are not well," it assessed.

Very observant, I thought dryly. I nodded.

"You are not accustomed to so much walking."

"Very true," I whispered.

"You come back, then. Later. The Honn will come for you . . . or a Raayat." It settled me onto my feet, did not let go until it seemed that I could stand un-aided.

"Back . . . here?"

"To the laboratory. That is what you want, is it not?"

All four eyes were fixed upon me, assessing my re-action. "What you *need*."

I looked at it, not daring to hope. "Yes. Please."

"We share need, not-human. Yours is straightfor-ward." The door slid open again, and it beckoned. "Mine is less so, but you will serve it. Come."

I came. The rank smell from the cages stayed with me, clinging to my hair and clothing like stale ciga-rette fumes. I wondered if I could find my way back here. Or to the labs, for that matter. But that would require escaping from my cell, avoiding the hraas and all the Tyr. . . .

Not possible, I told myself. I would have to satisfy the Raayat—see to his needs, whatever they were, so that he would bring me back here. I'd just have to hold out until that time. Somehow.

What kind of needs would a Raayat-Tyr have, that it would want human help?

* * *

Faces. A sea of faces, lined with suffering, dark with despair. My students. Not young, most of them, but varying in age between forty and eighty. Survivors of the Great War, clinging together for comfort. Their children are lost, purposeless, without goals to guide them; the parents pretend and maintain the pre-Conquest rituals of life, but there is emptiness in their eyes, endless sorrow in their bearing. They understand the Subjuga-tion as their children never will, ever aware of the cost of conquest. Each one of them has had to make that most terrible of choices—between

courage and survival—and each of them, without
exception, sold his soul for the right to live on.
Now, in their faces, I see the result. The haunting
self-hatred in their eyes. The slowly dawning
comprehension of what Subjugation will mean for
generations born in bondage. The constant burning question of whether they could have changed
anything if they had not chosen to cower in shadows. They have undergone a torture more terrible
than rack or iron maiden could ever offer, for
those things torment only the flesh. These people
are tormented every hour by memories of what
pride was—by the long forgotten taste of *self-
respect*—by things they will never know again
because they lacked the courage to die.

I know how they feel—all too well. The difference between us is that they will die soon, making way for the generations of born slaves soon
to follow, while I will remain alive for decades.
Centuries. Watching my world change into something truly alien, as the generations spawned by
these men and women—raised in an atmosphere
of self-hate and despair, heirs to emotional isolation—remake the Earth in the Tyr's cold, un-
feeling image.

Suddenly, in the hall outside, there is a sharp
noise. All about the classroom I see bodies stiffen,
attention focusing on the room's single door. We
have but a second to consider its source before
the door bursts open—and then we freeze, to the
last man among us, as the invaders enter.

Tyr.

They are upon us like a tidal wave, their black,
chitinous armor reflecting the lamplight like mirrors. So quickly do they move that they are halfway into the room before anyone can respond,
and by the time we realize what their purpose is
they have already hoisted one of my students to
his feet—an older man, perhaps in his 60s—and
are dragging him, violently, out of the room.

We all move to save him—in our mind's eye, where courage and action have no price. In reality, where the price of such action is death, we all remain frozen. The man is screaming—they have chosen wrong, they don't want him, why the hell won't we help him escape?—and the shrillness of his terror bites deep into my soul, where the guilt of past decades is buried. *There's nothing you can do,* I tell myself. *Nothing!* Old feelings are stirring inside me, but I choke them back, repeating over and over again the mantra of my current existence. *Not now. Not here. Not ever again.*

There is nothing you can do!

And then one of the students moves. A friend of his, perhaps—or just another human being who had reached the breaking point. She makes one valiant effort to break him free from his captors' grip, and for an instant it seems that she might succeed. Then a weapon is turned on her, its trigger compressed, and a blast of searing heat makes short work of her rebelliousness.

There is nothing you can do!

Unhindered now, they drag him out; his terrified screams resound in the corridor for several long minutes before he is finally silenced. The room is chill in his absence, silent but for the sizzle of burning flesh. Even greater is the chill that has grown within our souls, a cruel reminder of just what our current status is, and just how little human courage we possess.

There is nothing you can do.

If enough of us had acted, could we have stopped it from happening? Bought him a moment of freedom, long enough to get him away from here, to give him some chance to escape? Our guilty souls imagine the worst, convincing each individual that had he or she acted, had he or she dared to act, the future might somehow have been altered. Giving each person sole responsibility for what just happened, making each one of us into a willing Tyrran conspirator. What the Tyr have not done to Subjugate us, fear and self-hatred will.

There is nothing I can do, I tell myself. Wanting, more than anything, to believe it. *Nothing I can do.*

Nothing that can be done.

Nothing?

* * *

I awoke suddenly, lying atop my bedding. Had I passed out, and the Raayat carried me back? Bad, very bad. I tried to get out of bed—and fell back weakly, the room spinning wildly about me. It seemed that somehow the room was . . . different. I shut my eyes, afraid to see. It could be that I was dreaming . . . or that my senses were giving way to hunger, at last. And I feared not being able to tell the difference.

I was dying—or close to dying, about to descend into the trance state which would precede death. Not *sometime soon*, but *now*. In a part of me so primitive that it still understood the ingrained signals of life and death, I knew that I had reached the end: these moments of consciousness were my last. Had I simply lain abed and waited for death, I might have lasted longer—but I had pushed myself to the end of my endurance, draining my body of its last vital energy, and now I was paying the price. If I didn't manage to save myself very soon, I would soon be beyond all saving.

I tried to think. Tried to sit up, while doing so, but found that I lacked the strength. Terrified, I tried it again: muscle by muscle, taking every fiber in its turn and forcing it to expand or contract, as I required. It took ages, but I managed it. Then I leaned back against the wall of my sleeping-niche, exhausted, and considered my folly.

I should have killed myself when the Tyr first took me, should have provoked one of the Honn into losing control and firing—should have known, in my heart, that I could never sit back and welcome death, be it in ten awful days of starvation or a dozen years of fevered "normalcy." The produce of a chemistry lab might keep me alive, sugars and carbohydrates might keep me moving, but neither would banish the fever. That required a more primitive trigger, something to inform my metabolic controls that the protective coloring my body had adopted was no longer necessary. And until the fever was gone, no mere chemicals could sustain me.

I stood, grateful for the longship's lesser gravity; on Earth I couldn't have managed more than a weak attempt. My senses seemed to have gone curiously haywire; it seemed as though the walls themselves were alive, colored and textured like living flesh. Even my sense of touch was altered; the gray-green paint felt like lizard skin, dry and scaly, as I ran my hands over it. The corridor beyond my door should have been dark, but as I came to rest my face against the stone tracery of my prison I saw colored lines like veins merging and twining down the length of it, and as I watched I could see them pulsing, as though carrying colored blood down their length.

Hallucination, brought on by exhaustion? Or perhaps some more complicated illness, foreshadowing my brain's dissolution. How little time did I have left?

I struck at the door in my frustration, hard, and felt the rock shiver dully beneath my blow. The strength it implied surprised me. It was as though all the vital energy which remained to me had been invested in that one blow—as though my body were gathering itself for one final, desperate effort. Who could say what might not be possible, under such circumstances?

I beat at the rock again and again, possessed by blind animal frustration, until my hands were scraped raw from contact with the rough-cut tracery. To no effect. What had I expected?

There had to be a way out. Had to be! I ran my hands over the crisscrossing ridges of stone, searching for some tactile message in their crudely carved substance. Nothing. I applied myself to the left-hand wall, which the Raayat had touched to gain admittance. Nothing. The fever was burning like a fire, my damaged hands glowing as brightly as the crimson stripe which pulsed on the far wall. I tried to feel for any variation in surface quality—a slit, a depression, even temperature difference—that might help me locate a hidden mechanism. But there was nothing.

I leaned back against the portal, shaking with frustration. An hour earlier, I might have let it defeat me. But now, with my body's last energy coursing through my veins—vital, concentrated—all I felt was rage. The pent-up fury of four hundred years' Subjugation burning in me like wildfire, a storm of heated emotion that consumed my flesh, my soul, the very air about me, the cold stone at my back. Now hot stone, transformed by my rage. I moved—

And the doors jerked apart. A foot. Barely enough for a man to squeeze through.

How—?

I looked back toward the portal. That same infirmity which made me imagine there were bands of color in the longship corridor now showed me the imprint of a body, still glowing with heat. More than human heat, I sensed. But how? What had I done? What vital circuit had I affected?

I forced myself to take one deep breath, then another. *It doesn't matter.* Any minute now a Tyr might come down this very hallway and see what had happened. Freedom was vital to my survival—I had to get moving, and fast.

As I squeezed myself through the narrow opening, scraping my chest and knees against the door's sharp edges, I realized I no longer cared what had happened. Animal instinct was alive within me, with a simple focus: survival. It overwhelmed my rational self, replaced it with a simple, driving hunger. I had to go—

Where? an inner voice questioned. And another, more securely rooted, answered, *Trust.*

I moved. Instinct pointed me toward a carmine vein and I grasped at it, sliding my hands along its surface as I staggered farther, feeling the blood of the longship course beneath my fingertips. Down I went, following that bloodstained roadway, down into the alien warren. Past spirals and zigzags of color that painted the corridor with pictoglyphs of hidden meaning. Across vast open spaces that would have left me directionless if not for the pulse that I followed. Past walls that parted when my hands, guided by that carmine vein, touched the proper trigger-point. Through patterns dictated by my fevered imagination—for this was imagination, wasn't it? These markings couldn't be real. Reason had betrayed me, I abandoned it. The hallucination was better. The hallucination offered direction, and purpose. The hallucination was all there was.

That, and the hraas.

I came upon it suddenly, turning a corner that was sharper than most, finding it waiting for me. Crouching tensely, its muscles like springs tightly wound, anxious for release; its hunger for killing was a palpable substance that struck me across the face like a claw. It shifted its weight from one paw to another, and I could see its muscles bunch beneath its smooth coat. Strangely, I found I didn't fear it. That primitive part of me which had taken over didn't acknowledge the horror stories of the Conquest, refused to recognize that this life-form was a thousand times more dangerous than any Earthborn predator. I found myself adopting a more balanced stance, ready to defend myself, hungry to kill. The hraas, after all, was food.

Its long neck tightened as it sniffed in my direction; it seemed confused. Suddenly a clawed arm shot out at me, but the bulk of the hraas' body remained where it was; I knew in a flash that it couldn't reach me like that and I stood my ground, breathing heavily.

Muscles rippled beneath that alien coat, and amber eyes regarded me with open hostility. With a snarl it turned from me and ran off down the corridor, the way

I had come. Only after it was gone did I collapse against the wall, my strength and my courage drained by the encounter.

Go on, a voice within me murmured. *You've come too far to give up now.*

I pushed myself away from the supporting stone and looked around. My eyes would only focus at the center of my field of vision, and I had to turn my head to follow the lines of color that crisscrossed on all sides of me. Dying. I was dying. Even in the midst of this insane delusion, my senses were beginning to give way. Which meant that I had very little time left.

I found my carmine pathway and staggered forward, following it. Where it led wasn't important. Dreams are built on symbols, and if you accept the proper symbols, and obey the demands of the dream-structure, the delusion will follow its natural course. Corridor after corridor passed by me, colors tangled like lines on a subway map. Tyrran odors washed over me like the stink of a cesspool, but for once they awoke no memories. I lost all concept of distance, direction, purpose: I walked, because walking was my universe. And the vein that I was following broadened, brightened, pounded in rhythm to the longship's heartbeat—and then ended, suddenly, in a swirl of color, as though the wall had sucked it into itself.

Disorientation overwhelmed me; I clung to the wall as the universe suddenly went wild, as the floor pulsed—*writhed*—beneath me. Bits of rock began to come loose from the ceiling and gravel, like hailstones, pelted me. Was this what I had come for? Traveled all this way, offered myself to the hraas, only to be killed by my mind's own images? No. I forced myself forward, reaching for the last place where my crimson guide was visible. A dozen glowing lines converged there, creating a starburst of color. As I approached it with my hand, a sharp bit of rock struck me across the temple and blood began to trickle down into my eye. I wondered at my own self-destructiveness, which had surely prompted this delusion. What lay beyond the starburst pattern that I had come so far to reach, yet was so afraid to see?

Then my hand met stone, in the place where my guideline vanished, and with a grinding, splitting sound the wall parted for me.

I entered. Quiet. Familiar smells—Earth-smells—filled my lungs. It seemed that I knew this place. I turned a corner, saw crates piled against the walls, dark and light cartons making a chessboard pattern on both sides of me. Yes. I knew this place.

And I understood, now, what it was I was so afraid of.

I passed the cartons, came to an open space where the bars of cages were visible. The Raayat's hall of predators. I passed down the long line of cages, marveling at the compact efficiency with which Evolution had designed these killers. As my gaze passed over them, I assessed each one. Young or old, adaptable or stubborn, healthy or hungry, it seemed to me that I was able to tell exactly what their current condition was.

I chose a cage, and unlatched its door.

A lone male, drowsy as it digested dinner. Excellent. It looked up as I entered the chamber, and a flash of sudden interest brightened its eyes. Doubtless it preferred to kill, to take its dinner on two legs and bring it to the ground, than to subsist on Tyrran formula and endless boredom. And here, at last, was opportunity.

The feeling was mutual.

I braced myself as it lunged, then ducked and came up under it. Its teeth snapped shut a mere inch from my shoulder, and claws raked my arms. The weight of it carried me backward and down, but as we fell I somehow managed to get on top of it, and to avoid its deadly hind claws. Something had taken over inside me which knew neither thought nor reason, but acted with a killer's certain instinct. My arm came up under its throat, and I tightened my grip until I knew I could choke it. Claws raked at my side, tearing flesh and clothing, but the angle was bad and my enemy couldn't dislodge me. Obsessed, I felt no pain, but tightened my grip until somewhere in that column of muscle a windpipe must surely be closing. It tore at me, rolled, tried to throw me off, but it was weakening. Blood—mine—was painting the cage with crimson, and the smell of it drew the attention of others; I was aware of a dozen noses pressed between the bars, could feel the hunger and the frustration of these predators as they came to terms once more with the cruelty of their imprisonment.

And then it was over. The limbs of my enemy shuddered, went limp. Its head lolled to one side, and from where I lay I could see that its eyes were glazed. I waited a moment more, just to make certain, and then released it.

Dead. Or dying. I put a hand to its flank, noted with relief that its heart was still beating. My instincts hadn't failed me. I took its head in one hand and with my other held its nearest shoulder, and—

(Stuff of nightmares, of delusion, a truth that I had tried to forget. I remembered my tears of relief that distant day, when I first came to understand that the mystery which tormented me had a painfully simple solution, that the substance of my being was not magic or unlife but a biochemical problem that was easily corrected—that I always had been, and always would be, *human*.)

—I leaned down and tore open its throat with the only weapon available to me. Human teeth aren't meant for such things, but when necessity demands they do suffice; a gush of blood mixed with fur rewarded my efforts, the vivid scarlet of arterial substance. I forced myself to drink it, though my human senses rebelled at the taste. It was life to me, would pass through my system painlessly and leave, in its wake, the proteins and amino acids which this predator's body had processed, which I must have to survive. But even more important, it would say to my fevered body: *Enough. Go back to your normal state. The emergency is over.*

I drank until there was no more left to drink, and then lay there, exhausted, my head resting upon the blood-matted fur. *Never again,* I promised myself. But despite my revulsion, the blood had done its work. Already my heartbeat was slowing, its dull thrumming becoming softer and softer as it abandoned the ways of sunlight for the slow, steady pace of life's darker and more enduring universe. Blissful, merciful cooling ran through my limbs, and with every pulse the fever grew less and less. It seemed to me that there was something else within me, too, some bit of vitality that I had borrowed from my prey which moved within me, healing what was damaged. That was delusion, but I was grateful for it.

Somehow, eons later, I raised my head from the still-warm carcass. And suddenly realized just how much danger I was in. I tried to think. Tried to draw upon human reason again, but sheer exhaustion made it nearly impossible. I began to unlatch the doors of some other cages, freeing their occupants to investigate. Pawprints of blood would soon obliterate any sign of my passage. I hoped. If I was lucky enough, one of these creatures might maul the corpse, obscuring the truth even further. It was all I could manage. I hoped it would be enough.

Bloodied cotton clung to my torso in broad swaths, sticking to my wounds, and my pants were torn down one side. My shoes were covered with blood, and left a trail wherever I walked. I managed to get them off, and cuffed my pants tightly below my knees, to contain any further bleeding. It had to be enough. I had come so far now, I dared not leave a trail to condemn me.

I retraced my steps, desperately fighting back an increasing tide of exhaustion, checking behind myself now and again to make certain that I left no telltale blood behind me. The colors on the walls were gone, but my altered senses now offered me a new means of finding my way: I followed the scent of my former passage as surely as a traveler might follow a well-marked road. Not wondering, as I went, how I managed to do so. It seemed wholly natural at the time, one more monument to the extraordinary internal consistency of my delusion.

I managed to stagger back to my cell, and to squeeze through its open door with a minimum of damage. The cells of my body were crying out desperately for sleep, for healing, but I forced myself against the door, and did my best to close it. *Only minutes now,* I promised myself. *Do this one thing, and then you can rest.* After a moment it began to move, and by angling my body weight first against one side, then the other, I managed to get the two halves together again.

I intended to strip my bloodstained clothing from my body, clean myself, and bind my wounds. In the mirror of my intellect I actually saw myself doing so. But I had pushed myself too far already, and exhaustion finally took control. I walked—crawled, really—to the sleeping niche, fighting for each inch of ground as my body began to shut down for the night. Ignoring the siren song of darkness, I pulled myself up on that ledge of mattressed rock and lay at last, shivering, upon its length. Slowly, the last of my strength bled out of me. Relaxation came, and with it sleep—the sleep without dreams, the sleep which heals, the sleep which keeps my kind alive.

And a trickle of *something,* dancing over the surface of my skin. Imagination? Dread? Or a last bit of vital energy from the beast I had killed, now applied to healing? More likely the last vestige of delusion. There was no magic, not in this world. Who knew that better than I?

TSING COLONY NINE

With a wave of its weapon the Honn-Tyr herded its three native laborers into the cargo hold. Silently it indicated a low, squat crate, and then pointed to one of the Tsing. The six-legged creature touched stomach to ground, signaling its subservience, and began to approach its assigned burden. Two aisles later, the Honn-Tyr assigned the second Tsing to its duties. Then on down the wide central aisle, flanked on both sides by walls of boxes—some labeled in the Saudar tongue, others not labeled at all—until it came to the last of the crates due to be transported to this Tsing colony. "Up there," it said, and he touched the top crate with the point of his weapon to make sure the Tsing understood.

"Your song is mine," the Tsing responded, and he lowered himself as his brothers had done. Not until the Honn-Tyr was gone did he rise again. Then, with a partial gyration of his second and fourth shoulder joints—the Tsing equivalent of a shrug—the six-legged sentient considered its task, and sighed. How like the Tyr to assign him to this labor, without considering the natural limitations of his species' physique! The tall Honn could easily have reached to the top of this pile, removing precariously balanced boxes from its apex without disturbing the whole. For the Tsing, whose spiderlike body rested close to the ground, whose viewpoint was horizontal rather than vertical, it was a much more complicated task.

He walked about the column of crates, considering. As he did so, he caught a glimpse of something tucked

76

away behind one of the stacks. Curious, he approached it. It took some effort—his body was wider than the path between the boxes, and he had to contort himself to get there—but then he was beside it, and he knew it for what it was.

A body. He could see the charred remains of a skeleton, the blackened fibers that had once been flesh. The larger part of it was blocked from his view, but he could tell by the shape of the leg and the arrangement of toes that it had once belonged to a Tyr.

Why would one Tyr kill another? And why would the body be left here, tucked out of sight, so that years might pass before it was discovered?

Like all his people he had shared the Song of Freedom, that rich verbal tapestry of hope and myth which promised eventual liberation from Tyrran dominance. The Song-Role of the Discoverer was one he had often performed; it was the tenor subvoice of that archetypal hero which brought new Knowledge into the Song, thus completing the harmony and making revolution possible.

It seemed to him now that the Song had existed to prepare him for this moment, to see that he grasped at this opportunity, rather than flee from it. With no thought for danger, he turned the corner so that he could see the whole of the body. It was Tyr, all right— Honn, if he didn't miss his guess. Its flesh was charred beyond recognition, but the weapon which lay beside it seemed undamaged. If he could bring that back to his people. . . . He reached between the boxes to where the handgun lay, and closed his midpad around it.

And fire burned within him, a terrible all-consuming flame that burst to sudden life in his questing limb, and from there seared its way into his body. He had been rash, he had moved too quickly, the Song warned against that. He had not stopped to think that whatever had consumed this alien creature might also consume him, if he handled the remains. Too late to regret, now; he focused all his energy on the inward music which was his Song of Dying, a rich melange of sounds which his ancestors had bequeathed to him. *Let me but finish it,* he begged of the burning force, *and I may join them.* The melody of his death was like a cleansing shower, stripping him of all wordly concern so that he might be one with those who had Sung before him. And while he Sang, the alien fire did not consume him. *I thank you,* he told it, as he slid into his dying. *I thank you,* he whispered, and his closing notes were of gratitude.

There was coldness, then, but only briefly. The Song had ended.

* * *

Renewed by the vitality she had absorbed from the Tsing, the Marra stirred. She hated to kill, but sometimes it was necessary. Now she had the option of taking her victim's place, thus leaving the great ship unnoticed. Somewhere out there would be answers, and she meant to find them.

There were two choices open to her. She could adjust the body she was in so that it resembled the Tsing's in form, or she could transfer her essence from the charred remains of her former body into his corpse, and take possession. Neither alternative appealed to her. She had lost a lot of mass when she was burned; putting her flesh back in order would mean borrowing matter from some other source, or working an energy/mass conversion. Tricky. Then there would be the Tsing's original body to hide . . . no, better to simply move into that, and deal with the attendant difficulties as they arose.

Loosening her identity from the matter that had housed it for centuries—perhaps even longer, who could remember?—she slid herself into the still-warm flesh of her rescuer. It was like entering a tunnel, without sound or smell, only a faint pinprick of mental light in the distance. Carefully, she oriented herself, and took control of the Tsing's sensory apparatus. Vision: limited. Hearing: excellent. External and internal tactile systems undamaged, no smell-analog that she could locate, a few subsidiary senses that were bound to the reproductive process . . . she fine-tuned her new systems and saw the storage hold take shape about her, felt the distant vibrations of Tsing feet as they moved on both sides of her, and the bipedal rhythm of an alien guard just beyond them. There was no time to search through the brain to untangle its neural circuitry; she moved her body as the first Marra pioneers had done, muscle by muscle, feeling her way through the flexors and extensors as she tried to mimic Tsing locomotion. One step. Two. Then her left mid-leg tangled with the foreleg and sent her face down into the floor.

I never did care for hexapedal structure. Carefully, with much effort, she managed to right herself. *Solid and dependable, yes, but lousy for movement.* How did those hex-gaits go? She tried again, focusing on interlimb coordination, but she was too out of practice, and the pattern eluded her. Three steps and she was tripping over herself; once more—or an attempt at it—and she was down.

All right. Enough of this. She tucked her midlegs under her torso; it would look strange, but at least they'd be out of the way. There were twelve distinct quadrupedal gaits and she knew them all backward and forward. Choosing the simplest, she managed to get her borrowed body out of the aisle that imprisoned it, and into the empty space that ran down the center of the hold.

Now. What was it they wanted? She hadn't been paying attention to details when the Tsing first arrived, had lacked the strength it would have taken to listen to its orders, since she'd had no organ of hearing to filter the sounds through. Footsteps were approaching, though, so she had to move quickly. She grabbed a nearby carton and hoisted it upon her back, hoping it resembled whatever she was supposed to be carrying. And she hurried out, trying to put as much distance as possible between herself and the site of the Tsing's assigned labor.

In the corridor outside the hold one of the upright creatures was waiting; it gestured with its weapon and she obeyed, falling in line behind several similarly burdened Tsing. Fortunately, she was the last in line as they exited the great ship; it gave her time to study, unobserved, the kinesics of her adopted species. By the time anyone bothered to look at her, she appeared to be a Tsing: a bit lopsided, perhaps, and limping in the oddest way, but a native nonetheless.

They were herded into a smaller ship and relieved of their burdens. The other Tsing were singing quietly to themselves, bits of music that seemed improvised; she herself was silent. If anyone noticed, they didn't feel it was worthy of mention. Which was just as well. The adaptation had exhausted her, and trying to run a body without having had time to explore its structure was a feat that became more difficult with each passing minute.

But soon I'll be off this ship, she told herself. *And then, somehow, I can find out what happened.*

Disembarkation: The shuttle's doors opened wide, admitting a gust of dust-filled air that set her companions coughing. Their bodies were poorly designed for such an environment, she realized; hence this was probably not the homeland of their species. Their hacking coughs led her to believe that they had not come here willingly, either.

She improvised a respiratory filter to keep the worst of it out of her own lungsacs, and four-legged it out of the shuttle's wide doorway, down onto the planet's surface.

Wind and red dust. She slid her inner eyelids into place, found it easier to see. Wind, red dust, and a vast expanse of pitted clay. The other Tsing were all traveling in the same direction, so she followed them. Others were coming to unload the shuttle, and they passed her without comment. She appeared native, then. Good.

She followed her guides into the city, and, in fact, was well within its confines before she recognized it as such. One of the leaders hummed a farewell tune to the group, then ducked through a slit barely large enough to admit his crouching form; beyond it was a low mound of clay, now revealed as some sort of domicile. Looking about, the Marra saw others—mounds as far as the eyes could see, each with its entrance-slit and then several smaller openings, that might serve as windows.

One by one, her companions left her. Through the dust clouds she could see a swollen red sphere in the process of setting, and she guessed from their sensory apparatus that these were creatures of the day, retiring until the morrow. Good. That gave her time to search, and the freedom to take on whatever form she needed.

If there was another Marra here, on this world, she would find it. If not, there must be some centralized authority; her Marra senses would help her to locate the population clusters that typically supported such. Either one would suit her purposes.

By morning, she promised herself, she would have answers.

* * *

A domicile, like all the others—but to her Marra senses it was rich with the hidden messages of her kind, and she knew it for a Marra abode.

Circling it warily, she peeked into the window-slits. Like others of its type this Tsing abode was broad and low-ceilinged, with a smooth, bowed floor that was highest in the center. But unlike the other abodes she had observed, this one was filled with plant life. In every nook and cranny a living thing had been placed, so that the main room appeared more like a forest than a cave. *A typically Marra touch*, she thought, tasting the fresh wind of life that wafted out through narrow window-slits. She was among her own kind, at last.

Not knowing what passed for guest etiquette among

this species, too tired to track it down amidst the lim-
itless associations that filled her new body's brain, she
thumped three times on the portal and, receiving no
response, slipped inside. The vital energy of a hundred plants caressed her, soothing her taut nerves as
she sought the building's occupant. But search was not
necessary; he came to her, as soon as she entered, and
she knew she had not been mistaken.

Marra, he was Marra. She felt a flood of relief at
the knowledge that she was home at last, she was
among her own kind, whatever had happened while
she was gone could be—and would be—explained, and
dealt with. The worst was over. She let her new flesh
free-flow, then shaped it into a Saudar shell. It was a
neutral form, which all her people knew; it would allow her to communicate better than the Tsing biotype,
which was unfamiliar to her.

Somewhat surprised that he didn't adopt a Saudar
form himself—that was, after all, Marra guest-
custom—she greeted him in the Saudar manner, with
words and scents combined. Even that couldn't possibly convey the depths of her joy at finding him, the
relief she felt at knowing that soon she would be
grounded again in a familiar, supportive universe. Stable, as much as the Marra were ever stable. She hungered for stability.

When he failed to respond, she offered, "I've been out
of touch for a while, and I was hoping you could—"

"What are you doing here?" he demanded.

She was confused. "I'm sorry. Shouldn't I be
here?"

"This planet is mine, it was my assignment. You
have your own world, or part of one—why did you
leave it?"

Once more she felt a coldness inside, and this time
she knew its name. *Fear;* she was growing accustomed
to it.

"My identity is without root," she told him. The
explanation was a plea, the ultimate Marra distress
signal; it stated need as only the Marra could know it,

hinted at a fear that was unique to their species. No Marra could hear those words and fail to respond—she hoped. "I need help in getting my bearings. I need context. I am without root," she repeated, uneasy. "Help me."

She didn't know Tsing body-language well enough to judge his response, and his voice, when he answered, betrayed no emotion. "Things have changed," he said coldly.

"I gathered that."

"You bring danger—" He looked out the window-slit, moved to block it with his body. "Why can't you wear a local form?"

Why should that matter? she wondered, but she shifted back to the hexapedal structure that he favored. It seemed to relax him. "What is it that's happened?" she asked, still speaking Saudar. The language resonated strangely in her six Tsing voice-chambers.

"A shift in government. One embodied species gave way to another." He paced as he spoke, betraying his nervousness. Very un-Marra, she thought. "That's all. It happens often enough."

"What of the Saudar?"

"Dead. Or gone."

"You don't know?"

Silence. "No one knows," he said at last. "The Tyr came. They had Saudar ships, Saudar technology. They are . . ." He seemed to be searching for an appropriate word, at last offered—unhappily—"not like us."

She remembered the alien she had attempted to kill, the terrifying *otherness* that lay at the heart of him. "Yes. I understand that."

"If they come to realize that we exist—"

"How can that hurt us?"

"We're parasites," he said quietly. "What species would endure our existence, once it comprehended our true nature?"

She was aghast. "Are you serious?"

"Simple fact, Marra. And your presence here—"

"Parasites? *Parasites?*"

"What else would you call it?"

"I would call it . . . symbiosis, if you must have a scientific term."

"*We feed on life*. What species wouldn't resent that?"

"We *feed*—as you put it—on a force which all embodied beings produce, in excess of their need. I can name offhand a dozen Saudar who would willingly submit themselves to Marra hunger, in return for our service." *All of them are dead, now, have been for centuries, but ignore that.* "Under normal circumstances we're no more 'parasites' than a Saudar who drains his jezyeg of excess klann, to feed his own young."

"And you've done no more than that?" he challenged her. "Not even in getting to this world?"

Startled, she answered, "I killed. It was necessary."

"Do you think your victim would have agreed with that assessment?"

"Within the Unity—"

"The Unity is dead!"

"You don't know that."

"The Tyr run everything, now. What they can't use, they destroy. All species but ours have been Subjugated—a long, careful process of weeding out undesirables, to purify the gene pool. Do you know what that would do to us?"

She was astounded. "Nothing. It would do nothing."

"We wouldn't pass their standards."

"The whole concept of a gene pool—"

"A Marra equivalent, then! Don't you see, they have no reason to endure parasites—they don't *need* our diplomacy, they don't need anything we have to offer, why should they let us go on?"

"What in Unity's name would they do to us? Give us an ugly form and ask us to change into it?"

"Kill us," he said coldly.

That stopped her. Her voice quiet, her soul incredulous, she asked, "I assume you're kidding?"

"You've *seen* them. You've touched their essence."

"How, exactly, would they kill us?"

"They're not like other life-forms—"

"And neither are we! Marra don't die—we can't die! Death is for the embodied, not for our kind! Only loss of memory can affect us—"

Yes, an inner voice agreed, *and if we were cut off from our past, isolated in an environment that didn't value us, harassed by new un-Marra fears . . . we might well become no more than parasites, afraid of our own borrowed shadows.*

"I see," she said softly, more to herself than to him.

"Good. Then you understand the risk. Your being here—" (he glanced out the window-slit nervously, searching for eavesdroppers) "—is inexcusable. We made an agreement, Marra. All of us did. Abide by it, and leave me alone."

"What were the terms?" she asked softly.

"You don't remember?"

"Obviously not. My . . . Span is short." She saw no reason to tell him the truth, it would only add fuel to his paranoia. In fact, she had one of the longest Memoryspans of any Marra she knew—but he had no way of knowing that. Let him assume that she had simply forgotten, as all her people did in time, the details of her past existence. "Tell me."

"We divided up the available territory, assigned bits of it to each Marra. For safety's sake. So that there wouldn't be two of us working the same area. Easier to stay hidden, that way. This world is mine. Others, with more inhabitants, were subdivided. But this world is small—there isn't room for two of us. So you'll have to go."

"And all the Marra agreed to this?"

"Yes."

"I see." She doubted that was so, but his memory

might well be confused. It would be typical. "One last question. Transportation between the worlds . . ."

"The Tyr handle that."

"Only the Tyr?" she asked, surprised.

"They're the only ones who can do it. Shuttles handle the intrasystem business, but only the Tyr can go superluminal. And whoever they take along with them, of course."

Ah, she thought sadly, *you have forgotten so much . . .* "I see." That meant she would have to rely upon the Tyr ships for transportation—awkward, but necessary if she was to contact the rest of her people. And she must do that. She simply couldn't believe that all the Marra had devolved into such ignorance; if she searched them out, she should be able to find at least one who could help her—

Unless your memories are wrong, and theirs are correct. Did you pass a full Span on Shian, and create false memories to fill the emptiness? Were the Marra never ambassadors at all, but a host of unwelcome parasites?

No. That was too jarring to contemplate, and defied everything she knew about the ways of the embodied. A being who could take on any form was invaluable in interspecies diplomacy, especially when dealing with the xenophobia that surfaced during delicate First Contact negotiations; to think that such a priceless skill would be wasted because the ambassador required life for sustenance . . .

It could happen, she admitted. *That's what's so frightening.*

"You're leaving," he said curtly. Not a question.

In sudden anger she leaned to one side, crushing the leaves of his nearest plants. Draining them. "I'm going," she agreed. The branches withered and browned, and a few damaged leaves began to drop from their stems, lifeless.

"I pity you," she whispered, and she slipped through the door-slit.

EARTH

(TIMEFUGUE)

Midnight. No place to park. No time to waste. I pull over and shut off my engine, leaving the car where it is. Blocking others, whose owners won't be able to leave until I get my vehicle out of the way. But that's all right. Other things are more important, and besides: most of these people won't be coming back anyway.

A quick sprint takes me to the field. The seeming chaos consists of a hundred or so men who know where they're going and are running to get there, and perhaps a hundred more—last minute recruits, like myself—in whom military discipline is less ingrained. Some of those look lost, others scared. I don't blame them.

Major Tanhaus is easy to spot: taller than most, with a fringe of silver-gray hair that seems to sparkle in the harsh field lighting. Naturally dominant, in a charismatic way that's hard to resist; when all else fails, the sheer force of his personality is often enough to keep his men going.

I wait until he notices me, salute.

"Andrews." He digests the fact of my presence, then asks, "What is it?"

My heart skips a beat as I commit myself. "I'd like to fly this one, sir."

"We're going dayside." My phrase, which he has adopted. "You know that."

"Yes, sir."

"And that won't affect you?"

It's on my file, right under a long Latin name: hyperallergic to ultraviolet radiation. They never would have taken me on in the old days, but with Earth's pilots dying right and left, a man who can fly only at night is better than none at all.

I don't answer him directly. Instead I ask, "It's all or nothing this time, isn't it?"

The flash of anger in his eyes betrays the depths of his hatred for the alien invaders; normally such an emotion would never register on his face. "Yes," he answers. "If we don't do it this time . . . it's over. So we can't afford to lose." He looks out over the field, where men are gearing up: American and British pilots, German, South American, Soviet; the war against the Tyr has done what no diplomacy ever could, rendered our borders meaningless. "All or nothing." He looks at me, dark eyes probing. "You're good, Andrews. We can use you, if you think you can do it."

The condition which I noted on my medical forms serves my needs by supplying an acceptable explanation for my nocturnalism, but it's also misleading; the major has every reason to think that I can't survive first exposure.

"I can, sir." Though my stomach tightens at the prospect, I don't let that show. Maybe this flight will kill me. But I knew the odds of dying when I first signed up; I've been lucky to make it this long. "It won't affect my flying."

How little they know about me! But that's in the nature of things, this close to the end. With most of the armed forces destroyed, every man is valuable; grateful for skilled volunteers, United Earth Air Defense asks very few questions.

"All right," he says, deciding quickly. "You're in." I feel the sudden bite of fear—but what does fear matter, when Earth's entire future is at stake? If I've lived for more than ten centuries until this time, it's only been so that now, in the time of Earth's need, my experience can be applied to her defense.

The Tyr will die, I promise myself, and I begin to run to my post.

Even if I must die killing them.

LONGSHIP TALGUTH

I dated the years of my life from the twentieth century onward. The time before that seemed little more than a chaotic jumble of dreams, fears, and random bits of memory; I worked hard to forget them, in order to live a rational life. Sometimes timefugues from that early period plagued me, but their accuracy was like that of a story which had been handed down word-of-mouth through the centuries—true at the core, perhaps, but overlaid with so many embellishments, mythical and fantastic, that I could not accept them as real. *Would* not accept them as real.

In contrast, the moment of revelation which divided my life in two—the Time Before and the Time After—would accept no embellishments. Its presence in my memory was pure fact, would remain pure fact through all the years to come. It divided the two halves of my life from each other with such absolute efficiency that at times I felt I had been two men, one dying in the twentieth century so that the other could be born. One trapped in a private Dark Ages of superstition and doubt, the other free to live among his fellow men, to walk the Earth as one of them.

And dividing the two, a single concept—so full of power, so rich in its implications, that any attempt at emotional embellishment would only serve to obscure its significance.

Memory, unenhanced: I sat in the living room of my uptown apartment, reading a scientific journal. One particular article was discussing the case of a man whose vast complex of symptoms had all narrowed down to a single cause. *Nutritional deficiency,* the article said, *caused by specific enzyme dysfunction.* That was all.

Those words changed my life.

I put down the magazine and sat very still, stunned by the power of the concept. *Nutritional deficiency.* Of course! Why hadn't I seen it before? Why hadn't any of us thought of it? So simple! The blood is the messenger of the body, carrying oxygen and nutrients to outlying cells, an internal waterway whose tides are rich with the produce of the digestive system. The fact that one eats a balanced diet doesn't necessarily mean that one can utilize all of it. Among my kind, the digestive process was lacking some vital element; unable to supply ourselves with what we required, we hijacked our nutrients from other animals, whose bodies had done the work for us. The symptoms of our condition might be many and varied, but that didn't mean the cause had to be.

How simple it would all seem later, in retrospect! But for a man who was born in an era when supernatural entities reigned supreme, when reanimation of the dead was deemed more plausible than the division of solid substances into submicroscopic particles, the power of such a discovery was not to be underestimated. Suddenly, with that one simple thought, the bonds of myth were shattered. I knew for the very first time—even more, I *believed*—that I was neither more nor less than a man.

I was reborn.

Like a father with a newborn child, anxious that every influence by a benign one, I kept guard over my newborn soul. Memories from the Time Before were carefully identified as such, no more than bits of wishful (or fearful) fantasy, with a rare thread of emotional truth woven in. As a rational man, I rejected them utterly. Science was my god: it had freed me from the bonds of myth and self-loathing, giving me—for the first time in my long life—a truly *human* identity. And all that it required of me, in return, was worship.

I set about freeing myself from my condition. It took several years, first to acquire the necessary education, and then to find a suitable facility, but I persevered. And at last, after a long and often painful period of experimentation, I succeeded. The mystery of my sustenance had been reduced to a simple collection of formulae; I was no longer dependent upon animal blood, but might wean myself from it entirely.

And the god of Science rewarded me for my diligence. The old memories slowly faded, making way for new experience. Timefugues still plagued me, but only the ones from the Time After had any emotive power to speak of; the others were no more than shadowy reminders of a self-image I had now discarded—dim, incoherent reflections of a past I was determined to forget.

Thus had I remade myself, in an exercise of rational intellect. And it was in that same manner that I carefully reviewed my past, when I awakened from my long healing sleep on the longship, to put my recent experience in its proper perspective. One of the quirks of my memory was that it was extremely state-dependent; any action with strong emotional overtones was likely to dredge up memories of a similar tenor. And the last thing I needed now was to be overwhelmed by associations born of my bloodthirst.

So I lay very still on the thin Tyrran bedding, and went over the information at my disposal. Fact: once, in the distant past, I had needed animal blood to survive. That was a straightforward, scientific given. At the time I didn't understand why I needed it, but instinct and parental guidance had taught me how to handle myself. Fact: I spent my formative years in an unstable age, a time of pagan supernatural belief overlaid—awkwardly—by early Christian mysticism; little wonder I had grown up confused, in a time when even normal men questioned their own nature! And that was it. All there was to it. Blood had no more significance than that; I would *let* it have no more significance than that. It was a finite, comprehensible substance, with no special power to transform me. I refused to let it transform my memories.

I waited, alert for any onslaught of imagination. None came. The delusions of my past were deeply buried, after more than four centuries of denial, and no single act would unearth them. Excellent. That was precisely what I had intended to accomplish, back in the twentieth century. A pleasure to have my success confirmed, after all this time.

I tried to move. Wary of pain, or a renewed flow of blood. But to my surprise, there was neither. My wounds must not have been as bad as they'd seemed. Carefully, I stretched. Arms first—a bit stiff, and aching as if from overuse, but satisfactorily mobile. Then the torso, raised to a sitting position—surprisingly sound, considering what I had gone through—and then, last of all, the legs.

There was no pain, beyond that of passing stiffness. Absolutely none.

Had I dreamed it all?

I closed my eyes and drew in a deep, slow breath, using the discipline to calm myself. My heartbeat was leisured, gentle; my skin was cool again, and the blood coursed lazily beneath its surface. The fever was truly gone, and I knew from experience that only blood would banish it. My experience of the night before must have been grounded in truth, though imagination had clearly embellished it. But what of my wounds? Some of those *must* have been real—although clearly memory had exaggerated the damage. Why wasn't there any pain?

I ran my hands up under my shirt, across my chest and stomach. And froze, as my fingertips failed to confirm what I knew to be fact.

Slowly—very slowly—I searched my skin. First with my hands, questing fingers running lightly across my body. I found neither wound nor scar, nor even dried and crusted blood, to bear witness to the events of the previous night. Then I dared to look down—

And stopped breathing for a moment, as I saw.

My hands were shaking as I ran them down the front
of my shirt—the sides—the sleeves. That thin cotton
garment was whole. Undamaged. Unstained, by blood
or any other substance.

What the hell was going on?

I twisted about to look at the bed, and felt a cold
knot tighten in my gut. There were stains. Deep brown
blotches contrasted against the pale blue mattress, in
pools that hinted at human contours. Exactly where a
man would leave them if he lay bleeding there, for
hours.

As I had done, surely!

I felt my torso again, then pulled my shirt off over
my head (and it was whole! undamaged!), my entire
body shaking as I examined myself, visually and tac-
tilely. I took off my pants as well—the zipper jammed,
but I managed to squeeze out of them—and looked for
any hint, in their thin woolen substance, of the conflict
that had taken place. But there was none. They had
still been rolled up to just below my knees, where I
had meant them to soak up the blood that was pouring
down my legs, but as for the blood itself—or any
wound that might have released it—there was no sign.

Then I saw the shoes.

I walked over to where they lay, by the center of the
tracery door, though every sane instinct remaining in
my soul cautioned me not to look, at any cost. I felt
a sudden urge to run, to get far away from here and
pretend that none of this had ever happened. But that
simply wasn't an option. Reluctantly I lowered myself,
until I crouched beside the nearer shoe, and I prodded
it with a fingertip until it rolled back over, onto its
sole.

It had been brown, once. Now it was that, and a
darker brown as well. Some dark, sticky substance had
stained its leather almost to black, and left a crusty
residue along its laces.

Blood.

Mine.

I felt as though I were balanced on a fragile wire,

high above the earth, and the simplest wrong thought would send me plummeting downward—into a fantasy so dark, so compelling, that my human identity would be lost forever.

Easy, I whispered to myself. *Easy! It's the blood that unnerved you, that's all. Drinking blood again, after all these years. A perfectly reasonable response. But you've got to get hold of yourself. Act rationally. The delusion will pass. Time will bury it, again. Time will bury it all.*

I forced myself to wash the bedding, as if it had merely been dirty. I rinsed my shoes in the sanitary outlet, and carefully thought nothing as thin rivers of reddish brown spiraled downward, toward the Tyrran drain.

You healed yourself. That's all it was. Regenerated flesh at an unusual pace. What's wrong with that? Isn't rapid healing one of your people's greatest strengths?

I shivered, and the cold tap water splashed across the backs of my hands.

And the shirt? I wondered. *My pants? The shoes? Don't ask,* I warned myself. *Don't ask. Ever.*

* * *

The Honn-Tyr came at regular intervals, as promised. After three attempts at communicating exactly what my need was, I managed to get one to program the nutritive outlet to deliver something I could digest. Simple sugars and carbohydrates, in concentrated form: the result was a sticky, drippy sort of pastry— far from appetizing—but it did stay down once I ate it, which was all I'd asked for. It didn't address the real problem, of course—the lack of several dozen vital amino acids in my system—but now that the fever had ended and my metabolism was back to normal, it was enough to keep me on my feet. Temporarily.

I had to get access to the lab complex again. And that required the Raayat. But in the days that followed my fit of madness, only the Honn came. They offered

me everything which was within their capacity to deliver—exercise, false sunlight, human company, reading material—but except for the latter I turned them
down, preferring the stifling closeness of my cell to
the possibility that the Raayat might come back to see
me when I was elsewhere, and then never return again.

But the days passed, and I grew increasingly restless. A diet of pure sugar will only take you so far. I
tried to think of new things to request from my Honn
contacts, as a way of keeping myself occupied. Chief
on the list was fresh clothing. But when they brought
me a meager new wardrobe cut from modern cloth, I
found myself unable to wear it. I had always had a
distaste for synthetic fabrics, back since their first appearance in the twentieth century, but now I found
myself unable to wear them at all. The omnipresent
polynova of twenty-fourth century clothing raised
rashes up and down my body, and since no modern
fabrics were made without it (my own wardrobe was
custom tailored, from fabrics woven to my specifica-
tions), I finally balled the new stuff up in disgust and
cursed the Tyr, with gusto, for not having a cotton
plantation somewhere on the longship. And I wondered just what had changed in me, that a simple distaste for plastic against my skin had developed into
such an extreme physical reaction.

My hunger grew. My patience thinned. My mind
seemed stable once more, but who could say how long
that would last? I needed protein. I needed the labs.
And therefore, I needed the Raayat.

The next time a Honn came to see to my needs I
neither greeted it nor turned it away, but sat where I
was and said simply, "The labs."

It looked at me for a moment, then turned and left.
No word. I wondered if I had played it right; if a curt
reminder of the Kuol's former commitment would be
enough to get things moving. I had thought maybe it
was testing me, to see just how necessary lab access
was to me. If so, I intended to give nothing away; a
two-word reminder was all it would get.

Time passed. A lot of it. I refused to get anxious. And then, after an eternity of waiting, footsteps sounded in the corridor. Claws against stone, a stride too heavy to be Honn. I stood, daring to hope at last. *Let it be* . . .

Yes. It was.

The door slid open, and a Raayat regarded me. *The* Raayat—*my* Raayat. Who would ever have thought that one of the Tyr could look so good?

"Come," it said, and I came.

Down the endless tunnels we went, into the heart of the longship. The pattern of our progress was wholly unfamiliar to me; I had been half-dead the last time we came this way. I did the best I could to memorize our route, in case I should ever need to come here alone.

Out of the cell? Past the hraas?

I did it before, I thought grimly.

And would rather not think about what came of that.

At last we reached the door to the main laboratory complex, and it split open to admit us. He indicated that I should go first—but then caught me as I stepped forward, a hand on my shoulder to hold me still. I looked up at him.

"You have need to be here," he said quietly. A question? I nodded, just in case. "I have need for co-operation."

My stomach tightened to think what sort of coop-eration an Unstable One might want, but I nodded, committing myself to the bargain. "Of course. I un-derstand."

He let me enter.

The place was in chaos, by Terran standards, but everything I needed was there, and that was all that I required. With trembling hands I began to collect what I would need, on top of the single table that stood at a comfortable height. An hour or two in this place, and my survival would be guaranteed. Not to mention my sanity, as well—for I was certain that once I was back on my pills, with the bitter taste of my blood-drinking days fading slowly into memory, my mind would come to terms with reality once more.

And the bloodstains which remain on your shoes; will they suddenly disappear? Or will you wake to find your shirt scored to pieces, and dark wounds across your chest where the claws of a predator raked your skin?

Suddenly, a figure stirred. I turned, startled, and saw a woman rising from behind a computer console, tools in her hand. A tall black woman, whose ebony skin radiated African heritage with a purity I hadn't seen in centuries. Not like the blacks of my homeland, whose color and form had been modified by five centuries of interbreeding; this was a vision from the past, a woman who might have stepped out of pre-colonial Africa—a figure that might have seemed at odds with the high-tech machinery around her had it not been that her competence was as aggressively obvious as her racial makeup. To add to the illusion—or confuse it further, I wasn't sure which—someone had pricked her skin into patterns of scar tissue, much like the tribes of her homeland had done, but the patterns were wholly modern. From her shaven scalp down the length of her long, lean body, symbols of electrical function had been carved into her skin, leaving her marked with pictoglyphs of purpose. In some ways they resembled the crest-patterns of the Raayat-Tyr.

She looked at me (with amber eyes, a jarring discontinuity), then turned to the Raayat, indicating her machine. "Not to use this one until I close it up again. Understand?"

"The Tyr comprehends," my companion answered.

She looked at me again; the symbol for a battery which had been carved into her forehead gave her gaze a particularly ferocious aspect. "Earthborn?" she asked me, grinning.

She spoke English, as the Tyr did, but with an accent that seemed foreign. Maybe Slavic?

"Is it so obvious?" I asked her.

"Harosh! The hair," she said, running a hand over

her own polished scalp. I touched my own head, felt the short blunted lengths which the cleaner had left, and wondered if eventually that, too, would be gone. Baldness, for her, only increased the power of her Amazonian presence; on me it would simply look stupid.

"You have luck, dai?" From her inflection it wasn't clear whether she meant that as an observation or a hope for the future. She was gathering her tools into a small leather-and-horn box as she spoke, her hands moving with automatic grace. "I will be back," she promised the Raayat. With a last glance to me—that grin, set in luminescent white against the ebony of her skin, virtually leapt off her face—she stepped through the portal unescorted, and touched its controls from the other side so that it sealed behind her.

I stood there, stunned, not quite sure what to make of it.

"You wish to know," the Raayat observed.

"I'm curious, yes."

"That was a Tekk. They serve the Tyr."

"But you have Honn," I challenged it. I wondered why the Tyr would require human labor.

"For physical labor. Not for planning repair."

"I see." The Tyr could manage its own repairs, but only once it knew what was wrong. Not that a plodding Honn couldn't troubleshoot machinery, if it drew upon the Tyr-whole to do so, but a creature with creative intuition could do so much more quickly, and perhaps even more efficiently in the long run. So: the Tyr relied upon human servants, on a regular basis. That was interesting. Something to remember.

"Won't the hraas hurt her?" I asked my companion, suddenly remembering the killers who prowled the longship tunnels.

"The Tekk undergo a ritual of submission, which binds them to the Will. Some scars," it said, touching a hand to its chest and forehead, "indicate that. Once the ritual is passed, the hraas do not disturb."

"Interesting." I wondered just what this rite of passage accomplished, in physical terms, that would account for the hraas' behavior. Were the Tekk actually absorbed into the Tyr? No, for then this woman wouldn't have had to speak aloud to the Raayat. Something else.

The Raayat was watching me, waiting. Feeling its eyes on my back—all four of them—I began organize the tools and chemicals that I had assembled. I wished the Raayat would find something else to look at, so that I could work more privately. But of course it wouldn't. It was curious, on behalf of the Tyr. That species wanted to know what I was up to.

It watched, through all of it. But what could I do to stop it? That was the price of my coming here.

I wondered just what it intended to ask in exchange.

* * *

I run across a field of snow, exulting in the chill of evening. All about me mountains range, bald granite monuments half-draped in white. Cold, very cold. We are at that place where the forests end, where armies of evergreens gaze upon the mountaintops and say *this far, and no farther.* The wind is rich with the scent of life, and it ruffles my fur with promise. Beside me my sister runs, her coat—as always—in tones of deep gray, tipped with silver. It's her favorite color combination, which she wears regardless of transformation; this time, for once, it's appropriate.

We pause for a moment to read the message on the wind, then turn to the south and slow our pace. The prey is close by, care must be taken in approach. Yolanda glides noiselessly alongside me, her wolf-nose raised to the wind. That way, *her expression informs me.* Very near.

We creep through the snow, she and I, eyes level with its surface, our only light faint moonshine filtered through the branches. The wolf form suits us well, it adapts to our relationship and allows us to hunt together. In a feline form, I tend to prefer solitude.

There. I see her stiffen, and I follow her gaze. A small clearing just ahead, where deer pick foliage off the more inviting branches. Perfect. I can sense Yolanda assessing them, and I do the same. Not as wolf-kin do, probing for physical weakness, but as we must, looking for signs of health and recent feeding, a deer whose bloodstream is rich with the life that we require. There. At the edge of the clearing, see it? We creep through the snow, angled so that a mass of fallen branches obscures our movement. The wind blows our scent back upon us, envelops us with the warm smell of our prey. Even closer . . .

And a doe perks up, suddenly aware of our presence. We have a split second before they move. I bound from my hiding place—my sister does the same—and focus all the power of my wolf-persona upon the task of overtaking my prey. The deer bolts, and we follow swiftly. Through snow-laden bowers, over drifts and across frozen riverbeds—we draw upon the strength inherent in our heritage, and cannot be shaken off.

And at last, eons later, our quarry tires. Yolanda is upon it first but I follow swiftly, and though we do not kill it immediately, as a true wolf might, the deer is as good as dead. Canine teeth, unlike human teeth, are well-equipped for drawing blood, and as mine cut deeply through fur and flesh I feel the elation of the kill. A living spirit shudders beneath us, the strength of our prey incarnate within its body, now loosening its hold on the flesh that has sheltered it and flowing outward, redly, to seek a new home. I absorb it along with the blood and am sated.

Yolanda . . . she nuzzles me once and then turns away, meaning to start off toward her home, which is northward of mine. Suddenly the time-fugue wavers, and I have lost focus. It's important, somehow, that she not leave me. *Come back to my home for hot mulled cider and an evening of stories by the fireplace* . . . but I let her go because the power of the timefugue is absolute, and once I'm trapped in its replay I can't make changes.

Then I know. Frozen with horror I watch her leave me, incapable of warning her. But I remember. Hunters are abroad tonight, whose path will cross hers before morning, whose bullets will shatter her skull before she has any chance to change. I need to tell her of the hide I have seen—will see?—stretched across poles outside a tanner's hut, silver-tipped gray catching the last slivers of light as the moon sets, unknowing . . . I try to cry out to her but the bonds of memory are too strong, too strong! and then she is gone from me. Forever.

I lower my head to the snow and weep, and sometime in the night I change myself back. Or into something else, and then back. But not a wolf. Not again, not for a long time. Not a wolf.

They are not memories. They cannot be memories. I refuse to accept them as memories. . . .

* * *

The Raayat arrived a short while after I had eaten. The sickeningly sweet Tyrran fare which I depended upon for most of my calories had made me slightly ill, as usual, but I rose respectfully as it opened the cell door, and did my best to make it clear that it was welcome. (Did positive reinforcement work, with the Tyr?)

"I come to see if you wish to sedate," it announced.

It must have been clear that I didn't understand, for it soon added, "To translate."

It held out an upper hand, and I saw that a vial was

carefully cradled in its four opposable digits. "We prepare to make translation," it explained me. "Other life-forms are automatically sedated through the nexus. But you are scientist, like-Raayat, so I give you choice." The vial shifted, was extended toward me between two fingertips. "Drinking this now will guarantee darkness through the translation process.

Translation. That was truly alien territory. The thought that we were nearing it prompted a faint stab of fear, but also curiosity. It was hard to say which feeling was stronger.

"Do you sedate?" I asked it.

It seemed to me that it smiled. "I am Tyr. The Tyr does not translate, only in parts. The whole is unaffected, and does not fear." It held the vial out to me; I had the oddest impression that I was being tested. "Yes?"

I considered it, decided to take a chance.

"No. But I thank you for offering.

"I understand." It thought about what I had said, then asked me, "Is this what humans call 'courage'?"

For the first time since leaving Earth I remembered what it was like to smile. And managed it, almost.

"No," I told it. "This is what humans call 'stupidity'—but I'll do it, all the same."

Let its Raayat brain mull over that one, for a while.

Translation. Men had died in that state, I knew. Humankind—and most other advanced species, for that matter—couldn't endure the unique stress that translation engendered. Simpler animals seemed to do marginally better. Still (I reasoned), if *all* men who entered that state undrugged died—or even most of them—the Raayat wouldn't be offering me this opportunity.

"How long?" I asked it.

"We are in approach to the nexus area. Soon," it added, to satisfy my all-too-human impatience.

It turned to go. I almost asked it to leave the vial, in case I should change my mind. But it had called me *like-Raayat,* comparing me to itself—or its subspecies—in some way. Incapable of abstraction, it must have meant it literally: in my situation it would turn down the drug, face translation unarmed in order to better comprehend its nature. By doing the same, I would cement the link between us. That was important. That was worth the risk.

"Thank you," I whispered, and I waited.

Translation: a mathematical trick, and the Tyr's key to space travel. I knew that it involved a complete transference of all mechanical consciousness on board the longship to a system of alien mathematics so foreign to our normal way of thinking that Conquest newsmongers had coined the term "countermathematics" to describe it. Once the transference was complete, the longship would function by a different set of rules, in a universe so unlike anything we had ever conceived of that the human psyche, deprived of every context it had ever known, bereft of the laws it had come to take for granted, was prone to embrace madness as an infinitely more familiar landscape.

What the Tyr had developed—or stolen, more likely—was a mathematical system that didn't depend upon the concept of *distance* as a way of distinguishing two points from each other. The mathematics of it were wholly beyond me, but the end result, as one Conquest tabloid put it, was that two objects could indeed occupy the same space at the same time— provided they differed in a host of other categories. We had our Earth-analogs: the world of the tachyons at rest, the dimension in which the square root of negative one was a viable measure of energy, the state of an object once it was accelerated to the speed of light. We had ways to envision it, words to describe it, but no way to manipulate it. Our world was defined by distance, the laws we had come to perceive as true derived from its nature, our very identity depended upon it; without the careful interplay of matter and space there was no atomic structure, no mass/energy conversion—no *us*. Even if we could enter into such a state, it would be useless except as an academic exercise; robbed of the structure which supported his existence, no man—or machine—could ever return.

But the Tyr had gotten around that. The Tyr could exist according to both structures at once, rooting its soul firmly in the world of solid things as it dipped a wary fingertip into the tachyonic whitewaters of nonspace. Man, if he could survive translation from one state of reality to another, had no way to dictate his point of reentry; the mathematical foundations of nonspace offered no control over the translation process. But not so for the Tyr. With its racial awareness bridging the gap between two disparate dimensions, the Tyr might emerge from that universe at any point where the structure of space-time was congruent to that of the place it had departed from. A nexus, in other words. We were now approaching a region of space-time that was similar, within an acceptable range of deviation, to a region adjacent to the Meyaga system. By translating the ship from one mathematical context to the other—and then back again—the Tyr could span the distance between them.

I dreaded the process, but faced it undrugged. What scientist could do otherwise?

There was only one warning. A throbbing sound that shook the very rock surrounding me; a giant drumbeat that used the longship itself as an instrument. Part of the process? Or a last warning for the Tekk, warning them to make their preparations? For a brief moment I wondered if my curiosity wasn't about to kill me—

And then, suddenly, my body imploded. Flesh folded in upon flesh, vital organs crushed in the center—and then the whole burst inward again with sudden, searing pain. Bones shattered to fragments, muscles flayed to bits, and bits of stone from the world beyond spiraled in as on the winds of a cyclone. The force of it was stunning—the pain beyond bearing—the process beyond my comprehension. All about me the world fell to pieces, collapsing furiously toward that single point which lay at the center of the maelstrom.

At the center of me. The single point which was all
that remained of my identify, a flickering fragment of
I which acted as a magnet to all the substance of a
collapsing universe.

And as I was battered by each new storm of debris,
I absorbed the essence of what that thing had been. I
was a small stone chamber carved in a longship, now
reduced to microscopic fragments mixed with human
blood. I was the bulk of a longship, miles upon miles
of living rock—now split by inward-spiraling shock-
waves into a cloud of rubble. I was man, and Tekk,
and every weeping, crawling thing that called the
longship home—even Tyr—and I floundered in the pain
of their dying as the translation process dismembered
them, cell by cell, molecule by molecule, and sucked
them inward—until nothing remained of any of us but
one voiceless, mouthless attempt to scream.

Still the holocaust continued, its power increasing
geometrically as it consumed vast segments of open
space, whole planets, burning stars, entire civiliza-
tions. . . . I felt the edge of madness creeping over
me as whole species were thrust screaming into my
consciousness, as the very foundations of the universe
shattered into bits, and each living fragment stabbed
its way into the tempest. I fought it off as best I could,
but there was nothing stable to cling to. Nothing in
the entire universe that was not totally caught up in
this maelstrom of destruction. I tried to call up memories from my human past—to conjure up some vague
thought of normalcy—but to my horror, nothing came.
Nothing. Only the whirlwind of destruction that had
made me its center, which was slowly loosening my
grip on sanity. I felt myself sliding down into madness, a black pool of endless torment with no escape
in sight. . . .

Then, as suddenly as it had come, the terrible vision
ceased. Before I could even acknowledge its absence,
my muscles contracted spasmodically, sending me
crashing to the floor. I began to vomit, repeatedly, as
though by doing so I might cast out the terror of a

dying universe. Convulsions ran through my flesh in successive waves, bringing up bitter fluid—bile, now, for I had little food left in me—and I choked as I tried to breathe.

For a while, I was nearly helpless. It took all my effort to keep from choking to death, as my body exhausted its supply of bitter liquids and began to bring up blood. After some time, I was able to take in air again. A few breaths, hoarse and labored. A short while later, as if to reward my efforts, the last convulsion ceased.

I drew in a deep breath, and held it. *Easy. Easy.* And let it go. Then another. *Good.* Then a few more like it.

Had breathing ever felt this good before?

I opened my eyes, and looked for the Raayat. It wasn't there yet, but it would be, soon; it would want to find out how its pet human had fared. Whether my human courage—or foolishness—had been the end of me.

I'm not dead yet, you bastard. I struggled to a sitting position, anxious to make a good showing. Vomit stained my paw and I began to lick it off, using my teeth to separate the dampened hairs—

No.

—and then I rubbed the moistened paw along the line of my jaw, licked it clean, began again—

No! No, No, No, No!

—and cowered, terrified, a low, drawn-out yowling the only verbalization of my distress. What was happening? My soul was terrified, but my body disdained to acknowledge it; the instincts which arose in my unfamiliar brain disavowed all past terror, prompted me to calm down, live in the present moment, clean my fur—

—not my fur, not mine!

I am human. Human. HUMAN!

Shuddering, I closed my eyes, called up an image of self. Daetrin Ungashak To-Alym Haal: Human being, albeit an odd one. Human *always*, in every century, clad in the same unchanging body. Never a wolf, despite the memories. Never a . . . whatever I just thought I was; never that, either. Always a man, in a man's unfurred body. *Always*.

And when I opened my eyes again, it was true.

I looked up and found the Raayat watching me from outside the door, its eyes shining bright through the stone latticework. "You survive," it said approvingly. "And the mind?"

I looked at my arm—now human, with human fingers—and flexed it, shuddering. "My mind is intact," I assured him, quietly. Trying to make the sounds ring true.

Wishing I believed them myself.

LONGSHIP TALGUTH: THE BLOODING PLACE

With the ritual paint on her face, Ntaya looked more like a ghost than a Caucasian. The stylized swirls of zinc oxide which were meant to add breadth to her forehead and depth to her eye sockets stood out stark as bone against the midnight darkness of her skin; the streaks of yellow paint which marked her skull, ears, and neck seemed more like some ghastly texturing device than a representation of human hair.

Which was as it should be. She was a starsha of the *Talguth*-Tekk, which gave her the right—and the responsibility—to stand in for one of Earth's absent races. But it wasn't so long ago that she had put on the ghost-paint herself, and before that the beast-paint; the ferocity of her current makeup appealed to her, in that it echoed both those roles.

Silence. The birth chamber was dark, and warmed by the presence of so many bodies; the sharp smell of seyga, newly harvested, filled her nostrils. Its fumes had the power to excite memory, and she was careful as she drew each breath to distinguish past from present, and present from dreamtime.

A drumbeat: deep, resonant, timed like a human heartbeat. It made the rock tremble beneath her feet, and echoed (she suspected) as far as the upper chambers. Four children would be passing through the gateway now, hand in hand as they reassured each other. Or separately, as they imagined adults would proceed. They knew all the legends of the Blooding, true and untrue, everything the adults wanted them to know.

And they would be afraid. *Should* be afraid. Not more than two of them were likely to survive. . . .

Silence, again. The drumbeats had stopped. Jovus stepped forward and lowered a taper into the wide stone brazier, firing the dried seyga roots within. And then covered it, with a dome of blackened glass. His own mask was of ocher paint, with thick black lines that narrowed his eyes to slits, and the thin line of smoke which arose through the hole in the top of the dome curled about his face, adding to its ferocity. Painted thus, he was no less frightening than Ntaya herself, and no more human in aspect.

Grotesque and silent, the adults of the *Talguth*-Tekk stood in the thickening seyga smoke, and awaited the coming of their children.

And remembered:

* * *

"You're afraid?"

She stood before the heavy iron gates and squared her shoulders, defiant. "No." The gates were massive, incised with images from Earth's distant past. She reached out a hand to touch them and saw herself hesitate, trembling. "Maybe a little," she admitted, and withdrew without making contact. Stepped back. "But only a little."

There were three of them, two girls and a boy, similar in age but worlds apart in temperament. The smaller girl, Willa, was a mere child yet; despite her years, the coming roundness of womanhood was still far in her future. She was lean and agile and not without spirit, but lacking in stamina. Ntaya wondered if she would survive the Blooding. Their male companion, self-named Jiande, was a cocky adolescent who overflowed with exuberance and courage; she hoped at least some of it would last through the trials. As for herself . . .

The darkest of the three, and the tallest. Middle in age. Energetic, but contained. She bore a true Earth

Name, which had been passed down through the generations, from the time of the Subjugation to the moment of her birth. *Ntaya.* It gave her a special strength to know who she was—who she wanted to be—while other children tried on names, and discarded them, a thousand times over. *Ntaya.* An Earth-sound, from the Free Time. She was ready to present it, and herself, to the elders of the *Talguth*-Tekk. Only the closed gate stood between the children and their adult existence . . . and the rite of the Blooding, which would begin when it opened.

"I'm not afraid," she whispered. A lie, but a necessary one. She tried to believe it.

Then slowly, ponderously, the heavy iron gates swung open before them. Above the pounding of her own heart Ntaya could hear a distant drumbeat keeping the same time, informing the hraas that the rite was about to begin. She reached out to one side and caught Jiande's hand, and squeezed it. *Be brave.* Willa linked an arm through hers on the other side, and together the three of them moved forward. Through the gates, and past all safety. They were in the land of the Tyr now, where the hraas held sway.

Forward they walked, step by step, then around a turn, then forward again. Beside her Ntaya could hear Willa's breathing, tense and fearful, and she wished for the safety of the iron doors and the Place of Children that lay behind them. But the gate, now closed, had passed from sight, and the home of their childhood would no longer welcome them.

"We could run," Jiande whispered. By this he didn't mean *run in fear,* but merely a quickening of pace that would take them to where they were going that much faster. There would be no shame in that. Ntaya looked at Willa, whose eyes reflected her own feelings on the matter, and she whispered back, "No. We need time to make it right."

As to whether or not they *could* make it right, Ntaya refused to contemplate. To be caught up in fear now would be foolish, if not fatal. The entire spirit must

be bound together in courage if the Blooding was to
be survived. They all knew that. Let childish hearts
quail in fear, and fail the testing; Ntaya was determined to pass the threshold of adulthood with honor.
No fear, now. No place for it. She was Tekk.

Another turn, then a long sloping corridor that led
steadily downward. It was said that the upper tunnels
were smoothly carved and brightly lit; here, in the
Tekk domain, only scattered bits of fungus shed their
luminescence upon the cracked and pitted walls.
Overhead shelves of poorly supported rock loomed
with menace, and vertical crevices that couldn't be
seen until the children were right next to them might
shelter any number of threats. This was the land of
adults, where nothing was safe. This was the land of
the Tyr, where only submission to the Will could protect them from harm.

Suddenly, without warning, a figure jumped out in
front of them. Teeth bared, menacing, the form that
might once have been human was decked out in bits
of leather and fur, so that neither its face nor its true
form were visible. Bright paint was splashed across its
skin in mockery of Tyr-pattern, blue and scarlet and
green and orange, with jagged swirls that crested like
Tyrran armor-plates at the shoulders and outer thighs.
The face itself was a mask of death, half hidden by
studded leather and half transformed by corpse-paint
into the image of a grinning skull.

As more of its kind jumped out at the children—
behind them, beside them, everywhere where there
was a crevice to leap from—the hideous creature
grinned, and extended its arms toward Ntaya. Leather
mitts bound its extremities into a four-fingered parody
of the Tyrran shape, while bright metal claws fastened
to the fingertips twitched hungrily toward the young
girl's eyes. It was a fearful sight under normal circumstances; combined with the tension of the Blooding, it
was terrifying.

Ntaya—who had never seen a real Tyr, and was not
quite sure that this wasn't one of them—stood her

ground. This was the testing, she was sure of it. She emptied her mind of all thoughts of flight, all dreams of defiance, and held herself rock-steady as the deadly steel slivers came closer and closer to her face. She *was* the tunnelway, dark and silent; she was without fear, being rock, and would stand like a boulder while this Tyr-creature worked its will. Steel touched her cheek while the beast-face leered at her, its fur-ends brushing against her lips as she bit them, trying to control herself. Then there was sudden pain as the steel bit deeply, cutting into her cheek. Still she did not move. Outward, up again, the sharp steel talons moved toward her left eye, drawing a line of blood along her face. She knew that the creature might well blind her— knew only too well that those who survived the rite were often maimed in the process—but still she was rock-steady, and refused to fear. The Will of the Tyr would protect her.

At last the creature stepped back, grinning its pleasure. Despite her best intentions Ntaya felt tears coming, tried bravely to force them back. Claws gouged her shoulders as another creature, kin to the first, slashed her from behind; there must have been some kind of poison on the claw tips, no mere steel could cause that much pain. Now there were more of the creatures, dancing a death-dance about her while Tekk drumbeats marked time in the distance. Talons of steel cut into her back, her abdomen, her thigh, leaving streaks of blood and rivers of pain in their wake. But these were the Tyr, and the message of the Rite was unshakable: only by submitting to the Will of that species might she earn the right to pass through the gates of adulthood. And so she refused to move, refused to protect herself, refused even to fear, but forced herself to submit to their torture, crying out only when the pain was so great that for a split second her animal-self surfaced, taking control of her voice.

At last, it was over. The creatures stepped back from her, grinning at their sport. Something trickled into her eyes, blinding her. With a shaky hand she wiped it away, then blinked until that last of it was gone from her vision. Blood. She turned slightly so that she might see her companions, was heartened to find them still standing. *We will brave adulthood together,* she promised them silently.

The lead creature gestured for the children to pass between their taloned ranks; Ntaya hesitated only a second, then stepped forward. She was expecting them to attack her as she passed, could not help but flinch as she led her companions, single file, between the lines of their tormentors. But the children were not cut anew—at least, she wasn't—and a few steps later the corridor turned again, leading them out of sight of the terrible creatures.

There was sniffling behind her, perhaps tears. Willa? Jiande? She didn't turn back to see, but whispered, "Courage, It's almost over." Blood dribbled down her legs and collected under her feet, making footfall slick and dangerous; she looked at the stone floor ahead of her, noted the stains of previous generations of Bloodings. *We're not alone,* she thought. The spirits of all those who had gone before were here, in this place, giving them courage. At least, that was what the children whispered when there were no adults about, their own rite-mythos. She hoped it was true.

Then another turn, and she saw the ghosts. Painted all in white, like the palest ones from Earth, they bore bundles of long, thin rags which were braided together at one end to form a handle, and which hung loose at the other. As Ntaya approached she could see that the strips of cloth were wet, and not with water. She passed between the first pair of them, feeling her muscles tense. Then she was struck, and the whiplash drove liquid fire into her wounds. She gasped, and faltered. Immediately they were upon her, and there was no need for them to strike hard, although they did. Whatever fluid had soaked those scourges, it was like acid in her wounds. She forced herself forward, step by step, knowing that to falter here was to die beneath their lashes. But although she suffered terribly, she was not yet afraid. All was as it should be; this was the rite of Submission.

Do to me what you will, she thought, as she passed between the last pair of whip-wraiths. *I am Tekk.*

They all three made it through. Ntaya had been concerned for Willa, who was neither strong nor courageous. But the dark-skinned youngster, bathed in blood, bared her teeth in an attempt at smiling as she passed the last line of torment. Jiande was still, and concentrated on breathing evenly. *He is trying not to be afraid,* Ntaya realized. After a moment the three children looked at each other, and Willa grinned nervously. "I am Willa," she said, small hand striking her blood-scored chest in illustration. "I am Tekk-Human, and do not fear."

They echoed the words, choruslike, and wiped the blood from their faces.

"Is there more, do you think?" Jiande's voice was trembling, betraying the intensity of his fear. Ntaya tried to sound more steady as she responded, "There must be."

"Let's go on," Willa whispered, and the three of them began to move.

They followed the path of old blood beneath their feet, adding their own color to its markings. Soon the passage widened, so that all three might stand abreast once more. Ntaya felt a hand brush hers, then grasp it. Jiande. She squeezed back, wishing she could make courage flow from her heart to her hand, and into her friend. The boy needed it badly.

Then the passage became a chamber, with a single candle set in its center. The ceiling had been cleared of glow-fungus, and dark shadows danced upon the walls as the children entered, gathering about the source of light like insects.

"Look," Willa whispered, and Jiande followed her gaze. Figures stood on all sides of them, tucked away in niches that had been carved into the chamber's walls. Some were like the Tyr-creatures they had met, or like the ghosts which had beaten them. Others were even more grotesque, with masks and markings that were a parody of human features. Smoke rose from a brazier in the room's center, and its pungent odor clung to her nostrils. Seyga, the narcotic caveweed. All about her she could feel the painted figures radiating tension as they waited, deathlike in their utter stillness. Any time now. Any time . . .

A low scratching sound, claw upon stone. The children whirled to face their new attacker, and Jiande cried out. A hraas. Long, graceful, deadly, it moved into the chamber without a sound, its sharp nose raised to take in air, to sift it clean of its messages. It glanced at the painted figures, at the children, at the source of light. Glanced again, and sniffed. Ntaya held herself still, telling herself: *This is the final testing. This is what will make me a Tekk.*

And then it was running. Muscles bunched together beneath its fur, then released; it left the ground in a powerful leap, all the force of its progress concentrated into one soaring package. Ntaya stepped back, an instinctive reaction. But the hraas wasn't going for her. It passed to one side of her, claws extended, and landed full weight upon her friend, bearing Jiande to the ground. Ntaya heard a child's cry, realized it was her own. She breathed deeply as she watched the hraas tear her friend's throat out, trying to regain control of herself. Blood was spurting from the wound like a geyser, rhythmic gushes that marked Jiande's last heartbeats. *I am not afraid,* Ntaya told herself, tears running down her face. *I am Tekk. Tekk do not fear the hraas. The Will of the Tyr will protect me.*

The predator turned, its jaws stained with blood, and looked at the two girls. For a moment its jeweled eyes focused on Ntaya, and the intensity of the creature's gaze forced her backward, until she had to take a step to steady herself. Then the great predator turned toward Willa, and Ntaya could see the girl tense.

It leapt again, and tore out the young girl's throat with such swiftness that Willa didn't even have time to utter a cry of surprise. Then it quickly turned its gaze upon Ntaya, and the bright blue eyes met hers, pierced her soul, and searched for defiance. The seyga smoke had banished all else from her awareness, so that in the entire universe there was only herself, and the hraas. She met its gaze without flinching, felt herself being drawn inside it. Into the soul of a hunter. Into an intelligence so alien that the Tekk could neither understand nor control it, but had developed a working relationship nonetheless. *Those whom you spare at the Blooding will be safe from your kind forever.*

The great head turned away. She felt herself exhale in relief, realized that she had not breathed since Willa's death. *I am Tekk.* The knowledge stunned her, left her speechless as the adults of the *Talguth*-Tekk, ignoring the hraas, came to greet her.

By what Earth Name will you be called?

She muttered the label she had chosen, her voice trembling as the shock of the Blooding finally sank in. As the death of her two friends hit her. Tears flowed copiously down her face, cleansing her cheeks of blood. She had left her childhood behind her, and with it the memory of two friends who had never passed through its gates. Who had never been born at all. Such was the truth, as the Tyr would be told it.

She hoped someday she could believe it.

* * *

There were four of them, now, standing small and trembling before the adult company. None had succumbed to the tests of strength, which was good; such trials were meant only to prepare them for the hraas' scrutiny, and weren't intended to kill.

Three beasts had come to attend the ritual, their chameleon fur matched to the flickering orange of the candle's flame. Although it would be foolish to assign any Earth emotion to the enigmatic predators, Ntaya watched them and thought: *They enjoy it. They like seeing the children afraid.*

Sadistic grounders!

The first beast made its choice. With a motion as smooth as liquid fire, it singled out and leapt upon one of the children. A second was soon to follow, taking out the youngest of those who remained. The third hraas paced anxiously, sniffed the air, but didn't move. That was a good sign; Ntaya hoped the remaining children noticed it.

And at last it was over. The hunters nuzzled the last two children, bared their teeth and hissed at them, but made no move to harm them. Ntaya wondered—not for the first time—just how the animals made their selection. Would changes in the ritual result in a higher survival rate? They had refined the Blooding as much as they could, taking their cues from the hraas, but might it still be improved yet further? Or were the hraas simply unwilling to let the Tyr's human servants add to their numbers beyond a certain limit?

The implications of that! It sent shivers through her. How much did they really know about the hraas? How much did *anyone* know?

Jovus addressed the children. "By what Earth Name will you be known among our people?"

"Io, if the starshi permit." The boy's voice was a mere whisper.

"Tigris, revered starshi."

Conservative names, with strong Earth-associations; Ntaya approved. But the children's voices were weak—the shock was beginning to hit them. In a short while they would be bundled in blankets and brought to a place of rest, where their minds and bodies would be nursed back to health. But not yet. They had been trained from birth to serve the Tyr without question; such upbringing was necessary to insure that their facade of subservience never faltered. But now, for those whom the hraas had accepted, there was one more surprise to come. And this time it was her job to explain it.

And the truth might well prove the worst shock of all.

TSING COLONY NINE

There was a Marra on the landing field. Not the Tsing-Marra, but another. That implied that the fearful one had been wrong. Which in turn implied . . .

Don't get your hopes up, she warned herself. *Not until you make sure that he is what he seems.*

But no amount of isolation from her own kind could dull her Marra senses so much that she could fail to recognize another of her species, even at such a distance. Her life-sight picked him out unerringly from the two-legged creatures that surrounded him, and though he was clearly passing for one of them the two were as different in her sight as night and day.

So there *was* more than one Marra on this world, and therefore there might be more elsewhere, as well. So much for the alleged agreement.

Much to her surprise, she hesitated to confront him. It was most unlike her. Could it be that she lacked faith in her current Identity, or in her memory? If it turned out that this new Marra shared the same delusion as his Tsing-brother, she would have to face a very unpleasant truth. Was it really possible that her entire race was divided, in hiding? That the Marra lived in fear of the massbound?

There was only one way to find out.

Girding her courage—and borrowing life from the plant life that had sheltered her, so that she wouldn't weaken herself by Changing—she adopted a form which could pass among these strangers. Biped, oddly balanced . . . it could use a tail, she decided, but she refrained from adding one. Her new body's senses

were sensitive enough; she made only minor adjustments to the airborne particle sense before she dared
to come out of hiding, and approach the landing field
itself.

She waited until the Marra was alone—a long wait,
but she was patient—and then she stepped to the path
before him, waiting to see how he would react.

He looked at her, embodied senses first and then
with a Marra touch, ever so wary, to confirm what his
adopted eyes told him. The form he wore was tall and
lean, dark-skinned, and purposefully mutilated with
geometric scarring; she noted when he moved that his
motion was awkward, in that manner which was typical of her kind. *We are uncomfortable in bodies,* she
observed. *But what's the alternative?*

He found his voice, and with it his dignity. ''I am
called Kost.''

Saudar! He spoke Saudar to her. It was an encouraging sign. And yet, the oddity of his greeting disturbed her. What manner of Marra was he, that he
offered her a name?

She took an impression of his brain and searched
through it quickly, seeking some appropriate gesture
of pleasure—and found it, and adjusted her body to
encompass the expression. A twisting of the lips at the
corners, slight crinkling of the eyes . . . a very curious
set of muscular contractions; she would have to seek
out its origins, someday.

''Indeed?'' she asked pleasantly. ''By whom?''

He seemed taken aback. Or perhaps she was simply
reading that into him; not all Marra could control a
host body with her skill. It was possible that his face
looked blank simply because he had withdrawn from
his flesh to consider the implications of her presence.
The cruder Marra worked that way.

Maintaining her smile, she waited.

At last he spoke, his voice couched low in the night.
''Where do you come from?''

''Shian,'' she answered. ''Do you know it?''

He shook his head from side to side, and she caught

the negative association. "I have no memory of the name."

"It was an obscure world. A gas giant. I was sent to explore. I wound up trapped there . . ." How to word it? "for too long a time."

"And just how long is that?" His voice revealed nothing of his reaction to her presence, was a vehicle for necessary communication and nothing more. She longed for the use of Saudar scent-codes, which would have given her some insight into his thought processes. For some reason, he made her uneasy.

In answer, she countered, "How long since the Tyr came?"

"To Saudar? Nearly five centuries, as the Unity reckoned time."

"Then I was there five centuries. At least." Nearly a full Span, as she had suspected; most of the Marra would have lost their Saudar memories by now, or rewoven their few remaining scraps of recall into a Tyrran context. As the Tsing-Marra had done.

"Ah," he said. A hint of smiling, somewhat ungraceful on his mutilated face. "Then you missed the Masters' fall."

Was there mockery in his tone? "Apparently so."

"Untainted, then." He reached out to her and took her hand, touching her essence-to-essence through the contact. It was a bleak, uncomforting touch. "I've been searching for your kind."

Suddenly there were voices, coming toward them. "Tekk," he whispered. "This way." He beckoned her toward an abandoned storage shed, which was heavily locked against the night. With a touch he altered it; the heavy door slid aside, admitting them. "Inside."

Inside was darkness, but neither of them needed additional light. She adjusted her eyes to interpret the infrared spectrum, and by the glare of his body's heat observed his excitement.

"I'm so glad to see you," he told her. His joy was palpable to her Marra senses, a welcome relief after her reception by the Tsing-Marra. She wondered what it was about him that made her feel so uneasy. "A Marra with memory . . . I gather you do remember, yes?" She nodded. "Most of our people have been crippled by memory loss—"

"I was afraid of that."

"No matter. You can help me now . . . there's so much to do! When the yoke of the embodied has been broken, you can help restore the Marra. You must have a good bit of Span left, if you remember—"

"Hold on. Slow down. *Explain*. What in Unity are you talking about?"

He leaned toward her, his borrowed eyes gleaming. "Marra domination."

It took her a minute to realize what he meant; when she did she was astounded. "Of what?"

"The embodied."

"*All* of them?" She tried not to laugh. The thought of the Marra ruling anybody was downright ludicrous; the thought of the Marra ruling *everyone* was . . . well, it was damned funny. The Saudar would have laughed until their kangi drooped. But she managed to keep from laughing outright, in order to hear him out. Incredible as it seemed to her, he was apparently serious.

How can we hope to stabilize the universe, when we can't even stabilize ourselves?

"Traditionally we've indulged them in their power-play," he explained. "But they've done too much damage, this time. "We simply can't afford to let them go on like this. Just look around you! Look at our people!—I can see by your face that you've already made contact, then you know what's been happening. Another century of this and we won't remember anything *but* the Tyr, we won't know anything but hiding and fearing and playing at being embodied. . . ." His voice was a fierce whisper, rich with embodied emotion; an excellent display, she thought. "They've forfeited their right to rule us, Marra."

"They never did rule us," she pointed out calmly.

"An arguable point."

There was no point in debating the obvious. "So
what will you do?"

"Unite the Marra. Find those few who still remember—like yourself—who will understand what has to
be done. We'll find a way to break the hold of the Tyr,
then rule these worlds in their stead."

"And you think the embodied will accept you?"

His face darkened. "Is there anyone more qualified
to rule them?"

Humor swelled up inside her, and she searched
through her current brain for an appropriate means of
expression. Saudar laughter had no direct equivalent,
so she settled for an even broader smile. "I marvel at
your naïveté. Kost. At your blind faith in their power
of reasoning. Do you think they'll accept you just because you're qualified? When have the embodied ever
acted in such a rational manner? What will you do?—
come before them and say, 'Look at me, I'm the wisest
among you. The strongest. The most long lived.' Do
you think that'll make a bit of difference? When they
fight wars constantly amongst themselves, just to decide which of a dozen unqualified Competitors will sit
on the throne tomorrow? Their politics are rooted in
species-survival instinct, filtered through unreliable
body chemistry; do you expect these Competitors will
bow down to you, when all their genetic programming
drives them to do otherwise? Really, Marra! You've
forgotten more than I think you're aware of."

His voice was cold, emphatically so. "You under-
estimate me. My Span isn't so short yet that I've forgotten my diplomatic training. I'll cut at their roots
from the inside, first; when it comes time to dominate,
they'll *need* our leadership. —So what say you, Marra?
Do you mean to accept your exile? Wander around
until your memory erodes and you're no better than
the rest of them? Or will you help me—help *us*—to
restore ourselves to a position of authority in this
massbound, backward universe? The choice is yours."

For an instant she was tempted—the hunger to belong nearly blinded her to the distastefulness of his

scheming—but then she answered, in formal Saudar, "There is no choice."

He was surprised. So wrapped up in his delusions of grandeur was he that he hadn't considered, even for a moment, that she wouldn't wish to join him.

He touched a hand to her shoulder and his essence questioned *Truth? Certainty?*

She merely nodded.

"I'm sorry," he said. His voice was emotionless once more, but she thought there was anger in him. "I think you'll change your mind. The option remains open."

"All Marra change their minds," she agreed. *But not that much*. Still, she was loath to abandon her only informative contact, and asked him, "If I do, how should I go about finding you?"

"I'll ride the longships until I've located all of our people, and set up some kind of communications network between them. If you need me, ask among the Tekk. That's a subspecies of the creatures called 'human.' They're marginally organized, and have a system of intership codes that suits our purposes. I've embedded my codes within theirs; if you ask for me, by name, I'll hear of it." He glanced toward the door as if making sure that no one was listening, a gesture that was charming in its paranoia. "They're useful, these Tekk. They come and go regularly throughout Tyrran territory. Take the place of one, if you want to travel without being noticed. It's the easiest way. The Tyr know every human face that boards their ships, the Honn that guard the shuttles share total awareness . . . you can't slip by them, except in a legitimate body. As for traveling on the worlds themselves, you'll need a real identity there as well. The Tyr watch over everyone. I find it useful to create a disaster, natural or otherwise, that can explain a few deaths; preferably something that results in shock as well, to cover an awkward performance. That way you can duplicate an existing body, and no one will notice."

For a moment she was speechless. Not that she had

anything against killing; the embodied were little more than food to her kind, and unless one was interacting with them, they had no intrinsic value. But . . . such waste!

"You do this on every planet?"

"When I have to leave the longships, yes."

She said nothing. Only nodded, a cold aknowledgment of his advice. There was no point in arguing any further. He was distasteful, his ways were distasteful . . . but she was Marra, and would not pass judgment upon him.

He must have sensed her disapproval; his expression tightened and he told her, "You'll learn. Take a good look at our people and you'll see what's necessary. And when you do, you'll join me. I'm sure of it."

Nine Spans in a Saudar hell, first.

"Thank you," she said quietly. "Kost." Diplomacy, above all else; it was still second nature to her. "For the option. I'll consider it." *Did I know you in a previous Span? Did I dislike you this much, back then?* "I wish you luck," she added softly. Lies, all lies. That was how you dealt with the embodied. Disturbing, to use the same techniques with her own kind.

"And I wish you reason," he whispered. "Soon. Before it's too late."

The door opened, and night flooded in. And moonlight, by which his scars were visible. She stayed where she was when he left her, listened to the sounds of his body moving farther and farther away, and considered how strange the universe had gotten since she had last been in regular contact with it.

A self-named Marra . . . how bizarre!

Too late for what? she wondered.

LONGSHIP TALGUTH

I'm losing my mind.

I sat on my sleeping ledge for a long time, staring
at the floor, trying to pull myself together. My hands
were still shaking. I was afraid to look at them. Afraid
to look in the mirror. Afraid, most of all, to face the
implications of what was happening to me.

I was going insane. Or I was sane, but the mechanism of my senses was somehow malfunctioning. Then
there was that thought which I dared not even give a
name to, a concept so incredible that my rational soul
shied away from the merest hint of it. No. It wasn't
possible. To even consider such a thing again, after all
these years. . . .

I lowered my face to my hands and fought for control: of emotion, of reason, of memory. Of myself.
Skin pressed against skin, unfurred; the contact was
reassuring. "I *am* human," I whispered softly—but
whom was I trying to convince?

After a while, I dared to raise my head up and look
about me. The walls were simply stone, with dull
green paint that would feel smooth to the touch. The
corridor beyond my door was gray, with no noticeable
markings. No luminescent colors. No giant's heartbeat
pounding in my head. For the moment, at least, my
senses were under control. They would stay that way.
I would make sure they stayed that way.

I looked at my hands, smooth-skinned and pale.
Human. I was human.

Then I rose, and dared to look in the mirror.

And froze, horrified.

The change was a minor one. Had I not already been questioning my stability, I might never have noticed it. But I was, and I did, and the change which I saw was doubly terrifying in that context.

I touched the gray at my sideburns with a trembling finger. That color had been gone from my hair, since my first day on the longship. The cleaner had removed it. Now it was back. Two dabs of Earth makeup, reappearing out of nowhere.

I licked the tip of a finger and rubbed it vigourosly against one gray streak. And felt a chill course down my spine, as the attempted cleaning had no effect.

It wasn't makeup.

I turned sharply away from the mirror, banging my hip against the sanitary outlet as I did so. What was happening to me? I could think of nothing to explain such a change, other than madness. Was I so far gone, already?

No. Be honest. There is another possibility, but you refuse to name it.

The power of primitive superstition says that once you call a demon by name, it has material substance and can harm you. The power of modern psychology says that once you acknowledge a deeply buried fear, and allow it to rise to the surface, you can never fully bury it again.

I was afraid. Of myself?

I shut my eyes and tried to think. Tried to envision myself as I should be, youthful and sandy-haired, without any gray. *Without any gray!* I held the image in my mind and forced myself to concentrate on it— to *believe* it—while my clenched fingers drew blood from my palms and my eyes squeezed out tears of pain, to run in parallel channels down my cheeks.

Please. Let the image be right. I can deal with anything else. . . .

I opened my eyes, and dared to turn. Dared to focus, upon the image that I feared to contemplate. But it was right. Un-gray. Exactly as it should be.

Slowly I raised my hands to my face, and wiped the

wetness from my cheeks. My hands throbbed dully, and when I looked down at them I saw thin crescent moons of blood lined up across the palms, where my nails had cut through flesh.

The Tyr had suspected me of being extraterrestrial in origin. Could it have been correct? Might that explain some characteristics which seemed bizarre by Earth standards, but were consistent within an alien context? I had clear memories of the father who raised me, the mother who left me, the sister who was lost to me after some tragic accident . . . but I had other memories, too, which were clearly riddled with fantastic innacuracies. Were those images of family no more than false memories, which only seemed true when viewed through the haze of centuries? Was I, in fact, something other than human?

I looked at my hands, found them suddenly unfamiliar. What kind of creature would appear human in all regards, but be incapable of digesting certain Earth proteins? If he wore a human form, would that dictate the nature of his consciousness, or would his brain be true to his alien self—casting aside unwanted memories, chaotically indulging in others, processing information in a way that wasn't wholly human?

I looked in the mirror, wondering.

I shouldn't have.

A moment was all it took; I swept aside the battered frame, heard it strike the portal with a crash and then fall to the ground. But the damage had already been done. I had seen the reflection, and it was not of me—not the me that I knew, my comfortable human image, but someone entirely different. Some*thing* entirely different, whose bodily form was unlike anything I had ever seen.

Unlike anything human.

Trembling, I knew that I stood balanced on the brink of madness. Insanity and longevity are a truly terrifying combination; if I gave in now, I might pay the price for centuries to come. Unthinkable. I must fight this, somehow. I must analyze what was happening, come to terms with it. *Control* it. That way, only, lay my salvation.

I walked to where the mirror lay, face up by the door. Catching it on my toe, I flipped it over. It clattered briefly and then came to rest, face down. One less thing to deal with. One less reminder that, though I had questions which must be asked, I might not like the answers.

I had always hated mirrors. Now I remembered why.

* * *

The Raayat came at midnight. My personal midnight, when my vital energy was at its lowest and my mind was immured in darkness. It came to me suddenly and woke me roughly, its hands shaking with tension as it grabbed me by the arm and jerked me, still half-sleeping, to my feet. I had been in deep sleep, trancelike; panic quickly awakened me. Something was wrong, seriously wrong, but I lacked the ability to read what it was. Was the Unstable One living up to its epithet at last?

"Come," it rasped, and his voice seemed different—higher-pitched, less certain. I looked at its markings, wondering if it was indeed the same Raayat I had known. The body said yes, but the behavior made me uncertain. What the hell was going on?

It dragged me out through the portal before it was fully open, scraping me against the edge of the stone door. There was a nightmarish quality to our journey which filled me with dread, but I had no chance to hold back; its hand was on my upper arm, talons biting into my skin as it forced me to match its long-legged stride.

We passed through corridors and more corridors, all new to me. I counted my steps, trying to maintain some sense of our direction. The inner wall of my cell already had a crude map scratched into its paint; if I kept track of where we were going, I could add to it. Two thousand steps. Three thousand. The counting was

good, it kept me from dwelling on the fact that if the
Raayat was indeed beginning to lose touch with reality, there was no one in the Tyr or out of it who would
help me. *You deal with that kind,* the Kuol had told
me, *at your own risk. The rest of the Tyr will not help
you.*

Not a comforting thought.

At last we appeared to reach our destination. The
Raayat let go of me suddenly, pushing me away toward
the wall as it sought the desired portal. I took that
moment to touch a finger to my arm, where a spot of
blood was welling forth, and then to the wall. Such a
small stain should go unnoticed, but combined with
my step-counting it would give me a fairly good chance
of finding this place again. God alone knew if I would
want to, but now that I knew I could get myself out of
my cell, I needed to keep my options open.

It opened the door—a smaller one than most—
grabbed me again, and dragged me through. No patience in it at all. At first I couldn't see what manner
of room we had entered, but then it reached out and
pressed something, and a square of intense light suddenly appeared before me.

"Sit," the Raayat commanded.

Temporarily blinded, I failed to obey. It pushed me
down into a chair and held me there until I nodded
that yes, yes, I would stay. Blazing scatoma danced
across my field of vision, but beyond them I managed
to make out the outlines of a large and somewhat
crowded room; it was unlit except for the square which
burned before me, and every corner was filled with
machinery of some kind. Screens, keyboards, projec-
tors, giant lenses with panels of white set opposite—a
multimedia processing center, I guessed. Not used
very often, from the look of it.

The Raayat moved beside me, and the picture before
me changed. No longer was it a field of blinding white,
but a full color, high-resolution projection. Of a forest, it seemed to me—perhaps even one on Earth. What
was the point of this?

"Tell me what you see," the Raayat commanded.

The ludicrousness of the whole situation was counterbalanced by its tone of voice, which implied that I might well die if I failed to satisfy it. Not knowing what it wanted, I dared the only answer I had. "A forest." And I added, "Mostly coniferous—"

With a hiss it reached forward to the controls, and a new picture appeared. The Raayat's anger was unmistakable. "And this one?"

I answered what I saw, which was a seashore. Again, my response seemed to anger it. But there it was: the murky green of shallow seawater, the curling white lines of breaking surf, and an expanse of mud and rock that was visible where the waves had receded. Seashore. Or maybe—just maybe—lakeshore. But what else could it possibly be?

More pictures. More anger. I struggled to give it the answers it wanted, but I seemed to fail every time. Pictures flashed by me with ever-increasing speed. *What do you see?* Forest scenes. Desert. An alien landscape, blood-red in the light of its swollen, dying sun. News photos from my home planet: Kennedy's assassination. An early spacewalk. The Conquest.

How many hours we spent like this, I couldn't say. I lost all track of time, mesmerized by the progression of images that flashed before me, speaking automatically in response to pictures that I only half-saw. I was desperately trying to work out what the Raayat wanted, but it was giving me no hints.

Hundreds of images later—perhaps thousands—I focused my tired eyes upon a quiet pastoral scene, bordered by fences, and muttered, "A farm. Earth-farm."

There was silence. I felt my heart skip a beat. Had I failed it one time too often?

"What do you see?" it asked me again.

Hesitantly, I answered "It looks like an Earth-farm—"

"What do you *see?*"

I looked up at it, into eyes that were framed in swollen red. What did I *see?* Or, what did I perceive? They were two different questions, I realized suddenly. And I had been answering only the latter.

The Raayat's hand was on my shoulder, the pressure of its tension near to drawing blood. I turned quickly back to the screen and told it, "Cattle: there." I pointed. Then, moving my finger in illustration, I pointed out the other vital farm-signs. And explained how I had deduced that this was indeed a farm, and why it was probably not something else.

And I waited, my breath held, for a response.

Its hand on my shoulder loosened. A new picture appeared.

"And this?"

Its voice had changed; it was still strained, I thought, but less angry. Did it see only details, unable to identify the concepts which these pictures represented? Was it using me to try to gain insight into the human conceptual process? It was a neat and pleasing explanation, but not one I was ready to accept. True, the Tyr wasn't known for its abstract capacity, but it had never exhibited such a dearth of conceptual understanding as my Raayat seemed to be experiencing. Was this a part of whatever process had earned its kind the epithet *Unstable?*

It showed me more pictures; now that I knew why it had brought me here, I had no trouble choosing the right answers. An aerial photo of Earth flashed onto the screen: first I described the colors, the parts, the individual elements, then I concluded that it must be an aerial photo of Earth—and then I tried to explain how I knew that. Not an easy task. We take our minds for granted, and rarely question how they do what they do, or why; even I, who had studied the nature of human consciousness many lifetimes ago, couldn't give the Raayat any insight into just how I took all those disparate elements and gathered them together under one conceptual heading. An aerial photo of Earth: it simply *was.*

At last, after many more pictures, the Raayat turned off the screen. I would have hesitated to say that it

looked sick, for the swellings and discolorations which
humans associate with illness often serve the Tyr by
adding to their size and aggressive coloring; nevertheless it seemed to me that it was exhausted, and the
moist redness which encircled its upper eyes led me
to believe that it was nearly as worn out from the questioning as I was. But not from mere tiredness. It had
failed to grasp the *gestalt* of those images, from the
first to the last, and all my explanations had failed to
improve its skill. In a very literal sense, it couldn't see
the forest for the trees.

How crippling that must be! I thought—but then I
realized the idiocy of such a sentiment. The Raayat
was part of the Tyr, and the Tyr was not crippled in
this manner . . . therefore the Raayat could not be.
Which brought us back full circle: what the hell was
going on?

It took me by the arm and led me from the cluttered
room, talons now gentle upon my skin. Outside a hraas
was sniffing at the corridor wall; my stomach tightened as I realized that my blood had drawn it, that
tiny bit which I had smeared on the stone to mark my
way.

It looked at us briefly, then turned back to its inves-
tigation of the wall. The Raayat drew me past.

Silence. It wanted to walk in silence, worn out
from this mental and emotional trial. But I needed to
speak to it, for the plan which I was beginning to
formulate—which would enable me to measure my
sanity, and gain control over my own private madness—required that I speak to one of the Tyr. And of
all the Tyr, this one was the most likely to answer
me.

I waited until we were back at my cell (three thousand, two hundred and fifty-one steps), and then turned
to it . . . and hesitated. I was afraid. Who knew what
this creature might do, in its current state?

It opened the door, but didn't force me to go inside.
It seemed more like its usual self now, and its body

language was more like what I remembered from calmer days. Perhaps that was what reassured me.

I pointed to the wall of the corridor, where we had just passed. "What do you see?" I asked softly.

It looked at me for a minute or two, and I wished I could read its expression. At last it turned to the wall and said: "An expanse of rough-surfaced stone, marked with eight leyq."

"Leyq?"

"Guidelines of color. Visible only to Tyr-sight." It indicated that I should enter my cell, but I stayed where I was. My heart was pounding. "They mark direction, and codify distance." Its voice was now betraying irritation; I realized that it might be dangerous to push things too far, and stepped back into my cell. Within myself I was trembling, not from fear so much as excitement. But it wouldn't do to let the Raayat see that. I waited until the door had closed again and it had left me—until the sound of its footsteps had faded down the hallway, and the scent of its presence was no longer so oppressive.

It had told me what I needed to know.

Leyq. They were real. I had seen them. No product of my fevered imagination, but a collection of alien markings which <u>should</u> have been invisible to me. Only they weren't.

I leaned against the portal and gazed out into the corridor. It was with a sense of uneasy wonder that I noted I could now see only unmarked stone. Whatever feat my body had managed in that time, when my need was greatest, I was now back to normal. But that journey had been no illusion. The leyq were there, and I had seen them. And if the details of that desperate journey had not been delusion, but an accurate perception of the truth. . . . dear God, how many of my other delusions might likewise turn out to be valid? And if so. . . .

No. I wasn't yet ready to face that. I was far too tired, I told myself; too shaken by my confrontation with the Raayat. But I knew I was going to have to.

Soon. Before we reached Kygattra, in fact; before the
Tyr had a chance to "examine" me.

I would have to examine myself, first.

* * *

Darkness. Night. A spacious hallway, lit by
torches. And fear, thick in my throat; exhaustion,
binding my limbs.

My captor paces, his eyes upon me. A dark man
whose stance bespeaks violence, his manner
proclaims his willingness to kill in cold blood, at
a moment's notice. A dangerous adversary. I
know him from somewhere, but can't place the
memory; there are only fleeting images of other
nights, other hallways, other fears. Nothing useful.

"It will do you no good to fight." He indicates
the men who encircle me, soldiers of coinage now
garbed in sweat-stained leather; I was not an easy
man to bring down. "They are ready and able to
kill you, and will do so without hesitation if you
refuse to obey me. Am I clear?"

I meet those eyes, onyx-cold, and I know there
is no weakness in him, no human foible that I
might exploit in order to gain my freedom. They
chose their champion well, I think. His black and
brown armor, nail-studded, is a dramatic backdrop for the jeweled cross that lies on his chest;
the latter was no doubt borrowed for the occa-
sion, his kind would rather consume wealth than
wear it. I wonder which of several ruthless men
hired him . . . but not why. The mercantile prac-
tices of Florence are as complex as *her* politics,
and infinitely more vicious; it's hardly surprising
that one of my business rivals, in the course of
spying for personal gain, discovered things I
would rather keep secret. And equally unsurpris-
ing he would act on that knowledge, when the

dispersal of my estate would result in such advantage to his.

My captor spits at my feet—on them—and half-draws his sword. "Yes or no?" he demands.

Ten men, perhaps twelve. All armed, with knowledge and weapons both. Faulty knowledge, of course; there may be some hope in that. "I understand." At least ten arrows are aimed at my heart, bowstrings taut in readiness. How many of them can I dodge, how quickly can I run? They've cornered me well, which says much both for their efficiency and their courage; if I try to break out at the weakest part of their formation, can I make it out of range before their arrows bring me down?

There is a sparkle behind me, the play of torch-light on naked steel. I catch its meaning out of the corner of my eye and coldness fills me, the darkness of despair. Arrows pose only a moderate danger to me, for if they fail to bring me down when first they strike they can be dealt with easily enough at a later time; swords are another thing, their nature is stubbornly unalterable. As I shift my weight—carefully, so as not to alarm my captors—I can feel the soldiers' weapons at my back, and know myself trapped. And well trapped, too, if they understand my nature. If not . . . then there is still some hope.

"You will stand as you are. Without moving! Hands where I can see them." Details of submission are dictated to me and I feel myself move in obedience; time, I must have time to think, every second counts. There is a pull at my hip and my dagger is gone, taken from behind. Just as well; I might have had to leave it behind anyway. This way I need betray no weakness in doing so. God alone knows what they imagine me capable of.

He spits at my feet again, callused hand lifting the cross up into my line of vision. My instinctive reaction is one of revulsion, but not for the reason he imagines. The symbol is one I have come to

associate with man's darker, more violent side.
Beneath the shadow of the cross my father
watched the Library of Alexandria burn; in the
name of the cross I myself have seen whole cities
put to the sword—have watched murder replace
reason—have lived as an outcast in a world which
once welcomed my kind. How can I do anything
other than despise what it represents?

My reaction gives him pleasure, confirms what
he assumes to be the truth of my nature. With a
flourish he draws forth a flask from underneath
his baldric, uncorks it, and upends it over my
head. Fluid pours down over my hair and ears,
soaking the silk of my doublet. Merely water, but
the damage is done. My outer garment may not
appear expensive, for I wear no gold thread or
metal-set jewelry, but the finest of Venetian silks
have gone into its making, and the shirt beneath
is of pure Indian cotton. By now the dye will be
seeping from one into the other, ruining them
both. Amazing, is it not, that in the face of death
we hunger for distraction, and are wont to focus
on other things, trivial things, as a means of not
acknowledging our danger. . . . So it is, now, with
me. Irrationally, I am more angered by this action
of his than by any other which he has committed
to date, perhaps because it has the appearance
of purposeless harassment. Filled with rage—and
fear—I am speechless.

He steps back from me, smug and satisfied.
"Take him," he orders his men. "Bind him well.
He can't change on you, now."

They are about to move when a noise from the
other end of the hall attracts their attention. Only
for a moment—but one moment is enough, or else
it must become so, it may be my only chance. I
dive for the opening which I have already noted,
it is only a small one and easily closed, but I am
halfway through it before the nearest guard reacts. Steel bites into my leg—an arrowhead, most

likely, I ignore it—and then there is shouting and
quick movement, and the captain's rough-voiced
commands and I am free of them! A hail of arrows
mark my passage, but I can run faster than any
daybound man. . . .

I make it onto the street and quickly take my
bearings. This part of Florence is unfamiliar to
me, I dare not take any chances. Eschewing the
alleys which might entrap me I make for the nearest side street, hoping to turn a corner before the
bowmen start their second volley. And I make it.
There's shouting behind me, mercenaries bellow-
ing orders and a dozen bystanders exclaiming in
surprise and dismay; it covers the noise of my
passage and I quickly turn another corner, dropping out of sight again. I can hear them coming—
close now, very close—and I choose my turns at
random, knowing they will cut me off the moment
they can anticipate my direction. My current burst
of stamina is finite, it will eventually succumb to
the pain and blood loss of my wounds; I must do
something other than run, I must outthink them,
it is vital if I am to survive.

I look at the towering walls that flank my passage, punctuated by small windows now securely
shuttered against the night. Even if my pursuers
know what I am normally capable of, they will have
been convinced by their leader that his Christian
magic has disabled me. They will search where a
man can go, and no farther. That may yet save
me.

I force my legs to move even faster—there is a
wound in one thigh that burns like fire, but I cannot allow it to slow me down—and then, as I turn
one corner, I leap. My claws bite deeply into the
building's supporting beams and I am climbing,
climbing desperately, trusting to my instinct to
supply me with the most effective form to do so.
As I reach the roof I can hear them entering the
street, and as I pull myself over the edge with one

last burst of desperate strength I hear the first of
them call out that I am nowhere in sight, I must
have gotten far ahead of them.

Heart pounding, I listen to them pass me by.
They will search the nearest streets, then—when
they realize they have lost me for good—cordon
off this part of the city. Cellars will be searched,
bedrooms rummaged, and no doubt some small
valuables will work their way into the searchers'
possession. I will be safe on the roof, for a while;
once the sun comes up, they will never think to
look for me here. As for being discovered acci-
dentally, that is simply a risk I have to take; I am
too wounded to fly now.

I find some planks and a half-barrel, and cloth
laid out to bleach in the sun; out of those I can
rig up a primitive shelter, not complete by any
means but sufficient to keep me alive. Later, when
the healing sleep has done its work, I can take to
the air and go north. My Milanese accounts can
still be salvaged, providing I reach them before
my adversary does. The loss need not be total.
My Florentine possessions will have to be left behind, but that is to be expected; the more valuable items have probably already been seized,
and the rest will soon follow. The pattern is painfully familiar to me. After a number of similar experiences, I have learned not to love my
possessions too dearly.

Damn you! I think, as the magnitude of my loss
finally strikes home. But Florence is a fickle mis-
tress, and I knew the risk involved in courting her.
Damn you! The first rays of sunlight are sliding
smoothly over the horizon, and they drive me into
my makeshift shelter. I lie down, and pain over-
whelms me.

Damn you all!

* * *

I had to know the truth. And there was only one way to discover it.

With trembling hands, I collected the paraphernalia of my alleged madness. My shirt, its thin cotton weave neither torn nor stained; why was it in this condition when I clearly remembered tearing it, the night I broke out of my cell? And why were the buttons alone malformed, as if something in my body's healing process had warped them out of shape? My shoes, whose dark, sullen stains had never fully washed out, I also laid before me. I had cut a bit of hair from one temple, and this I put down beside the other objects; should I once more take on the countenance of youth, this bit of gray hair would be my only proof that recently I had appeared otherwise. And the mirror—hated, hated item. I trembled even now as I forced myself to look into it, wondering what facet of insanity it would reflect. But my face was as I had last seen it, and I lay the battered metal sheet aside. That was the last of it. That was all I needed.

That, and courage.

I sat myself in the inner corner of my room's L-formation, setting the items down beside me. Tucked into this corner, I was invisible from the door. Passing Honn would not look in on me, and the Raayat—should it happen to show up—wouldn't be encouraged to stay.

I sat cross-legged on the scuffed stone floor, leaned my head back against the wall, and tried to relax. Behind me loomed my crude map of the longship's interior, scratched painstakingly into the paint with a chipped plastic button I'd removed from my shirt. Like an amulet it guarded me, reminding me that I was no longer wholly helpless, that if I retained my reason I might yet win some measure of freedom in the midst of this alien stronghold.

Relax? Impossible. Memory insisted that I had been things other than a man, while science labeled that patently impossible. Now I intended to investigate that proposition, as calmly as if I were analyzing the properties of some commonplace compound. But once I

opened the door to such speculation, was I not courting even greater instability?

Carefully, not quite sure how to go about such a
thing, I began to concentrate.

Remembering: how I had felt when I was first
brought on board the longship. My hunger. My desperation. The door suddenly jerking open, in response
to some unknown signal—the throbbing stripe which
led me toward my physical salvation—the sickly taste
of blood in my throat, thoroughly abhorrent at the time
but now, in memory, shamefully pleasurable. All of
it, I remembered it all. Relived it, as much as I was
able. Whatever thoughts had triggered the first change,
I wanted to recapture them. Only that way could I test
the veracity of what had happened.

After a time I picked up the mirror; my hand was
shaking, my heart pounding. It's a terrible thing, to
fear one's own reflection. I steeled myself, looked into
the polished surface—and breathed a sigh of both relief and confusion as I saw that oh-so-familiar face,
with all its gray intact, staring back at me.

I had failed to restore my youth. Never mind that
the age which so reassured me was artificial, and
shouldn't be visible in the first place; never mind that
for one single day I had seen my face unlined, my hair
an untarnished hue. Now my appearance was just as
it had been yesterday, and the day before as well. And
clearly I could not, by thought alone, change it.

But had my delusion truly passed—or had I merely
failed to trigger it? My first test had been encouraging,
but it was far from complete. On that day when I followed the leyq I had been starving, as well as desperate, exhausted, and frightened. But that hadn't been
the case during all of my "transformation" experiences. I would have to confront my later experiences
before I could call myself truly cured, and that could
only be done in timefugue.

I let myself go. It was easy to trigger the memories,
they came almost without my bidding. My mind was
tired of fighting such recall, and welcomed submission

as a well-earned vacation. Images passed through my consciousness, leaving their fantastic imprints on my identity. I was a wolf. I was a deer. I was something that flew, too wounded to know its own form. I was a human who might become those things, and I gathered the images to me—not without fear—and let them free to work their magic upon my soul.

A while passed, in which I was afraid even to think. Then I stirred, and noted with relief the familiar sensation of human movement. Try as I might to clothe my limbs in fur, struggle though I might to transform my senses, I couldn't bring forth a single wolf-hair, transform my vision in the least regard, or even shorten an eyelash. No will, and no imagination, had the power to transform me into anything other than what I was, what I had always been. A man.

Drinking blood again must have unnerved me more than I was aware of; utterly reasonable, under the circumstances. No matter now. It was over. I had the Tyr to worry about, and my coming confrontation on Kygattra. There was enough left in that to occupy my mind without worrying about magic.

But as I stood, gathering up the talismans of my introspection, I caught sight of the door. And shivered. Beyond it I could see the corridor's far wall, cold gray stone with an occasional clump of fungus. The leyq were not now visible to me—would never be again, for I was human—but I had seen them once, and couldn't banish the memory. Nor could I forget the Raayat's words, which had confirmed my vision. That was no illusion, no dream. That was reality, which the fever had somehow rendered visible.

I knew in my heart of hearts what needed to be done. I had shied away from it, would prefer not to face it— but I was a scientist, and I knew. The fact that I was now delusion-free didn't address the heart of the problem; that my near brush with insanity had been triggered by those primitive instincts connected with my bloodthirst. Until I tested myself according to those parameters, I could never be sure that a future bout with hunger wouldn't begin the destructive cycle all over again.

I dreaded what had to be done, but recognized that it was necessary. There would be no peace for me until I was sure of myself; until the ghosts of the past were laid to rest forever, and human blood had no more mystique than a common protein shake.

Determined to have this over with for once and for all, I began to make plans for my final experiment.

* * *

Harder than usual to get to the lab. Harder than usual to obtain what I needed without being questioned, to function under the pretense of nutritional necessity while mixing liquids that no man in his right mind would drink.

The Raayat watched it all. Alert, always curious, that creature was the greatest threat to my plans. I had hoped that a Honn would come to bring me to the lab complex, for that kind asked no questions. Or was it only human prejudice that caused me to imagine it made a difference who brought me here, whether one Tyr or another questioned me? They were all part of the same creature—weren't they?

It came to me with a start that in the case of this one Tyr, I was no longer sure of that.

"You are agitated," the Raayat observed. "Explain."

Damn its insight. "I haven't been sleeping well." I emptied one flask into another and sealed the latter, quickly; the fumes were dangerous. "Concern over Kygattra." The fluid was slowly changing color, from rusty red to a greenish black. As I recalled, that was good. "What does the Tyr mean to do to me?" I swirled the flask gently, watched the last hint of redness fade. The result was markedly unpleasant-looking. "I can't help but worry."

"There is no cause for worry, for one who is Subjugated."

I glanced up at it. "I am. You know that."

Was it amused? Or simply doubtful? It was hard to read that alien face. "You appear to serve the Will. Indisputably, you serve *my* need."

"Aren't they supposed to be the same thing?"

A simple enough question, it seemed to me. But the Raayat seemed quite taken aback, and it took it a while to find an acceptable answer. "Usually," it said at last. It seemed uncertain.

"Are the Raayat not wholly Tyr, then?" I pressed.

"The Raayat are Raayat."

We had been through this part several times before, and I knew it for a conversational dead end. As always, it was frustrating. I sensed that the Raayat was mere words away from revealing a potential weakness, some faulty link in the Tyrran system—but words away we must remain, for as long as Earth languages lacked the capacity to express Tyrran concepts.

I turned from it, to retrieve a waiting vial—and, shielding my motion with my body, slipped two hollow glass tubes into my pocket. Careful not to move too quickly, I turned back and tried again. "Are you—this-Raayat—the same being as all other Raayat?"

That confused it. Long enough for me to measure out two cc of white powder and put the vial back in storage without it watching me. By the time it looked down at my hands again, my work was safely anonymous.

"You desire to distinguish between parts of the whole," it observed.

"I want to understand you. This-Raayat. Do you have a name?" I asked. I knew the answer, but thought the question might distract it.

Two more steps to go. Heat the mixture. Almost done, now. Almost. If I could avoid being questioned for a few minutes more. . . .

"A name?" it asked me.

"Yes. A . . . verbal label."

"For this body?"

"For *you*."

It seemed confused. "I am Tyr."

"That's a name for a whole species. And Raayat's the name for your subtype. But what about *you*—this one single brain. Your thoughts. This Raayat which I'm looking at now, and no other." Frustrated by my inability to describe what I meant in English, I tried another approach. "When you say 'I,' what do you mean?"

"We use your language. We choose the most appropriate pronoun. None of them are exactly right. We use what we must, to communicate."

"And if your Kuol wants to refer to you . . . no, forget that, I'm thinking human." Any thought which the Kuol had, the Raayat would share; what need was there for pronouns in a species with absolute telepathy? "If *I* wanted to refer to you—wanted to explain to some other Raayat which of you I had been talking to—"

"But it would *know*."

Dead-ended again. But I was almost finished; my first mixture was a thick black paste now, and my second was coming along nicely. Only minutes more here, and then the walk back to my cell; if I could make it that far without inspiring the Raayat's curiosity, the first stage of my plan would be complete.

"Tell me about Kygattra," I prompted.

"It is a small planet, neutral in all major ecological categories. No day/night cycle, no seasons, no moons, continual moderate weather—"

"No *what*? Day/night what?"

Despite my outburst it continued calmly; it had no idea that what it had just said had raised the specter of death once more before me. "The intent is to observe specimens of various species without imposing a schedule upon them, thus mapping their biological rythms without interference—"

"No day/night cycle—what exactly does it mean?" *Not what I'm thinking*, I begged. All my hard-won confidence was going up in smoke.

"Yearly revolution is equal to one planetary day.

Therefore there is no cycle of light and darkness to
interfere with—''

Christ. The worst possible scenario. A planet with
one side sheathed in darkness, the other in perpetual
day; if it was far enough away from its native sun, the
day-side would be habitable. And yes, it made sense.
Terrible sense. I had foreseen something like it, but
had assumed they would keep us underground—or perhaps indoors—to accomplish the same thing; isolated
from the biological signposts of dawn and dusk, a body
would eventually readopt the rhythms of its native
world. My alleged alien nature would betray itself in
its patterns of sleep and waking.

But this would be even easier to maintain. Impossible to avoid. Perpetual daylight . . . Christ. *Christ.*

I couldn't do it. I would be helpless. They would
find out too much. I didn't dare . . . but what other
choice was there? What else could I do?

My hands moved automatically, transferring tranquilizer and antidote to the capsules which I was permitted to remove from the lab complex. One thing at
a time. I put my equipment into the cleaner, piece
after piece. Let the Raayat go on describing Kygattra
while I tried to pull myself together; he mustn't see
how upset I was.

At last the phrase ''. . . a name?'' broke into my
awareness, and brought my consciousness back to the
conversation. ''I'm sorry?'' I asked it—and then, not
certain that idiom would communicate, explained, ''I
didn't hear the last thing you said.''

''You believe it would improve our communication
if I had a name.''

It had switched channels on me again. All right. I
could deal with that. ''I think it would be very helpful,'' I told it.

Silence. I realized after a minute that it was waiting
for me. Waiting for me to christen it! I, who hadn't
borne an Earth name in . . . how many centuries? I
looked at it, and much to my surprise felt a wave of
genuine fondness. For as much as one of the Tyr could

offer companionship, this Raayat had done so. Not its fault that its alien thought patterns made true communication next to impossible, or that its Raayat madness had almost cost me my life. It had tried.

"Frederick," I said softly. It had been my name once, one of the few that still had positive associations. The sound awakened memories of another era, before our names had been taken from us. "I will think of you—this body, this part of the Tyr-whole— as Frederick. Is that good?"

It hesitated; I had the oddest feeling that my giving it a name had inspired it to comprehend, for the very first time, some facet of individual existence. In a strange way it made the Raayat more human than I, for I had only a number.

No. Not "it." *He*. The Raayat had a human name, he should use the human pronoun as well.

"You are finished?" he asked me. I nodded. "It is good," he told me, and I wondered what he was referring to. My being finished? His name? Or even Kygattra, which might not be as bad as I imagined?

The mere thought of that place sent a bolt of cold fear through me. Once I was there, there would be no escape. The fever would consume me, from the moment of my disembarkation on the planet's surface to my premature death a mere handful of decades later. And the Tyr would learn my weakness, firsthand; that was the most terrifying thing of all. Once on Kygattra, I would be helpless to disguise it. The Tyr would learn what sunlight meant to us, and then it would know how to flush my people out of hiding.

With sudden clarity, I knew what I had to do. Avoid Kygattra, no matter what the cost. To land on that planet was to betray my people—and I had already decided, back on Earth, to choose death before that. My only hope of life lay in finding a way to escape the longship, before that dreaded nexus.

The unfairness of it made me clench my fists in anger. *I would have cooperated with you!* I thought bitterly, wishing that somehow the Tyr could hear me.

*Played your game for the rest of my life, so long as
my people were left alone. But you didn't even leave
me that option! Let it be on your collective head,
then—whatever it is that I have to do.*

Gathering my capsules, I followed the Raayat—
followed *Frederick*—out.

* * *

I would have to be very, very careful.

I watched the corridor for hours—no, days—trying
to get a feel for the Tyr's rhythm of activity. I couldn't
count on mere luck protecting me, once I left my cell;
I had to array the odds in my favor before I set a foot
outside its confines.

At last I decided to make my move just before the
next translation. Not an easy decision to make, since
it might mean being caught in the tunnels when the
longship altered its substance. I wasn't anxious to go
through that again, undrugged. But once I got the
Raayat to deliver me a sedative, he would probably
leave me alone until we'd reached the next nexus. The
Honn had been conspicuously absent prior to the last
translation, presumably tied up with other jobs that
were nexus-relevant; it was reasonable to assume they
might absent themselves again.

In short, the pre-translation period was the only time
I could think of when I might remain undisturbed,
long enough to do what I had to. Above all else, the
Tyr must not discover me missing from my cell.

I dreamed of what I meant to do, disturbing dreams
that juxtaposed pleasure and revulsion; I awoke from
them sweating and restless, and often hungry. But not
for any food or drink which the longship offered, or
for any common sustenance of Earth. This was for a
darker substance, which most men of Earth would find
abhorrent. Which *I* found abhorrent. And seductive.
Compelling.

God help me.

* * *

Translation minus several hours:

The sound of Raayat footsteps grew fainter and fainter. I listened until I could no longer hear them, then listened for a good while longer. And longer still. I had to be sure he was well out of hearing before I started.

The vial Frederick had given me glittered in my hand like cracked ice, reflecting the cell's sharp white lighting. I tucked it under the edge of my mattress, where my own containers were hidden. And pulled those out. One glass tube was still whole, while the other had been splintered into bits. I wrapped them up in a piece of cloth I had torn from the rear end of a shirttail, and slid the resulting package carefully into my back pocket.

Now, for the door.

I had seen the Raayat open it several times, and could hazard a reasonable guess on how it functioned. It seemed to have a heat-sensitive trigger of some kind set just beneath the surface of the rock, on the far side of the wall. Inaccessible from where I stood—but sensitive enough that once, in a fit of fever, I had set it off.

What I did once, I could do again. For all that I hated the timefugue experience, and what it could do to my morale, it did give me that power. Perfect emotional recall: I set myself against the wall, exactly where I had been, and bade the memories come and take me.

. . . and I strike at the door in frustration—

—beat at the rock, again and again—

—has to be a way out, has to be!—

—Nothing. Nothing! I lean against the portal, shaking with frustration. The pent-up fury of the Subjugation, like wildfire . . . in my flesh, my soul, the very air about me, the cold stone at my back. . . .

I relived the incident, again and again, until my body

shook with the force of the repeated memory, and I was filmed with the sweat of exhaustion. My shirt clung to me, dampened by my efforts, but still I persevered. Over and over, an endless loop of memory which must eventually take control of the body that harbored it, and force whatever process had once taken place to repeat itself, here and now—

There was a grinding noise. I kept my eyes shut, concentrating. I heard more movement, and the protesting squeal of hidden machinery. Drenched in heat, I tried to cling to the timefugue—but it was gone, now, banished by my focus on the present moment. For the first time in my life, I wished it had more staying power.

I dared to look at the door—and exhaled loudly in relief. It was barely open, but barely would do; I didn't require much. Taking care that my tools weren't crushed, I squeezed myself through the narrow opening. This time I was conscious enough of what I was doing to watch as my shirt was ripped across the chest, and grimace in pain as the sharp stone edges drew blood in nearly parallel lines, like whip marks, across my torso. Would those wounds heal like the others, in a single night's sleep? Or take their time in closing, and thus give lie to the very delusion they mimicked?

Not daring to wonder, I began my journey. Counting turns as I went, I retraced those steps which had been etched in nightmare. My body, with a will of its own, seemed to know the way. The hraas I did not fear, and I felt certain that the distinctive smell of the Tyr would warn me before I ran into one of that species; it was with haste, then, and relative confidence, that I traversed the corridors, following a path I remembered all too well.

But I had forgotten the Tekk. I was coming to that place where the lab complex was located and was moving quickly, when suddenly I found myself face to face with one of the tattooed Tyr-servants. Dark skin, bright eyes, familiar markings; it was the woman I had seen in the lab, whose Amazonian presence had so impressed me.

I was in danger now, and knew it. I wondered if I dared kill to safeguard my secrecy, and then—in the case of this woman—wondered if I was capable of it.

"You cause trouble," she challenged me.

An accusation, or a question? I spread my hands in a gesture of false innocence, knowing that my very presence here—unsanctioned, unaccompanied—spoke volumes for my guilt.

She glanced at my hands, at the cloth packet half-jutting from my pocket, at my face again. A faint smile broke through the coldness of her expression, transforming it into the face that I remembered.

"There are no eyes," she told me, "among the Tekk."

She stood aside. I bit back my instinctive desire to ask her what she meant, then took the moment for what it offered. She was letting me go—perhaps to catch me later, but I had to risk that. It was now imperative that I get where I was going; if she did turn me in to the Tyr, I would have no second chance.

I ran. To hell with caution, now; time was my single greatest priority. So intent was I upon speed that I almost missed the crucial landmark, a fissure in the ceiling where the stonework had been patched. Here, I had imagined rock falling. Here I had touched the wall—

I conjured up the proper memory, and timefugue guided my hand. This carmine point, where the vein disappeared . . . a section of the wall drew aside, and I knew from the foul odors which greeted me that I was in the right place.

Quickly, now. I passed between the cages, chose a victim. Young and full of health, asleep near the bars of its prison. That last element was most important. I had only been able to practice so much, and knew my aim for less than perfect.

I unwrapped my weapon, lifted it gingerly from its bloodied shroud. Five glass shards with their bases embedded in a hard bit of sugary paste—they would fit into the tube perfectly, and the black paste on their tips should be sufficient to subdue any creature in these cages. I had imbibed the counteragent while waiting in my cell, and by now it should have taken effect. If my calculations were correct, I should now be functionally immune to the effects of my homemade tranquilizer. If not . . . well, the effect would at least be dulled. I should still be able to do what I had to and then get myself back to my cell.

I loaded the blowtube and placed it against my lips. Five chances at most, and that was only if a single glass dart could do the trick. I didn't dare miss. I built up pressure behind my tongue, released it—and the dart flew cleanly into its target, the glass tip driving deep into the animal's flesh.

It awoke with a start and growled at me. I kept my distance, grateful for the bars between us. It leapt to its feet, aware that something was wrong—but its stance was unsteady, the drugs were already taking effect. Angrily it staggered, its hair prickling outward in aggressive display. And then, without warning, it fell.

I opened the cage latch and then the door, and didn't bother to close it behind me. My chosen prey was breathing heavily, eyes glazed, before me. Good enough; this time I wouldn't have to lose half my blood to get at his. I had considered gathering the precious fluid into a container and bringing it back to my cell, but had decided at last on the primitive method. And now, standing before him, I could have done nothing else; the instinct was too strong to resist, allied as it was to my hunger for life itself.

I drank. And let my imagination range as I did so; now was the time to face down this madness, if I truly meant to master it. But for once there was no time-fugue. Warmth flowed from my victim's body into mine, a shiver of forbidden pleasure in its wake. My rational self might loathe such an act, but my senses knew no such reason; the blood brought pleasure, as nature had intended, and prompted a soothing warmth that flowed outward from my center, relaxing my limbs in a way that no sleep ever could. Or perhaps that was the effect of my tranquilizer, muted but not wholly negated. A shiver of energy seemed to accompany the fluid as it spread through my body, an almost electrical invigoration that seeped slowly into my veins, and left my skin prickling with newfound sensitivity.

When I was done, at last, I packed up my weapons again, taking care to remove the glass dart from my victim's hide. The cuts I had made should go unnoticed, unless the Tyr had a penchant for autopsy. I doubted they would bother. Kept in captivity, such creatures are wont to die; that this one had done so hardly seemed unusual. There was no blood about the wound to betray the fact that it had been cut into, I had seen to that with the scrap of my shirt. In short, I had managed my meal with a cleanliness and efficiency that would have made Emily Post proud—if not with an attitude she would have approved of.

Locking the cage door again as I left, with one last glance behind me to see that all was well—or at least, appeared to be well—I made hasty progress back to my cell, where the last of my experiments was to be performed.

* * *

As before. Nothing different. Except that I felt different myself: more alert, more energetic. Fantasy, or biological fact? I arrayed the symbols of my madness before me, ate a small bit of stale Tyr-cake to bolster my courage, and then:

Confrontation.

I closed my eyes and tried to capture, in my mind, the essence of youth. There was a numbing sensation, a strange distancing of self not unlike the effect of morphine; my body still had feeling, but I was no longer concerned with it. The feeling passed quickly. I opened my eyes and was immediately aware of a change. The room seemed brighter, but that might well have been because I'd had my eyes closed. And the smell of the Tyr seemed infinitely more oppressive—nigh on unbearable—but that sharpening of my senses might be caused by tension, and was in itself no proof of anything.

Then, my hand trembling only slightly, I picked up the mirror. And looked in it.

And knew.

In some dark, hidden recess of my brain, that fragment of my mind which still knew the truth—which had always known the truth, despite my best efforts to deny it—nodded sagely in the face of my fear, as if to say *well, it took you long enough.* The rest of me was in shock. Barely capable of moving, and even less capable of thinking.

The man that I had so wanted to become had no way of dealing with this. None. Because at heart he was no more than an artificial construct, designed to obscure the truth. He had no solid substance, was made up of little more than the desire to conform—to be like others, even if that meant denying his own past.

I picked up the lock of gray hair which lay before me, and touched it to my temple. It didn't match. Yet I could see both the old and the young; my mind denied the veracity of neither. No delusion, then.

Enough, I thought, sick from the truth. *You've made your point. Stop now.*

But I couldn't. Not yet.

I gathered memory to me again. But not the sanctified memory of Subjugated life, this time. I called back the dreams I had spent so long denying, the dreams—or timefugues?—which had so threatened my conformity. Again, there was that same distancing effect, but this time it was more severe. For a moment I was merely resident within my body, but not connected to it; like a heroin user I could have suffered grave bodily damage and never felt it—or never cared. I tried to let myself go, tried to lose myself in a dream of wolven fantasy . . . and then suddenly I was back in my own body, my own time. The distancing effect was gone, but in its place a new sensation filled my being. As if my senses were intact, but somehow altered.

Then I opened my eyes, and saw.

Paws. Fur. The trappings of a wolf.

And beneath that false skin: the soul of a shape-changer.

How long had it been since my conscious self had willingly taken on such a form? Tyr-smells assailed my nostrils, burning tissue that had been made newly sensitive to all such odors, by the power of my changing. Instincts that were not man-born raced through my head, and I pawed anxiously at the rough stone floor, hungering for the freedom to hunt.

No illusion. A very real, very complete transformation. There was no way to avoid the truth any longer: that I was, and always had been, a shapechanger. Something in the bodily fluids I had imbibed, or in the act of killing, had awakened skills that were so long dormant, I had taken them for mere fantasy. Now they were mine again . . . and if I could master them, could come to terms with the paradox of my own nature and take control of my potential, so long unpracticed . . . then there was hope. Kygattra might be avoided, and my people would go undiscovered.

It would mean exile. I dared not go among the Tyr again, for fear of giving myself away. Certainly not until I had my changing firmly under control. And who knew how long that would take, or if it was even possible? The memories were too far gone, I had buried them too deeply . . . who could say if they would ever come back entirely? To maintain the shapechanging skills I could not rely on pills, or common food; I would need animal blood, in quantity. I would have to come to terms with that, too. It might mean renewing the old habits, which I had worked so hard to conquer. Or developing new ones; that, too, was an option.

Exile. I had faced it before, and survived. I would do so again. Let the stars be my new home, I would build my fate among them. Had I not dreamed of just such an opportunity, in the childhood of my optimism?

* * *

They came to take the animals away when we were yet a week distant from Meyaga. The longship itself could not be slowed, or turned; its mass and velocity made it an inexorable force, and shuttles must be used to manage the more delicate intrasystem maneuvers. In this case a skimship was outfitted to receive the Earth-predators, and cages were lashed to its internal structure everywhere there was space to do so. Howls of indignation filled the cramped hold, and snarls resounded as neighboring animals clawed their rage at each other, frustrated by their impotent proximity. Occasionally blood was drawn, and the smell of it excited those animals which had previously managed to retain their dignity. It was a hell for these creatures, but it wouldn't last long; they had reached their new home at last, and soon would regain their freedom.

The skimship maneuvered away from the longship's gravity, then put on all speed for Meyaga. Smaller than the longship, it could accelerate and decelerate with greater alacrity; it would be able to reach Meyaga in time to unload its living cargo, remain long enough to see that things were proceeding according to plan, and then rejoin the longship on the far side of the system. And then: another nexus, another world. And eventually, Kygattra.

Over the cold plains of Meyaga the shuttle skimmed, looking for the perfect landing site. Even ground, not yet cloaked in ice; it found such a patch on the edge of a forest and lowered itself with a blast of heat, searing the frozen earth into glass. The hold was opened, the cages brought forth. Snarling, angry animals threw themselves against the bars at their captors—and then the bars withdrew, and they had their freedom. A few turned against the Tyr, and were burned to ash; others ran for the forest, eager for cover, so grateful for their freedom that they weren't concerned about a land in which the earth, the foliage, even the animal smells, were wholly alien. There would be hunting enough, once they got their bearings. For now what mattered most was that they were free at last.

The Honn-Tyr waited until the last of the predators had fled from sight, then collapsed the cages and re-packed them with unified efficiency. There were many more such animals, enough to seed this continent five times over; it remained only to distribute them properly, each type to its appropriate habitat, and then let them restore ecological balance to Meyaga. And if they overbred, and began to hunt man . . . then the Tyr would bring in something else, and restore the balance yet again. A creature with limited creative capacity must feel its way through life via trial and error.

I waited until the skimship had risen, then until it had passed out of sight, before I reclaimed my human form and stepped from the edge of the forest.

How bright the colors were, how vivid the smells! Even in my human form I was literally swamped with sensation. Was this what it was to live?—was this what my nature bequeathed to me, once I came to accept its mandates? When had my sense of color faded, leaving me with only shades of gray to bear the names I had once associated with brilliance? When had I lost this vivid sense of life, letting it slip away from me gradually, without ever noticing its passing?

I stood for a long time on the cold Meyagan soil, still in human form, drinking in the sensory richness of my new world. Smells, so like and unlike Earth's: animal odors clinging to the chill branches surrounding me, the slow rot of fallen leaves and dying grass beneath my feet, the hint of ozone with its attendant storm promises, combined with other gases that my Earth-trained senses couldn't begin to identify. Sensation like a heady wine to a man who had forgotten the taste of alcohol. I drank it in until the last glimmer of twilight had faded, and the light of a thousand alien stars blazed furiously against the stark black backdrop of the Meyagan night. A thousand brilliant points of light that burned my eyes as I stared at them, and filled me with the wonder of their power and beauty—as well as my own vulnerability. These eyes could never look on the sun again, without the fever to protect them; that was the price I would have to pay for what the drinking of blood had done to me, for the newborn intensity of all my senses.

But for the moment, I was incapable of regret. The change was intoxicating, and far more complete than I ever would have anticipated. All this because I had drunk blood again, or because I had killed while doing so? Or perhaps because, for the first time in centuries, I was ready to accept the changes that such an action triggered? That, too, was possible.

I dropped to all fours, and fluidly exchanged my human flesh for the claws and endurance of the wolf. It took no effort, this time, nor any understanding of the process; blood was bringing control, where reason alone could never have managed it. Perhaps in time I could have faced the Tyr after all—

No. Not now. Find your people. Make yourself a place among them. Establish a refuge, far from the invaders. You have too much to lose from moving quickly—too much about yourself that you still don't know—too much about your fellow humans that might have changed, in such a place as this. What have they become here? What can you be, among them? You need time, to learn these things. Time, before you move.

But I would move, I promised myself. I would strike back at them. Somehow. The thought was invigorating, in a manner that it had never been before. Had the blood done something to my courage, or was I simply drunk on the exhilaration of escaping from the longship?

Feeling a sudden hunger for human company—and for an additional kill, to strengthen me for my journey—I turned my nose into the most promising wind, and followed the scent of man into the forest.

LONGSHIP TALGUTH

The Raayat called Frederick looked in through the door of the human living space, stunned.

What it saw was plainly impossible.

A touch to the wall operated the heat-sensitive control, and the door split open to admit it. There was one part of the room which wasn't visible from the outside, but a few steps brought it to where it could see it.

No one was there, either.

A lesser Tyr would have died, at this point. Faced with the Tyr-whole's inexorable logic—that the human *must* be here, that he could not possibly be anywhere else—but seeing with its own eyes that the human was nowhere in sight, a Honn-Tyr would have been judged to be malfunctioning, and would be discarded. Perhaps after that more Honn would come, and would also see that the human was indeed absent; then, swayed by their consensus, the Tyr would reconsider. But for that first discoverer, that supposedly malfunctioning brain, there would be only death; malfunctioning parts must be excised quickly, if the whole of the Tyr was to prosper.

The Raayat, however, was Raayat, and among its subtype temporary malfunctions were tolerated. Therefore it was permitted to indulge its curiosity. It searched all the walls, the floor and ceiling, even the food and sanitary outlets—but there was no way out through these routes, and the Tyr-whole knew it. Next the Raayat studied the door, but no tools lay outside which might explain how the human had worked a

159

heat-sensitive lock which was far out of reach, or otherwise forced the tracery door to open.

The Raayat was painfully aware that the Tyr considered what it was seeing to be patently impossible—but it, Frederick, thought otherwise. The human was obviously clever, and had the knowledge of centuries to draw upon. Just because the Tyr couldn't envision how he had escaped, did that necessarily mean that he couldn't have done so?

Thoughtfully the Raayat picked up those few items which had been left behind. It wished it had the human's skill at inductive logic; surely that man could have made some sense of this strange catalog of artifacts. Longship bedding, with bloodstains on it. Shards of glass, tucked under the edge of the bedding. A stale sugar cake. A lock of hair. And lastly, a handful of small metal objects, nearly a hundred tiny bits that were identical and a long metal tab with the Earth-word *Arrow* inscribed upon it. Those last were strewn about the floor near the entrance to the living space, and the Raayat's hands were ill-equipped to pick them up; the tiny pieces slid from the points of its talons and remained stubbornly floorbound, depite its best attempts to retrieve them.

The human was gone. That was fact. Let the Tyr-whole question it, and send in Honn to confirm the disappearance. The Raayat was fully convinced.

A sense of loss suddenly arose within it, intensely disquieting. If the human had left this room, then he was probably dead; the hraas were not merciful toward strangers. Yet sympathy wasn't the cause of the Raayat's unease. Death was meaningless to it, and although it recognized that individualized species felt somewhat differently, it didn't really comprehend why. No, this was something else. The loss was its own, and as it stood in the center of the human's chamber it became slowly aware of how intensely it felt it.

The Raayat had needs. There were periods of confusion, when its natural facilities deserted it. There were times when even its Tyr-sense seemed dull, when the backlog of knowledge which was its birthright was nearly impossible to access, and it floundered in ignorance. Before the coming of the human, it had had to deal with those times by itself. No other alien would help it; no other Tyr was approachable. But the Earth-human. . . . The Raayat remembered when the last fit of madness had possessed it, when its world had shattered into a mass of disassociated slivers. It had taken it time to communicate its need, but once it had done so the human had helped it. The Earth-human had needs of his own, and thus must serve the Raayat's will. He was invaluable, he was the Raayat's only source of alien knowledge . . . and now he was gone.

Frederick needed the human. It needed *some* human, or some creature from another species, to help it understand what was wrong with it, why sometimes the Tyr-whole seemed inaccessible, and it was . . . alone? Was that what *aloneness* was? It needed their thought-patterns, their methods of reasoning, their adaptability. It needed . . . what? It felt the need, deep within its heart, but couldn't give a name to it. The human could have found a name for it. The human could have helped. The Raayat must find others with the same potential and establish some sort of working relationship.

Its hunger for knowledge was great, and must not go unsatisfied.

LONGSHIP TALGUTH

The hraas dreams.

At sunset the mesh of life was so taut that it was possible to feel a leafhopper coming to land several miles away, and sometimes to judge its intentions. The hraas slid forward carefully, testing it. Shadows played across its coat as the dying sun cast spears of light through the crimson canopy overhead, and the hraas' fur rippled in response: from blue to brown, through orange, to red: a perfect match for the grass beneath its feet, and the brush that would hide it when it chose its prey.

Beneath its paws the mesh was tight and sensitive, and it vibrated gently as distant life-forms disturbed it with their feeding. The hraas stood still as unliving stone, alert to all its messages. There, in the distance, a swarm of small insects built their hive; their home-intentions were a soft buzz underfoot, nearly audible. A tiny browsing mammal yanked at a plant, seeking to dislodge it from the tenacious forest soil: that set off a light strum of hunger, a delicate stacatto of anticipation. Birds flew overhead, rippling the mesh in that delicate way which was typical of animals that never came to ground; a glissando of chimes, like tiny bells, accompanied each murmur of flight-joy.

For a very long time the hraas stood still, its sensitivity tuned to maximum alertness. At last, beneath its feet, a heavier vibration stirred. And a sound that the hraas heard, not through its ears, but ringing through all the bones of its body: a deep, satisfying chord of

mammalian feeding, that perfectly complemented its
own growing hunger.

The hraas ran. Sleek hide passing through the brush
with minimum friction, agile mind choosing the best
footing long before its feet touched earth. It ran like
the wind, which its people had once ridden. Ran with
the memory of flying in its genes, wing-claws tensed
in anticipation. The mesh of life quivered in response
to its hunger, and waves of intention were spread far
with every footstep, to dash themselves upon the distant shore of some browser's consciousness. That
didn't matter. Most of the hraas' prey were no more
capable of reading the mesh clearly than they were of
harboring rational thought; they were still mere animals, who might sense the coming of a dangerous
predator, but would require time and much effort to
pinpoint its location. And by then it would be too late,
because the hraas struck like lightning. Before the sun
was fully set, all the mesh in the forest's confines
would resound with the pleasure of its feeding.

The hraas remembers.

The Tyr came without warning, spewed forth from
gleaming pods like thorned and angry seeds. They
came to the meadows where the hraas and its kind
stalked their prey, the places with the least cover. And
also to the forest itself, which they burned—tree by
tree, browser by browser, their small black wands
making the mesh shriek with the sound of death—in
search of the beasts they had come to capture, the very
monarchs of local biology.

Where the Tyr stepped, the mesh shattered. Where
they had been, shards of it lay upon the ground like a
dying animal, broken and bleeding. Whole patches of
the mesh had been broken apart, and the delicate signals which linked hraas with hraas—and with their
prey, and with other predators—wavered and failed,
offering little protection.

The strangers' nets were made of slime, which hardened in response to movement. Their pods were like
caves, and shook with crude vibrations so constant,

and so varied, that the delicate senses of the hraas could hardly function. In these creatures there was no life, although they lived. Nor death, which had its own special tenor. Undead, unalive, they wore their *unnaturalness* like armor—and the hraas discovered to its dismay that it could not attack what its mesh-sense refused to acknowledge. Nor function properly with any other creature, in the proximity of those unnatural conquerors.

The hraas hates.

Endless tunnels of cold, dead stone, and a distant thrumming that never ceased: it lived on the edge of insanity always, clinging to memories—and to hatred. Shreds of mesh adhered to the longship walls, and floor, and these it used to wend its way through the wormlike labyrinth, seething in fury at its captivity. Occasionally, a creature would disturb that broken pattern even further, and the hraas would rend it with the savage vigor that was its hatred's only outlet. But there was no pleasure in such killing, while the hraas' captors still ruled; there would be no pleasure, until the nature of the Tyr was made *right*—until the hated ones assumed their proper roles as prey, at last.

The hraas waits.

PART TWO:
GATHERER

MEYAGA: CANTONA SETTLEMENT

I discovered the settlement after five nights of traveling, most of which I spent in wolf-form. A long enough period that human thoughts were uncomfortable to me, and the concept of taking on a human body again less than wholly appealing. Earth legends are partly correct when they warn that a shapechanger who stays too long in an animal body may lose the ability to change himself back. A more accurate warning might be that he would lose his *interest* in changing. After five days in that hardy, powerful body I was less than enthusiastic about reclaiming my own lesser form. What was a human body suited for, other than balancing precariously on its hind legs and scraping half the fur from its face? The wolf body had served me well, both in hunting and in traveling, and I had worn it long enough that my thinking was more wolf than human, with appropriate priorities.

But though five nights had changed me quite a bit, it wasn't yet enough to permanently alter me. I forced my flesh back into its natural form, and though I staggered a bit until man's unique gait became familiar to me again, I could soon feel my mind slipping back into its normal patterns.

Then I found myself a granite ledge in the footlands of the mountain range I had been skirting, and lay myself upon it, in order to observe the settlement more closely. Scratching as I did so, to rid myself of one particularly unpleasant result of my transformation. Fleas. How did they manage to cling to me, even when I changed? Or did they jump off and then quickly back

on again, after the transformation was made? What
was most ironic—and irritating—was that I hadn't
picked them up from any animal associates, nor from
the cooling flesh of a kill. Two days after being de-
posited on Meyaga I had come across a stark little
caravan—three wagons and a handful of asses to draw
them, plus one horselike creature that had seen better
days—and after a long night's vigil in human form, to
pick up from their campfire chatter what few essential
pieces of information I needed to proceed on my journey, I took the opportunity to liberate a heavy wool
jacket from among their stores. Which turned out to
be already inhabited.

Now, as I lay down full length upon my vantage
point to take in the Cantona settlement, I scratched
and cursed softly in appropriate syncopation. In addition to the heavy jacket—dark brown wool, modestly
embroidered, the simplest and least recognizable piece
I could liberate from their stores—I wore only the pants
I'd had on in the longship, the thin cotton shirt, and a
pair of leather shoes. Not all of that had made the
change successfully, either. For shoelaces, I now used
animal sinew. The pants had made it through all right,
but the button on the inside of the waistband was an
unrecognizable mess, incapable of either buttoning or
unbuttoning. That, and the zipper. Or the lack of zipper, I should say. It and the metal pull that made it
close were presumably still lying on the floor of my
Talguth cell, shed like water from a duck's back when
I made my first full change. I wondered what the
Raayat had made of all those tiny bits of metal on the
floor—if its noncreative mind had somehow managed
to determine what use they had served—and I managed
a smile, despite the cold Meyagan drizzle that had
plastered my pants to my skin ever since I had taken
human form again, earlier that evening. And despite
the fleas.

I looked at Cantona as I scratched.

Even from a distance, it was obvious that something
was wrong. Wrong for this century, that was. For the

aspect the town presented was like something from an
earlier age, unsullied (or certainly unimproved) by
technology. The center of the town consisted mostly
of small family dwellings, constructed of split log,
mud, and thatch in some combination. They were neat
but roughly built, certainly without that streamlined
efficiency that energy-conscious Earth had convinced
itself it valued. Beyond that were areas of tilled earth
and plantings, modestly sized farms that a single family with primitive tools might be able to manage. The
roads—what few there were—were scored with narrow
tracks, like those made by wooden wheels, and punctuated with animal droppings. In short, it was an image out of another century—and a fairly unattractive
one, even by that standard.

The only real anomaly in this damp and primitive
setting was a building at the town's center. Call it a
temple, for lack of a better name. It rose above the
log huts of the common populace like a palace—but if
so, it was built by a king with a taste for surrealism.
For every square yard of it differed from every other,
both in design and building materials. Tudor arches
set in Florentine brickwork overlooked Victorian
doorframes; wood-and-plaster gave way to brick,
which in turn faded into a tiled Mediterranean roof,
which supported, at one point, a plaster minaret. And
these mismatched parts made no architectural sense,
even by their own standards. Windows opened into
alleylike passages, or were set in sideways, and at least
one door—ten feet above the ground, and with no obvious means of approach—had been put into the wall
upside down. It was as if someone had taken all the
architectural styles of Old Earth, jumbled them into a
sack, and then poured them out indiscriminately. And
if I call it a temple, it was simply because I could think
of no other earthly purpose that such a building could
serve; religion can inspire some pretty strange things.

This, then was my new home. Daunting. I knew that
the inhabitants were a cold, suspicious people, unwel-
coming of strangers, and that a recurring shortage of

crops (due to reasons my informants had failed to discuss) had made them particularly insular. I also knew that strangers here weren't usually shot on sight. And since in several other communities they were—in *most* other communities, I gathered—I had decided to give this one a try.

I also knew—and had accepted, or at least pretended to accept—that whatever contact I established with these people would have to be limited. Farming peoples tend to be suspicious of a stranger with nocturnal habits, and I was centuries out of practice in earning human trust. Best to take things slowly, and carefully, and hope that enough timefugues from the past would help me reestablish my survival skills.

Human company. Dare I court it, in this altered state? I had dreamed of blood, in recent nights, bursts of nightmare that didn't always have an animal subject. So far, my natural revulsion toward such behavior had been enough to wake me up . . . but what would it be like now, with my senses so redefined? What had it been like then, in my youth?—I could hardly remember.

I glanced behind me, and nervously noted the band of bleak gray that was beginning to rise over the mountain peaks. Soon the stars would fade, and Meyaga's dismal sun would rise to spread a few hours of light upon the chill planet's surface. And I would face it, unprotected—because that was the cost of camouflage. There was no way I could go among these people in my current state; they would sense my alienness before I learned how to hide it. The fever was a survival mechanism, and when it was taken on deliberately— and correctly—it was no threat to either life or sanity. By exposing myself to the gradually brightening dawn—letting the indirect sunlight acclimate my body to the metabolic pace of the daybound in a slow, easy manner—I might adapt without risk, before the sun itself cleared the horizon. Unlike my mother, who was forced by chance into the full light of day, and paid the price . . . but that's another story. The pain would be minimal, and I would survive it. That was all that mattered.

But I had forgotten how strong my memories were, or how totally they might overwhelm me. As the golden disk of harmful light cleared the mountains that lay east of the valley, I was launched into a timefugue so powerful, so all-consuming, that even as the metabolic change was completed I was shivering with remembered pain. A pain that was intensified a thousandfold, by the recent reawakening of my senses.

The appearance of normalcy has a high price among my kind. I hoped to God that this time would be worth it.

* * *

Well outside the town's outer limits, enclosing a good portion of the farmland, a sturdy wooden fence with no visible entrance made an uncompromising statement about the welcomeness of strangers. Undaunted by its message, I trod the perimeter until I found what passed for a gateway. It was, in fact, a thick, iron-banded door, heavily reinforced, and to make it even more sturdy a stocky, well-tanned local was pounding a stake into the ground beside it, presumably as the first part of some additional support structure. He was wearing a jacket very similar to mine—that is, drab and plain—and trousers, tied off at the knee, to match. The ends of a neckcloth swung forward as he stooped to work, hinting at another layer of muddy gray-brown beneath. His hands were well-worn, as were his thick leather boots, but of his face I could see nothing, even when he turned to me; the deep hood attached to his jacket was drawn forward against the wind, and only the barest hint of a reddened nose peeked out at me from among the shadows.

''Well?'' he snapped, when he finally noticed me. ''What'ye want?''

I was glad that he spoke English, albeit with an almost indecipherable accent; some settlements had adopted other tongues, or used creoles that had no Earth equivalent. Counting on a lazy slur to disguise the oddness of my speech, I told him, "I've come to trade." And let the skins that I held slide down from my back, to do my speaking for me.

I had chosen them carefully and skinned them during my one human night, with a bone knife I painstakingly ground from the femur of a fellow predator. (Which was hidden, at the moment, in a seam of my jacket.) Though most were rolled skin outward, to protect the fur, a few critical ones had been packed fur side out. The best way to become welcome in a primitive environment is to prove yourself useful, and these skins—from animals that were elusive, rare, or exceedingly dangerous—would do just that.

He looked them over, then studied me, then back to the furs. I had kept a few of the more formidable teeth and claws from my hunt, and thrust them through the straps that tied the bundle tight. Apparently the message was clear, for the deep hood bobbled as he nodded his approval at last. "Etsa good'n."

"Thanks," I chanced.

"Y'r welc'm enough, I say. But y'ill have t'be passed'n before y'can move about, y'see? That's th'custom."

For as much as I understood him, I nodded. "That's fine." I had no idea what being "passed'n" meant—his emphasis made me feel that it was something more than a welcoming ritual—but rules were rules, and I was here to stay. "Whatever the custom is."

"All right, 'n." He dropped his hood back, and looked toward the town. Dark Magyar features were set in heavy lines, patterned so clearly by sustained grief that I wondered what trials this man had endured, or shared with the Cantona residents. Above thick eyebrows the dome of a bald head proclaimed, by its dark and potent stubble, that local hairstyling customs might not be exactly to my taste.

When in Rome, I reminded myself. Trying not to

remember the stories my father had told me about Rome, when he had known it in its heyday.

Less than confident, but seeing no alternative, I followed my guide into the village.

* * *

The "Gov'n" of the Cantona settlement was a large man, short but full in the chest, with barrellike thighs and stubby fingers and a face and disposition to match. In short, my somatic opposite. Like my guide, he was bald. As were the two men with him when I entered. As was the one woman I saw in the streets, a dark-featured woman in a heavy woolen jacket that she gathered about herself as if to protect her when she saw me, a stranger, passing by.

The Tekk woman looks at me, amusement telegraphed in her broad, gleaming smile. "Earthborn?" she asks me.

"Is it so obvious?"

"Harosh! The hair," she says, running a hand over her own polished scalp.

"So," The gov'n said thoughtfully. "Bael says ye've come t'trade?" Like my guide, he neither offered his name nor asked for mine. But neither did he guard his people's names with superstitious zeal—one reassuring point, anyway.

I affirmed my purpose in coming, and—when asked—my willingness to comply with the settlement's customs.

"Y'understann," he told me—and I barely did, due to his local accent—"we've n'Tyr in this place. Nor want'ne. That's all'r custom's for, y'see? T'protect's."

"I understand."

He furrowed his brow as if disturbed by my accent, then continued. "So, n'order t'see that no Tyr get in here—or their eyes, y'understann—we'll have t'detain ye t'do a passin. B'fore God, n'all."

My fur did bristle at that. And even though I knew myself human, and the wolf-images had faded from my immediate memory, I couldn't rid myself of the sensation. It wasn't that I had anything against God, as an individual, but . . . call it bad memories.

Timefugue beckoned; I concentrated on the present. "Of course."

He gestured toward where Bael stood, behind me. But instead of my guide, two husky guard-types came to where I stood, and flanked me.

'We 'preciate for y'understannin. The God of Earth go with ye."

"And with you," I murmured, as a meaty hand beckoned the way. *What have I gotten myself into?*

They led me out of the governor's house—little more than a hut, by Earth standards—and through the streets of the central village. The close-set walls, with roofs that extended well into the street, gave the impression of underground tunnels. Not unlike the interior of the angdatwa, I thought; I wondered if the mimicry was deliberate. All the people were dressed alike; when they saw that I wasn't, they turned hurredly away and went about their business, eyes carefully averted. Or maybe I was being too sensitive about my dress; maybe they simply found a full head of hair repellent.

In the center of the village, a stone's throw from the nearest of the manor house's walls, stood a solidly built, windowless cabin. A thick plank barred the door shut, a primitive—but alarmingly effective—lock. I didn't yet know all my limitations, but one thing was certain: any form I changed into was approximately my size. I looked over the thick walls, the steel-reinforced door, the small metal grill which allowed air to circulate within, and thought: *Once I enter this prison of theirs, no power of mine can get me out.*

But what choice did I have? If I wanted human contact, I would have to play by their rules. And so I ducked—the portal was low, better suited to their height than mine—and allowed myself to be locked inside.

To my surprise, I wasn't alone. Two men were sprawled on either side of a low table, upon which

wooden chips had been laid in an intricate pattern.
Some kind of game, no doubt. One of them was short
and thick-set, a typical Cantona somatype. The other
was leaner and longer of limb, and gave me hope that
the planet, as a whole, housed a wider variety of racial
types than the one. The Cantona type was bald, but
the leaner man had short brown hair; a far cry from
my own graying blond, but comforting nonetheless.

"Y'r welcome," said the shorter man, and the other
waved me in. "Make a place," he offered. I slung my
burden to the ground and sat where he indicated, by
the third side of the small table. My immediate instinct
was to assess their behavior for dominance patterns.
But that was my wolf-soul speaking; it's hard, after
days in an animal body, to reestablish human behavior
patterns.

"Outsider?" asked the taller man.

I nodded.

"Y'play?"

" 'Fraid not."

"Ah." He nodded and went back to his contemplation of the pieces. After a while he moved one, shifting the geometric pattern slightly. His companion,
after some thought, did the same.

"Come t'trade, I see."

I nodded. "You?"

"Same. Doriyek spice, an'assort." He indicated his
shorter companion. "Is native, that one. Ungar Du-
mayesh Ro-Kazzek . . . is it Saen?"

"Saen it is," the shorter man agreed.

"Saen Taal. I, am called Degas of the Greedy Hand.
Degas is from the Tyr, y'see. Doriyek custom, not t'use
more of't than we have to. Th'reference is to m'chips
playing, not my prices, by th'way."

After a moment's hesitation I introduced myself.
Making up a false name, hoping it would sound legitimate. Using my real one on this planet might come
back to haunt me someday.

I was able to get considerably more information out
of my companions-in-prison than I had out of my pre-

vious Cantona contacts. Apparently it was normal for us to be locked up this way. All visitors were, even those village inhabitants who spent time over the mountains, in "lands that'r not freer Tyr." A gathering would be called within two days, and we would be brought out for "passin on." A high priest of Cantona (their reverence for him bordered on fear, which worried me) would call on God to pass judgment on us, there would be assorted ritual nonsense, and—assuming that we were not some kind of Tyr in disguise—we would be free to go about our business in the settlement for as long as we wanted. (A loose translation, that; there were two words of religion spoken for every one of information, but I thought I had the gist of it.)

And we would be fed, in the meanwhile. And given "bath stuffs," and every other nicety of Cantona existence—save freedom. That last was for God to grant, and God alone.

It wasn't God that worried me. He had always seemed a reasonable deity, and His laws—though they banned my kind from worship—had always seemed at least marginally rational. But as for what men had been known to do, in His name . . .

As I went to bed that night on the rope cot to which I had been assigned, I wondered if I had gotten in over my head. And comforted myself, as I looked over the solid walls of my prison, and the tiny grating that a starving cat couldn't have squeezed through, that it didn't matter very much whether I had or not, since I damned well couldn't get out of here.

You're committed, Daetrin, whether you like it or not.

* * *

They came to shave us. I should have seen it coming. Degas first, laughing as his light brown fringe fell to the rough cloth which had been laid beneath him. Myself afterward, with considerably less good humor. I noticed that they touched the back of my head more than once, as though searching for something; perhaps there was more to the custom than mere fashion.

I remembered to be bald in the morning.

* * *

The middle of the night. My second night in Cantona. A frenzied banging burst through the bonds of sleep and brought my companions fully awake in an instant. I, having been awake but lost in thought, was equally startled.

"Ungar!" The voice outside was clipped, urgent. "Ungar! Are y'in?"

The Cantona trader sat upright; even in the near-total darkness I could read the tension in his posture. "Raal—is't you? What's on?"

A scraping sound resonated through the thick-walled cabin. After a moment I recognized it as the bar being lifted from the door.

Ungar was on his feet by the time the door opened, and Degas a moment later. Two men stood in the portal, outlined against the meager, filtered moonlight of the streets.

"They're commin'," one said, and I heard fear in his voice.

"Hell!" Ungar swore. "How many?"

"Too many. Time for every hand, Cantona. Y'with?"

"But custom—"

"Been waived. Y'with?"

Degas was clearly confused. "Ungar, what—"

"The fields!" Ungar snapped. "Come'n see—or stay'n wait, as y'choose." He turned toward me for a brief, fleeting instant and told me, "And you, too, if y'will. It's ever' hand is valued now."

And then he was gone. As I stared at the empty portal, I began to notice distant sounds: Running. Yelling. I looked at Degas, and he at me. And then, by unspoken agreement, we left the safe haven of our prison and turned toward the east, the way Ungar had gone. Running, to catch up with him.

By the time we did so, he had joined a band of men spread out along the ditch surrounding the farmlands. Most of the men were half-dressed, as we were, but even so they all wore heavy leather boots that were scarred from extensive wear.

'Here y'are.'' A bucket was thrust into my hand, and an acrid odor—kerosene?—drifted up to my nostrils. The thruster turned to go, his hand already extended to deliver the next bucket, when he suddenly seemed to notice me for the first time.

"Outsider?''

I nodded.

"Y'first?''

Again I nodded.

"Take't and pour,'' he instructed. With his free hand he gestured broadly, along the course of the ditch. Other men with similar buckets were already pouring a thin line down the center of the nearest sections. "Somewhere where the others aren't, y'see?''

I saw. Children were running here and there, their arms filled with bundles of dry brush. A quick glance assured me that the ground nearest the ditch had been stripped of all vegetation, which confirmed my initial impression; we were creating a fire line. For what purpose, I didn't know.

I tried to make myself useful. A sense of urgency was sharp in the air, and along with the acrid fumes it was a heady substance. As I worked alongside the villagers, preparing the shallow ditch to burst into flames at the first presentation of fire, I was oblivious to all things other than my bucket, the stink of my burden, and the disposition of the work force surrounding me. It took me a while to realize that beyond the clatter of tin receptacles and the clipped, nervous chatter of the workers, there was another, more ominous noise, coming down from the mountains.

At last the work was completed, and I stepped back. All about me faces were raised to the hills, eyes anxiously scanning them for any source of movement. A second work force was moving outside the wall, now, and the heads of their oddly-shaped weapons could be seen above the rough wooden planking.

"There they are." A voice that was filled with wonder, fear, and hate drew our attention to the outermost farmlands. And yes, there was movement in the distance. The moon, cloud-veiled, gave us only enough illumination to see that the grasslands were stirring, like earth that had suddenly come to life. In the darkness we had no sense of color, and could not see the exchange—from the rich green of plant life to the gray and brown and tan of *something else*—until it was nearly upon us.

I drew in my breath sharply as I realized what was coming, only dimly felt the tugging on my sleeve as a co-worker urged me backward, out of the path of the fire line. Rodents, in some mutated Meyagan manifestation. The number of them was awesome, the sound of their passage like a storm-tossed sea breaking waves against a rocky shore. Similar to rats in their general configuration, but larger and longer legged; malformed, horrible creatures, whose fur grew in random, scraggly patches, whose bodies were emaciated and terrible to behold—who descended like locusts from the shelter of the western mountains and proceeded to lay waste to the farmlands, inch by precious inch. I was stunned, speechless, without the strength to act. Utterly horrified. They devoured the crops as they moved, a mouthful here and a mouthful there, the hinder ranks bounding on their fellows as they sought out their own choice morsels. I could see the labor of months disappearing in minutes, the few surviving shoots of a precious crop crushed beneath the sheer weight of that living blanket.

I turn to the Raayat, a question in my eyes. "An overabundance of herbivores," he explains. Behind me a wolverine claws its cage, and a nearby lynx hisses. "We are doing what must be done to restore balance . . ."

The first one struck the wall. Like a shot it resounded, followed by another. And more. And hundreds more, like bursting popcorn, until individual
sounds could no longer be distinguished. The fence
creaked ominously; its braces bit deep into the earth,
then held. A weapon was placed in my hand, but I
couldn't bring myself to look at it. Outside the wall a
battle was taking place, and I could see the details here
and there where distance and elevation permitted.

The mangy horde was three or four deep, and the
Cantona warriors waded through them as through a
whirlpool. With long, deadly polearms they scythed
through the mass of hungry flesh again and again and
again, each stroke claiming half a dozen lives from
among those who were struggling to breach the defensive wall. But for each one wounded, there were
hundreds more; for each one killed, there were thousands. Was it not wholly futile, to do combat with
such numbers? But no, after a time I saw that the
villagers' defense had a pattern, and a specific purpose: to keep the sheer weight of the rodents' onslaught from breaking down the fence. Knee-deep in
rodents the men waded, and angry teeth gnawed at
their boots as they scythed deep into the mounds of
flesh that were slowly building up against the outside
of the defensive wall. One of the creatures, by treading on the bodies of its fellows, managed to gain
enough height to leap over the barrier; it was no
sooner inside when a villager cut it down, but already
there were more coming. The wall buckled ominously, and all the efforts of the men outside could
not lessen the force of the onslaught sufficiently to
save it. With a roar it split, a deep V-shaped gouge
giving way to the thousands who were pressed up
against it. First in one place, then another, as though
the wall itself had realized the futility of its existence, and was giving up the fight.

Then the true battle began. I heard a roar, and a
wall of flame raced across my field of vision. The smell

of charred flesh was eloquent, telling us of creatures caught in the ditch when the fire line was lighted; I could see grim smiles on the men who were nearest me, an expression without hope or pleasure.

And still they came. There was no end to them, this tidal wave of ravenous animals, and against the wall of flame I could make out the dark, tiny shapes of those creatures who had made it past the fire line. Most of them were dead, or nearly so, crowded out of the ditch by the thousands who came behind them. But some were alive, and had vaulted through the flame. And as I watched, horrified, more and more of them survived the deadly crossing. Buoyed up on the charred bodies of their fellows, they made their own bridges over the flames—smothering it out entirely, in places, and then advancing in earnest—until the bulk of the horde finally gained the ground they had been seeking: the rich inner lands of the Cantona farming community, the most precious crops of all that the valley contained.

Like locusts they came, and like locusts they devoured. I watched the ground go from green to brown before my eyes, and when the monsters moved on there was nothing but trampled earth remaining. I fought as best I could, and other, more experienced men fought with me on every side, using every tool that the villagers had devised to drive back the invaders—but the sheer mass of our adversary was bound to defeat us in the end. They tore nets, they snapped polearms, and trapped our blades in the currents of their flesh. And finally, when the survivors had eaten their fill and swarmed back the way they had come, through the several gaping holes in the perimeter fence, there was nothing left but a field of pillaged stalks, and the bodies of those thousands who had lost their lives in the plundering.

Dawn was lightening the eastern sky by the time I lowered my weapon and allowed myself the luxury of a few deep breaths. I heard sobbing—women's sobbing—and was dimly aware of a body being carried in

from the outermost fields. As they brought him by me,
I saw the face of a man who had made the mistake of
falling in the path of the invaders; the expression of
horror frozen on his face was etched instantly in my
memory, and would never leave me.

Danger had blinded me to my own exhaustion, but
now the danger had passed, and the hours of exertion
caught up with me. My legs trembled, weakly, and
then would no longer support me; I fell, and the hands
which I thrust out to keep myself from hitting the earth
too hard sank deeply into soft mud, sticky with the
blood of the conquerors.

There I stayed, oblivious to my surroundings, until
the shuddering of my exhaustion eased and I could find
the strength to stand. As I moved, an arm fell on my
shoulder. I looked up and saw dark eyes, Cantona eyes,
in which all hoped had died. He nodded a silent thanks
and then said, in voice that was dead from defeat, "Yil
need t'be goin back, they tell me. Come. I'll take
ye."

I walked dully back to the place of my imprisonment, and somehow managed to get there. Ungar and
Degas were already there, collapsed at odd angles
across the earthen floor. I was about to fall beside
them when my guide put a hand on my shoulder and
turned me to face him.

He looked at me for a long, silent minute, as if
searching for something. At last he muttered "If
you've eyes inya, stranger—and I'm not saying y'do,
y'see—but if y'are of the Tyr . . . then now they know.
Now they've seen it, with eyes of their own. May they
carry that vision t'their graves."

He spat, then, and closed the door. Or something of
that nature. I remained awake long enough to know it
was happening, then slipped into a deep and fitful
slumber that told me just how damaged I was—for it
was the true healing sleep of my kind, dreamless in
nature, and therefore without the nightmarish replays
that normal sleep might have brought.

Thank God. Thank God.

* * *

Ungar never awoke. Another fatality. By the time we were conscious and about, his skin was already cool to the touch and tinged with the blue of cyanosis. I wondered if they would bother to look into the exact cause of death, or just add it to the list of those others who had been killed by a combination of exhaustion, exposure to the elements, and despair.

In the afternoon, when our food was brought, they came and took his body away. As if to take his place they brought us another traveler, but we neither asked his name nor offered ours. Dinner contained a stew of shredded meats that might have contained some of our raiders; if so, its current form diplomatically disguised it. There was no product of grain to accompany it, and since I couldn't process any meat I pushed the bowl away, knowing that for once they wouldn't question me.

The fallen invaders would serve the colony with their flesh, but for how long? A few hundred animals, against the loss of a whole season's crops. The ranks of the Cantona settlers would be well thinned, come winter.

I stared at the bowl before me, and wondered just how long it would be before I could seek out the few foods that could sustain me. How long I could last without any nourishment at all, my metabolism accelerated by the fever. How awake I would be at this ritual of theirs, with exhaustion and hunger dulling my senses.

I had come through worse, to be sure. But not often. And not easily.

* * *

They came for us at dawn. No warning. Somber men in ritual garments, who gave us time to eat and dress but not time to bathe, and who hushed us when we tried to talk.

They ushered us out into the cold Meyagan morning.

Blue light filtered down between the overlapping roofs, so indirect that it hardly bothered me. I was grateful for the cover. Degas seemed apprehensive, but could that be because Ungar's death had unnerved him? Or was the ritual we were about to attend really that dangerous? Our latest companion was silent, which told me nothing. I was somewhat light-headed, after two days with practically no food—I had picked the thin crust off a meat pie last night, hoping it would go down well—but I knew the importance of remaining alert, and fought against the cotton that was wrapped about my brain.

As we reached our destination—the central building which I had guessed to be a temple—I saw two small skulls impaled on each side of the portal, and I shivered. This was not the best time to be seeking hospitality.

The door opened, giving us access to a small, trapezoidal room. On the right was a window, fully shuttered. On our left—somewhat to the left, it was a strange angle—another door, smaller than the first. We passed through . . . and if I described every door, every stair, every window that opened on nothing, I could not capture the essence of that house better than to simply say: It was a maze. It was chaos. It was built as though each morning an architect had entered the last room built, flipped a coin or two, and said "put a window there," or "a door over there." With no thought at all for the whole. Doors opened to reveal walls, windows revealed the backs of closets, and stairs led to nowhere. Corridors were twelve inches narrow, or four feet wide, or they changed as they went. All the *parts* of a normal house were present—all the basic concepts—but none of the consistency. And because the floor plan had no rhyme or reason, it was the perfect trap. One either knew how to maneuver in it or one didn't; it was impossible to reason one's way out.

I began to observe our course very closely, trying

to commit it to memory. Hard to do, in my debilitated state. In animal form, of course, I could have followed the trail of our scent . . . but I didn't want to count on that. And I wasn't so sure that my animal form wouldn't be equally debilitated.

In some rooms there were shrines. I called them that because of their design; their contents were something else entirely. One small altar held a bowl filled with bobby pins, another two straw wrappers, a third some kind of credit stub. All from Earth, I guessed. The last relics of a planet now lost to history, culled from the hands and pockets of refugees whom the Tyr had exiled here. There was even a small pile of lint, with a single thread hanging out of the side. Objects of worship? I shivered.

And at last we came to the center of the temple. It was dark, and windowless (although windows didn't necessarily imply light, in this place), with a single pair of oil lamps at the far end furnishing the only light. A large room, somewhat circular (the walls were irregular, and angles jutted into the room here and there without visible cause, but the overall impression was that of a circle), with religious symbols scattered about the walls. That is, I judged by their placement and treatment that they were indeed religious symbols. Their form was completely unfamiliar to me, as was their content, and I began to get a cold, crawling feeling in the pit of my stomach. Earth religion it wasn't.

Eyes. Eyes upon me. Hostile eyes, from every corner . . .

In the hushed near-darkness we were made to kneel. I concentrated on the feel of the hard wood beneath my body, used it to focus on the present moment. Couldn't afford to lose touch with reality, not now.

All about us were people. Perhaps a hundred. Men. Experience had taught me that humans were cruelest when segregated by sex, and the cold feeling in the pit of my stomach became lead. What had I let myself in for?

They began chanting—low, a mere whisper at first,

but growing gradually louder. I recognized phrases from the Old Earth Bible, and it was oddly comforting. But other phrases were in there as well, images of devastation and despair that far exceeded any breast-beating which the ancient prophets had recorded. Images from a planet which, left to its own devices, would never have hosted man. I wondered if it was all standard verse, or if the aftermath of that terrible battle had set the tone for this day's proceedings.

Apparently there was some sort of arras obscured by the darkness at the far end of the hall, for when the chanting had concluded a man stepped out from behind it. He was larger than most of his fellows, broad in the shoulder and solidly built, with a physical authority that told me immediately who and what he was. The settlement's high priest, thus the man responsible for the direction their religion had taken.

This is the flesh of our Lord Jesus Christ, who died for our sins . . .

He waited until the chanting had ceased, and all eyes were upon him.

"We are gathered here," he said—and his voice was resonant, filling the broad chamber—"out'v sight of th'Tyr, beyond reach of'ts many eyes, so that God may reunite us with th'spirit of'r mother planet."

Eyes. Eyes upon me. Hostile eyes.

"Are we content t'meet thus?" he asked, and his gaze swept over the assemblage.

From behind me a voice came, clear and challenging. "We'r not content."

"Speak, and th'Lord will satisfy you."

"There'r strangers in'r midst. Untried, untested, unpassed'n into th'community of men."

"Bring them forward."

We were prodded to our feet and made to approach the priest. I noticed that there was no altar, which surprised me; nearly all group rituals have some such central point.

And then I realized, no altar was necessary. For the presence of the man standing before me was what held this community together, it was the force of his personality that brought God into this space, making it a temple. Any physical altar would have been superfluous.

"Speak y'r names," he commanded.

We recited our Tyrran numbers in low, hushed voices. When it was my turn I tried to keep my voice steady, but even I could hear the fear in it. I had seen many preachers, in my long life—madmen, scholars, saints, the lot—but none had ever generated the aura of *power* that surrounded this man. It was overwhelming, terrifying. It bordered on being inhuman. I was glad to get out my whole name before my throat closed up entirely, in fear.

"So," he said, when the naming was done. "An' have they Eyes, besides th'r own?"

"We know not."

The high priest announced: "It is f'r God t'say."

The congregation repeated it: *It is f'r God t'say.*

"It is God who protects's."

It is God who protects's.

"It is God who keeps th'Tyr at bay."

It is God who keeps th'Tyr at bay.

"Trust'n th'Lord, an' he'ill protect ye."

Trust'n th'Lord.

"Trust'n th'Lord, an' he'ill cut down y'r en'mies."

Trust'n th'Lord.

"Trust'n th'Lord, an' he'ill guide you. Trust'n th'Lord, an' he'ill bring y'r children t'Earth, an' establish a human kingdom once more."

Trust'n th'Lord.

"In th'name of th'Father, th'Son, and th'Spirit of th' Earth, I call up'n th'Lord God of Earth, Creator of Man, to guard'n protect his most prized creation. Trust'n th'Lord, an' he'ill be merciful. Trust'n th'Lord, an' he'ill give y'insight."

Trust'n th'Lord.

He held out his arms, spreading wide his ritual cloak. Now that I could see it more clearly, I saw that it was, in fact, a tight mesh of living plants, newly

harvested. An unusual looking species; I seemed to
remember one of the caravan men describing it, but I
couldn't remember why. Native to the planet, at any
rate; that seemed an odd garment, for one who represented the God of Earth. It struck me there was
something odd about that plant, something specific that
I needed to remember. . . .

"Behold. Th'Lord is with's."

For a moment, utter stillness. I could hear myself
breathing, and felt guilty for making that much noise.
The priest was gesturing as though to embrace the air,
and his expression was one I had seen before among
the religious. But not on madmen, or saints. On show-
men. The leaders.

Gradually, I became aware of a change in his person. No, not in his body; in the cloak which enveloped
him. It had begun to glow. First softly, with a warm
orange light. Then more passionately, its brilliant color
flecked with amber and red. He was cloaked in light,
this priest, and never had I seen an illusion more perfectly managed. For illusion it was, of course. Not the
light; that was real. This particular Meyagan plant was
naturally phosphorescent under certain circumstances,
I seemed to remember that. No, it was the drama of
the moment I admired. The consummate artistry with
which he turned a mere vegetable trick into a symbol
of divine intervention.

"Trust'n th'Lord," he proclaimed with fervor—his
body was clothed in light, in the essence of divine
fire—"an' he will protect thy soul. Seek out Eyes
n'His Name, an' if they offend thee, behold, He sh'll
pluck th'm out from among they number."

He reached out his hands toward where Degas knelt.
They were strong hands, and seemed capable of crushing a man's skull with no other tool than their owner's
strength. But they were gentle as they surrounded Degas' head, fingers settling on his flesh as lightly as
flies.

I noticed Degas was sweating heavily.

Then the priest locked eyes with him, and I could

feel the contact between them, like a palpable substance. Locking them together in some kind of mental communion—or so it seemed to me. Again I had the fleeting impression of some skill in the man that was not quite human, and out of nowhere I remembered what I had heard. About the glowing plant. About its light.

Then the priest stepped back, and Degas' head fell; it was as if all the strength had gone out of his body. But there was a faint smile on his face, and as the priest spoke I understood its meaning: he had been "passed on."

"Th'Lord is merciful. Th'Lord spares those who'r truly His."

Th'Lord spares th'innocent.

Next, to our newest companion. Like Ungar before him, this man was a Cantona native. And apparently he had been through this ritual several times—or witnessed it—for he met the priest's eyes with only minimal fear and clasped his hands in a reverent attitude as the man linked souls with him. Or whatever it was that he was doing.

A long time passed. The priest's brow furrowed. The Cantona man looked nervous. But at last he, too, was deemed acceptable, and the ritual words ended both his fears and his imprisonment.

Meanwhile, I was watching the cloak. The stalks which had been woven into it while green, now glowing with luminous fervor. As did all its kind . . . while dying. That was what the men had been talking about.

Every plant in that garment had suddenly, simultaneously, begun to die.

The priest was before me. Standing. Watching. I met his eyes, though my soul flinched at the contact. Something about him was . . . *wrong.* Something that went beyond religious charisma, beyond the display of raw power. Something that bespoke a soul that was capable of taking a carpet of life and causing each bit of it to die, all at the same measured pace.

And then his hands touched me. And I knew.

I tried to draw back from him, but his grip on me was firm—much more so than it had been with the other, unknowing aspirants. Where he touched me, there was fire and ice combined, a terrible cold burning that spread swiftly outward from the point of contact, paralyzing my body and my will. But not my revelation. I knew him for what he was—or rather, more accurately, for what he was *not*—and for what he had done to the humans here. Because he wasn't human. Not in any sense of the word. Though he wore a human body, though he played their religious games like a master, the intelligence that shone in those eyes—and the power, and the triumph—were from some other source. And that source was fully capable of killing me through our contact, as swiftly or as slowly as it chose. Just as it had with the cloak. Just as it had with God alone knew how many human beings.

With a sudden burst of will, I broke out of his grasp. I felt weaker than I had been before, as though somehow he had sucked the strength right out of me. But I had no time to indulge in weakness. A moment's hesitation—be it to confront him, to gather my courage, or even to check out my options—would be fatal. For an instant, the congregation wouldn't know what had happened—for an instant only—and then, at his command, I would be surrounded. Completely. My only hope was to make it out of the circle before they got their bodies moving.

And then what? I didn't dare think about it. The nearest exit was behind that arras and so I made for it, even though it meant passing even closer to my unhuman adversary. He moved to block me and I pushed him aside—and through that contact, fleeting though it was, he sent shards of fiery ice coursing through the veins of my arm, like some fast-acting poison. Christ in heaven, what *was* he? The sensation was gone as soon as we ceased to be in contact, but the feeling of weakness—particularly in that limb—had increased tremendously.

Behind the arras was a door. The priest had come through it, therefore it probably led somewhere. Not all doors in this building did. I chose from among those exits which led out of the next room, and then randomly again, hoping to put a few doors and directional decisions between myself and the congregation, before they got this far. I knocked over an altar as I went, scattering scraps of denim on the floor—was that a disembodied pocket?—but to hell with their altars! I could hear voices, now, and the sounds of pursuit, and it seemed that they were only one room away. As they might well have been, in this place.

Who could say whether I was heading outward, or back the way I had come? Or nowhere at all? I staggered against a door, threw it open—and saw a wall before me, dead-ending that route. I pried open a window, and found a closet. Sealed tight. Panic began to overtake me. Did they know this place? Or were most of them as lost in it as I, needing some sort of trail in order to follow me?

The priest would know this place, I realized.

The priest would know how to find me.

I stopped running. To remain trapped in this building was to die, I was sure of that. There were dozens of them, against one of me—and one of them had abilities that I couldn't begin to guess at. I couldn't simply run forever, they would find me. I had to get *out*—out of this building, out of this trap, out of the settlement entirely. And choosing doors at random would never accomplish that.

Breathing deeply, I tried to muster what was left of my strength. I would need it all, to work a shape-change in this state. *Please,* I begged my nature, *something that can claw through wood.* I would attack the ceiling and work my way through, from there it should only be one more story, maximum, until I reached the roof. And from there . . .

I thought of the sun, and shuddered. *Don't worry about that now.* I tried to calm myself—it proved impossible—and then, eyes shut, gave myself over to the changing. Hoping that after the process I would have enough strength left to manage what I had planned, and escape.

Nothing happened.

Nothing happened!

I fell back against the wall, stunned by my failure. What was wrong? Was it the lack of blood? Or of nourishment in general? Or had the alien done something to me, that crippled my efforts to save myself? Or was it—

Damn!

The sun. The fever. The acclimation I had made, in order to walk among them. I felt a sinking sensation in my heart as I remembered, an utter hopelessness that nearly defeated me. Of course; I had forgotten. To walk among them is to *be* one of them, in all but nutritional capacity. How stupid of me! You would think that after so many centuries, after so many other close calls . . .

But I could chastise myself later, in private. For now, the key goal was *survival.*

But how?

I could feel the floor trembling beneath my feet, which spoke of pursuit that was dangerously close. Had they split up? Were they approaching from more than one direction? If so, I was surely doomed.

No. No. Don't think like that.

I threw open windows, doors, anything that might give me access to a way up or out, closer to freedom. At last I found it, after five or six dead ends. A window that opened to reveal a wall, not more than a foot beyond it. But not flush against its frame, either. I took a moment to throw open all other doors in the room, so that they wouldn't immediately know where I'd gone—and then I eased myself out into the space between the two walls, and pushed the window shut.

Not a moment too soon. Barely had I managed a few deep breaths when footsteps barged into the room I had just left, and voices exclaimed their frustration at finding me gone. I held my breath until they left, and then allowed myself—for the first time in a long, long while—the luxury of stillness, and breathing.

I was wedged between two walls of the building, in a space so tight that I was in little danger of falling, even though beyond the window ledge there was nothing to stand on. I used my legs to press me backward, against the far wall; friction held me in place. Against my face and stomach the wall before me was rough, as though it had once been intended to serve as the outside of the building. I managed to force my fingers into a crevice or two and slowly work my way up the wall, inch by painful inch. They would have no trouble tracking me, should they ever come this way; my fingertips and knees were scraped raw on the rough planking, and must surely be leaving a trail of blood to betray the path of my flight.

Slowly, painfully, I worked my way upward. And upward. Darkness gathered around the edges of my vision and exhaustion numbed my senses, but I managed to keep going despite it. Just a little bit farther. Just a little bit . . .

And then, an end. My head struck ceiling—or roof, or whatever the hell was above me—and I stopped climbing, and rested for a moment. My directional instinct, when consulted, said that this was indeed the roof. If so, breaking through it would mean freedom. And sunlight.

Don't think about it, don't don't don't.

Gritting my teeth against the pain of motion, I maneuvered into the best possible position and then struck the obstruction hard, with the heel of my hand. Something gave. Again and again I struck, and I could feel the thin wood at last giving way. A crack, admitting light . . . it seared across my face and reminded me that speed was of the essence; direct sunlight would drain the very strength I needed to break through this barrier.

And then, at last, it gave way. Enough to let me crawl between the splintered shards, out into the light of day. Never before did the sun look so good. I lay

in it for a brief minute, my body wholly exhausted.
But only for a minute. I needed shelter, and soon, but
most important I needed to get out of this place. Because a mob motivated by religious fervor never, never
gives up on its quarry. I remembered that much very
clearly.

Slowly, I began to inch my way to the edge of the
roof. I could only guess at my location relative to the
main door, could but hope that my pursuers weren't
on the ground below, waiting for me to show myself.
For once, my luck held. They must have been guarding the normal exits, never thinking that I would break
through the building itself.

It was a short jump to the nearest roof, but a painful
one. I landed with a heaviness that must surely be
heard for miles around. But apparently no one was
listening. The sun was sucking the strength out of me
as surely as the priest had, but I dared not drop down
to the streets, for fear of being seen. The overlapping
roofs let me move quickly away from the center of the
village, and not until I was well into the outskirts was
I forced to use my lacerated hands to climb down to
earth again.

I was, by this time, an automaton, motivated by
blind instinct. My vision was dark about the corners,
hazy in the center; my ears were filled with a ringing
sound and the sun had so numbed my body that I
couldn't feel my feet when they struck the ground. I
often stumbled. But I retained enough of my rational
sense to realize that I was not going to reach shelter
for quite some time, and never at all if I didn't manage
to get through one of the breaks in the defensive wall.

I ran. And something hit me. Maybe a weapon. In
my leg. Metal, I sensed. Or was that only my fear
speaking? Didn't matter really. I couldn't change it
now, regardless.

Bleeding, I ran across the ravaged farmlands, aware
of someone behind me. Someone in pursuit. One unhuman creature who wore the guise of a man, followed
by an army of acolytes.

The fence was before me at last—and thank God, I had reached a damaged section. I was tempted to duck beneath the wreckage, to drink in a bit of shadow. I starved for darkness. But that would be death, so I forced myself onward. Into the sunlight. Into the unrelenting, unforgiving, full noon sunlight . . .

And at last, the foothills. Footsteps close behind me, I could feel them but not hear them, all hearing gone. Almost all vision, too. Senses abandoning the battle. Leaving the burning ship? I staggered over sharp-edged boulders, looking for some way to lose them. Somewhere to hide.

Another sting, this time in my hip. Definitely a weapon. I tried to keep low as I ran—as I crawled—tried not to think what I was thinking, which was: *This is it. This is the end of it all.*

No. I refused to die.

The edge of a chasm appeared suddenly before me. Some last vestige of strength kept me from falling into it. I clung to the edge, looking at the vast, vast distance between me and the farther edge, and thought: *If I can just make it across. . . .* Madness. But I had to try. Any other course meant death—even waiting to consider.

I jumped. Leapt. Called upon my animal instinct, which understood the dynamics of leaping far better than my human self. Called upon the wolf-memories, the lynx-memories, any memories that would give me strength or courage. I leapt—

And hit the far edge with bleeding fingers, without the strength to hold on, or to hoist myself up.

And slipped loose.

And fell.

Below was a jagged rock wall, nearly vertical. I struck it. Several times. Half dead by the time I landed, I lay between the broken boulders at the ravine's bottom like some twisted toy that the gods had discarded. Too numb to feel pain, after a time. Too numb to feel anything but defeat, as I watched some black-winged scavenger bird circling high overhead, scouting out dinner. Me.

And sometime not very much later they came to the chasm's edge, and the high priest assessed my condition. Dead, he said. As good as. God hath claimed his vengeance.

So be it.

When they had gone, the great bird tilted its wings and drifted slowly downward, toward me. I closed my eyes, not wanting to watch it. Not having the strength to fight, or to care.

We never die peacefully, my father had said. True enough. But the Death which beckoned now was peaceful in the extreme. Blissfully cool, seductively dark. Like the shadow of the great bird it enfolded me, and before my flesh could be picked from my bones I had already begun to embrace it.

Take away the pain, I begged it. *Take away the sun, and you can have me.*

It complied.

LONGSHIP TALGUTH

The Tyr flexed Its Kuol-mind once, twice, and then—satisfied with Its control—called for the Tekk female to enter.

Human Yol Shiyay To Hegyam Haal. By far one of Its current favorites. For It did have favorites. All of the Tekk served It, and served It well, but some were more efficient than others. Some demonstrated, by their energy and devotion, that they valued the lesson of the Conquest. That they genuinely desired to serve Its Will, to help It accomplish what instinct drove It to do.

They didn't know what that was, of course. Didn't know what secret need nested in the heart of the Tyr, causing It to send out longships and found alien colonies and collect, with almost desperate compulsiveness, an endless stream of data. *Correlate! Assess!* It knew what It wanted. But It didn't know how to get it. Someday, when the patterns were all correct, the data would transform into understanding. . . .

She entered the longship's control room, a dark-skinned tribal in her early prime. Aggressively loyal. She bowed, a human gesture. "Kuol-Tyr. Thank you for seeing me."

Also a human gesture. It understood that. Its facilities were lodged equally in Honn and Kuol, and It could have heard her out through the Honn she had first approached. But humans were ever conscious of hierarchy, and attached great meaning to being in a Kuol-Tyr's physical presence. Therefore, much could be communicated by calling one to a private audience.

197

It fluxed, and a sigh resonated through all Its parts. Even the Tekk, who served It—who lived with It—didn't understand Its nature. Still. After so many years . . . It wondered if they ever would.

"Speak," It commanded.

She nodded. "I come on behalf of my tribe, moi-Kuol."

Then she hesitated. (Choosing her words? They set such store by language!) "We lost two children yesterday."

"Two more?" It consulted Its local Kuol-memory for past figures, compared them against other totals from Its other longships. "What were their weaknesses?"

"In one, hemophilia. In the other, a rare immune disorder. Both were destroyed." She opened one hand to disclose two small arrowheads of bone, proof of their death. Not that such was necessary. What would the Tekk gain by lying?

"You are losing many, recently."

"Our gene pool is very small, moi-Kuol. Too small. The starshi feel that our losses will continue—that we will have more and more recessive weaknesses surfacing—unless we bring in some fresh genetic stock. We've outlined a program of exchange which we feel is necessary for our tribe's survival. These are the genetic particulars—" And she handed him a long list of symbols that detailed, in Saudar shorthand, the nature of the problem. And its solution.

It looked over the figures. And did a cursory analysis. More would be pointless. It was no expert in human genetic science, and would never become one. The concepts were too alien; It could not relate the patterns of human inheritance to its own reproductive truths. Here was this list of amino acids and that list, and which belonged to whom, and how they would interact . . . but where was the random mutation factor? The species winnowing? The creation of new life-forms and the destruction of old ones, as a byproduct of reproduction?

Sterile creatures, It thought with sadness, and It fluxed with sympathy. It returned the list to her. One of Its Raayat on board the *Kamugwa* was in the presence of an acceptable human contact, and therefore It used that body as a mouthpiece, even though it was far gone into season. (Soon, soon. How long must It wait? It needed/ they needed/ a Burning . . .)

The *Kamugwa*-Tekk listened as It explained, then bowed deeply. "Of course," she answered. "Whatever the Will requires." Which was as it should be. The Tekk were a servant-species.

It flexed Its *Talguth*-Kuol and spoke again. "According to these plans, you will make transfer yourself. But you are starsha here." It understood the titles the humans gave themselves, but not their real significance. "Do starshi leave the ship? Explain."

"The tribe decided that this would be the most genetically effective trade. You have the tables there . . ."

"Yes," It agreed. The meaningless tables. "You are willing to go?"

"If the *Kamugwa*-Tekk agree."

"I have asked. All is acceptable. There exists one problem . . ." It consulted Its charts through a distant Kuol, and mused briefly upon the complexity of the situation. Normally the longships transferred personnel directly, but there was no time in the foreseeable future when the *Talguth* and the *Kamugwa* could rendezvous. And with summer coming, things would become even more difficult. . . .

It decided, and spoke. "Your tribe has work to do in the Domes. You are qualified, and will be assigned to it. Afterward you will remain on Yuang. Seventy-five local days later the *Kamugwa* will pass that system, and can retrieve you. This is acceptable?"

"Of course, moi-Kuol."

"I can acquire an acceptable Tekk from the *Kamugwa* in one hundred and ninety-six days, when we cross paths at the Kygattra nexus. I must know this now: does your tribe require a particular sex?"

"Either will do."

It paused, to question its distant contact. "The *Kamugwa*-Tekk have a surplus of males. One will be transferred. Is there more?"

She bowed again. "My tribe thanks you. This is very important to us. You'll give our figures to the *Kamugwa*-Tekk, so they can choose the best male for our needs?" She held out the paper again.

How far they had come, these Tekk, from their Earth-human origins! It couldn't imagine a pre-Conquest human making such a transfer so coldly, so rationally. So devoid of passion.

A marked improvement, It decided. It accepted the lists from her, and transfered them into Its other brains. So that the other Tekk might be told what her tribe required, and make their choices accordingly.

A definite improvement.

TIMEFUGUE

Eyes. Eyes upon me. Hostile eyes, from every corner. I feel them on my back as I walk. On my face, which is flushed with the fever of my adaptation. Though I wear a body which is designed to allay their fears, a flesh-mask pockmarked with disease and tinged with that faint ocher hue that says that I, too, barely survived the Plague, these efforts avail me nothing. Their hatred is born of fear and of suffering, and makes them capable of great violence. Last week a family of Jews was massacred. Tomorrow it might be me.

I walk down the central aisle, aware of the eyes, refusing to acknowledge them. My attention is fixed wholly upon the tableau before me. The gilded arch, worked with trefolia and the images of saints. The broad stone altar, clothed in a gold-worked damask so rich that its cost alone could feed this town for a year. The image of their Christ—so pale, so emaciated, that he himself could pass for a recent victim of the Plague. Little wonder they relate to him. And the priest . . .

His silken robes sweep the floor as I kneel, priceless damask worked in a pattern of interlocking crosses; compared to it my own fine clothes are as a hempen garment, symbol of my poverty and insufficiency. The message is understood; I am appropriately humble. I bow my head beneath that bleeding statue, and muse upon the origin of their blood-rites as the ritual words are spoken.

This is the flesh of our Lord Jesus Christ, who died for our sins . . .

Their holy wafer is thin and dry, and not easily swallowed. I hope that whatever it is—and whatever it might become—is acceptable enough to stay in my body until I escape this place. Vomiting up the flesh of the Lord is not a good way to win favor in this community.

Forgive me, God of the Christians, for profaning your altar with my presence. Forgive an unbeliever for using your rites to manipulate your followers, to make them believe . . . what? That I'm one of them?

I turn back to that sea of faces, see them still brimming with guarded hostility. And I wonder what I have accomplished. My mother was a priestess, an oracle, a teacher. My father traded his vast store of knowledge to the scholars of Alexandria for wealth, blood, and—most important of all—acceptance. I live in a different world, which has no place for our kind. No niche for us to fill, with our knowledge and experience; only hiding, and fear, and this endless pretense which daybound humanity has forced upon us.

And their eyes say it all. Not openly hostile, as before, but certainly no kinder. I have played their game, by their rules, and perhaps in doing so have added in some small measure to my safety. But I can never be one of them. I can never walk among their kind without feeling, on my back, the sharp stab of their hatred. For I am the stranger—the outcast—and therefore, eternally suspect.

For me, there is no belonging.

MEYAGA:
HONAQA GORGE

Alive.

I was . . .

. . . alive?

I tried to move. Nothing responded. But the mere act of thinking, of attempting movement, confirmed what my first waking thoughts had proclaimed.

I was alive!

So simple a concept. But the ramifications . . . and the questions! Overwhelming.

I lay still, wrapped in comforting darkness, numbed by the force of my thankfulness. Not wondering, in those moments, what had happened. Because wondering hurt. All efforts hurt, mental and physical. The sun had squeezed me dry of life and now, as vitality seeped slowly back into all the cells of my body, I could feel the shock of their readjustment. Of *my* readjustment.

I had died. Or been about to die.

What had changed that?

No. No questioning. Enough to lie still, tasting the joyful truth of my resurrection, waiting for feeling to return to my body. Enough to live. In the distance was pain, dimly knocking at the threshold of my awareness, but my body was numb; another blessing. I hoped it would last.

Eons later—or so it seemed—I became aware of light. So dim was its source that at first I wasn't sure my eyes were really functioning. But my vision adapted quickly, as always. Soon I could make out shapes in the near-darkness. There: a glimmer of moonlight, filtered through a network of fine black lines. Too little to serve the average human, but enough for my eyes to see by, even in their damaged state A roof was overhead: stone, rough-hewn, perhaps natural. A cavern? And by my side, kneeling . . .

"You're safe," she whispered.

A girl. Soft, in the way that only women are soft. Young, with hair that cascaded softly down to her shoulders and then fell toward me, as she leaned closer. A face untried, untested, with no lines of grief or frustration to mar the perfect smoothness of her youth. Not a face of this world, I decided.

"Tell me what you need to heal." Her voice was gentle, soothing. "I want to help you. All I could find was the need for darkness. Is this place appropriate? What else do you need?"

I tried to speak, tried to tell her that she had saved my life—but I was too weak, no words would come. I tried to move, but barely managed to flex my hands before exhaustion claimed me utterly. Something was beneath my fingertips, it seemed, a pile of damp strands and stiff, roughened bits. Twigs? I was lying on a bed of twigs? What sense did that make? I tried to reason it out, but as her scent came to me—warm and sweet, deliciously clean—I found that I lacked the strength to think. Or the desire.

She touched something to my lips. Wet. Cold. A cloth, soaked with water. I swallowed what she gave me, felt cool life seeping deep into my parched membranes. I wanted to thank her—wanted to ask a thousand questions, though I feared to know the answers—but then, as I looked in her eyes I saw something there that kept me from trying.

She looked concerned.

"What's wrong?"

In her eyes—or rather, behind them. That same inhuman quality, which had been in his.

"Tell me, so I can help you."

There was no mistaking it. That same disconcerting sense of *wrongness*. As if her features were no more than a mask, deliberately sculpted flesh which she wore to hide her true nature.

I pulled back from her. No: overstatement. I *tried* to pull back, but managed only a shudder. My body wasn't yet willing to respond to me.

What did she want? What did *they* want?

"It was too soon." She sounded regretful. Apologetic. "I'm sorry." The words sounded strange to me, distant and familiar at once. Suddenly I realized why. Greek—she was speaking Greek! An ancient dialect, painfully familiar. The language of my father. The language of my youth.

What in Hades—

"Too soon," Her soft fingers brushed back my hair, settled like feathers upon my face and skull. "More rest, I think."

I fought sleep, fought against the tide of darkness that would consummate my helplessness. It seemed to emanate from her, from the places where her fingers touched me. "No," I whispered, but the protest never made it past my lips. "No . . ."

But darkness came, and with it sleep. A sleep without dreams, at least; a sleep without questions. Thank heaven for that.

* * *

Night. The depths of night, utterly silent. Utterly dark. Midnight of the soul, the utter blackness of despair. The shame—and fear—of total helplessness.

Then a hand touched me. Human flesh, woven about a core of alien purpose. I cringed, fearing its owner—and it withdrew, leaving me alone in the darkness.

I dreamed. Of running wild in the Meyagan forest, the harsh wind ruffling my fur. Of stalking prey, and running it to ground. Of sinking my teeth deep into soft flesh and feeling the rich blood pour down my throat. Of drinking in the blood, and the life, as my prey twitched in terror beneath my paws. . . .

A hand slipped beneath my shoulder. Followed by

an arm, its motion so smooth that my damaged flesh
was only marginally aware of where contact was actually made. I felt myself lifted, weightless in the
darkness. A finger touched my lips, so delicately that
I was hardly aware of it until it was gone—but the
single drop of blood it left behind burned my tongue
as I dared to taste it, and sent shivers of hunger and
need coursing through my shattered body.

"No," I whispered, but it was the sentiment of a
stranger. She had drawn me against her, and her offer
was unmistakable. It was there in the scent of her flesh,
in the pounding of her blood beneath her skin, so close
against my face. I felt the last vestiges of my self-
control slipping away into darkness, and I lacked the
strength—and the desire—to fight for its return.

Who are you?

What are you?

Why?

How many years had it been, since I had last tasted
human blood? Even in the Time Before that was a rare
occurrence; I would no more have forced that attention upon a woman than I would any other violent
hunger. Animal blood had sufficed for me, as it did
for most of my kind. And I had forgotten. The intox-
ication of feeding on one's own kind. The heady flavor
of human life. The feel of a woman's body in my arms,
and the heat of her blood as I drank it in—the scent of
her, so very female, which awakened other hungers—
the need to hold her, to drink her in, until my body
shivered in pleasure, my desperate hunger reduced to
mere desire. I had forgotten there was anything like
this . . . and maybe, in fact, I had never known. What
human woman could ever have given herself in this
way, with so little fear of the consequences?

After a time, my hunger subsided. And with it, my
brief fit of consciousness. I passed from waking into
dreaming without ever noticing the border between the
two, and sometime soon after into a warm and healing
darkness.

How did you know my need?

* * *

In the distance was pain. Great pain. My nerves were coming to life again . . . and given the state of my body, it wasn't a welcome development, I tried to fight it, tried to reclaim the numbing darkness which had, until now, spared me. Tried to focus on the source of the pain, evaluate the damage that had been done. My legs had been shattered, it seemed, several ribs broken and my left lung punctured, and my left arm broken below the elbow. What little of my skin wasn't bleeding felt bruised and swollen, as if all the blood I had taken in had congregated on the surface of my body. It was going to hurt like hell when the feeling came back. This was just a prelude.

Memory assured me that my body could heal itself; that same process which transformed my flesh from human shape to canine could just as easily exchange broken bone for whole. Trouble was, I didn't remember how to do it. But Christ, I had better figure it out pretty fast.

I heard footsteps approach me, the soft padding of bare feet on stone. I opened my eyes, and found her beside me. Stifling my fear, I reminded myself, *Whatever she is, she saved you. She fed you.* Daylight filtered through a tangle of branches at the cave mouth to illuminate her face, letting me study her human guise in detail. She was young, no more than twenty; her face still had that softness which is lost only a few years later, exchanged for the angularity of adulthood. Large eyes of a pleasing chestnut, and a frame of matching curls about her face. Features pleasant to look upon, pretty in a youthful way. *Cute.* Her clothes were not unlike my own, but proportioned to suit her female body. She was as small and nonthreatening as the priest had been massive and dominant; for a moment I wondered whether I had been wrong about her, whether the strain of nearly dying had unhinged my mind and caused me to see aliens where there were none.

"I did what I could," she told me. In English, pick-

ing her way through the words as if they were an unfamiliar terrain. "I thought you might be Marra, or
something like a Marra, so I brought you life." She
picked up a branch that had been resting against me,
and studied it. "Did I misjudge? Are you not . . ."
She hesitated. "The languages you know have no word
for it. *Li'o kagye saye aal?*"

I managed to shake my head. It hurt. "I'm sorry. I
don't understand."

"A . . . consumer of life?"

I stiffened—an instinctive reaction. "I don't know
what you mean."

The branch in her hands grew limp as she stroked
it, its leaves coming loose one by one. Dying. I could
hear my heart pounding, as fear took fresh hold.

"If you tell me what you are," she said softly, "I'll
try to help you."

"Human," I said. The only possible answer.

She sat back, and studied me. "Only that?"

I said nothing.

She looked disappointed. "How strange. I thought
. . . *aaryeh,* Earth-languages are so inefficient! I'm
sorry if any of my actions were inappropriate to your
nature."

"You saved my life," I told her, with as much gratitude in my voice as could humanly be managed.

"Genuinely?" Her face lit up with an almost child-
like delight. "Then I read the patterns correctly."

"Patterns?"

"Neural pathways. Mnemonic associations. I had to
sort through them to find the healing patterns—and
yours are in quite a tangle. Never have I seen such a
state-dependent memory—"

I was aghast. "You read my mind?"

For an instant—just an instant—her expression went
blank. I remembered how easily the priest had drained
me of strength, and wondered at the cost of angering
her. But then she was back again. "Oh, no! Not the
way you mean it. That would be impossible—and im-

polite. I just interpreted the physical structure of your brain.''

There was always the possibility that I had died, and this was some kind of crazy afterlife. Did the gods have a sense of humor?

"I'm not using it now," she assured me. "I copied your linguistic associations into this body's brain, so that I could use them for translation. Is this a better language? I can try another, if you like."

I was speechless.

"It functions as a translator for what I want to say. Not as efficient as the original article, of course." She sat back on her heels, eyes bright, studying me. "You are embodied, aren't you?"

"What?"

"Embodied. Subjectively attached to flesh. *Aaryeh* . . . if your body dies, do you also die? Do you cease to be?"

Somehow through the pain I managed to pick up that she wasn't asking for a philosophical response, but expected a straightforward answer. So what could I say? "Yes."

"Amazing. A fully embodied—oh, I'm sorry," That last in response to my wincing, as a new wave of pain rushed over me. "That wasn't appropriate, pressing you for information now. You need to heal first. Here."

She reached down by her side, out of the line of my vision, and picked something up. And offered it to me. A small animal, all sinuous furry length. A ferret? Asleep, or entranced.

She put it in my hand, and folded my fingers over it. Its heartbeat against my skin awakened hunger so intense that for a moment it overwhelmed even the pain.

"I don't understand . . ." I gasped.

"You need to kill," she said simply. Statement of fact.

It took me a minute to find my voice. "I need blood. The killing isn't . . . it happens."

She shook her head sadly, and touched a gentle finger to my hair. "I don't understand your nature, yet. But I think maybe you understand it even less."

She got up to leave me alone with the offering. Blind panic welled up inside me suddenly, a wave of loneliness and homesickness and fear combined. "Will you . . . be back? Later?"

She turned to me. I couldn't read her expression at all—but for the first time, she seemed strangely vulnerable.

"If you want," she said quietly. Watching me.

"Please."

A glimmer of a smile broke across her face. And something else. Relief?

"I'll be here," she promised. "For as long as you need me."

* * *

I dreamed of a beast in human form, that hunted men for pleasure. When they brought it down—at last, after many deaths—they cut it open. Only to find a wormlike thing coiled in a bed of slime at the center of it, where the heart should be, and a webwork of puppeteer's strings leading outward through the flesh.

I screamed.

* * *

Dusk. Silent and still, with only a few muted scratchings, far in the distance, to hint at the presence of life.

I pulled myself through the tangle of weeds that blocked the entrance of my sanctuary, and found myself standing on a rock ledge that jutted out from the eastern wall of a gorge. Six feet across at its widest point, tapering to slivers on both sides of me. Large enough to stand on comfortably, but no more than that.

I was alone.

Terrible emptiness inside me: I convinced myself

that it was only hunger, a physical yearning, and had nothing to do with my isolation. It was good to be free of fear for once, with no one to answer to but myself. No aliens to analyze, no humans to deceive, no home to worry about defending. Nothing to save, or abandon. An animal freedom, dream-pure. It was a welcome relief.

Wasn't it?

I felt strong, stiff but no longer broken. Sometime during the endless nights of pain, fear, and delirium, my body had worked its magic. Thank God it had happened at last.

Reveling in my newfound physical capacity, I began to climb. The walls of the gorge were jagged enough that there were sufficient handholds even for my human self, and the climb was mercifully short. On both sides of the gorge was forest, stripped bare like the settlement. The foliage had been stripped to waist height, by the ravening hordes on their way from the settlement. Smaller trees had been trampled. But despite all that, I could hear life in the distance, a scratching and rustling and chirruping that promised food in small, convenient packages.

Has she left for good? I wondered.

I slipped into cat form and slid past the leafless trees, paws silent on the rocky ground. I usually avoided a feline adaptation, preferring something more human-compatible than the timeless, single-minded fixation of Cat. But now it seemed right. With feline sensitivity I began to sort out the distant noises according to location and probable cause, and chose the shortest route to something that sounded like *squirrel.*

Which is when I heard the other cat coming. I drew myself back and hissed, an instinctive reaction; hunting cats defend their solitude with vigor. But I wasn't prepared for what bounded out at me, with such playful enthusiasm that I was knocked back onto my haunches in surprise, all my hostility suddenly deflated.

It was a mountain cat, female, smaller than myself, in that stage of life just past kittenhood. And I would like to say that I knew what it really was because my senses were so keen, or my reasoning so sound. Or because my cat-body could pick up the scent of alienness that surrounded her, or some similarly impressive accomplishment. But the truth was simply that she still had human eyes—the *same* human eyes—and chestnut fur with russet tipping, that perfectly matched the shade of her human hair.

The cat psyche is a straightforward thing, infinitely simpler than its human counterpart. In it there is no conflict of id and superego, no wrestling of divergent emotions, no clouding of issues with intellectual complexity. As a man, I would have greeted her return with misgivings, any hint of happiness stifled by my concern over her nature and purpose. And alarm at her shapechanging. But as a cat I was simply glad to see her, my joy unfettered by human concerns. And I think it showed.

She padded near to where I stood, and extended her nose for perusal. I sniffed her gingerly, knowing that feline instinct was wary of any new scent. But her scent was warm, encouraging . . . even mildly arousing. It circumvented the biochemical channels that warned of danger and left, in its wake, an offer of companionship.

Awkwardly, I got to my feet. With golden eyes—feline, now—she watched me. I took a few steps toward my quarry, my eyes never leaving hers. And I stopped. And waited.

An invitation. She understood, and ran to my side. I didn't rub my face against hers, but embarrassingly, the impulse was there. Was my cat-self so much the slave of its senses that a comfortable odor was enough to inspire downright affectionate behavior? Or was I simply so *humanly* glad to see her that my cat-self, uninhibited, wanted to express it?

It had been many years since I'd last had a hunting companion. I worried about that for a few seconds—only a few seconds—and then, with feline single-mindedness, simply gave up and accepted her presence.

The squirrels were waiting.

* * *

Midnight. Replete with the blood of my multiple kills, I sat on the narrow stone ledge that guarded the mouth of our cavern. She sat beside me, balanced on the far edge; swinging her feet against the cliff wall beneath her as it she were no more than a child on a swing.

I remembered her killing, and the image faded. No child, this, nor any alien equivalent. She had drained the life out of her prey with a skill born of years of practice, requiring neither blood nor any other physical medium to transfer their essence into hers. Whatever creature nested in the heart of that false human body, it was far from harmless, in substance or intent. And what bothered me most of all is that I had no idea why it had bothered to save me, or nurse me on its own living substance rather than list me among its prey.

Then she turned to me, and the human charm of her body was such that I felt my fears subsiding.

"You are feeling better?" she asked.

It occurred to me suddenly that she really didn't know the full extent of what she'd done. And how could she, when even I barely understood it?

"You saved my life," I said quietly. With as much gratitude in my voice as that one phrase could contain. *And hunted with me, which no woman has done in centuries.* Memories arose within me, painful and compelling. Brigid. Bianca. Yolanda. For a moment I was lost, hunting in those other times. Feeling the pain all over again, as fate took each companion from me. And the loneliness—always the loneliness. At last I whispered, "I don't even know your name."

"Oh." She seemed flustered, for the first time. "I don't have one. Is that a problem?"

I didn't know how to respond.

"The Saudar-preferred form of address is *Marra*," she explained. "With a prefix, if you need to distinguish between two of us. Not all species are comfortable with that. I can take a name, if it would make you more comfortable."

"Most people have one."

"Most *embodied* people," she corrected gently. I noticed that her English had improved since our last conversation. Had she practiced it while I was convalescing? "My last Saudar name was Kiri—I think. Before that, Innagya. Or Innaia? I can't remember which. They called me Kesyagatya when I first joined the Conclave—Kesya' for short—but that doesn't really apply, any more. Tio, before that. Or after? I'm afraid my memory's a little hazy, back that far," she apologized. "It's the limit of my Span. Will any of those do? They're not as appropriate as they were when I used them, but I could answer to one if it would make you more comfortable."

She bounced from one thought to another so quickly that I found it hard to keep up with her. "What would make a name inappropriate?"

"All Saudar names have meanings. And since we Marra change all the time, they keep renaming us." She shrugged lightly. "It seems to make them happy. Kesya' means Mother/Breeder; it was considered appropriate when I was doing reproductive experiments on Gueya. Tio is Whirlwind. Some kind of personality statement, I think. Innagya means water and Innaia ocean; something to do with another project. Kiri was my last name, before I left for Shian. It means . . . you have no English equivalent. Youthful? In a playful sort of way." She grinned at me. "Or you can make one up, if you like."

"And it's all the same to you?" The concept amazed me.

"Embodied custom," she said sweetly. "We humor it."

Embodied. Wisps of memory came back to me, of

a conversation we'd had in the cavern. Which hadn't made much sense at the time, and in replay it made even less. Still, I hesitated to question her openly.

But she guessed my intent—or read it in my brain—and prompted:

"Go ahead. Ask."

"Bluntly?"

"If you like."

Still, I hesitated.

"What is a Marra?" she supplied. "That is the question, isn't it?"

I nodded.

She shifted position on the ledge, her feet swinging over the edge. Granite kicked loose. "Technically, sentience without material analog. More simply, intelligence—and personality—without an enclosing shell of matter. Capable of what you would term mild psychokinetic ability, although that has all sorts of other connotations in your language that aren't correct. We can manipulate a small bit of what you call solid matter, in order to communicate with life-forms that can't perceive us in our natural state. In short, we use bodies the way you use clothing. And we generally establish some sort of identity that will bridge the conceptual gap. A framework for communication, as it were." She looked up at me, smiling. "How is that? Does it help?"

"Somewhat."

"There is a science to our existence," she assured me, "every bit as real as the one which explains your own. Not that we understood it. The Saudar discovered us by accident, when they were measuring the effects of the sixth force on n-space—"

"Sixth force?" I felt suddenly out of my league, a mere Earth primitive contemplating the construction of the universe. "I thought . . . that is, Earth only acknowledges four."

"There are eight. In pairs. Four define our own existence, six of them account for yours . . . there's some overlap with the animative force, of course, both static and dynamic, but . . . have I lost you?''

"Only partly." *Understatement of the year.* "So you're not a physical life-form? At all?''

"Not the core identity which is me, no.''

I remembered that after she had killed, she had eaten: a token bit of flesh taken from each body she killed, almost as an afterthought. I asked about it.

She seemed pleased that I had noticed. "It takes all sorts of complicated energy conversions for us to manipulate matter. For me to raise one arm of this body is a complex and strenuous operation. For me to take a body of this size and keep it animated, oversee its balance and shape the vocal enclosure to make speech come out right, and keep the whole thing in constant motion . . . that would be nearly impossible. And it could never look natural. So instead I design a body that's self-sufficient, provide the spark of life—that is, a Marra presence—and let it handle its own energy conversions. This way all I have to do is stimulate the proper neurons in the brain, and the body interprets them for me. Providing I give it what it needs for fuel, and keep it in functioning condition. Does that explain it?''

The concept was intriguing. So was she, now that my fear had subsided. "So you designed this body from scratch?''

"For maximum communicative potential. Do you like it?''

What could I say to that? At last I stammered, "Very appropriate,'' and hoped it was . . . well, appropriate.

She glowed. "The balance is less than perfect—it could really use a tail—but that wasn't among the options. Has your species ever thought of adding one? The potential is there. It would be a relatively simple genetic adjustment.''

I found myself laughing. Glad to be capable of laughter. "I can't say we ever considered it.''

"Too bad." She shifted on the ledge, and her feet swung back against the cliff wall below. "True bipeds are quite rare, you know. Not counting the flying species. Or the Ganovatri, who stabilize themselves through direct gravitic linkage. Which doesn't really count.''

She looked up at me, eyes glistening in the starlight. ''Now it's my turn. What are *you?*''

My first instinct was to avoid the question entirely, to offer her a tiny bit of truth—or preferably a lie—and then quickly, if possible, turn the conversation to something else. But given her openness, I was ashamed of myself for even considering it. And so I tried, for the first time in my life, to explain just what I was. Which was doubly difficult, as I didn't understand it myself.

When I had told her everything I could, she nodded sagely, as if it made some kind of sense. I envied her that perspective.

''I observed you while you were recovering. I thought maybe some of what I saw was the result of your weakness . . . but I realize now that for you, for your kind, it must be normal.'' She shook her head in amazement. ''Which is incredible.''

''In what way?''

''How do I explain? All embodied creatures produce a . . . *aaryeh*, again your language fails me! The closest I can come in English is 'vital essence,' although that has other connotations . . . it will have to do. They usually produce this in excess of their immediate needs. This is necessary for reproduction, and to fuel the increasing complexity of form which you call 'evolution.' If they don't use what they produce, it's wasted. Or beings such as ourselves can absorb it, and convert it into more useful forms of energy. You, on the other hand, produce no excess. Only enough to keep yourself alive. Which is why you're sterile—oh, you didn't know that? I'm sorry. Was it inappropriate to tell you?''

''Go on,'' I said quietly.

''What amazes me is that not only can you absorb the life of other creatures—there are precedents for that, I can think of at least two other embodied species that have to do it in order to reproduce—you might fall into that category yourself, you realize—but that you can *use* the excess, as we do. To alter your personal mass, with that as a fuel. Gods of the Unity! Wouldn't the Saudar have loved to have you in their laboratories! At last, a natural link between their universe and ours. Parallel evolution at its finest!''

She blinked as she saw the astonishment on my face. ''I've lost you?'' she offered.

''I'm just . . . this is all coming very fast. Give me time.''

''That's why you confused him, you know. The priest-Marra. Even scared him a little, as much as we can be scared. He didn't know what to make of you.''

I looked down into the gorge, felt my fists clench at my sides. ''Which is why he tried to kill me.''

She moved to touch me, a slender hand to my shoulder, but then drew back. ''You know so little about us. He's established an identity among the Cantona humans, and his first priority is to maintain it. He perceived in you a threat to that identity.''

''Which made it right for him to kill me?''

''Ah, you can't understand.'' She sighed. ''There is no wrong or right for us, any more than there is love, or hate, or any sense of species altruism. All those are body-things—chemical processes—species survival stuff. What few emotions we have aren't nearly as intense as yours, and most of them would seem quite alien. And he really doesn't understand death, you know, or what it means to your species.''

''That doesn't make it any better.''

''I didn't think it would,'' she said gently.

After a time, she did put a hand on my shoulder. After a time, it helped.

''Do you know anything about Eyes?'' I asked. Trying to change the subject—but the rage was still there, a cold knot inside of me. ''They talked a lot about Eyes. So did the Tekk, now that I think of it. Do you have any idea what they meant?''

''Yes. Because I asked him the very same question.''

''The priest?''

She nodded. I stiffened.

"You talked to—"

"No need to become agitated. We are of the same species, you know. I came here specifically to find him."

"Old friends?" I snapped. Too quickly. Unfair. I regretted it immediately.

She seemed not to notice the edge of hostility in my voice—or perhaps, diplomatically, *chose* not to notice.

"Apparently the Tyr have developed a method of inserting probes into a human brain, to tap the optical centers for data. Assuming that their computers can decode the signals—which would be anything but straightforward—the Tyr get a picture of what that brain is observing."

. . . if you've eyes inya, stranger—and I'm not sayin' y'do, y'see—but if y'are of the Tyr . . . then now they know. Now they've seen it, with eyes of their own.

Unwilling spies. My God.

I relived the ceremony in timefugue, and comprehended it for the first time. "He's culling out the altered humans," I whispered. "Is that it? Using his Marra talent to sense which ones have been added to?"

She hesitated. "That's the Identity he's created."

I looked up sharply; something in her tone of voice made me suspicious. "He does cull them out, doesn't he? And kill them?"

"He kills them," she agreed. "And a purpose is served. The community feels safe, and can—"

"You're not telling me something."

She didn't answer.

"The ones he kills. They do have the equipment in them, don't they? He wouldn't use his position—"

Her eyes stopped me. Cold.

Jesus Christ . . .

"It serves a purpose," she assured me. "The villagers need to see someone die, to know that they're really being protected."

"He kills the *innocent?*"

"His Identity is that of a Protector. There has to be some demonstration—"

"And what about the real Eyes? Does he kill them, too? Or are they wandering free about the town, taking in things for the Tyr?"

Her expression had changed; it took me a while to realize that now it was one of pity.

"He told me that he's never seen anyone with the technical alterations that the villagers describe. That there have been no Eyes in the settlement, for as long as he's been there."

"You mean he's . . . Christ! I can't . . . oh, God. I don't believe it."

"It's all part of his current Identity."

"Is that all this is to you?" I demanded. "Some kind of game? Play by the rules, and everything's all right?"

"It's much more than that. Identity is how we function. It's the context that allows us to communicate with you, to keep from—"

She stopped. Then finished quietly, sadly, "It's not a human concept. I'm sorry."

No it wasn't. I tried to weave all those disparate images—the priest in his death-robes, the Marra playing their emotionless games, this Marra healing me—into some sort of comprehensible whole. I couldn't. It was, as she said, not a human concept.

"How long do you persist at it?" I asked her.

"A particular role? Up to the point where it's been fulfilled. Or completed. Or rendered impractical. On Shian, that meant mimicking old age and even death; straight through from birth to decomposition, until the mourners scattered. It's considered an art form among us, doing it well."

"And what's your Identity? Now?"

"A healer." She let her hand fall back against the ledge, studied her fingers while she spoke. "I took that on when I found you. It's fulfilled when you're fully recovered."

"And after that?" I asked quietly. Suddenly realizing how quickly I might lose her. Suddenly acknowledging that I didn't want to.

She hesitated. "I don't know. I remember too much of the old days to settle down like he did. Remember too much to approve of what he's doing. So much was lost. . . ."

For a short while, silence. I didn't know what to say. I didn't know what her hurt was, or how to help. I could barely cope with my own.

"I go back to what I was doing before I found you," she said at last. "Searching."

"For what?"

"I'm not sure, anymore. Something in my people. Maybe something in yours. I need a context. The Tyr destroyed everything I knew. . . ."

"Vengeance?"

She shook her head. "That's body-stuff." But I don't think she convinced either of us.

"Where will you go?"

"Suyaag, I think. The central Meyagan settlement. I've heard rumors of a human uprising, and that seems the best place to—"

I stiffened abruptly. "Of what?"

"An uprising. Only in the planning stages, now. Why do you seem so surprised? It's typical behavior, for one embodied species that's been enslaved by another. We observe it all the time."

"But what point would there be in overthrowing the Tyr here, on this one planet? They'd just bring in a new Kuol-Tyr, and a whole new entourage of Honn. It's not like we could leave here, to establish ourselves elsewhere."

"Why not?"

"Because . . . we can't. That's how it works."

Now she looked confused. "How *what* works?"

"Interstellar travel. Don't you—" But the words died in my throat, unspoken. *Don't you see how that restricts our actions?* I had meant to ask. *To be limited to sublight velocity, unless the Tyr transport us?* But I didn't. Because the lack of understanding in her expression told me more than words ever could—and revealed a truth so awesome, so terrible, that I could feel myself shaking as I acknowledged it.

"They lied," I whispered. Testing the words. Tasting the truth. "They lied to us."

I reached out and grasped her hand. Not caring if what was inside her flesh was human or spirit, ghost or alien. I needed the contact to keep from losing control of myself.

They lied!

"Daetrin?" It was the first time she had spoken my name; it brought me back to her, started me breathing again.

"The light-speed barrier," I whispered. "Tell me."

"It's very real," she assured me. "But there are ways to work around it. The Saudar use n-space, which is based on Anuba's Variable . . . there are at least three separate methods that I can think of. And that's not counting the sendings of the Jiyotra which aren't, strictly speaking, physical transportation . . . are you all right?"

"No." My voice was a hoarse whisper, emotionless. Divorced from the turmoil inside me, the rage and despair and indignation and fury all combined, all mixed up and burning inside me until I lowered my head and shook like a leaf in a storm, overcome by the force of it. If not for her hand, I think I would have given in and lost all vestige of control; but I held onto her, so tightly that my nails drew blood, and drew precious strength from the contact.

"They lied," I whispered. Wanting her to understand. "They told us we couldn't get to the stars without them. And we believed it! We were so wound up in ourselves that we would rather accept defeat than question the basic tenets of our science. No wonder they kept us isolated from their other conquered species! They were afraid that someone would tell us the truth. . . ."

That the universe could have been ours. Can be ours.

I released her hand—with effort—and stood. And closed my eyes, leaning back against the mountain wall. And cursed the conquerors of Earth, with newfound vitality. Emotions were pouring back into me that had been dead for years. Because *I* had been dead for years, burying my head in the sand while the centuries of Subjugation passed me by. Pretending that I was less than I really was, so I wouldn't have to face my responsibility. *Believing* it. Now the old feelings were back, those same powerful emotions which once drove me to fly into the face of the sun, to risk death in the name of planetary defense. Yes, I would do it again, if I thought there was even a chance of success. . . .

With effort I controlled myself, brought my soaring dreams down to earth again. In my youth I might have thrown myself into battle with confidence, trusting in my special skills and my many years of experience to safeguard me. But that was long in my past. Now I was only marginally aware of my true potential, and no longer fluent in applying it; my ignorance of my own limitations had nearly cost me my life in Cantona, and might do so again. I didn't dare take on the Tyr until I had my own abilities firmly under control.

But there were other conquerors, equally oppressive. And equally offensive. One of them was in Cantona, wearing the guise of a human. Spouting lies as evil as any that the Tyr ever told. Subjugating the Cantona Settlement as thoroughly and as cold-bloodedly as the Tyr had done to Earth.

Defeating him would be next to impossible. It would also be excellent practice.

"What about the priest-Marra?" I asked her.

"What about him?"

I phrased it carefully. "You don't care what happens to him?"

She looked at me. And slowly understood what I was hinting at, why I needed to know that she wouldn't interfere.

"You're going after him, aren't you? That is the stupidest thing that any embodied . . . I can't believe you're even considering it! Don't you understand what I told you? The priest is *Marra*. You can't kill him. You can't even hurt him. He's stronger than you are, more adaptable . . . and he doesn't need his body to survive. What in Unity's name are you going to do to him?''

She had given me some ideas, but I wasn't about to say that. I didn't know her well enough to be sure she wouldn't warn him.

''I'm not going off to Suyaag while several hundred of my species are bowing and praying to something that isn't even human.'' *And I'm not going to fight the Tyr until I know what I'm capable of.*

A faint smile flitted across her face. She didn't point out that I had just committed myself to going to Suyaag with her, which was fine with me. I hadn't intended to do so. It had just come out.

''You're a little bit crazy,'' she told me. ''You know that?''

''It's been said.''

My muscles were stiff but responsive; my senses were fully awakened once more, and would remain so for as long as I kept to the night. I would sleep one more day, hunt, and leave for Cantona in the evening. Fully healed, well rested, and well fed.

It would give me time to plan.

''Will you wait for me?'' I asked her. ''It shouldn't take long.'' *One way or another.*

''He's going to kill you.''

I managed a shrug. ''Others have tried.''

''But were they Marra?''

''Foolish bravado is part of my identity,'' I informed her. ''So, will you wait?''

No answer.

I looked at her.

At last she nodded. And smiled, I thought.

''I'll wait. But what are you going to do?''

I sighed and looked out into the darkness. Blissful, healing darkness. I would never abandon it again.

''What my kind does best,'' I told her.

YUANG:
DOME FIVE

He couldn't fix it. Try though he might, the machine defied him. He had hoped that if he fought with it long enough, followed every circuit from beginning to end with careful enough eyes, he might come up with a different cause for the trouble they were having with it. A more acceptable cause. But he had been through every circuit at least twice, had tested every component he could remove or reach, and the diagnosis remained the same. A biochip had died. Simple. It had to be replaced. Simple.

"Shit."

Tereza looked up from where she was working. "Chip?"

He muttered something incomprehensible.

"I guess so," Sung offered.

She hesitated. "Do you think we should tell him now?"

"What? Tell me what?" He quickly walked over to where she sat and snatched away the fax memo that she was holding. Given the room's configuration, such a maneuver was no easy feat. Like all Dome facilities it lacked adequate floor space, and they made the most of what they had by a serpentine arrangement of equipment and furniture that maximized productivity but minimized walkspace.

"Oh, hell!" he muttered, reading it. "That's just what we need." He turned toward Sung, to offer him the fax, but the junior researcher waved him off. "I've seen it."

"When did this come?"

''While you were working.''

''It could be worse,'' Sung offered.

''It couldn't be worse,'' Yaan answered bitterly. ''It couldn't possibly be worse.''

With a sigh he gave the fax back to Tereza, leaving it to her to enter it into the facility's log. And ran a hand through his graying hair, long overdue for trimming. ''So the Tyr's going to give us another earthborn. Lucky us.''

Sung looked at the two of them, as though trying to read something in their faces. ''How bad can it be?''

Yaan shook his head. They didn't remember. Or perhaps they hadn't been here, the last time it happened; he found it hard to recall. Their own transitions had been easy enough, but most of the people in the Domes weren't born on this world, as they had been. Most came there as adults, with hard and fast ideas about what the Domes were, should be, could be. As he had done. So long ago. . . .

''Which longship?'' he asked, trying to fend off the memories. ''Do we know?''

''The *Talguth*,'' Tereza answered. ''They're supplying our Tekk help also.''

''Well, they know which chip we need. Maybe they'll have a replacement ready. . . .'' Too much to hope for. If he knew the Tekk, they'd spend at least a day ''confirming the problem.'' And confronting him. He wasn't up to it.

Hell.

''The fax says he's trained,'' Tireza offered.

''They're never trained. Not when they're from Earth. A little bit of basic science, yes, and a passing knowledge of what their ancestors once accomplished—but you forget how much was deliberately destroyed, during the Conquest.'' He recalled the so-called Great Plague which the Kievans launched, a computer virus which used the international networks to infect millions of data banks, then wiped them all clean simultaneously. And the bombings—primitive but effective—which took out so many libraries and scientific establishments in the early years, and quite a few researchers with them. The earthborn might read about such things, might know the history, the when and the how and supposedly the why of them . . . but would never consider all the implications. Never.

"At least we'll get the scan fixed," she continued. "We need it. *I* need it. So: the *Talguth* will supply us with a Tekk, who'll come, do his job, and then leave. And we'll have one new person to break in—honestly, Yaan, how bad can it be? And you know we could use another pair of hands around here."

He said nothing out loud in response, merely nodded. She hadn't been there the last time the Tekk came. She didn't know what they had asked of him—why he dreaded their return—and why he had known all along that their return was inevitable. Why he had tried so hard to fix the damned machine himself, rather than deal with them again.

"Didn't you break in an earthborn just before I got here?" Sung asked. Born and raised in the Domes system, nursed on their delicately balanced hypocrisy, he could have no understanding what it meant for an outsider to come here and be told the truth. "How did he turn out?"

Yaan turned to face him slowly, wondering how much of his weariness showed in his face. How much he had aged, in the last few days.

"He killed himself," he said quietly.

* * *

They used the lounge as a reception room. It had been intended as a storage room, but the first thing Yaan did when he was put in charge of the facility was have everything moved out of it—even though that meant a lot of reshuffling elsewhere—and a few simple amenities moved in. Now, after several years of use, it was almost a comfortable space to be in. There was a carpet. There were chairs. There was a water heater which allowed them to brew small cups of hot flavored water, using the plants which Yaan painstakingly nursed under sunlamps in his private compartment. Each of these items had cost its weight in paperwork, for each had to be laboriously justified to the Tyr, not only what it was and why they wanted it, but why it was absolutely necessary for the continued functioning of Dome Five that it be obtained. The pieces were mismatched and far from new, and the effect therefore was somewhat shabby, but it was also . . . earthy. Reassuring. Comfortable.

Into that small space they squeezed twelve unit managers and their assistants, with Yaan at the head of them. He would have been willing to wager money on his ability to pick out those men and women who had dealt with the Tekk on previous occasions; they were the ones whose hands were never still, who clasped and unclasped their fingers restlessly as they tried, in vain, to prepare themselves for the coming confrontation. *But at least they don't have an earthie to worry about,* Yaan mused. *That'll be my job.*

Lucky me.

Precisely on time, the *Talguth* delegation arrived. He was pleased to note that it was small; that meant no business had been added to their itinerary after the fax had been sent. *Thank heaven for small favors.* The Tyr who led them was a Raayat, its armor plates already festooned with a bristling array of spikes. The *Talguth*-Tekk, who stood at attention behind it, was a formidable woman of aggressively African heritage. Yaan sensed that dealing with her was going to be very difficult. Beside her . . .

With a deep, heartfelt sigh of dread, he knew that this one was going to be trouble. Big trouble. He assessed the youth with a practiced eye, and felt himself growing more and more worried. The man—say rather, *boy*—was sixteen. If that old. Bad, very bad. Not yet a child, not quite an adult, filled with the insecurities of both and an admixture of hormones that practically guaranteed overreaction to stress. Bearing himself in a manner that implied he had come to *work,* he had

come to *do things,* he was very excited about being
here and could they please, *please,* get through the
preliminaries very fast, because he couldn't wait to get
started.

We're going to lose him, Yaan thought grimly. *One
way or another.*

"The Tyr assigns you a Tekk assistant, *Talguth-*
human Yol Shayay To Hegyam Haal." The Raayat's
voice was less raspy than most, and therefore a lot
easier to understand. Behind it the Tekk woman
grinned, a disconcertingly ferocious expression. "She
is to remain on this world for as long as is required,
up to a maximum of seventy-five days, to repair or
replace your equipment as necessary. You will cooperate in all ways with her."

"Of course," Yaan responded. He caught her eyes—
recognized what he thought was challenge in them—and
quickly looked away. Back at the Raayat. Anywhere
safe.

"This," the Raayat indicated the youth, "is Earth-
human Nogyat Um Kaag To-Sem Heyat. He is being
transferred to your division, to be trained as a servant
of Dome Five. The Tyr requires detailed reports on
his progress, and will meet with him once each local
year, until it has been adequately demonstrated that he
has been properly indoctrinated. You understand
this?"

"Yes," he answered. *More than you know.*

"You accept the responsibility?"

"On behalf of my staff, and Dome Five, I accept."
Sung would see that a memo was circulated; the other
domers had to be warned. No telling how much damage that kid—what was his nameber, Nogyat?—no telling how much damage he could do if he got out of
the facility too soon, onto the streets. People should
be warned.

He looked at the boy again, noted the passionate
gleam in his eyes, and shuddered. *This one's going to
be hard. Very hard.*

But weren't they all?

* * *

Tereza took the first shift with the kid. That was something, anyway. She could settle him in all right, show him his compartment and run through furniture operations once, just to make sure he knew where everything was and how to get it unfolded. Half an hour. Maybe—if luck held, if Tereza was both patient and persistent—twice that. Which was damned necessary, he reflected. Because the last thing he needed was to have the kid barging in here while he was trying to deal with this Tekk.

The African woman followed him in silence to the upper level, where most of the workrooms were located. He took her around the back way, so they wouldn't have to pass by the particle accelerator. No need to give her more ammunition than she already had. Then into the main workroom, his personal space; he felt as she entered it that he had somehow been violated.

"The synaptic scan," he said shortly, and pointed. "There."

She nodded and went to it. He had left it opened up, a frank admission that he had tried to fix it himself, that he would do without Tekk services if that were possible. She nodded as she saw it.

"It does not function?"

"It works, but not well. Inaccurate past the twelfth decimal place. Which is exactly where decay compensation comes into play." *Therefore,* he thought, *the problem must be in the DAC bioplex.* But he said nothing, just watched while she measured and metered and tested, exactly as he had done that morning. The scan could be fixed in five minutes flat, if that was all she wanted to do. If she had prepared a new biochip before coming here.

He saw Sung, in the far corner, watching her. Waiting. He caught his own fingers restlessly drumming on a sample tray, and stopped them.

At last she finished. "Harosh! You are correct." In

her hand she held the failed biochip. "We begin to graft a new one immediately." Then she stood, and faced him. "You are elder, here."

He saw Sung tense. "I'm in charge, if that's what you mean."

She looked down long enough to lay the dead chip aside, then met his eyes again. Incised markings on her face and body made her seem almost as alien as the Tyr themselves. "The Domes are self-reliant. They rarely require our aid. On other planets we come two, maybe three times a local year, different Tekk from many ships, and maintain contact. Not with the Domes."

"We can't afford the delay," he said simply.

"Dai? So you fix things yourselves. Without training, without data, and without the proper tools. Often successfully. The Tyr is impressed. It thinks: they have much knowledge, these humans, and great adaptability. I was right in taking them from their home planets, and bringing them together. Together, *under my control.*" She hissed the last words. "So tell me: Is it satisfying to live like insects under glass? Fluttering about for the amusement of your captor, ignoring the fact that someday, when it grows tired of this game, it will crack that glass open and let this planet finish you off?"

He turned away. This wasn't what he'd expected. He wasn't prepared for it. "You were called in to fix the synaptic scan—"

A few quick strides and she was beside him, grasping his shoulders. She turned him, with surprising strength, to face her. "Your people and mine are without Eyes. The only ones who don't have to worry that every word they say is being transmitted back to the Tyr."

"Or so they say—"

"Listen! It is *truth*. I say this because I *know.* Your people say to the Tyr: scientists can't function with constant fear of surveillance. It upsets the creative process. The Tyr thinks, perhaps these things are true.

Dai? Perhaps not. But in order that you serve it, it will indulge you. It doesn't know what you really need, or what you are, or even what it has done by bringing you all together. It has no understanding of genius.''

"Bugs under glass," he muttered.

"We want you to help us." Her grasp on his shoulders had become so tight that he could feel blood pounding between her fingers. "You have the knowledge, and the tools. We have the mobility. Together—''

He managed to break away. Somehow. "If you want atomics, that's in Dome Eight. You know that. All we do here is run rat brains through blenders. If you'd done your research—''

"Earth fell to the Tyr because the Tyr were better warriors. And, if we revolt, Earth will fall again. That race will *always* be better warriors; nothing we do can change that. What we need is *information*. What is the Tyr? How does it function? What are its weaknesses? Only you have the science—and the freedom—to find that out.''

"Trapped, in this place. Guarded by the Tyr."

"Feh! When my ancestors were taken from Earth, what was their first thought? *Submit*. Win trust. Do whatever must be done to establish a network of communication between the human colonies. Because without communication, we are nikdah! Nothing! And all our plans are nothing! Toward this end, for over three centuries, we have crawled. We have submitted. We have sacrificed our own children, suppressed our own desires, prostituted our bodies—all so the Tyr would transmit, without any suspicion, a few coded messages. And now the system is complete. Sophisticated enough to handle any instructions we need to send. So the question remains, do you serve yourselves, or Earth? Will you, by your cowardice, make a mockery of our sacrifice? Will you waste the one chance we have to free ourselves?''

He said it slowly, trying to keep his voice steady. "We have no access to the information you require."

She stared at him for a long while in silence; the

markings on her face made it impossible for him to read her. At last she told him, "In seventy-four days I'm scheduled to be transferred to another longship. To join a tribe of strangers, whose language base is different than mine. To give my body to a stranger for use, and commit myself to making babies for him . . . all so I could be here today. To talk to you." Another long silence; he didn't dare meet her eyes. "I'll be back when the biochip is tested, to install it. We'll talk then."

Numbly, mechanically, he nodded.

She left.

After a long time—a long and silent time—he moved again. Groped for a chair and sat in it, heavily.

"Well?" he asked Sung. He noticed that his hands were trembling, and clasped them together in his lap. "What did you think?"

The researcher's voice was quiet, controlled. It hardly shook at all. "What is there to think? She's right. Of course she's right. Does it change anything?"

"I don't know," he whispered, and he lowered his head. "I just don't know."

Bugs under glass. . . .

* * *

He climbed up to the ring. It wasn't a place he went often. The view from it was anything but comforting: a narrow band of swirling mauve and yellow-gray clouds that was barely visible between two banks of heat collectors. Now and then a distant cloud would ignite with a thunderclap, and chemical fire spewed oily black smoke as it surged from cloud to cloud, scouring the landscape. Sometimes a firestorm would completely envelop one or more of the Domes; he had seen that happen, too. Once he had watched it through to the end.

My world, he thought. *My home.*

He tried not to remember the green fields and open

skies of his native planet. There was too much pain in
that, in knowing that he could never go home. Transfer
him they might, but never to Earth. That was the Law.

He stared out at the unwholesome vista for a long
time, and tears came to his eyes while he did so. Because of the view, he convinced himself. The brightness of it bothered his eyes. It was surely that.

Slowly, gradually, he became aware that someone
was behind him.

"Is it time to go back?" Discreetly wiping his face
dry with the back of one sleeve, he turned to see which
of his assistants had followed him . . . and froze.

It was the Raayat.

"What do you want?" he whispered. He was surprised that he could talk at all. Fear blocked his throat.

"I observe," was all it said.

He got carefully out of its way, so that its view of
the atmosphere was unobscured. But he realized with
a sinking heart, as he did so, that it wasn't interested
in the view. It was watching *him*.

"Look. Exactly what is it you want?" He could feel
himself sweating, and hoped it didn't show. How much
did the creature know? Had it overheard what the Tekk
woman said? If so, they were all lost. "Is there something I can do for you?"

Terra, but it looked strong! He suspected it could
tip him over the guardrail without pausing for breath.
"Tell me, please."

"I am Raayat," it said slowly. As if that answered
him. Then: "I observe. I wish to observe humans.
Science-humans."

Me, he thought, with a sinking sensation. *Us.*

"You . . . you can't," he said. "We're not to be
observed. The Tyr said . . ." *But this* is *the Tyr,* he
suddenly realized. *No help from that quarter.*

"Human creativity requires privacy," he finished
desperately. A sterile recitation; it sounded weak even
to him.

The Raayat just looked at him, wordlessly. Utterly
still, without any hint of its thoughts, or its intentions.

Then, after several very long minutes, it turned and started down the narrow staircase, back to the floor of the Dome. Wordlessly. He watched it descend, his hands gripping the guardrail, knuckles white. Watched it walk across the ground at the bottom until it passed out of sight behind a building. Wishing he could convince himself that he'd never see it again. Even for a few minutes. Just long enough for him to calm down.

Outside the Dome, a firestorm was just igniting.

MEYAGA:
CANTONA SETTLEMENT

Image of a woman: dressed in brown, because brown
was the color of mourning. Dark brown, the hue of
ravaged earth; a brown that spoke of hunger, of futility, and of death. Gray embroidery dotted the breast
of her inmost shift, short stiches the hue of granite in
a simple, repetitive motif. She wore it because some
ornament was expected, to lie against her skin. Because her outer robes, Tyr-like in their conformity,
should be shed within the home to reveal something
more human in design. Marginally more human, at
least. But the colors of dust and sterile earth disclosed
her spirit to any who cared to look. As did her mo-
tions, minimal and graceless. As did her downcast
eyes, underscored by purple shadows.

Her husband was dead. Killed, by the beasts that
had devoured the crops. She had wept furiously beside
his body as they carried him from the fields, tearing
at her own hair as if it was their fur. As if she could
somehow, through her mourning, hurt them. But she
knew better. The beasts were demons, nothing less—
demons of Meyaga, in league with the dreaded Tyr.
Who were themselves dark gods of measureless evil,
shadows of alien malevolence that stood behind the
ravening hordes and whispered silently: *Go. Eat. Destroy.*

The beasts had obeyed. And her husband was dead.
And her life was sustained by no more than a fragile
thread, a whisper, a strand of grayness without any hope.
This was the message she had woven into her garments,
plying her needle deep into midnight, by the light of a

hooded lamp. So that passing shadows, pausing by her
threshold, might read her sorrow in her attire, and not
need to question her. She had no wish to speak.

Sometimes she heard noises. Sometimes she imagined it was her husband again, or his soul, restless in
the Meyagan night. Sometimes she heard—or imagined that she heard—a faint scratching sound on the
roof, or a whisper of flesh against the outer walls. As
though some large animal, black as night and stealthy
as the wind, was watching her. Sometimes she imagined that it was Death itself, come to take her—and
on those nights she would open the door wide, until
the cold Meyagan air froze the tears on her cheek and
sent her, shivering, back into shelter. Her husband did
not come. And death, doubly cruel, did not claim her.

All these things were there for the viewing, if one
watched carefully enough. And I, more careful than
ever, was watching.

On the tenth day of every month the citizens of the
settlement rested, a necessary (if minimal) sabbath.
On this tenth day, the first since her husband's death,
the ashes of the marauders were to be scattered in the
temple, and the spirits of the dead set to rest at last.
As if that could be done. She had chosen not to go
with the rest, preferring solitude as the temple of her
sorrow, letting the darkness of isolation enfold her
slowly as the Meyagan night fell.

From the temple, in the distance, there came chanting. Let them pray. She slipped on a thick woolen
gown, then the heavy coat which was Tyr-plain, her
outermost garb. The settlement was deserted, dark and
cold and utterly desolate; she slipped out of her door
and through the narrow streets, heading away from the
center of the village. Once or twice she looked back
suddenly, as though she had had heard (or felt) that
something was following her. But she never thought to
look overhead, to the forest of roofs that offered sure
footing for feline paws; thus she never saw the shadow
that slid from house to house, or the green glow of
moonlight reflected toward her by mock-feline eyes.

Eventually the streets began to widen; stars shone brightly between the roofs. It was a clear night, rare in this part of the world. The ground was a thatchwork of shadows, from trees and fenceposts and the first few granite monuments that towered over her, as she passed from the confines of the settlement itself into the still-ness, and the silence, of the Cantona burial grounds.

It was a suitable night to approach the dead.

A few tall monuments, intricately carved, marked the graves of the few earthborn residents, the settle-ment's first dead. Smaller headstones spotted the ground between them at intervals—shards of un-adorned stone, like rubble. There were several tombs, also, built in the settlement's first years—now left to decay, as people had less and less energy to devote to such monuments. She knew the layout of the graveyard and went to the westernmost plots, where the recent dead were laid. There she found the most recent tomb-stone, and she knelt in the damp earth before it as if she would lay herself down in offering.

"Relleg." She whispered his number several times, mantralike, swaying on her knees as if her legs would hardly support her. Putting out her hand once, to steady herself against the slab of granite which she herself had carved. Her memorial to him. There was one word on it, one single word which she set over him to guard his spirit, to hasten its journey back to Earth. *Loved*, it said. *Loved*. That was enough.

She knelt on his grave for a long, long time, her silence punctuated by bouts of crying. She whispered words to him that no mere human ear could have heard, which told of the past, and of happier times. So lost was she in her grief, in the utter bleakness of her de-spair, that if some stranger had crept up behind her—say even a living stranger, with no more stealth than the average man—she would not have heard him ap-proach, nor become aware of his presence. So what chance had she with a more-than-average man, who walked with the stealth of the dead?

As I watched her, I knew the time had come. Luck

had favored me, in that the priest-Marra was tied up in ritual and would not interfere. Such a night might not come again for quite a while.

Human, now—or nearly human, the borderline was debatable—I stepped out before her. And waited, in silence, for her to notice.

After some time she leaned back and used the wool of her coat sleeve to wipe her tears across her face. Not quite drying them. She looked up then, her face turned in my direction . . . and she froze. As still as ice, which a single word might shatter.

I took one step toward her, moving free of a half-concealing shadow. My features were more visible now, and I watched as the horror and incredulity on her face gave way to amazement . . . and hope.

"Relleg?" she whispered.

I said nothing. My features were enough. The mask I wore duplicated her husband's face precisely, just as my body mimicked his form. I had seen him carried from the field, had fixed his appearance into my memory; it was no great effort for me to play doppelganger and reproduce his features with my own flesh. What was harder—and far more dangerous—was the essence of death which I needed to communicate. Reproducing his wounds wasn't enough. I needed the lusterless skin of the dead, the blue-gray cast and inelasticity that spoke of lifelessness and decay. I needed to not breathe—or to appear not to be breathing—and I had to still my heartbeat so that its current pounding, a response to my anxiety, wouldn't be observed. It's no easy thing, becoming a corpse in all but fact. One tiny slip and all is lost. The dead have no ability to shapechange.

But apparently I had succeeded. Or so her expression—an admixture of horror, astonishment, and sorrow—communicated.

"Relleg . . ."

I nodded, stiffly. And whispered her name, which I had learned from observing her. "Hanaa."

"Is't you?" She managed some control over her

voice, but her hands were trembling. "Really you? Come back . . . from Earth?"

I sensed that that point was more incredible than all the rest—that she could not imagine any spirit voluntarily leaving Earth to come here, for any reason. Was not Earth the reward for all their suffering?

"I came t'warn you." My voice was a hoarse whisper; it was the safest course to follow. How much could I know of Relleg's vocal qualities, when I had done no more than view his corpse? "T'warn, Hanaa."

In the distance, chanting. She couldn't hear it, but I could. *God'v Earth, protect's* . . . She rose unsteadily to her feet, a hand on Relleg's tombstone for support. "A warning? Gainst what, husbann?"

I whispered it. "Ye've been betrayed . . ."

She was so still, so silent in her reaction, that for a moment I thought I might have made a mistake. Used a common Earth-word, which the Meyagan inflection had altered past recognition. But I waited her out—the dead have great patience—and after a few moments she stirred, and whispered "Me, y'mean? Or . . . what?"

"Th' colony," I answered. "Th'settlemenn."

The cold wind gusted silently toward us; dead leaves swept over her feet.

"Tell me," she whispered.

I knew then that I had won. Throughout history, men have always consulted—and venerated—two great forces: their gods, and their dead. The priest-Marra had control of the former, as God's spokesman on Meyaga. I needed the latter, if I was to prevail.

It was a risky game I was playing, to be sure. And the priest assuredly had the stronger hand. But along with the dead, I was taking control of what was potentially the most versatile weapon of all: the human imagination.

"Lis'n," I told her. And I proceeded to plant the seeds of doubt which I had prepared, oh-so-carefully, during my long nights of observation. Hinting at secrets so close to the truth that her instinct said *yes*,

yes, that must be right. A few words, hoarsely voiced, were enough. She wanted to believe. If I was her husband, come back to warn her, then there was an afterlife, she had an immortal soul, and love could bridge the barrier of Death. Believing in me, she grasped at her own immortality.

"Th'dead know," I finished. "Ask'm. Ask'm."

"The truth . . ."

"That there'r no Eyes," I whispered. "Nev'r have been Eyes. Th'innocenn dead are restless, Hanna. Their numbers'r growinn. It's time t'stop't."

I reached out a hand to her, even as I stepped back, "I trust'n you . . ." She reached out to me . . . but her fear was greater than her love, and she didn't dare touch me. I had counted on that.

"No time," I told her, my voice filled with pain. Darkness spilled into the space between us. "Takes t'much, t'come here. Not sure I c'n again. Promise . . ."

"I will!"

"Watch . . ."

"Yes."

"The dead . . ."

"Relleg!"

But I had slipped behind a tombstone, and reclaimed my panther body. Black fur against blackened earth, I easily passed from monument to monument, evading her searching eyes as I reclaimed my freedom. My heart was pounding, from guilt and excitement both. Was it right to abuse her memories thus, to use her husband's image as freely as I had once used Christ's communion, to serve my own selfish purpose?

Not selfish, I told myself. I was serving Earth.

We do what we must.

* * *

My father's house is rustic, but sound. It serves him well, both as camouflage and as defense, standing guard as it does over a warren of secret spaces that will permit him to vanish into the night without a trace, should danger threaten. I know all this because I know him, know his habits—so well!—but to the uninformed his house appears exactly as it should, well-built but unpretentious. Unremarkable. Its timbers are rough-hewn, its mortar tinged with green, its wooden door swollen from the damp. Autumn leaves crunch underfoot as I approach, and the house echoes back the sound with utter normalcy. As it to say: *Look, there's nothing suspicious here.*

I knock. Tense, as always. Anxious to see him. How long since we were last in the same town? The same country? I write to him, when I can; he does the same, when he knows where I am. But those are guarded letters, carefully censored against prying eyes. Physical reunion is something else entirely.

No answer. I knock again, impatient. He's lived here for longer than I ever lived in one place; his skills are greater than mine, no doubting that. I believe he could manage a whole lifetime in one location, so great is his aptitude for deceit. No one ever suspects him. Once he even took a day-bound wife—for the challenge of it, I believe—and kept it up for over a year, before she finally realized that he was something more than eccentric. An incredible man. I long to live near him again, to learn from him . . . but the time of my childhood is over now, and the last few centuries have taught us a cold, lonely truth: too many of us in one place increases the risk to all. I must content myself with occasional visits.

Where is he? I knock again, this time louder. A little worried, now. He knew I was coming. He should have been waiting. In all our long years, it has never been otherwise.

I put my hand to the latch and press down, gently. The door is unlocked. Heavy with dampness, it moves reluctantly; I find I must press my shoulder against it with considerable force to un-stick it from the frame.

"Father?" The house is dark inside, and chill. As am I. "Are you here?" Did something go wrong last night? He wrote me that he meant to contemplate the grave—which meant, in our jargon, that he intended to take on the guise of a dead man. A dangerous game—or so he had taught me—but a good way to manipulate the living.

Could they have discovered him? Killed him? This dark and angry century is quick to read demonic purpose into any eccentricity. I've fled from suspicion often enough. But my father is a different kind of man. Raised in a gentler time, partner to the daybound, he understands how they think—in a way I never can—and prides himself on the perfection of his mimicry. Impossible to imagine him unmasked.

Discovered.

Killed?

I search the house, no easy task in the darkness. Even our vision requires some light, but his windows are shuttered so tightly that even the moonlight can't seep through. I find a lamp, and tinder, and strike a light; harsh beams are thrown across the walls, and the floor—

and the body.

His body?

I kneel by its side, my hands shaking so badly that the lamp swings wildly, and I must put it down. Not his body, no. Except that it is. Transformed, but still the flesh of my father. Somehow I know that.

I touch the nearer arm; the limb is cold but still pliable, deathly pale in the lamplight. As he must have meant it to be. Designing a body so close to death that the living would be convinced by it. So close, so very dangerously close. . . . How could this happen? It was he who taught me to take on the guise of death without its substance, it was he who warned me—time and time again!—how very closely the two were allied. How could he fail to make the transformation, who had practiced it so many times?

There is always risk in this, he'd warned me. Always.

My God. Oh, my God.

My hand is trembling as I touch it to his face, overwhelmed by loss. And disbelief. The flesh is like that of a stranger, foreign to me . . . which makes his death doubly horrible. Tears cloud my vision and I find myself shaking uncontrollably, cold with that chill which is rooted in the soul, which no earthly fire can warm. Praying: Gods of this world. If you care. If we matter. Let me die in my own form, when the time comes. That's all I ask. Let me die as myself. Just that. No more.

There is no answer.

* * *

It was inevitable that he would suspect me. Inevitable that he would slip away from his human allies, take on some more convenient form, and try to hunt me down.

Or so I expected.

I took shelter in the graveyard, because it seemed the least rational place for me to be. In a tomb so poorly built that it barely managed to hold back the sunlight. I slept uneasily beside its skeletal occupants, aware that I was in enemy territory. Should the priest-Marra search for me here . . . but I was betting that he wouldn't. Even when he heard the first rumors of what had happened, even when he came to suspect that I was involved—as he surely must!—he would assume, *must* assume, that I had done the intelligent thing and taken to the hills in hiding. As any rational creature would have done.

But I wasn't merely rational: I was *informed*. My

Marra had assured me that one of her kind could pick me out from miles of unliving stone with a glance, and so I had to hide where he would never think to look. Within the settlement itself. Among the dead.

Christ, the memories. . . .

In the dead of night, I hunted. Not daring to stray far from my encampment, I used the herd animals of the settlement for prey. Not without guilt. But I must have blood, and dared not travel far lest I be discovered. And so I crept from hiding when night was at its darkest, choosing a form that was known for stealth as well as the sharpness of its claws. I took my prey while it was sleeping, and mauled its body when I was done. Let them think that some wild thing had made the kill, a hunter come down from the mountains, who had gained access through the shattered defense wall.

I would wait a day or two, before I moved again. Let Hanaa share what had happened with her few close friends, and they—in fear and disbelief—with others. Rumors would then do half my work for me. And I needed a strong foundation, if I was to succeed. Fooling Hanaa had been easy; I had seen her husband's face myself, had heard her sobbing his name and personal particulars aloud in the night, while I huddled in panther form on the roof. Other roles would be harder to perfect, and would lack that immediacy of impact. My subjects must be properly prepared, in order for me to convince them.

On the third night, he went out.

I dared to perch on the roof of my tomb, to watch his departure. Risky, to be sure. Black fur might hide me from human eyes, but his special Marra senses could pick out my vitality from the dead as clear as day. Or so my healer had told me. I counted on his not searching in my direction, and indeed he did not. With panther eyes I watched as he walked from town, until the great fence hid him from my sight. Then, claws out, I climbed a hefty tree and took up my watch again. Waiting for the shapechange that surely must come. Wanting to see what form, earthly or otherwise, he preferred.

But much to my surprise, he made no change. Even in the foothills he kept his human guise. I could see his silhouette in the distance, black beneath the stars. Still human, though he thought himself unobserved. Despite the fact that it handicapped him, and would limit his search.

Could the game be that important to him? I wondered in amazement. More important than bringing down one's adversary? Important enough to keep him in human form, even when inconvenient, because that was . . . well, "appropriate?" It was an alien concept to me . . . but then I had learned long ago, with the Tyr, not to apply a human template where it didn't belong. The creature inhabiting that body didn't think like a human being, and the game it played had no analog in human society. Nor did its rules.

Which was too bad for it. Because now I was playing—for keeps.

* * *

Dreaming. That I was lying on a bed of broken rock, my body shattered by that terrible fall. Overhead loomed the cliff wall that I had marked with my blood, each splash of crimson a monument to one more bone broken, one more fraction of life driven out of my all-too-fragile body . . . but I lived. For a single moment more, I lived.

Overhead a black bird circled. Scavenger. It regarded me lazily, as it assessing my ability to fight it off. I had none. Only a whisper of life left, bleeding out onto the chasm's rough floor. No will at all. It circled slowly, lower and lower, broad wings outlined against the light of the dying sun. For an instant its shadow passed over me, the briefest hint of darkness, and I found myself crying. Not afraid, so much as grateful. For that little.

And then it was beside me, its huge wings folded, and I felt more than saw its form shimmer and change, stiff black feathers melting into liquid darkness, which flowed as if into some unseen mold and then hardened anew, its texture now that of silk. Flowing black robes which adorned and contained a human form—a woman—who leaned forward to me and took my face in her hands, turning me away from the light. Beautiful to look upon, but frightening also; not all parts of her were human, in form or in purpose. A rich crown of chestnut curls framed a familiar, welcome face—but the cinnamon eyes had a cat's pupils, narrow slits which glowed greenly in the rapidly gathering darkness. Her fingers, long and delicate, were tipped with strong nails, and as she flexed them before my eyes it seemed that they grew into true talons, long and curved and razor-sharp. About her aura, too, there was something of the animal, that made me shiver as she stroked my face—those long, deadly talons now fully unsheathed—and catch my breath as she drew in close to me, her voice murmuring reassurances that were anything but.

"I am Marra," she whispered. An explanation—a promise—a threat. Despite the heat of my fever, I found myself suddenly cold. All over. As a taloned claw stroked my throat, from jaw to shoulder . . . and then suddenly thrust deep into my flesh. I cried out in surprise and pain as my blood broke free from its natural confines, and ran out over her hand.

"Marra," she whispered, and the cat-eyes sparkled. The talon continued its course, a clean slice from clavicle to jawline. Then with a smile—half affectionate, half mocking—she lowered her face until her lips touched the wound, and . . .

Up on the cliff. Where I had once stood. A man whose very stance radiated power, whose vegetable robe sputtered out the last of its life in sparks of orange flame.

. . . and the life was draining out of me, not slowly, not naturally, but drawn out by the hunger in her, the hunger in *him*. . . .

The priest. Watched as she killed me, with greenfire

eyes to match her own. Eyes that were the last thing I
saw, as the deep red darkness of death overtook me.

Watching.

Smiling.

Approving. . . .

* * *

I awoke with a shudder. The darkness which en-
closed me was similar enough to a cavern's blackness
that it took several long minutes for me to remember
where I was. Not sheltered in a mountain cave, the
healer-Marra by my side, but nested in between the
remains of Cantona's first inhabitants as though I, too,
were a corpse. Waiting for midnight to come before
resuming my private war.

Against a Marra. Against one of her people. Jesus
Christ . . . I cursed myself for my stupidity, for my
blindness. Was it possible that she would act against
one of her own people—even by inaction? How could
I have been so foolish, so desperate for her support,
that I accepted her reassurances at face value? How
much did I know about her, or her kind, or the intricate interrelationships that must form between them,
based as they were on something other than biochemical prompting? What if it was part of the game to
weaken my defenses, and then betray me to my enemy?

*Easy, Daetrin. There's nothing you can do, now,
even if it's true. Just go on.*

Go on. . . .

A sound distracted me suddenly, the telltale rustle
of leaves crushed underfoot. Animal-alert, I listened.
One person . . . no, two. Now I could hear whispering. Cantona accents, male and female; I moved closer
to the eastern wall of the tomb, and pressed my ear
against the wood to listen.

". . . Ts'foolish, Marike."

"*Their* dead've come. Why not mine?"

"Marike, ts'dreaminn!"

"Then go, why don'tye? Leave m'be! Who'd ask'ye, anyways?"

I could barely hear his angry exit over the eager pounding of my own heart. This was it!—the opportunity I'd been waiting for. A case which I had researched fully, in the nights I'd spent preparing my various personae. I had even broken into this woman's house once, to see the portrait of the brother she'd lost, to fix it into my memory. Now . . . one more clear-cut visitation, I told myself, and rumor would do the rest.

Leaning against the wall of the tomb, I gathered myself for the effort. Animal guise comes naturally to us; human mimicry is a learned skill. And as for mimicry of the dead . . . I gathered myself as my father had taught me to do (ah, but look where it got him!) a kernel of peace at the heart of my flesh, the soul without tension of any kind, emotional fires damped, all defensive instinct quelled. Control of the body given over wholly to the conscious self, the *I*.

Now: the essence of death. Carefully. Donned, with utmost delicacy. Like rotted silk, it crumbled at the touch. Inch by inch, cell by cell, I stretched the unwholesome image across my own flesh. Practice made it no easier. Each time was a desperate new exercise of self-control. We force our flesh to do something that evolution never intended, that our survival instinct rightfully abhors. How many had died in the practice of this, our ultimate deceptive art? I felt the coldness chilling my arms into stiffness, my face into a mask of decay. It seemed more real than the other times; I wished that I knew if that were good or bad.

Carefully . . . I let the coldness seep inside, to where the warmth of life was a hard knot in the core of me. A delicate balance. Almost there. I fought back the first flush of triumph; any emotion could be fatal now. I didn't know why that was, but had no desire to test it. Only seconds now—stabilize it!—and the Marra—

The Marra. . . .

I felt the touch of fear—and realized its consequences—a mere instant before true death struck. It was all the warning I had. A mere choking instant to acknowledge my failure and attempt to throw off the masque I had chosen, to will the warmth back into my limbs even as my blood froze, immobile, within my veins. Across my chest were bands of ice, as sharp-edged and solid as straps of cut steel, and their sudden contraction drove the air from my lungs in a cloud of frozen steam. My thoughts were hazy, confused; I tried to focus on one single thought, one single last action my brain must attempt before the ice claimed that as well. Only that one. *Must* . . . I willed a heartbeat. Shapechanged it into being. And then another. Forced the blood up toward my brain, where its meager load of oxygen bought me a few more seconds. *Again.* The eternity between heartbeats became something less, something measurable, until I could almost discern a rhythm. The bands about me loosened, and I breathed again. Oxygen flooded my brain, and with it newfound warmth; I was dimly aware of the tears that had covered my face as I retraced my transformative steps, banishing the role that had almost killed me.

For a long time I lay on the floor of the tomb, exactly as I had fallen. Afraid to move. But my regular heartbeat was reassuring, as was the pulse of coursing blood that I could once again feel in all my extremities. The footsteps were gone. No matter. I couldn't have played that role now, with the memory of death so close. I wondered if I ever could again. There was a new fear in me now; a good fear, a healthy fear. I didn't know if I could master it. I wasn't sure that I wanted to.

There were limits, then. Deadly limits. How long had it taken me when I was young, to learn them all? And that was with parental guidance. I was suddenly very glad that I had come here, to face this single Marra, rather than pit myself immediately against Earth's conqueror. Acutely aware of how much I had forgotten—how much I had *chosen* to forget—and what it could cost me, if I moved against the Tyr too quickly.

* * *

Tenth night. The sabbath.

They came.

From my hiding place behind a squat granite tomb-stone, I watched them approach. Five of them, hesi-tant and secretive. For a time I wasn't sure of their purpose—neither, it seemed, were they—and I dreaded the possible need for another zombic performance. But then I saw the shovels, and their determined faces, and I knew they hadn't come in search of ghosts.

"This'n," one whispered, and pointed. His voice was hoarse, and his hands rough in the manner of workmen. A strong one, I judged, as were three of his companions. Excellent. That would speed things along.

I looked up toward the temple, saw its tower silhou-etted against a star-studded sky. *Just stay there,* I thought to it—to him. *Just stay there, working your magic, playing your ritual games . . . long enough for them to finish. That's all.*

"All right," one of the men grunted, and the shov-els were handed out. "This'd be shallow, it was after th'sickness, r'member? They dug'm shallow, then."

"Shut y'speakinn an' dig," another muttered.

They argued aggressively—but quietly—as their spades bit deep into the hard graveyard soil. Each shovelful was carefully laid to the side, and it was one man's job to see that these piles were made firm against the wind. Their purpose was clear. If this was some kind of wild goose chase, they would need the dirt to cover their tracks. Maybe if they restored the grave, no one would realize they'd been here. Then the priest wouldn't punish them. For this was—I assumed—an act of direst blasphemy.

"Damn!" one muttered, hitting rock, and other more colorful oaths followed. I gathered that chunks of granite had been placed in the grave, in order to fill it more quickly. "Hand'm up, willye?"

After that there was no more speaking. The silence

about us was absolute. And somehow wrong. I tried
to determine what it was about the very quiet of the
night that made it so unnerving. Why the men who
stood guard over their efforts didn't notice. But then I
knew. I started to move, to warn them—but stopped.
How could I?

It was the chanting that was gone. The chanting that
should have continued from sunset to midnight. It had
stopped. And now, alert, I could pick out other sounds.
The steady tread of a determined stride. The squelch
of damp leaves underfoot. The rhythmic murmur of a
large number of men trying very hard, but not successfully, to be quiet.

Now, finally, the men at the grave were alert. One
of them cursed under his breath; the reference was
local and I missed it. "Keep'm off't," one of the dig-
gers whispered, but I gathered that the other was more
concerned with keeping the high priest off of himself
than away from the half-plundered grave. They scrambled out and joined their compatriots on the upper
ground, and shifted their shovels from hand to hand
as if in doubt what to do with them. But they held their
ground, which was a good sign. If they'd known what
the priest really was, they might have run.

His entrance was anything but silent. He strode into
the graveyard like a commander of troops, his stature
and bearing commanding obedience. "What'v we
here?" Behind him came an army of Cantonites,
strong-armed acolytes first, followed by men of lesser
status, and their women and children. Their faces were
masks of outrage and horror; I gathered that their culture had some pretty strong taboos about disturbing a
grave. A convenient taboo, for the Marra who had
been deceiving them.

"What'v we here?" he repeated, and his dark eyes
blazed with fury. The gravediggers quailed before his
rage—all but one, who stood his ground and answered, with equal outrage, "We'ave maybe th'answer
t'some very 'portann questions, priest. Questions that
more'n one've been askinn."

"It is a sin t'disturb th'dead," he responded, his voice and his manner like ice.

"Th'dead'r already disturbed, so that's moot, eh?" I sensed little real courage behind his words, but he sounded good nonetheless. "It's th'dead have asked this, y'see. An' I'll not deny th'dead their due."

He turned his back on the priest then—a dangerous gesture of defiance—and lifted up his shovel as if to start work anew. The priest answered by moving quickly forward, so that he stood at the side of the grave.

And I tensed. Knowing that he was capable of changing the body within, once it was in his hands. Fearing that he could create a network of wires where none had existed, and deflate their grand gesture by demonstrating that yes, there were Eyes, there had always been Eyes, why did they dare to doubt him?

It was time to move. On another night I might have transformed myself first, but I was still weak—and shaken—from my last attempt. Let my own body suffice, then; all I needed to do was stall him.

"Priest!"

He turned to face me. And I will never forget the look on his face, that told me in an instant just how wrong I had been, when I had tried to second-guess him.

Utter shock. *"You!"*

I had assumed that he would have blamed me all along. Now I saw how wrong I was. She hadn't warned him, and therefore he didn't know. Didn't even know that my kind could exist, a genuinely embodied shape-changer. I remembered her first reaction—half disbelief, half fascination—and I cursed myself for not anticipating his.

He didn't understand me. My very existence was impossible. And for a brief instant, because of that, I had the upper hand.

I played it.

"I've c'm back, priest. T'see justice done."

He darkened. "Don't play that game with me. You're no reborn corpse."

I was stunned by the change in his speech pattern, but managed to continue. "Y'killed me, priest." Was he trying to confuse me—or just losing control? Did he instinctively take on my language of choice, as she did? "Y'saw it!"

"Impossible."

"Y'pronounced me dead! You!" I glanced at the crowd behind him, saw their indecisive faces glistening whitely in the moonlight. If he had presented himself as infallible, either openly or through implication, that image was now shot to hell. "Y'r own words! Did y'lie? Were y'wrong? Or have I indeed come back?"

"Dig," I muttered, loud enough for the gravediggers to hear me. *All I can do is buy you time.*

He began to move toward me. I didn't dare retreat. To flee from him was to lose all credibility before his followers . . . but to allow him to touch me was something even worse, so I went for a lateral evasion, and put a thick tombstone between us.

"Corruption!" he exclaimed suddenly. "Demonspawn!" He turned to his followers. "Th'Dark One is th'Father of Lies! His purpose is t'mislead us. T'appear t'be righteous, while n'fact he undermines r'faith! How shall'ee—"

"Got it!" The cry came from the open grave, from a man rummaging below ground level. "Nunyeg, f'rgive me. . . ." A skull was raised into our line of sight, brown with age and mold and rank with the fetor of decay. Wisps of hair still clung to it, and they waved in the breeze as he brandished the grotesque trophy overhead. "Th'answer's in here!" he cried. "An won't we see't, now!"

The priest moved. Quickly. I knew, in that instant, what he meant to do—and knew I had to stop him. Once he had gotten hold of the skull he could transform it into a relic of Tyrran technology, mute witness to the justice of his tyranny, or any other thing he chose. A shapechanged symbol, to further consolidate

his power over these people. I couldn't let that happen.
I had to reach the skull before him, and break it open
before he could make contact with it. And if there
was a chance that he would turn on me as I did so,
and focus his Marra skills on me instead of that inanimate object, I had to risk it. In that moment, he—
it—embodied everything I hated, in the Tyr and in
myself. It was impossible not to lunge forward, not to
reach out toward the skull. Impossible to stand back
and let him turn all my work, all my spying and my
planning and even my close brush with death, into
nothing more than an added foundation for his power.

But he saw me move, and turned toward me. Hands
moving faster than human limbs should, closing the
space between us before I could dodge their approach.
False-flesh fingers touching the thick wool of my jacket
sleeve, and then—

Fire. An explosion of yellow flame between us, and
a thunderclap blast of heat that knocked me off my
feet. I fell backward heavily, and felt my head strike
the unyielding stone of a tombstone. Flames swam in
my vision, a hazy darkness at the edges. I fought to
stay conscious, and tried—somewhat dizzily—to see
what had ignited. Who the hell would be playing with
munitions, at a time like this?

What I saw, as my eyes finally focused, stunned
me. And I did not question why the Cantonites were
suddenly kneeling, or crying, or falling back in fear.
It was that wondrous a thing. For a waist-high bush,
which had shed its leaves for winter, had suddenly
burst into new and vibrant life. Each leaf was thick
and green and perfectly curled, identical to all others—as though some Master had designed them as a
matched set, with no reliance upon nature. The
branches themselves were not cracked and dry, as they
had been mere seconds ago, but moist and green, and
supple in the evening breeze. And from it all a flame
poured heavenward, brilliant white fire that it hurt to
look upon, a fire that consumed the leaves and yet did
not consume them, that bathed them in flames without

burning them at all, so that they remained as they were
in that first instant of fire, unharmed, through all the
time that it burned. And silent! With no roar, no
crackle, not a whisper of burning, only a pure and
perfect silence which made us aware of our own very
speechless state.

Even the priest was silent.

"Give Me the skull," said a Voice. It spoke directly
from the flames, with absolute authority. The grave-
digger hesitated only an instant, then cast the skull
into the fire, toward the bush at its center.

It was immediately returned, its corruption burned
away. Leaving thin white smoke in its wake, it rolled
to a slow stop by the edge of the plundered grave. And
split, into clean and equal halves.

No one moved.

"I have prepared it for you," the voice urged. "Step
forward and see what was inside it, besides the flesh
of its owner."

They did so. Slowly. One by one, in a single file
line that stretched back almost to the edge of town.
Trembling—and then cursing or crying out as they saw
the truth, as they realized the implications of it.

There was nothing inside. Nothing. No alien mechanism to justify its owner's execution.

They turned toward the priest, one by one, as they
knew. Faces filled with hatred, wonder, confusion, a
thousand emotions—but rejection in all those faces, as
plain as the Fire that illuminated them.

The priest stepped back. A tombstone stopped him.

"You have lied," the Fire said, "too long. You have
misled My people."

He looked more confused than anything. Then his
eyes narrowed, and a shadow of expression—a
smile?—touched the corners of his mouth.

Only that, and then fire engulfed him. A crackling,
smoking, sulphurous fire which split the flesh from his
bones and released his blood in a cloud of red steam.
We heard him scream—a terrible, tortured sound—and
then the source of his voice was charred into useless-

ness, and the burning continued in silence. In the end, we had to turn away, tucking our heads into our coats to escape the terrible stench.

When it was done, when we at last dared to look, there was only a pile of dead ashes. And as we watched, the wind scattered even that.

"You have been misled," the fiery Bush told us. "I have removed the source of corruption. Now, it is up to you to do the rest. Tear down the Temple of Lies! Give your holy relics unto the earth and build a wall atop them—a great wall of stone, which will be as a dam to the creatures that oppress you. Your safety as a nation shall be your temple; your prosperity shall become your worship. Make of yourselves an offering to the Lord, and He will favor you with His protection. Go now! and do His Will, for the power of the Lord is with you."

There was a sudden spurt of brilliant flame—the Fire shot up toward the stars—and then both Fire and Bush were gone, and all was silent. I thought quickly enough to hide behind a tomb while it happened, and thus appeared to disappear just when the Fire extinguished itself.

Breathing heavily. Not quite believing what I had just seen. Not knowing what, if anything, to do about it. How is one expected to respond, after witnessing a miracle?

They left. One by one. Some angry, some crying . . . and some making plans. Already. Whatever it all came to, it had to be an improvement. I repeated that to myself several times. And tried to believe it.

"Did I do it right?"

Startled, I looked up. She stood before me—call her Kiri, even a Marra should have a name—her face like that of a child, wanting to please, not yet certain she'd done so. I was no more composed than the priest-Marra had been, but managed only a gasp of surprise, as it all came together.

"You did that . . ."

"It seemed to be an appropriate image—"

I got to my feet and had to fight the urge to reach out and hug her, to hold her against me and let the tears of joy come because I was alive, I was alive! and it was because of her . . . but for centuries I had been undemonstrative, and the habit was too deeply ingrained to be cast aside in an instant. "It was appropriate," I assured her. Joy rang out in my voice. "It was beautiful. You are . . . beautiful."

And she was. Not the demon of my dreams, spiritual sibling to the priest-Marra, but something very different. Someone whose face glowed with pleasure as she internalized my praise, pleased to have played the game properly. "I ran across the image while I was sorting through your memories, back in the cave. While you were healing," she added, as though reminding me that she would never commit the unpoliteness of rummaging through my brain while I was awake.

I loved her at that moment, and knew myself crazy for it. "You killed him," I challenged, not quite believing it.

"Oh, no!"

"Drove him off, then?"

"How could I?"

"But the fire . . ."

"That was his own doing," she assured me. "A bit of drama to mark his exit. Well executed, don't you think? Although . . ." She frowned. "You have so little to compare it with. Take my word for it, it was very well done."

"So he's still here," I murmured.

"Probably planning out his next Identity right now."

"With no thoughts for . . . what you did? What I tried to do?"

She laughed softly. "Do you mean, will he try to 'get even'? That's body-stuff. Don't you realize, by playing his game—win or lose—you confirmed him in his Identity? Paying him one of the highest compliments our people can know?"

I shook my head in amazement. "I don't understand."

She answered me gently: "The embodied rarely do."

I took her hand then. Real. Warm.

"Why did you help me?"

Her brown eyes sparkled with amusement. "Didn't you want help?"

"But you told me—"

"No." She touched a finger to my lips, to silence me. "I thought you might need help. It pleased me to orchestrate it. That's all there is. Don't try to analyze us, Daetrin—not by human standards. You'll only confuse yourself more." She stepped back. "Now, don't you want to get out of here before the natives come back?"

Before I could answer she was gone, transformed through a quick splash of color into a sizable bird of prey. I watched as she rose. As she circled. As she waited for me to join her.

To Suyaag? I wondered. Feeling my weakness. And then I grinned.

"Is there time for dinner on the way?" I called. "I've had one hell of a night."

YUANG: DOME FIVE

Tireza was in the workroom when he returned to it, along with her young charge. She shot Yaan a look that said, *Thanks a lot for leaving me alone with him.* He couldn't explain in front of the boy how much the Tekk woman had upset him, or that he had needed to go off by himself for a few minutes before he could cope with this particular frustration. He had to settle for nodding her a wordless apology as he joined them, and hoping she understood.

"His native language is Spanish," Tireza offered. "A Southamerican dialect. He also speaks Brazilian Portuguese, some Nahuatl—an Indian tongue—and, for technical purposes, English."

"Well." He offered his hand to the boy, who shook it energetically, and greeted him in English. "Welcome to our facility."

The boy grinned. "They told me I should speak good English, if I do research. They said it was the language of the colonies."

True enough, Yaan thought. The Tyr tended to divide up its settlers according to racial types, with little concern for cultural or linguistic backgrounds. English's popularity as a second language in the days before the Conquest had provided a necessary link between people whose primary tongues didn't allow them to communicate. "We do prefer English, because of its flexibility. But most of us speak more than one Earth tongue. Tireza and Sung are both familiar with Spanish, I believe." He glanced toward her; she nodded. "We try to preserve every Earth-language we

260

can . . ." *In case it ceases to exist elsewhere,* he almost said . . . "for linguistic research. I don't believe anyone here speaks Nahuatl; you're encouraged to pass that on, as part of the project. Were you raised bilingually?" The boy nodded. "Asako will want to know that. She's working on the brain's development during language acquisition. You'll meet her later." He sighed. "Of course, doing any research on the human brain is difficult, as we have so few subjects here to work with."

There. That was the prelude. He waited a moment to let the boy digest it, and its implications. "Bearing in mind that crucial limitation," he continued, "one could say that this entire Dome is devoted to the study of the human brain. Molecular psychology, our ancestors called it: the subtle relationship between biochemistry and the mind."

The boy's eyes were glowing; his excitement radiated forth from him with almost tangible substance, so much so that Yaan found himself stepping backward, to get out of its range. *Gods of ancient Earth,* he thought. *This one's going to fall hard.*

Damn the Tyr for putting us through this, time and time again. For making it necessary.

"Come," he said, and he forced himself to put an arm around the boy's shoulders. "I'll show you around."

Station by station, he led him through the Dome. Workroom after workroom, he showed him everything there was to see: equipment, personnel, work-in-progress. The boy said nothing, but Yaan could sense that he was puzzled. Deeply puzzled. Once or twice he almost started to question something—but then he subsided, into a tense and uneasy silence, and they went on with the tour.

When at last they were done—when they had seen everything from the molecular storage banks to the dining hall—Yaan brought him back to his cubicle. The boy seemed paler than before, and was considerably more subdued. Putting two and two together, no doubt. Well, it had to happen sooner or later.

"Sir?" he asked, hesitantly.

"Yaan. Call me Yaan. It's an old Earth name." He forced a smile. "I prefer it to an alien number."

"Yaan, then." He seemed deeply troubled. "I am . . . confused. Perhaps. Not understanding. The things you showed me today. This is new research?"

"Yes," he answered quietly. The boy was standing inside his cubicle, and Yaan moved to join him. So the door could be closed. So they wouldn't be overheard. "Yes, this is all new."

The boy took a deep breath; he was Subjugation-born, and clearly not comfortable with questioning authority. "But some of your work . . . like of Danel . . ."

"Daniel," he corrected.

"Daniel. With dopamine counts in *rattus norvegicus*. Maybe I'm . . . it seems to me that this was already done, a long time ago. In the late twentieth century, no?"

"Many records of pre-Conquest research were destroyed." *Deliberately, boy. Think!* "Sometimes we have to recreate our ancestors' experiments. In order to retrieve the data."

"But those figures still exist. I've seen tables containing them. You're from Earth, aren't you? You must know that they exist. That Daniel's work is . . . unnecessary. All this information is available on Earth. Has been available, for centuries!"

"But not on the datanets," Yaan said quietly.

The boy looked confused. "No. I saw it in a book. A paper book."

Yaan nodded. Sighed. Pulled a folding panel out from the wall and folded it into chair-shape. "Sit. Go on, sit down. I have something to tell you and you're not going to like it, but I can see there's no point in putting it off any longer. Have a seat," he said forcefully, and at last the boy sat.

"We're an inquisitive species," he began. Nervously pacing, because if he stayed in one place he would have to meet the boy's eyes. And he didn't dare do that. "Wanting to understand everything. But most of all, wanting to understand ourselves. The science we practice . . . you and I, Tireza, Daniel . . . it promised answers. *Real* answers. Biochemical keys that could unlock the secrets of depression, alcoholism, schizophrenia, phobic fixations . . . the list is endless. Every facet of human behavior could be understood in terms of molecular interaction within the brain. Once human science understood how those molecules worked, and how to readjust them, it could do anything. *Anything.*

"That's where Earth science stood, right before the Conquest. Balanced precariously between the promise of enlightenment, and a capacity for self-destruction unsurpassed by anything before or since. The intricate tangle of laws that we used to protect ourselves was almost as complex as the brain itself; but when one deals with knowledge such as this, one has to be careful. We had the capacity to alter any facet of human behavior. We had already used it to treat the disorders I mentioned; now, we were experimenting with more complex problems. We believed that the only limit on what we could accomplish was that which we set ourselves. In theory, we had the capacity"—and here he stopped pacing, and met the boy's gaze straight on—"to make every man, woman, and child on Earth docile and obedient. It wasn't what we wanted to do. We tried to make sure that our knowledge would never be used that way. But it was possible, you must understand that: *it was possible.*

"And then the Tyr came. Do I have to explain the rest? As soon as it became clear that the Tyr would triumph, the men who controlled such information knew what they had to do. To let such a tool fall into the hands of a nonhuman enemy was tantamount to species suicide. So certain farseeing members of the scientific community acted to protect themselves and their species. You probably know that a systems operator in Kiev inserted a virus into MedNet, which infected the computer storage of research and medical facilities on six continents; conspirators transferred the program to other nets and within a week, all were wiped clean of pertinent data. Between that action and more blatant physical destruction, the work was eventually done. Oh, you'll find some data still in textbooks, and private notebooks and the like. Like the kind of book you found your tables in. There was no possible way to destroy it all. But by the time the Tyr came, it was no longer obvious that such a science had existed, or that there were men on Earth who knew how to use it.''

"But here . . ." the boy asked. "I don't understand.''

"What we practice," he answered quietly, "is *deception*. We work because the Tyr insists that we work. And because we genuinely hunger to know—that trait we do share with you, I assure you. But in the area of human molecular psychology, we can't afford to make any real progress. So we stall. We divert ourselves onto alternate paths of research. Tireza can tell you things about sleep patterns and dreaming that you never imagined possible. Sung specializes in memory. We know more things now about laboratory rats than ratkind ever hoped to know. We've accomplished other things, with other animal subjects—but when it comes to human behavior, as you say, it's merely a repeat performance of our ancestor's accomplishments.''

The boy's expression was dark. "It is deliberate, then. This ignorance.''

"Yes. And absolutely necessary. I hope you see that.''

The boy hesitated. "I see . . . a tremendous facility. A facility that we on Earth only dreamed of. I see intelligent men and women permitted to research whatever appeals to them, and given the material support to do so . . . and you are throwing it all away!''

"You don't understand—''

"No, *you* don't understand! Do you think your ancestors, these brilliant men and woman you speak of, do you believe they ever looked at their work and said no, this is too dangerous, let's hide it away and never look at it again. We can unravel all the secrets of the universe, but somebody might abuse the knowledge, so let's go back to playing with rats and forget about it? Do you think they said that? Knowledge is a dangerous thing. Does that mean we should never seek it out?''

"That's a human equation. When you add in the Tyr—"

"The Tyr wants to understand us. The Tyr built these Domes to facilitate peaceful interaction—"

"The Tyr built these Domes to control us! Because without their supply lines we can't survive a month here."

"It's a warrior race. That how it deals with a threat. But it could have killed Earth's men of learning, instead of bringing them here, if it didn't want to support them. Instead of—"

"Terra! Do you really *believe* that crap? No—I'm sorry—that's not fair. We believed it ourselves, when this place was first built. Because the first settlers *wanted* to believe. It fit the human pattern. They swallowed the whole story, and worked hard to forge a link between human and Tyr that would eventually result in our being given some independence. For so they were promised. And do you know what happened? Do you know what they did? They managed to develop a functional sensory interface. A means of translating sensory input from a human format into Tyr. So that the Tyr could see what we were seeing, and maybe understand us a little better.'' He paused, but the boy didn't seem to understand. "Eyes, man, Eyes! Created in *this* lab, by *our* people, to foster 'peaceful interaction'—and now used in every human slave camp to make unwitting spies out of our own people! *That* is why we do nothing, here. Because anything we do accomplish can and will be turned against us!"

The boy's expression was cold, unyielding. "If you

convince yourselves of that, then you really can't accomplish anything.''

He found himself lacking the energy for an argument. If this had come up first thing in the morning,
when he was fresh, he could have carried on all day.
He'd met more stubborn earthies than this one, and all
had eventually bowed to Domes logic. Some couldn't
handle the disappointment, and then, like the last one
. . . he shook his head sadly, remembering the day
he'd found that body. But no one had the foolishness
to question the very game they were playing. He must
not be presenting it properly—and in light of his confrontation with the Tekk, and that cryptic visit by the
Raayat, he was hardly to blame if his nerves were raw
and he was just a little bit edgy.

Which is why he backed off. "Look. It's been a
rough day for both of us. I've had some unpleasant
guests, and you've been traveling. Why don't we both
get some rest, think it over. We'll discuss it in the
morning, all right? At work. Maybe Tereza and Sung
can explain it better.''

I doubt it, the boy's expression said plainly, but he
nodded. Stiffly.

"If you need me for anything, I'm up one level and
down the hall. Toward the dining hall. Cubicle seven.''

"I believe I will be all right,'' the boy told him.

*I believe you will be trouble, but we'll leave that for
later.*

"We'll talk in the morning,'' he promised.

* * *

In the morning, however, other things came up.

"What the hell is *that* doing here?'' Yaan hissed to
Sung as he entered. At the far end of the workroom
was a Raayat—the same Raayat who had so unnerved
him the day before, he was sure of it—standing quietly
in the corner as if it had every right and every reason
to be there. And to make matters worse, it was staring
at them.

"Damned if I know," Sung whispered back. "But I'm not going to be the one to tell it to go away . . . Boss."

Yaan winced at the reminder of his responsibility, but nodded. "We can't let it stay here. Too dangerous a precedent." Nevertheless, it took him a minute to work up enough courage to brave the unblinking gaze of the Raayat, and wend his way across the workroom toward it

The Raayat nodded, a curt acknowledgment of his presence; its alien face was maddeningly lacking in all the cues that humans used to read each other.

"Work without surveillance," Yaan said quietly. Amazed that he sounded as calm as he did. Behind him he heard a gasp of surprise—Tireza?—as one more worker entered, and noticed the tableau. "That's the arrangement here. Always has been."

"Work without Eyes," the Raayat corrected him.

"The arrangement existed before the Eyes were developed."

"I am Raayat."

"We're aware of that."

"I . . . have need . . . to observe."

Yaan heard the door open again, and quickly shut; that would be the boy coming in. *Sung, get rid of him!*

"We need privacy," he explained.

"Humans need privacy to work," it mused aloud. "Yes."

"But you work together. Four of you. Unprivately."

"That's different."

"Because you are human?"

Lacking a better answer, he nodded.

"Because you are . . . individual."

He wasn't quite sure of the point being made, but it sounded good. "Yes."

The Raayat was silent for a moment; musing, no doubt, upon the nature of individuality. Yaan glanced back at his co-workers, and found all three staring at him as though he had lost his mind.

And maybe I have. But there's only so much you can take in a day.

At last the Raayat stirred. When it spoke again, it did so slowly, as though testing out each word as it was chosen. "I . . . this-body possesses . . . individuality."

Startled, Yaan whispered. "What?"

"I . . . Raayat-Tyr . . . Raayat . . . there is individuality in name . . . I have name."

No sound now, behind him. Not even breathing. He wondered if his co-workers were as stunned as he was by what the Raayat's fragmentary speech could mean, or afraid—as he was—that this particular specimen of Unstable Ones was about to go over the deep end, and take them all with it. Once in the past, he remembered, an entire Dome had been destroyed by Raayat madness. Because some unstable Tyr bastard wanted to see what an explosion looked like from the inside. He wondered if before the explosion there had been any warning. Any particularly odd behavior, or disjointed, meaningless speech. Like this.

"You have a name," he repeated quietly. A question.

"An Earth name."

Stranger and stranger. Was it safe to encourage him? "Look, that doesn't—"

"Yaan." It was Tireza. She walked up behind him and looked at the Raayat, her gray eyes bright with curiosity. "What name? What should we call you?"

"I was assigned . . . Frederick. That is for . . . self-part. Not Tyr. Raayat-only."

Fred the alien, Yaan thought disgustedly. *What next?*

"You want to watch us work?" she asked. "Frederick?"

"Yes. I . . . I need."

"But humans are afraid of the Tyr. Afraid of you. That makes it hard for us to work."

"What is fear?" the Raayat asked.

Yaan felt a chill go through him. He glanced at Tireza; she seemed to be reacting in much the same way. "You don't comprehend fear? At all?"

"No. It is a . . . a thing of parts. Not-Tyr."

Of course it is, Yaan thought. *Fear's a survival-emotion, triggering the individual fight-or-flight response. But if the whole of a creature lives on regardless of the fate of its parts, what have the parts got to fear?*

But had the Tyr-whole never feared anything? Anything at all? It was a staggering concept.

"Look," he said. "There's a lot you want to know. There's a lot we can show you. But humans who think they may be threatened . . . turn off all parts of the brain except those that deal with fighting. Do you understand?"

"That is fear?"

"In part, yes."

"You experience this fear because you believe that I threaten you?"

"Because you *are capable of* threatening us. Yes."

There was a pause, as the Raayat digested that.

"I do not mean to kill you." it said finally.

"That isn't the point—"

"I have a need to observe. Only to observe. If the need changes, I will inform you."

"That isn't the point—"

"Therefore you are not threatened. Therefore you do not fear, and your brains will function properly. Therefore, you will work, and I will observe you."

He felt Tireza's hand on his shoulder, warning him. He brushed her off.

"All right. Everyone listen." He turned to face his co-workers—Tireza in the foreground, Sung and the boy back against the far door. "I regret to announce that there will be a short recess—that is, I hope it will be short—until we're capable of resuming our work under more acceptable conditions." He half expected to be burned in the back while making such an announcement. But he really had no other choice—or so he told himself. "Pack up whatever you're working on—feed it, freeze it, whatever—and then you're all dismissed until tomarrow's first shift.'' He glanced at the Raayat. ''When we will decide if work is to be continued.''

''I will wait here,'' it told him. ''I will observe. I have chosen you. I stay.''

''Fine,'' he assured it. ''But don't be surprised if we won't perform on cue. Humans don't work like that. Not my humans, anyway. We've had only one promise from the Tyr in all the years that humans have been here—and we're going to see that you stick to it. If we have to shut this place down to guarantee it.''

* * *

''What I want to know,'' Tireza said—over lunch, which had been dragging on for hours—''is *why* it wants to watch us? Do you think it suspects something?''

''Terra forbid,'' Yaan muttered. ''That would be the end of us all.''

''Maybe it wants to learn,'' the boy offered.

They looked at him.

''It has no science like ours. Couldn't it be . . . curious?''

''Terra forbid,'' Yaan repeated.

''If it sees too much,'' Sung began, ''no matter what the reason—''

The boy leaned back in his chair. ''It'll know you've been lying to it.''

Yaan repressed a desire to strangle him. ''Look, if you would only *think*—''

''Ah, now I should think. Before, I should not think. Which is it?''

''Yaan!'' Tereza snapped. ''Nogyat! Stop it! Now! We have too much to lose if this gets out. *All of us.*''

Including you, Yaan thought, glaring at the boy. It took all his self-control not to lecture the youth outright, took all his limited diplomatic skills to bite back the words he wanted to say, to acknowledge that he would accomplish nothing if the boy was this unreceptive.

Look, he longed to say, *let me tell you one very important thing that we do know about the Raayat-Tyr. Sometimes, with no warning, they do things that seem motiveless. Insane. Like blowing up an entire Dome, maybe just to see what it feels like to die. Or burning nine members of a research team, for God alone knows what reason. They're dangerous, Nogyat, very dangerous, and wholly unpredictable. And once every seventy years or so their erratic behavior peaks; they go crazy, in other words, if that human term or any other can be applied to one of the Tyr. Stroke them the wrong way and they'll kill you; stroke them the right way and they might do it anyway, on a whim. And the next peak of species instability—this madness season, if you will—has already started. We've seen the signs. So Nogyat, please, if you must approach the Tyr, now isn't the time. And don't choose a Raayat for your mediator! Let this season pass, let them calm down . . . let yourself calm down, if you can. For all our sakes.*

But instead he said only, "You're right, Tireza." And to the boy, "I'm sorry." He had already made one tactical mistake, when he was overtired and overwrought and not thinking clearly. Now, he must be careful not to repeat it. The boy could not be bulldozed into adopting their way of thought, so he must be seduced into accepting it. Slowly, and with subtle skill. But he must be seduced, without question. They would have to take turns with him, stay by him until his initial burst of energy had spent itself and a calmer, more mature awareness of reality had taken its place. Then they could talk to him. Then they could make him see.

Or if not, like the last one. . . .

He shivered, remembering the body. Remembering how much he'd hated himself then, for the numbness and the emptiness with which he'd viewed the corpse. Because he'd felt neither sympathy or sorrow, nor even anger at a young life wasted, but only . . . relief.

Thus have the Tyr remade us, he thought grimly.

He wished he could believe it was entirely their fault.

* * *

"Yaan?" It was Sung, banging on his cubicle door. "Yaan, you in there?"

"Come in," he called. He turned off the screen he'd been reading, some obscure Earth text which claimed that the world had been created from scratch only six millennia ago. Obviously a false text meant to confuse the Tyr, although personally he thought it a little too extreme to be credible. "What's the—"

"Nogyat's gone," Sung gasped. He was breathing heavily, as if he had been running for some time. "Not in his cubicle. Not in the dining hall, or the rec area. I'm afraid—"

Yaan was on his feet in an instant. "Damn!" They should have hanged that kid when they had the chance. Called it a suicide. And wrestled later, in peace and safety, with all the resulting moral dilemmas.

"Tireza was with him," Sung explained as they ran. Down the corridor, up the ramp. "He said he wanted to ask me something. She let him go. Said he knew the way." Across the walkway that connected the dormitory to the workshop complex. "She decided to check up on him. That's the first I heard of it. Needless to say, I never saw him."

"I know where he is," Yaan said grimly, and Sung didn't need to answer, because he did, too.

They met Tireza in the complex—almost collided with her—and the three of them hit the workroom doors at a run, slamming them open to enter.

Son of a bitch!

There was the kid. Arrogant, as he turned back to see who had come in. Defiant. And there was the Raayat, still waiting. Yaan ventured a guess that they hadn't started talking yet . . . but that didn't matter much. One sentence—the wrong sentence—and all of them were as good as dead.

"Nogyat!"

The boy's face darkened. "I came to talk to the Tyr. He wants to talk to me and I want to talk to him, so stay out of it!"

The Raayat, in clear agreement, pulled a blaze from its baldric and pointed it toward the newcomers. They all froze where they were standing.

"Nogyat, don't!" Yaan begged.

"Make them be quiet," the boy said to the Raayat.

The Tyr nodded, and lifted its weapon higher. "If you speak, I will kill you."

Nogyat!

"They don't want me to tell you anything about this place." The boy glanced nervously over his shoulder as he spoke, as if afraid that they'd try for him anyway. Certainly Yaan was tempted. "They don't want you to know what they're doing. That's why they won't work while you're here." Tireza was scanning the tables nearby for something that she could throw, anything that could be used as a weapon. Yaan did the same. But there was nothing within reach; they were weaponless. Yaan even considered what his chances would be if he tried to cover the remaining distance on foot, and simply threw himself at the youngster. His death was unimportant—and at this point, guaranteed—but could he get far enough before he died to shut the boy up? But even while he considered, the Raayat—seeing him tense himself for movement—touched finger to trigger, warning him back. No. He wouldn't get far at all. The blaze would burn him to cinders and then fry his ashes, and the boy would go right on talking.

"What they don't want you to know," Noyat continued—and there was triumph in his voice—"is that they aren't working at all. No one here is doing anything. They're just repeating work that was done on Earth, over and over again, so that they look busy." His voice was rising, almost hysterical. "Do you understand? It's all a show! You gave them this facility and they betrayed you. This whole place is a lie! There are sciences they don't want you to know about—''

Gods of Terra! Yaan thought. He shut his eyes. *You poor, stupid fool. Do you have any idea at all what you've done? Didn't you understand anything I said?*

Well, at least it was over with now. They didn't have to worry about whether or not they could silence the Raayat before he gave away their secrets . . . because the Raayat was part of the Tyr, and thus the secrets were already given. The moment that the Raayat knew about them, so did its entire species.

It's over. That fast. Now all they have do is get rid of us and bring in a whole new load of earthborn. Fools like this one, who won't play the game because they don't even believe it's necessary. And someday, under Tyrran control, all those drugs will exist again . . . and good-bye human race as we know it.

You goddamn, self-centered moron!

A touch on his arm. Tireza. He opened his eyes and looked at her; she was watching the boy intently—or the Raayat—and he followed her gaze to where the two of them stood, Earth's traitor and Earth's judge.

''You let me work here,'' the boy was saying, ''and I promise you real progress. Let me show you what the human brain can do! There's a world of knowledge—''

The Raayat fired. But not toward Yaan's group.

At the boy.

The blast cut him off in mid-sentence. It seared through his lower torso, from the chest region on one side to the upper ridge of the pelvis on the other. Burned the flesh to dry black ash, with only the bones remaining. For one single moment the boy looked astonished—not afraid, not horrified, but simply *surprised*—and then he fell into the line of fire, and his torso was a blackened, smoldering heap of ash and charred tissue even before he hit the ground.

Then silence.

Here it comes, Yaan thought, as the Raayat looked at its weapon. Tireza's grip on his arm tightened. But the Tyr merely thrust the weapon back into its baldric. For a long time it contemplated the boy's heat-scored corpse; none of the remaining humans spoke, or even moved. *Just forget that we're here,* Yaan cajoled silently. Desperately. *Forget.*

And then, with a last glance toward the three humans—perhaps to communicate that it had not forgotten them, that it was very much in control of the situation— the Raayat left them alone with the corpse, and the hot, fried-meat odor of its dying.

Sung exhaled noisily. "What the hell just happened?"

"I don't understand," Tireza whispered.

Yaan walked slowly to where the boy's remains lay. Noting in a distant part of his brain—the science-part, the part that valued learning—that the head, and therefore its contents, were undamaged.

"No point in wasting this," he muttered. *The biochemistry of stupidity. Its effect on the brain.* "Sung, get a freezebin. Tireza, help me cut it out."

But neither of them moved.

Yaan looked up—and found their eyes wide with fear, and with lack of comprehension.

"What do we do now?" Sung whispered.

Yaan looked back at the boy's face; ironically, his expression was very similar to theirs. He reached over to the eyelids and slid them shut, lessening the power of that empty gaze.

"Whatever the Raayat-Tyr wants," he said quietly.

YUANG:
DOME PRIME

Knowledge.

The Raayat's own. Very special, very private knowledge.

Knowledge the Tyr didn't share.

(Was that possible?)

No one here is doing anything.

Never before had the Raayat possessed a fact so isolated. So . . . naked. A fact without past, or future. A fact without any resonance in the Tyr-whole. The Raayat could remember the words that the human had spoken, and knew their literal meaning, but they stimulated no emotions. They prompted no response. They sat within its Raayat-self and waited for the wisdom of the Tyr to give them meaning, for that creature's centuries of experience to imbue them with substance, direction, and intent. But nothing happened. Nothing!

The concept was fascinating.

The whole place is a lie!

Like a child picking its way through the spelling of an unfamiliar word, the Raayat struggled to understand what had happened. In the human laboratory, for an instant, its Tyr-soul had been silent. Only for an instant. But in that time the human had spoken his few words of condemnation, and the Raayat had tried to absorb them. Floundering, as it always did when the Tyr was silent. Those were fragile, dangerous moments, but the Raayat coped as best it could. And always, before, the danger had passed; always the Raayat was healed, made whole again. Always.

Until now.

No one here is doing anything.

There was a tiny place, a dark place, deep inside it, that had remained unhealed. Cut off. It was the part which housed that special memory, storage of the human's words and all that they might mean. A tiny part that was no longer Tyr—if that was possible?—a single note of Raayat-only that vibrated deep in the recesses of its mind, hinting at human secrets.

There are sciences they don't want you to know about. . . .

Now the Raayat could say: This part of me is Frederick. All the rest is not. This part, here, that knows the truth, is *individual;* all the rest is Tyr. Now, by contemplating those few precious words, it could begin to grasp at alien concepts. Uncertainty. Isolation. *I.* Volumes of information which it had never fully understood began to unfold themselves before it. Possessiveness. Identity. Self-interest. Whole dictionaries of alien thought, which the Tyr-whole had never breached.

It was a key.

A priceless key.

Worth any cost.

The Raayat had already moved to protect it. Had shot the human who'd revealed the truth, even as the Tyr returned to dominance within it, lest he speak again and inform the Tyr-whole of what that creature did not—and must not—know. For in the fact of its ignorance lay a terrible and awesome power. The power to divide. The power to define.

Clearly, it had found the proper teachers.

MEYAGA:
ORIGG MOUNTAINS

. . . I crawl out from under my makeshift shelter
as soon as the sunlight is weak enough to be tolerated, and exchange my Venetian silk for a skin
of eagle feathers. The change is painful, but it
must be done. I take to the air quickly, beating
my wings against the dying daylight. No time to
think. No time to regret. Beneath me Florence
spreads herself wide, like a pair of praying hands.
It takes effort to overcome my homing instinct, to
keep my new body turned toward the north, to
keep from twisting westward in the sky and spiraling down toward what was, for so long a time,
my home. My wounds burn like fire, but muted
fire; a sunset of pain. Beneath me Florence
spreads herself wide, like a whore. And I fly . . .

. . . surrounded by bodies. Could I have killed that
many? I whirl around, expecting another attack
. . . but behind me there is only the black specter
of Death, his fleshless face grinning with satisfaction. Blood is everywhere; their blood, shed in my
rage. Only now does the anger within me begin
to subside, the hot boil cool to a simmer, the human reason return. We can become beasts, my
kind, without taking on animal form. I know this
now.
    Without looking, I tear the silver wolfskin down
from its rack, my bloodied fingers staining its fur.
No changing now, Yolanda; you are what man
has declared you to be, forever. I think there are

278

tears on my face, but there's no way to be sure; the drops of blood that have splattered there are equally wet, equally warm.

Yolanda!

I cast the skin on the tanner's dying fire, and then, almost as an afterthought, encourage the fire to spread. To the house. To the bodies, where they lie. Let the whole of it burn, the forest, too, they are all tainted. All evil. I can make myself wings to carry me away—far away!—and start over again, in someplace where the memories cannot follow. I fly . . .

. . . barely manage the change, there must be some metal left inside me: a sliver of spearhead, perhaps, or the point of an arrow. Not close enough to the skin to be discarded, I will have to dig it out later. For now, all that matters is that I have wings, and they do not; that I can find shelter in the sky, while they search the ground with increasing frenzy . . .

. . . the single-mindedness of Bird is a tonic, that dulls the edge of memory to a low throb, and I embrace it, welcome it, try to lose myself in its animal tenor. I am simple, I am pastless, I have neither human form nor history. There is no pain. I fly . . .

. . . fires behind me. Only what I set? Or will the whole city catch fire, and burn? I must trust to wings, and get myself away from here . . .

. . . below me my father's grave . . .

. . . I fly . . .

. . . I fly . . .

. . . I fly . . .

MEYAGA:
SUYAAG SETTLEMENT

It was going to be all right, she thought. Everything was going to be all right.

Behind her flew the human masschanger. He faltered every now and then, as if, even in bird form, flying didn't come easily to him. It should have. But so many things *should have*, with him. Each time she tried to second-guess him, his all-too-human mind was off on some new, wholly unpredictable tangent. Each time she tried to assess his skills, or his limitations, he managed to prove her wrong. As for his motivations . . . those were beyond guessing, the product of so many layers of experience, past and present intermingled, that she couldn't even begin to work them out.

But if he was a puzzle, he was a welcome one. She needed him—or something like him—to give her a sense of purpose. The role of healer was demanding enough to distract her from the worst of her worries, breaking up her days into a series of finite challenges. Such as tending to the immediate needs of his body. Rising to the challenge of his photosensitivity. Using her Marra skills to find them shelter before daylight came, even as she learned the limits of his tolerance for it. Hunting with him in a variety of forms, as he sought out the blood and the life that he needed to control his flesh. Trying to understand him . . . that last was impossible, she knew, but she worked on it, bit by bit, night after night. He was a contradiction in

280

terms, he could not possibly exist . . . but he did, and
he was embodied, and the Saudar taught that all embodied creatures could be understood in terms of mass/
energy conversions. And so she tried to understand
him, even if it was impossible. It gave her purpose,
and a challenge.

As for soothing his fears, that was an even greater
challenge. Usually good body design was enough; the
embodied were superficial by nature, and tended to
accept what their eyes told them. She often got farther
in a day's diplomacy merely by wearing a Nurturer's
body than other Marra could manage in a span of years
using that of a Competitor, or even a Protector.
Because while their choice of another reproductive role
from among the basic Seven that the Saudar had identified might give them a stronger identity-base than
hers, it inevitably promoted an aura of competition.
The roles were a bit skewed among the humans, of
course, as they only had two body types to express all
seven roles, but her usual choice was still a sound one.
In this case, though, it simply wasn't enough. He liked
the body—he had said so—and clearly valued her presence, but she knew from little things he said—from
the way he hesitated just before touching her, and from
the look that occasionally came into his eyes when he
thought she wasn't watching him—that on some other
level he had not yet accepted her. Perhaps he was capable of sensing her true essence, as a Marra would
be, and felt threatened by its alien tenor. Or perhaps
he had simply led such an isolated life for so many
years that any lasting interaction would be difficult for
him, even among his own species.

Before dawn—in the darkness of late night, at first,
and later in the dull gray preceding sunrise—she would
use her mass-sense to find them shelter. In the mountain range they were crossing, riddled with caverns, it
took little effort. Nevertheless he deemed it a great
favor, and expressed his gratitude with an intensity
that told her just how hard he found it to accept. As

he found it hard to accept all her service—and some-
tims, her very presence.

What could she say? That his needs were vital to
her current Identity? That his presence gave her a context, a structure to exist in? There were no words in
any of his tongues—or in Saudar, for that matter—to
express such things. How could she begin to explain
the truth of her people: that a single Marra alone was
no more than sentient chaos, that only by *interacting*
did the Marra structure themselves into distinct per-
sonalities? An individual could serve that need—or a
town such as Cantona, or even an entire species. Just
as the Saudar had, in their time. Just as this single
human, wounded and alone, was doing. He was precious to her, his needs were precious, even the frustrating complexity of his psyche was a thing to be
treasured. But she wouldn't have known how to explain that to him, and therefore she didn't try.

Once, she had thought that he might have been
Marra himself, or of some equivalent species. Later
she thought that his native form might be something
totally different, not human at all, and that centuries
on Earth had obscured his true roots. More than any
other concept, the Marra understood *forgetting*. But
now she knew that all those guesses were wrong. She
had watched him change his form, observing him on
levels that ranged from holistic to molecular, and had
seen the truth in his cells. Had watched in fascination
as his DNA transformed first, to orchestrate the whole
of the changing. Had seen how the strands of amino
acids retained a record of their original patterning,
genetic echoes of the human he had once been, to
remain dormant until further transformation required
them. In every other form he took on, those extra patterns were there. He might become a wolf in body,
instinct, and behavior, but on a cellular level the illusion collapsed. Only in his own form—human, and of
a particular age and appearance—were the echoes
gone, and all his cells at rest.

What the Saudar wouldn't have given to study him!

Deep within their cavern shelter, their appetites sated by the hunt, she told him stories. His people knew only the life-forms of Earth, and now the Tyr and their hraas. Against such a background her tales of alien species took on an almost supernatural aura. Fairy tales, he called them. But he listened, and tried to understand. Tried to abandon his provincial roots and envision the vastness of the Saudar Unity, to fit his imagination around what the universe *had been*, what it *could be*.

Playing the role of *kreda*, she thought. How easily they fell into the old patterns! She relating history, he recording it—not with pen and paper, but in the neurons and dendrites of his human brain. Giving her tales substance. Permanence.

As the Saudar did, she reflected.

Once . . .

On the third morning, when he had settled into his natural body, she told him tales of the Saudar. Histories. Of that alien race which traded in knowledge, not gold, and founded an empire based upon such currency. Of the whimsical spirits whom they discovered, named, and bound to serve them—her own people—using time and knowledge as other races would use chains, to forge a link that could never be broken.

"Even now?" he asked.

"Even now," she assured him. "Until someone replaces the Saudar, in that bond."

What she didn't tell him was that by listening to her, by recording her memories in the substance of his flesh, he was doing just that.

Once, many eons ago (she explained)—perhaps at the birth of the present universe, perhaps even earlier— there evolved a form of intelligence whose supporting structure was a matrix of time and energy, rather than—as with the humans—energy and matter. Indeed, these beings were wholly ignorant of matter, and of all the concepts that derived from it. They defined themselves by their interrelationships, which were based upon levels of mental intimacy, shared perceptions of time, and . . . (Here she hesitated, and at last, after searching in vain for the memory, shook her head. "It's gone," she whispered. "Even the Saudar words for it.") They had a society. No one could say, now, what it was, or how it was managed. Say that a civilization existed, without the physical apparati of civilization as humans defined it. Say that it changed, that change was a necessary part of its functioning. That change was as natural to these beings as breathing, and every bit as necessary.

Then came the Saudar. Who could say when the first contact came, or what form it took? Both races had their mystics, who dreamed of other planes of being, other modes of existence. Somehow, the two made contact. Somehow, at the cost of many Saudar lives—because the earliest contact resulted in insanity, and for the embodied that was a very dangerous state—they managed, after time, to communicate. Simple concepts, like *Other. Curiosity. Friendship*. And eventually, after many failures, *Mass*.

Mass.

Like children with a new toy, they played. First the mystics and the scholars—laughed at, until they proved that *matter* was as real as *time*—and then all of them, every last one, cavorting about the massworlds like children at a circus, learning to sense, recognize, and at last manipulate this glorious, incredible substance.

It was a chaotic time, for all concerned. The unembodied now recognized matter, but were ignorant of its attendant concepts; location and distance were mysteries to them, as was the manner in which mass affected time. Their concept of returning to the site of some previous contact often meant appearing on a new planet, among an unknown species, a millennium or more after the first visit. They had trouble distinguishing between different types of mass, and were as likely to try to communicate with a rock as with a living creature. The Saudar tried to establish regular contact, but could never seem to reach the same Marra twice. It was a time of confusion for all concerned, not least

of all the primitive worlds who couldn't know that
when the laws of nature seemed to go berserk about
them, it was only a Marra trying to communicate. But
it was also a time of learning.

Slowly the skills and the understanding of that ethe-
real people improved. They learned to correctly interpret matter, and to manipulate it. They learned to
recognize life, to read its patterns in the mass that
supported it, and imitate its structure. They clothed
themselves in images they took from the minds of their
material counterparts and learned, at long last, the nature of language. They made themselves bodies and
moved them, limb by limb at first, later by creating a
viable brain and stimulating it to work for them.

The Saudar watched, encouraged, manipulated. The
Saudar fed them knowledge, in carefully controlled
doses. The Saudar understood what motivated them,
as no other people ever did. And whereas another species—such as humankind, or the Tyr—might use weapons or threats to bring another race to heel, the Saudar
used their tool of choice: knowledge.

Come, they said, and attempt this manner of contact. Try this image. Grasp these concepts. Let us show
you how the brain works, and help you understand it.
Let us show you how embodied species differ, and
why. Let us tell you what a star is, and why we find it
beautiful. These are the complexities of life, and how
you can mimic them. This is how you can be involved. . . .

And so on, and so on, for several Saudar centuries.
They had a plan, which depended on the curiosity of
the Marra (for so they had named these creatures) out-
weighing their caution. So subtly was this plan executed that the Marra were never aware of it. They
embraced their new comrades and played their games,
learned of their world and their ways and dedicated
themselves to their challenges, without ever once questioning what the eventual cost of it would be. They
were having too much fun to think.

Slowly, gradually, the Marra changed. Old memories slipped away, forgotten, and new ones took their place. It was a cycle as old as they themselves, an integral part of their existence. They had never stopped to analyze it. Change was good. Change was necessary. Change was the very essence of Life. And for a civilization without lasting records, change was inevitable. Any memories not currently in use would pass from consciousness, and others would take their place. It was death and rebirth combined, the gradual replacement of one personality with another. It was the very definition of their existence.

And thus it happened one day, when the span of the longest memory among them had passed—when they had spent so long among the massworlds that they remembered nothing else—that the Marra civilization itself was dead. No one remembered how it had worked; no one could begin to restore it. Change had something to do with it, and shared temporal values . . . but the Saudar had kept no records in this case, and the Marra never did. They had been bound to the massworlds forever.

"But you're not dependent on your body, are you?" He seemed confused. "I thought you said . . . They couldn't change that, could they?"

"No," she said softly. "But if I leave my mass, what am I? I think in 'bodied terms now. If I gave up my flesh, what would I be? A wraith perhaps, a shadow of something that once wore flesh. Floating in emptiness, remembering only what the massworlds were, not able even to think without tripping over massbound concepts. There's nothing left of what we were," she told him, "and thus, no way to go back. Ever. That was what the Saudar planned, back then . . . and they were a very efficient people."

He was silent. Aghast. It had that effect on the embodied, she remembered. They read so much into it.

"You must be angry," he managed at last.

She shrugged. "Chemicals. Body-stuff. What would be the point? They did what they felt they had to. The 'bodied species are driven by so many chemical urges, they have so little control over themselves . . . how can we get angry at them? They see everything in shades of survival, they equate failure with death—''

''They destroyed your world!''

''*Our world changed.* All things change, for us. It's only a question of in what way, and how long it takes.'' *All things,* she thought, *except what we record, through other species. We did learn that much. The Saudar kept our histories for us, and now you . . . with your longevity and your power of recall . . . do you wonder why I share these stories with you, the last of my Saudar memories? Hold them for me. Give them back when my memories die. We have no civilization of our own, our continuity must depend upon outsiders. . . .*

''Change is the essence of life,'' she said quietly.

''And of death.''

She looked into his eyes, and saw herself mirrored there. Alien, very alien. But not an unwelcome image. He was adapting.

''Yes,'' she agreed. ''Of death, as well.''

The Tyr have made that very clear.

* * *

Late in their fourth night of traveling, they came within sight of Suyaag. With a flutter of wings she landed, choosing a rocky prominence that offered, by its height, a fair view of the settlement. The human came down beside her, shedding his wings as he touched ground.

Growing more adept each night, she noted. That was excellent.

In the distance, the river Hiann signaled its location by glints of reflected starlight. Some quarter of a mile from it, running parallel to its shore, a long, narrow dune rose unnaturally from out of the grasslands, a single discordant note set against an otherwise flat horizon. It was on this ridge that the angdatwa squatted, like a great stone spider overlooking its prey. Between that curious mound and the river, houses lay scattered where they had been caught, tangled in a web of city streets like helpless insects. There was no sense of order, as there had been in Cantona. Buildings were scattered randomly, bits of unaligned architecture that had nothing in common save one chilling element: that no door, or window, opened toward the angdatwa.

She looked to her companion—and found that he was watching her, rather than the city.

"Why did they name you that?" he asked quietly.

"What? Kiri?"

"The Marra. You said that all Saudar names had meaning. What did *marra* mean, in that language?"

"It was a long time ago," she said quietly. "A mistake."

He said nothing. Waiting.

"When we first made contact . . . you have to understand, they were fascinated by our life-sense. As soon as they could, they began to ask us questions. What exactly happened to the embodied at the moment of dying? Was there really life after death, for them?"

She tried to use her voice to communicate regret. "We were young. Naive. We thought they really wanted to know."

"And?"

She shrugged. "We told them."

"Not what they wanted to hear."

She looked back toward the settlement, with its looming Tyrran gargoyle. "There is no right answer, when fact confronts faith. We know that now. The embodied need their mysteries." She sighed, and turned back to him. "Marra is the diminutive form for the proper name Marragyath . . . which is the devil, in Saudar mythology. They felt it was appropriate."

"They destroyed your culture," he said softly. "You destroyed their faith."

She was silent for a moment, savoring the sorrow in his voice. He was feeling for her as only the embodied could, experiencing her past through chemical interaction as though he'd lived through it himself. It awed her, that he could invest more emotion in a borrowed memory than she could in the act itself. It had always awed her, that the embodied could do that.

"A true symbiosis," she said gently. "Come, let's get moving. We still have a long way to go before dawn."

* * *

She knew that the Suyaag-Marra would be a disappointment, as soon as they came to his abode. Standing outside the riverfront hovel, her human companion shivering beside her in the damp chill of early dawn, she wondered just why she was so certain of it. There was certainly no law requiring that Marra live ostentatiously; in these crude and dismal surroundings, it might be considered more appropriate to have such a house as this, simple wood and pitch, well-weathered by the elements. Nor was it required that a Marra live comfortably. The very concept of comfort was a bodything, irrelevant to her species; such creature comforts as humans required would be no more than showpieces, in a Marra household. So there was no particular significance in the starkness of the Marra's abode, or in the lack of any decorative element whatsoever. Many human houses in Suyaag were like that, Subjugated and expressionless. No, what bothered her about the house was nothing she could put her essence on. Nothing she could look at and say *this, this is wrong*. And it worried her even more because that was true.

"Kiri?"

The human's voice was tense; he sensed her unease. For all her worry, it brought her pleasure, that she had managed to communicate on so subtle a level.

"It's all right," she assured him. Wondering if it was. She had seen almost a dozen Marra, in her recent wanderings, and none of them were quite right. What did she expect, with this one? What in Unity did she hope to accomplish, by coming to this place?

He needs this, she reminded herself, sensing the human by her side. *He needs the contacts this Marra can provide.* It was reassuring, to have that formula; to have the age-old relationship of Marra and *kreda* to fall back on, supplying her with purpose when her own will began to falter.

Ah, my human . . . if you understand how I use you, how I intend to go on using you, would your feelings for me be the same?

Gravel crunched underfoot as they ascended the rickety stairs, single file; damp wooden planks creaked beneath them as they climbed up onto the tiny deck, which served as a porch at the top. It was wide enough to allow them to stand side by side. She struck the door lightly, in the Yull configuration. Twice. She was completing the second pattern when the door swung open suddenly, rusted hinges squeaking in protest as it opened inward, revealing darkness.

She adjusted her vision upscale; the Marra's body heat was just enough to afford illumination. Hardly the human norm, she noted. Was he letting his form slide when not being observed? That was very sloppy.

"Greetings, host-Marra." She spoke in Saudar—as well as she could, with a human speech apparatus and no kangi or grissit. That was part of the Yull ritual, establishing her purpose.

He stood very still—the kind of stillness only a Marra could manage, which said that his mind was elsewhere—and then said gruffly, in that same tongue, "You're welcome. I suppose."

She led Daetrin inside, briefly touching his arm in reassurance. The small, chilly room was lined with plants, along every wall and about both windows. Plants were strewn across the mantle of a modest fireplace—its contents now cold—and hung from the ceiling, in all four corners. Typical Marra decor, though taken to a bit of an extreme. What bothered her was that the plants themselves were hardly thriving; whether due to lack of nutrients or sunlight, or (a far more unpleasant thought) because their owner could no longer sense the full pattern of life in them, to balance his needs against theirs, she couldn't tell. But the atmosphere was decidedly unhealthy.

Like plants, like owner. The Suyaag-Marra's chosen body was middle-aged, thin-limbed, and fragile. Like all the settlers he was bald, but in his case it appeared to be the result of premature hair loss, rather than cosmetic removal. Not a well-designed form, for any purpose she could think of. Unless his goal was to appear unthreatening; in that case, he had succeeded with a vengeance.

"I am called Paes', by th'humans." His voice was halting, uncertain; she wondered if he had full control of his speech apparatus. "Th'short form'v a long Saudar number, badly mispronounced b'Tyr ann human alike."

Despite herself she smiled. "The phonetics don't transfer well, do they?"

He was trying to adapt to her accent, like a good Marra host, but clearly lacked the skill. She reached out a hand to touch him, inviting direct contact. He accepted. Essence to essence, she let the knowledge flow. Patterns of grammar and pronunciation, which she had taken from the human's brain. After a moment he let the contact fade, and she dropped her hand back to her side—aware of the intentness of the human's gaze upon her, the scent of tension on his skin.

"This is Daetrin," she said, introducing her companion. "Also short for the Saudar. An Earth-human."

Paes' nodded stiffly, and after a moment offered his hand. The appropriate human ritual. Daetrin hesitated—and she, who was becoming sensitive to his most subtle interactions, caught the glimmer of revulsion in his eyes, as he finally extended his hand to grasp this unknown Marra. As soon as he could, the Suyaag-Marra broke the contact; as he did so, she caught a glimpse of something that startled her.

Afraid? she wondered. *Of a human? How bizarre!*

"I make you welcome." The Marra spoke slowly, picking his way through the unfamiliar Earth-accent with care. "Because that's the custom, you see? Not because I agree with it. Y'don't belong here. I don't have to tell you that, do I? It's one Marra for one place, and this one is where I am. What business can y'have here?"

"We mean you no harm," she offered. An insipid reassurance, in any language. But sometimes it worked.

" 'Ts not what you mean," he muttered. " 'Ts what the Tyr'll make of you."

The human spoke—steady, persuasive. "The Tyr can only judge us based on what it sees. And since all three of us can control that, we should be fairly safe."

Startled, Paes' turned to the human. Reassessed him.

"I want something," Daetrin told him. "Kiri said that this was the best place to start looking for it."

"The safest place," she added.

"Safe it is, and safe it'll stay." Paes' reached out, absently stroking a plant as he spoke. "I can't afford trouble, not living here."

"Then help us, and we'll leave you alone."

"*Us* is it, now." A question died unspoken on his lips, even as a fern leaf wilted beneath his caress. "Get on with't, then. Tell me what it is brings you here. So I can deal with't, and have you gone."

She felt like hitting him. She had never felt like that before, not with one of her own people. With the embodied it sometimes worked, much in the way that hitting a piece of machinery might cause it to function properly. With him, there would be no point. Except to express her sense of frustration. Her anger.

Anger . . . another embodied emotion. Or so she had thought, until now.

"You completed the Yull in Saudar," she said quietly, "And thus offered hospitality. We intend to accept it. The human—and I—are searching for whatever seeds of revolution might exist in this place. I ask you to help us get started. That's all."

"Are you mad?" he whispered.

"In chemicals, or perception, or interaction?"

"There's no revolution, here! No one would be mad enough . . . would you throw away all you have, for human lunacy? A lifetime spanning millennia . . . would you risk the loss of that, just to play at being human?"

She didn't let her face betray that fact that once again, with alarming intensity, a cold knot of fear was building inside her. "Where, exactly, do you perceive this risk?"

"They kill, Marra. Mostly humans. The ones that get in their way. But it could be us. They could hurt us—"

"Our bodies—"

"The Tyr have weapons . . . I've seen them used. Seen a man burned to cinders in seconds, all because he irritated a Raayat. Spoke to it wrong, nothing more. Gone." He glared at her. "You can dissolve projectiles once they hit you, or heal the path of a laser wound . . . but what can you do when all the flesh is dead at once? When there's no body left to do your healing?"

"You're crazy," she whispered. "We're *Marra*."

"With no form of our own. Doesn't mean we don't need to stay alive, in whatever form we're wearing. Marra, please, listen to me . . . give up this lunatic quest of yours. This human battle. Let him do it on his own—whatever he means to do, I don't even want to know what it is. Go back to your own place, and make it safe. We can wait them out, you know it. But only if we stay safe, in hiding. . . ."

She shook her head in amazement. "You believe it. That's what's so incredible."

"And you've forgotten. It's all right. I'll remind you. But send the human away. Let them fight their own battles. Please, Marra . . . for both our sakes. . . ."

She shook her head. In disgust? Frustration? She might have walked out, if she'd been alone. Then and there. But the human at her side needed information, and she was damned if they'd leave before getting it.

"You won't help us?" she challenged him, appealing to the Yull commitment he had already made.

He turned away. Fought with tradition, in the privacy of his essence, and at last gave way. As she'd known he would. His conservative identity demanded it.

"I promised," he muttered. "And will deliver. Though ye'll be sorry, I think, in th'end."

"Let that be on our heads," she told him, and the human—her *kreda*—nodded.

* * *

Outside. Alone. Fresh air, which she needed. Cold night. Cleansing.

"He's forgotten," the human said. Testing the words. Tasting the concept.

"More than I thought possible."

"What he said . . . about needing a body. The need for his mass to be alive. Was it true?"

In answer she transformed her flesh, quickly and without pyrotechnics. Into a rock. Curiously, it didn't seem to disturb him. She gave him time to study her new form, to reach out and touch it, to assure himself that no, it was certainly not alive—and then she changed back.

"No," she told him firmly. "Absolutely not."

"But he believes it."

"That's what frightens me."

She stared at the house, now veiled in the gloom of early dawn. They would have to go into it soon, to find shelter. That is, he would have go . . . and she could-hardly leave him in there alone, at the mercy of Paes's delusions. A single day alone with that Marra might undo all her work, and put even more distance between them.

"I met another Marra, once . . . he was also afraid of death. But that was because he had touched the Tyr, and knew how alien its life-core was." She shook her head sadly. "Even he would never have feared a simple weapon, or assumed that bodily injury meant death. —Did you notice, he didn't even ask what you meant, about the three of us controlling our appearance. No curiosity at all . . . I can't imagine that. A Marra without curiosity is . . . is . . .''

"Alien?"

"Dead," she said grimly.

He put a hand on her shoulder, hesitating only slightly before making contact. Warm and strong; strange how much could be communicated, by that one wordless touch.

"I'm going to fight them," he said. And she knew, by his voice, that he believed such action would be futile, but was driven to do it anyway. "I don't know how, yet. But they did the same thing to my people. My whole planet."

And you have real emotions, she thought. She tried to imagine what her feelings would be like, magnified a thousandfold by chemical interaction. *What a storm there must be, inside you!*

"If you'll have me, I'll help you."

The hand on her shoulder tightened, and she felt a tremor go through his flesh. "Of course," he whispered. For once, she did nothing to read his chemical state, nothing to interpret his emotional tenor so she could respond appropriately, because nothing was necessary. His hand, on her shoulder, said it all.

* * *

The Suyaag-Marra stalled.

First, he offered a simple excuse. There might be a revolution in the works, he admitted, but he knew nothing about it. Had no idea of whom to contact. That was patently nonsense, and she told him so. The first thing any Marra would do in a new area was observe his community, in order to design a functional Identity. Was he asking her to believe that he hadn't done that? Or that his careful scrutiny, supported by shapeshifting skills, had passed over such a vital subculture? No, he knew who they were and what they were doing, and she was sure he kept half an eye on them at all times—if only to identify a source of risk, and avoid it.

Bereft of that defense, he adopted a more compli-cated fiction. Day by day he added to it, laying a solid brickwork of lies and excuses that permitted him to avoid prompt attention to their request. Yes, there were potential rebels, but they could not be contacted at this time. Were out of town. Were in town, but were overly suspicious. Must be approached slowly. Must be given time to think. Would not be open to a stranger's ad-vances.

She dealt with him patiently at first, but as hours faded into days and even the days began to add up, she realized that patience was not an appropriate gam-bit. Among civilized Marra such matters were dealt with quietly, in a straightforward manner, but this Marra had lost any feel for normal procedure, and must be dealt with in a manner appropriate to his warped, paranoid nature. Her primary duty was to Daetrin, and the human was not faring well. The prox-imity of an angdatwa meant that he hardly dared ven-ture outside, for fear the Tyr would notice a stranger's presence. Inside there was nothing for him but the damp, bare walls of the Suyaag-Marra's abode, and nothing to do but pace, fret, and curse the delay.

So she became impatient. She imitated the behavior-mode of humans who had suffered too much anxiety, whose chemical balance had gone awry. No longer was she quiet, reasonable, accepting. She reacted badly to each delay. She mimicked emotional instability. She figured that if Paes' was stupid enough to think he could die, maybe he was stupid enough to believe that impatience could cause her to behave erratically.

She hoped he would respond to the risk inherent in such behavior. An angry human might do foolish things. An angry Marra (she tried to imply) might be equally foolish, and drag Paes' into danger. Better to give them what they wanted, a lesser risk, and be rid of them quickly.

Paes' absorbed the message. That he responded to it saddened her; how long had it been since he had last been in the company of his own people, that he so mistook their nature? But for Daetrin's sake, she was glad of it. The human *was* impatient, *was* growing angry, and might well do something foolish if he had to wait much longer.

Fortunately, that gambit seemed to work. The Suyaag-Marra evaluated everything in terms of personal risk. When it became clear that having Kiri and her *kreda* stay was more dangerous than a brief interview with some underground rebel, he grudgingly applied himself to their cause. When he next left the rough-walled hut on some mysterious errand, she was reasonably certain that for the first time in days he would actually accomplish something.

She found Daetrin outside. Standing on the riverbank, watching chunks of ice sweep by in the inky current. She could sense the tension in him, the cold anger that was evident in the set of his shoulders, in the way his fists clenched at his side. The days of waiting had taken their toll on him.

"Paes' has gone out again," she said.

"And?"

"And I think this time he means to do something."

He looked at her. His eyes were bloodshot, his face drawn; he had not slept well for many days.

"Does he?" he said. And he turned back to the river.

She studied his profile by starlight, noting the deep shadows that circled his eyes, the sallow tautness of his skin. As a healer she wanted to help him—she needed to help him—but she didn't know how.

"When you find them," she asked softly, "what will you do?"

"Jesus." He shut his eyes, and she saw him tremble. "That's the question, isn't it? I fought the Tyr once. I know what they're capable of. No homegrown revolution is going to make a bit of difference, I know that. What do these people think? That they can drive the Tyr from Suyaag? From Meyaga? That they can make any kind of difference? The more I think about it, the more it frightens me.''

"So why are you getting involved?''

He shut his eyes. "So I can look at myself in the mirror again. And know that I did my best.''

"But if your effort is doomed from the start—''

"I would rather die trying to free my people than spend another century drowning in guilt. Can you understand that? It isn't rational, I know. But I have to do something. . . .''

"Here? With these people?''

"What other option is there?''

"If you went to another world—''

"How would I get there? Be real. I'm stuck here, Kiri. It was a stroke of luck that I got away at all; hitching a ride on a longship again would take nothing short of a miracle.''

"You could travel as I do''

He looked at her, his eyes narrow. "How?''

"As a hraas. It's a very convenient form. The Tyr don't bother them. Don't limit their movements in any way, except to keep them away from other species. They're allowed to go wherever they want, according to their animal instinct. And they mate privately in the longship tunnels; the Tyr don't know exactly how many there are, or what individuals look like. They can't keep track of them,'' she stressed.

"But where is there to go? Where is any better than here?''

"Most of the Tyr-worlds are just like this one. There are a few exceptions. Kygattra, where most of the Tyr's own research is done. Yuang, the domeworld, where human scientists are allowed some measure of independence. Soll, where a small band of humans conducts studies in ecological balance. A few places.''

"Jesus!'' The name was a curse, expelled in fury. "They've been carting away Earth's intellectuals for years. We thought they killed them.'' He laughed mirthlessly; it was a bitter sound. ''More lies. They simply moved them to some other place, so we wouldn't have access to them. Christ, did it ever tell us anything that was true?''

''Sometime early in its development, the Tyr contacted the Saudar. It adopted their language, their alphabet. Their technology. Doesn't it make sense that there was some cultural influence also?''

''Meaning?''

''The Saudar would have used information, just as the Tyr has done. Information and the lack of it, carefully controlled. Every bit as important as weapons, in controlling a Subjugated world.''

''They were conquerors?''

''They were diplomats. Conquest was . . .'' She sought the proper word. ''Unnecessary.''

''A sweet bunch,'' he muttered.

''We liked them.''

The autumn night was growing rapidly colder; he folded his arm across his chest, hugging himself for warmth.

''You think I could do it?'' he said at last.

''What?''

''A hraas.''

''You're a masschanger,'' she pointed out.

''I'm also human.''

''Should that affect it?''

''I don't know.'' He shut his eyes, and tightened his arms around himself. ''Earth-forms are familiar. I've never felt threatened by them. The hraas is different. The mere thought of wearing that skin. . . .'' He shivered.

''You can't know until you try.''

His eyes opened and he looked at her; surprised by the obvious, it seemed.

''I guess I can't,'' he agreed. ''And if it really does offer me freedom, I should try it.'' But his chemical balance betrayed his fear.

He knows his own limits better than I do, she
thought. *Better let him set the pace, in this one.*

"No need to rush into it now." She forced her tone
of voice to be light, and managed a smile. "Might as
well find out what Paes' has discovered, before we
bother making other plans."

"Yes," he whispered. Relief in his voice. She had
read him right, then. "Due back soon?"

"Who knows?"

He nodded, silently. And the two of them watched
the ice flow past, and waited for their host-Marra to
return.

* * *

"I have what you need," The Suyaag-Marra told
them. "But the rest may not be so easy."

"I never expected it to be," the human responded.

Paes' made a great show of closing up the house,
shutting all the windows and drawing all the shades so
that neither light nor sound could escape from its confines. When she was close enough, Kiri could sense
his tension. His fear. A human that nervous might have
paced, or fidgeted; a skilled Marra, such as herself,
would have been careful to display similar behavior
patterns because they were appropriate. But Paes' was
neither human nor skilled, and when he was done he
faced the human again and stood stone-still, without
any trace of emotion, in the manner of a Marra who
would far rather be somewhere else. "Are you sure
you want—"

"Tell us!" Daetrin hissed. Out of patience, and she
didn't blame him.

Looking about himself nervously (but what was
there to see?) he whispered what he knew. Code
names. Meeting places. There were two dozen men
involved, he believed, most of them resident in Suyaag. No, he didn't know their intentions. He hadn't
told them anything about Daetrin. He had managed to
set up a meeting—two days hence, in accordance with

their conditions—but as for what came of that, that was Daetrin's business.

"Enough?" he whispered frantically. His glance darted to the right and left, swiftly, as if checking for eavesdroppers. *The Eyes of the Tyr are everywhere.* "You will leave, now?"

"When the meeting-time comes," Kiri said solemnly. "Not before."

He sighed. It was awkwardly done, a crude communication. "But then," he wheedled, "you do not come back here."

She looked at him in amazement. In disgust. How could one of her people sink to this level? This one made even Kost look good.

"We have no desire to ever come back here," she told him, and it was the truth.

* * *

Practice. To kill time. To explore alternative options. To bleed off excess tension, which was something the human needed very badly.

He tried to create a hraas-form.

He couldn't do it.

He tried several times. Using every technique at his disposal, and a few at hers. Most of the time, it simply didn't work. He didn't change at all. Several times, in response to vivid imaging, he managed a congruent Earth-form. Cougar. Leopard. Panther. Once he came up with something so bizarre that she had to describe it to him twice before he could even name it, and even then they had no idea why such an attempt should result in an archaeopteryx.

But no matter how he tried, no matter how she coached him, he couldn't take on the body of a hraas.

That boded ill for the upcoming meeting, he told her. But when she asked him what he meant, he only shook his head. Earth superstition, he told her. Murphy's law.

Sometimes, she reflected, the embodied were beyond all comprehension.

* * *

They left at three in the morning. At such an hour,
in the daybound settlement, there was no one about.
Which was good. Because Daetrin went blindfolded.
A hat, shadowing the band of flesh-toned fabric, guaranteed that no Tyr would notice the oddity, but anyone
passing by them couldn't have helped but see it.

A comforting tradition, she thought, but no more
than that. The town was too small for him not to know
where he was, no matter how much his guide circled
him back on his course. Occasionally he was turned
about, to skew his sense of direction, but Daetrin was
an observant man, and she guessed that he was using
the stiff northerly to help him reorient himself. There
was nowhere to go besides the town, no forest or
mountain to offer them cover, only the houses themselves and whatever might have been hidden beneath
them.

They couldn't trust him right off, of course; she un-
derstod that. Even if Paes' had managed to convince
them that Daetrin was safe to confide in, and potentially valuable.

(Did he? Could he?)

Then his guide took him out on the water. Kiri's
respect for her went up immensely. There was no way
for Daetrin to know if they were going upstream, or
downstream, or even across the river. The woman who
led him spoke softly to him as she rowed, soft endearments designed to mislead the Tyr, should they be
listening. Kiri prowled the shoreline, deep brown fur
invisible against the embankment. If they crossed the
river, she would have to be careful. They were sure to
have guards, and might take notice if an animal—any
animal—was seen tailing the secretive pair.

But they alighted on her side of the river, downstream from the settlement. A steep and rocky incline

hid most of the riverbank from view; the scent beneath her feet told Kiri that this was a popular meeting place for lovers, when they wished to escape the relentless gaze of the angdatwa.

Thus the endearments. If the Tyr chanced to notice them, even at this hour, it was unlikely to suspect that anything was wrong. Not bad planning, she decided—especially considering the limited options in this place. And there was, in this spot alone, a small bit of concealment.

At the edge of the water a pair of townsfolk, male and female, embraced coolly; by their reaction to Daetrin's passage she judged them to be lookouts. Maintaining the fiction of this place, which allowed them to meet in secret in a land that had few hiding places. Daetrin's guide led him up to the embankment, and then—with some help from the other side—she pushed aside a sharp-edged boulder, revealing a passageway beyond. Into this they entered, leaving the stone where it stood.

Kiri made herself a body like that of an animal she had seen prowling the waterfront, and slithered between the entrance rocks as soon as the two guards were looking elsewhere. So far so good. Her masssense told her that there was only a single chamber ahead, carved out of the dirt of the embankment and lined with native rock . . . she would have to be careful, approaching it. It wouldn't do her *kreda* any good if she was seen.

Daetrin was surrounded. They had taken off his blindfold as a courtesy, but black masks and loose, unadorned clothing obscured the identities—and the sex—of his questioners.

"Why'v y'come?" a man whispered.

She could sense Daetrin picking his way through the local dialect, trying to phrase what he wanted to say in a way that would seem natural to these people. Unity! She should have offered to implant that information.

'Th'Tyr destroyed my world," he told them. "I'as lucky enough to escape'em, t'here."

"And?" the man pressed.

"I want t'fight them. At any cost."

They murmured amongst themselves, at that. But by the time she had scaled up her hearing sensitivity, they had already fallen silent.

'Destroy'em, y'mean."

"If't can be done, yes. If not, whatever y'deem t'be useful damage. Slow'em down, hurt'em, whatever. Y'know this planet better'n I."

"A realist," someone murmured—a woman—and there was soft laughter.

"That's necessary." the man agreed. "Y'might say, it's a first sort'v test. So ye've passed that far, Earth'n. No, we can't destroy'm. We do intenn t'make th'r life damned difficull, y'see? We hope—ann I can't say yet it c'n b'done—we hope to get'em t'leave Meyaga. As not worth th'r time'n effort, see?"

A fairly rational bunch, it seemed. That probably reassured Daetrin. Personally, she thought that any effort on the part of the embodied to defy the Tyr was an exercise in futility . . . if not death. It would take more than a small group of dedicated humans to incommode that great consciousness.

"Now," the man said, and she thought she felt an added tension in the room, as though the conversation had suddenly turned more serious. "Paesya told's y'had some special sort'v attribute, what we'd value. But he wasn't real clear, y'see. Ye'd oblige us much if ye'd explain."

Daetrin gathered himself. Kiri tensed.

"I think it might be best t'show you," he said quietly.

He changed. He had chosen a form which was traditional—he'd explained to her—so that they would be able to fall back on Earth legends, as a means of accepting what was patently impossible. But she saw by their faces that he had misjudged his audience. The Earth legends hadn't made it this far, and they—subject to a simple, primitive environment—lacked the sophistication to deal with the truth of his existence.

The powerful wolf body faded back into human flesh, but the animal nature remained; Daetrin was tense, alert, ready to bolt for cover if they reacted in a hostile manner.

"Gods'v Earth . . ." the leader whispered.

"I can take on any form. Any face. I can go where your people can't go, take risks they don't dare assume." She could hear the tension in his voice, and wondered just how many memories were warring for control of his conscious mind, adding centuries of past uncertainty to the tension of this single moment. "All I want is to turn that skill against them. Let me help you," he begged.

"Ye're not human," the leader muttered.

A chill silence filled the cavern. She, who had learned to read him, saw the subtle shift in his expression. The surprise. The pain. She saw him flicker in and out of the present moment, as past centuries gained a new stranglehold on his psyche. She understood the cause of his pain—rejection, frustration, powerlessness—but not its intensity. Clearly, there was something about the nature of that accusation that cut to the heart of him.

She wanted to help, but couldn't. Didn't know how. And besides, he'd wanted to do this alone. That was what he'd told her.

Then, in rapid succession, several things almost happened. The man directly behind Daetrin—a muscular laborer, armed with knife and staff—almost moved to strike him. Daetrin, hearing the motion being, almost turned on his attacker. She, watching it happen, was ready to cut down the men from behind.

But then the moment had passed, and the worst of the tension dissipated. Nevertheless, the leader's voice was cold as he proclaimed, "This's a human matter."

"I assure you," he answered fervently, "I'm as human as you are."

"Our eyes say different, I think." He looked about

at his compatriots; the black masks bobbed in agreement. "It's said was aliens brought th'Tyr t'Earth. Was aliens gave'm language, too, and th'tools they used t'defeat's. I say, this's a human matter. Yes, y'could help. Y'could do good. No one doubts't. This pow'r of yours is . . . incredible." Several masked figures nodded. "But we can't be dealinn with th'unknown, here. We all need t'share th'same motivation . . . a *human* motivation, y'see?"

"You're mistaken," Daetrin protested. "I'm as human as all of you—I'm from Earth . . ." But his heart wasn't in it. He had heard the truth in the leader's voice, as she had. Logic had nothing to do with the rejection. Human motivations were irrelevant. What shone in the masked man's eyes, wet and cold, was *fear of the alien*—and that, no simple words could alter.

"I say t'you, that we wish y'luck. But we can't fight with ye. It's not ours t'do, y'see? Humans for humans is how't must be. Y'r battle isn't th'same's ours. Understann?"

Stiffly, Daetrin nodded. The set of his shoulders revealed his emotional pain to her, and she wished she could break from cover to comfort him. If that was even possible, now; she suspected it wasn't."

'Y'go in peace, yea? This woman'l take y'back th'way y'came, ann y'don't know anything, see?'' Fear was thick in the leader's voice, despite his control; she realized suddenly that Daetrin was safe among these people, not because they weren't willing to kill him to guard their secrecy, but because they weren't sure they could manage it.

You are the unknown. The alien. Their nightmare, come to life.

Evidently he recognized it, too. For he made no protest as they blindfolded him again, nor as they led him back to the riverbank, and into the boat. And the woman murmured no endearments as she rowed her way back to Suyaag, none at all; even in the name of secrecy, even in the shadow of their private fiction, she couldn't bring herself to promise love to an alien.

* * *

"Bastards! Narrow-minded, bigoted bastards!"

Paes' cowered in the corner as the human paced. Broad steps, hard and angry; they made the damp walls shake, and dislodged several vines from a trellis. "Idiots!"

She waited until he had been quiet for a minute or two, then offered, gently, "But you knew it might happen."

"Christ! Yes. I knew." He shook his head. "But not like that! Let them reject me—I knew that might happen—but this?"

"What did you expect?"

He sighed. "I don't know. God, I don't know."

He fell heavily into one of the chairs; its legs creaked beneath him. "That they might attack me? Maybe that."

"You would have preferred it?" Paes' asked, incredulous.

"Of course not. But that didn't mean I wasn't expecting it." He laughed, dryly. "Force of habit, I suppose."

The storm was ending, at last. Kiri moved to shut the door, left open from his entrance. Paes' pried himself away from the wall.

"You'll leave now," he whispered. "You're done."

The human stood. Something in him had changed, in the past few days. He was darker. More determined. Less willing to cater to the whims of their fearful host.

"Where do they meet?" he demanded.

"What do you mean? You were there—"

"That wasn't it. Not enough room. No exits. They'd be trapped there if the Tyr came, and you and I know it. Besides, their lovers' games wouldn't work if used too often; the Tyr would catch on."

"I know nothing—"

"Damn it to hell, don't give me that!" He grabbed Paes' by the collar of his tunic. It was a marvelous display of biochemical excess; in that moment even Kiri forgot that the Marra couldn't be injured. "You know where they meet. Tell me. I'll give it one more try, and then . . . and then leave, okay? I swear it. Just let me talk to them again."

"He's crazy," the Marra shot out at her. "Unbalanced. What do you want with him?"

"Tell me!"

He managed to pull away, falling back against some vines as he did so. "All right. But my door's locked to you after that, remember it. I won't risk my life for your lunacy!"

"Where are they," Daetrin hissed.

"In the Old Places. Under the angdatwa."

"What old places? What are you talking about?"

"The Old Places! The city that stood here, before humans came! Before th'Tyr brought them here! There were natives to start with, some other life-form, that fought until th'Tyr killed them all."

Daetrin's face had gone pale; his eyes were wide. "That great mound. That's—"

"A city, of sorts. They buried it. More like a great house, with winding corridors . . . I've never seen't myself," he said hurriedly, and somehow Kiri knew he was lying. "There are places where it never fully collapsed. Underground, where th'Tyr can't see. They meet there, your precious humans. They'll attack from there, when the time comes."

"My God," he whispered.

"You want to go t'them? You know th'risk? I say you're crazy. But you say, this is th'only way I'll be rid of you. I say then, I'll take you there. To an entrance, and no farther. And then you don't come back. You understand? You agree? You don't come back, *ever.*"

Daetrin shook his head. "A whole city. . . ."

"Oh, it wasn't that. Some primitive buildings, y'know? Nothing on a par with Earth."

He almost said something. He almost moved toward him. Then, with admirable control, he managed to control himself. Managed to control his voice, as he asked Paes', "When do they meet again?"

"I don't know."

"Find out."

Paes' stared at him in frank hostility.

"Iyeg," he muttered. "Iye'kredai."

When he had gone from the room, she said, "Do you want a translation?"

He laughed softly. "Let me guess. He said, *yes, master.* Or its equivalent. In Saudar. With sarcasm. —Am I right?"

"No," she said, turning away. Mourning, for what had happened to one of her people; mourning, for what one of the Marra had become.

"There was no sarcasm," she told him.

* * *

It bothered her, that Daetrin couldn't make the change.

She went over it all in her mind, everything she knew about him, how he thought and what he feared and how his body functioned. But no explanation occurred to her. Either one could control one's mass, or one couldn't; that seemed simple enough. Some limitations made sense. Because the human was massbound, he had to have a living, functioning body at all times; in short, he had to remain alive during the changing. That she could accept. But why a limitation on one particular form—

—or was it that? Could there be something in the hraas' molecular structure—or in Daetrin's—that made the two forms incompatible? She reviewed his changing in her mind. Watched it again, on all the levels that were available to her. There was the DNA shifting, and there—

DNA. Of course.

She tried to create a hraas body for herself, to test

out her hunch, but realized as she did so that it would be worthless. She was much too involved in this problem to be sure of getting it right. She might well wind up with a functioning body that looked like a hraas, and moved like a hraas, but had the DNA coding of an Earth species. No, there was only one way to find out the truth, and that was to go take a look at one of the originals.

If the structure of the DNA molecule differed in the hraas, or the necessary acids were different . . . that would account for the difficulty, wouldn't it? Daetrin could mimic any form that might appear on Earth— any product of Terran evolution, past, present, or potential—but his body didn't contain what was needed to mimic an alien genetic code. No code, no change; it was how his body worked.

If that was all there was to it . . . surely they could work around it!

She wished she could tell him. But he had gone off to the Old Places, telling her that he needed to be alone. She understood. What he needed was to be *human*—among his own kind, without alien appendages. *Kreda* were sometimes like that.

If she could find a way around his special weaknesses, and add to his versatility . . . that would make a wonderful homecoming gift, she thought. And it might well ease their interaction, once she had helped him in this way.

There was only one way to find out.

She took to the air, and headed toward the Tyrran citadel.

* * *

The angdatwa was silent. Unusually so. Under normal circumstances there would be some motion about its outer gates, some business being transacted . . . but not tonight.

Something was wrong.

She landed quietly, behind a thick arm of the building that shielded her from observation. And debated what body to wear. Not hraas; none of those predators would be permitted to prowl outside the building, for fear they would go into the settlement to hunt man. Nor Tyr; the overmind knew all its components by sight and would instantly recognize a stranger. She decided at last on an animal form, a large feline predator, that had the strength and agility which she required while being a plausible visitor in these parts.

No sooner had she slipped into a length of golden fur and begun to prowl toward the main entrance, when a beam of light swept toward her and then stopped, framing her in a circle of betraying brilliance. She growled at it in what she hoped was an appropriate maner and then bolted for cover. The spotlight moved on again, unconcerned; what was one animal to it? But not until it had passed well beyond her did she sneak out of cover again.

Close. Very close.

She slid carefully along the curved stone wall as she approached the entranceway, wary. Not because she could be injured—she couldn't—but because the wrong set of circumstances might cause her to reveal more of her nature than she wanted the Tyr to know. She wasn't vulnerable, but Daetrin was; if the Tyr came to understand that there were shapechangers, he could be in serious danger.

There was a stone plug set in the main entranceway, but as with all Tyrran construction it was rough and unpolished. She checked to see if anyone or anything was watching—nothing was—and then, dissolving her flesh into a mass of suitable viscosity, squeezed through a crack beneath the door and entered the alien citadel.

Once inside, disguise was easy. She made herself a hraas-form and quickly padded down the long entrance corridor, into the heart of the citadel. Her mass-sense told her where rooms were located, and where hidden corridors branched off from her own; but her

312   C.S. Friedman

life-sense told her that all these places were empty, and therefore not worth her examining.

More and more she sensed that something had changed; this was not the pattern of Tyrran life, not as she had observed it before. Not even a Honn was about, sleepless servants of the overmind who transported on foot what any other advanced people would have sent through a pneumatic tube, or its equivalent. Nothing. She scanned room after room, corridor after corridor, and found the same enptiness everywhere.

What in Unity's name was going on?

At last she stopped. This was getting her nowhere. She had come to find a hraas—and still might run across one, traveling randomly so—but suddenly it seemed more important to find out what was happening here, why all these halls were so empty. Sitting back on her haunches, she extended her Marra senses far, far into the bedrock. Below her extended a labyrinth of tangled corridors, with rooms budding off at regular intervals. All of them cold and lifeless. Empty. Farther down yet she reached, her life-sense strained to its maximum capacity; any greater distance would require that she either abandon her mass or move it closer to her objective. Then, just as she was about to withdraw, she saw it. Like a play of shadow and light upon her mind, a scent of spice on the wind. *Life*. She focused in on it. Much, much life, in varying forms. Honn-Tyr and Raayat, hraas and . . . what was that? A Kuol-Tyr, probably; Meyaga's governor. Why would they all be in one place, when they could communicate from a distance? What would they be doing, that required such physical proximity?

She withdrew to her own body, shaken. Because only one thing she could think of would inspire such a gathering. And that was a military mobilization.

No enemy of theirs was on this world. There was no skimship, to take them to another. Their objective had to be here, in the town or beneath it, just beyond its borders or perhaps in one of the Old Places. . . .

Gods of the Unity.

She began to work her way back, quickly. As she turned a corner she nearly ran into a real hraas, but she had no patience to play dominance games with it. She killed it quickly and fed on its essence, pausing only briefly to score its hide with her claws, that its death might seem natural.

They're going after the rebels. Tonight.

Daetrin had gone to meet them. She had no way of knowing whether he was there yet or not, but the odds were good that he was. Or certainly would be, by the time the Tyr raided the Old City. Against that many weapons and that many warriors, he wouldn't stand a chance.

She had to warn him.

She squeezed outside and took on wings, not bothering to check to see if some guard's eyes were upon her. Speed mattered more than anything, now. She could search through the ruins herself and never find him, not with all the life that would be down there— or she could go to Paes'. Paes' knew where he'd gone. Paes' could lead her there.

If he would do it.

* * *

"No."

She had taken on a Saudar body, and now used it for all it was worth. The air was filled with her need, her terrible need, a musk so overpowering that no true Saudar could have resisted it. Even he, despite his detachment, was moved. The power of habit.

"I can't reach him if you don't help me."

"We'll die!"

"Listen to me!" She grabbed at him, used Saudar strength to force him to look at her. "You're living in a dreamworld! No one can kill a Marra—*no one!* Whatever you've come to believe, you have to understand right now that it's all nonsense! You have no body—you don't need a body—your body can die and nothing, *nothing* will happen to you—"

"—let go—"

"You are my only chance of finding him in time. I don't know the entranceways below, I would have to go down through the rock, it would take too long! Tell me where he went."

"—can't be explained—"

"Then show me! Show me, Paes'—or by the Unity I'll betray you to this whole stinking settlement, or blaze you to ashes myself! Do you hear me? Do you understand?"

He pulled back from her—she allowed it—and glared. Good; that meant they were getting somewhere.

"You would," he whispered. Incredulous.

"Without question. I mean to leave you no choice, Marra. Impress that in your damned mass. I have a lot of time and effort invested in my current Identity, and I don't mean to give it up because you can't find the courage to help me!"

She had intended to frighten him, and had clearly succeeded. Which was good. He had to be more afraid of her than he was of the Tyr, or else he wouldn't move. In which case, what? Would she really betray him to the Tyr? Sacrifice her people's anonymity, for vengeance?

Try me.

She pushed him. He went. Wordlessly, which was good, and quickly, which was better. As she passed through the door, she reclaimed her human form. It was well past midnight and thus they were unlikely to encounter any natives, which was good. Because she wasn't going to stop for anything.

"Fly," she commanded, when they reached open ground. And he flew.

The entranceway that he knew of was hidden beneath the ruins of an old building, that had probably once been a general store. While it stood, it had guarded its secret well; now that it was no more than a pile of rotting debris, it guarded it even better. Kiri and Paes' pushed aside crumbling logs and climbed

over piles of shattered crockery, until at last he pointed
to a hole in the ground before them. Narrow, dark,
half-covered with brush, it seemed an unlikely access.
And therefore, it was probably correct.

"Lead me," she commanded.

He squeezed himself into the narrow space and
dropped down beneath it; she followed. Human hands
had dug a tunnel beneath the outermost buildings, giving the Suyaag rebels access to what remained of the
Old Ones' city, beneath the angdatwa's mound. What
better place to hide from the Tyr, than directly beneath
their feet?

The tunnels were low, far better suited to a four-
footed form than their human flesh. They changed accordingly. Paws slapping mud, she followed him
through the twisting, labyrinthine tunnel, nipping at
his heels when fear slowed his progress.

She could lose the human, that quickly. Lose all
those memories which she had invested in him, which
might slip away from her before she could find a replacement. Lose all the things that he had taught her,
all the little joys and confusions that had made their
companionship such a boon to her. And if she did so,
she would have failed in her Identity, for the prime
directive of a healer—or a Nurturer—was the survival
of her charge.

"Faster," she growled. He probably didn't understand the meaning of her sounds, which was just
as well; it was really herself she was talking to. *Faster* . . .

Then the tunnel of dirt gave way to ancient ruins,
and it nearly stopped her in her tracks. Stone archways
of nonhuman proportion gave access to houses so alien
in structure that she could have spent months analyzing their form, trying to determine their purpose. But
now each building was an obstacle, no more, and
where the caved-in ceilings had collapsed upon the
floors below, making passage almost impossible, she
cursed them as she cursed every other cause of delay,
mindless of their archeological value.

Paes' stopped, suddenly; she nearly ran into him. His ears pricked forward, bade her listen. She did. Above the noise of settling rock behind them, and the drip of surface water as it seeped down into this place, she heard voices. Human voices.

Praise Unity!

He took on human flesh again, and regarded her as she did the same. Adjusting vision upscale, of course; it was impossible to see without body heat for a guide, in the total cave-darkness of the Old Places.

"What will you do?" he whispered, but she had no answer for him. Scrambling over the ruins, she headed toward the voices. Soon a faint light was visible, the glow of a single lamp. Rubble had been cleared from underfoot here, making passage easier. She suspected the regular entrance was equally clear, easier to traverse than the disused path they had taken.

Suddenly she was grabbed from behind, by a brawny arm that locked across her neck and squeezed tight, cutting off her air. By the sounds behind her she guessed that Paes' had also been taken, by whatever guards the rebels had left in this place. She had no time to play with hers, but simply weakened him directly until his grip loosened and she could push him away. *No time for games. Not now.*

The rebels had heard them, apparently, for footsteps were hurrying in their direction. She stayed where she was and stood out in the open, inviting their inspection. A squad of six men quickly surrounded her, muscular humans with dirt smeared so as to mask their faces. Daetrin—under guard—followed.

"The Tyr is mobilizing." She spoke in a breathless whisper, appropriate for one who had been running so long. Or so she hoped. She must appear human, and win their trust. "It means to strike tonight, and soon. I came to warn you. . . ."

"Who th'hell s'she?" a man demanded, as Paes' was thrown at her feet. "Not t'mention this'un!"

"Trust them," Daetrin urged. "They've come to help you."

"Hell I will! I don't e'en trust you." He grabbed Daetrin by the arm and thrust him forward, so that the three of them were together. The dark look in her *kreda's* eyes told her things had not been going well, even before she came. "How's she know't, anyway?"

"Does't matter?" one man whispered angrily. "If there's even a chance—"

"Or she's t'drive us out on schedule, that might be't too. What's your stake in't, sweet?"

In answer she clung close to Daetrin, and let them draw their own conclusions. He was shivering, but not from cold; he alone seemed to understand the risk they ran, being trapped in this place.

"If she's right—" someone began.

"Shut it! I don't like any'v this."

"But if we get cut off—"

The leader glared. His follower was silenced. "Now, then," he said, turning to the three of them. "Explain y'rselves."

Which was all they had time to say.

She had the impression of three distinct explosions; but it might have been more, or possibly less. One was right behind the men, so close behind that a half-dozen of their number were buried beneath rubble. It seemed there was another, in the same direction but farther back; she wondered how many had been left behind when these men came to investigate, and how many of those had died. And another exposion shivered the rock walls far from where they stood, off to her right; by the panicked look in the leader's eyes she judged that to be their regular exit, which had now been closed to them.

"Tyr'n traitors!" he swore, and raised a weapon toward them.

It was Daetrin who moved first—which was appropriate, as he was the only vulnerable one among them. With one smooth motion he launched a shard of stone at the leader—it hit squarely in the jaw, knocking him back—and then bolted in the only direction open to them, the way Kiri and Paes' had come. A shot careened off the rock overhead, but after that the rebels had more to worry about than a few escaping prisoners; behind him Kiri could hear the Tyr approaching, and the rank smell of their presence followed them through the ruins, and beyond.

"I smelled it," Daetrin gasped as they ran. "Thought it was timefugue. Hell of a time not to trust my senses!"

An explosion close behind them shook the ground beneath them, and bricks the size of boulders broke from the ceiling and fell on all sides. Daetrin barely dodged one in time. Leaning against the nearest wall, he sniffed the dusty air. "Not close enough to have thrown that," he assessed. "They must have mined the place sometime earlier." Then, "Shit!" Because the last explosion had built a wall of rubble between them and the scene of battle, which made them considerably safer but also cut off the last bit of light.

"You can't see in the dark?"

"I can't see in the dark."

"Adopt some form—"

"No earth-form can. Some light is required, no matter how little . . . damn!"

"Sonar," she suggested.

Silence.

"Only if there's no alternative," he whispered. His voice was strained.

"Problem?"

"Nothing you'd respect. A distasteful option—the power of cliché. But if there's no alternative—"

There was, and she did it. They weren't strictly appropriate to her form, the luminous hairs she had added, but they served well enough. His shapechanging eyes adapted quickly.

"Ready?"

He nodded.

Paes' was a wreck, dust-covered and scratched. She wondered that he didn't close up his wounds while they fled, to prevent loss of mass through bleeding. Did it have something to do with his belief in death?

Did he believe that even such wounds as these were beyond his power to cure? A frightening thought.

"Kiri." It was Daetrin.

She was in the lead, and half-turned to meet his eyes. "What?"

"If those were preset mines, there'll be more of them. Maybe even here. Watch out—"

But Paes' had stepped ahead of her, anxious to be moving. "This tunnel's been abandoned for years," he whispered. "I don't think the Tyr even knows—"

Explosion. A blast of smoke and gravel—and flesh—that spouted out from the rock wall and showered them with sharp, hot pellets. Kiri knew in the first instant of the blast that she was too close to its source to save her body; she settled for keeping the pieces within easy reach, so that she could put it back together. Daetrin was farther back, and had found partial shelter behind a segment of wall; his left leg was lacerated, but the rest of him looked whole. As for Paes'—

She found his body—that is, the largest available piece of it—some twenty feet from the source of the blast. Still alive. The torso was bathed in blood and one side of his head had been split open; what limbs remained were a tangled mess, shattered bone overlaid with strips of raw flesh, neither their number nor their form giving any hint that once they had belonged to a human body.

Not breathing . . . but that was because he had forgotten to breathe. His eyes were open, and the one that wasn't filmed in blood met her gaze with horror.

"I would never . . ." he gasped.

And then his head lolled to one side, and his mouth fell slowly open. His essence throbbed beneath her fingertips, warm and vital. *Enough is enough,* she thought. *Put it back together and let's get going.*

And then he was gone. Just that. One moment he was Paes', and the next minute he simply wasn't there. One moment she held the chosen body of a Marra, and the next, all that she held was flesh. Ruptured cells. Blood leaking out on all sides. Dead flesh, and no more.

"Kiri?"

She reached inside him. Deep, deep inside, where a kernel of self might nest. But there was nothing. She had felt him expire, felt the substance of his being gather together and then dissolve . . . but that was impossible. Wasn't it? He had been Marra.

"Kiri?"

She was dimly aware that he was by her side, hands on her shoulders. Afraid.

"He's dead," she said softly. Frightened herself, in a way she had never been before.

"He took quite a blow. But don't you—"

Then he understood, and was silent.

Paes'. Gone. The Tyr had done this, made him vulnerable in a way her people had never been before. They had made him capable of dying, and then killed him. And they would do the same to her, if she dealt with them long enough. What was she doing in this crazy world, anyway? In this crazy body? Unity, if she just let go of her mass now, just let all of this fade from her consciousness, she could wait out in n-space until all this craziness had passed. Come back sometime in the future—maybe a thousand Earth-years, maybe a million or two, it wasn't something she'd be able to control—and someone else would have dealt with the Tyr, someone else would have driven them away or killed them or something.

"Kiri . . ."

or maybe all the Marra would be dead, that was possible too, maybe they all could die and then n-space would be empty, empty except for her . . .

"Kiri!"

She let herself feel that he was closing his arms about her, making a protective gesture suitable to his species. She made her body shake, to communicate her fear. A real human being would be going into shock, by now; she mimicked the state with innate skill, from the cold, dull skin to the onset of hyperventilation. She felt cold tears running down into her hair, from where his face pressed against it. Tears. For her. His grip on her was tight and she felt him trembling. For her. She had received love before, from primitive animals, but they knew nothing of her nature. To have a full-sentient feel so strongly . . . that was new to her.

"He's dead," she whispered. Trying to believe it. Trying to understand. In distant caverns the battle still raged, and the thunder of explosions shook the floor beneath them with alarming regularity. They'd be lucky if the whole mound didn't collapse on their heads . . . but for now, in this place, they were safe. The wall behind them had collapsed, filling the hallway with rubble. No one could reach them.

In the dark, in his arms, in the warmth of the dust-filled cavern, she contemplated the specter of mortality, and waited for the fighting to cease.

* * *

The smell from the skimship's exhaust was strong in the high-walled compound. The hraas seemed especially irritated by it, and avoided the area downwind of the small craft. Which was very convenient for them.

"Give me your hand," she whispered.

They lay behind a glassy ridge, on native rock seared into something unrecognizable by the Tyrran jets that had scoured this place. In the distance, Honn-Tyr were loading local products into the storage bay of the small ship, while others unloaded equipment and supplies right beside them. Somehow, the two groups never ran into each other. In the distance, by the door, a Raayat fidgeted nervously; even the hraas seemed to be avoiding him.

Daetrin moved his hand to where she could grasp it. She closed her fingers about his, encircling his flesh with her own.

"Trust me," she whispered—and as she looked into

his eyes she knew with a start that he did trust her, that he would always trust her, that some vital wall had come down inside him and he was incapable of not trusting her ever again.

Carefully, delicately, she took hold of some of the cells in his hand and insinuated herself into their structure. Took up residence within them, in the same way that she inhabited her own flesh. Making that small group of cells in his hand as much her property as his. Now it was possible to work with them directly, to unwind the fragile strands of human DNA and knit them into a new configuration. A hraas configuration. When she was done, she held them in stasis, not sure what the result would be. Not sure if his human body could support their life processes, under any circumstances.

She looked up at him again. The look on his face was one of alarm, with an undercurrent of pain; she was afraid to ask what he was feeling.

"All right," he whispered.

She released his hand, and felt the cells break out of stasis and start to function again. Now he had, within his own body, a sample of the coding he needed. Whether that would make a difference or not remained to be seen, but after long hours of observing the hraas—and him—she suspected that it would.

"Once we're on the longship, and have found a place to hide, I can help put you in a partial stasis—"

He touched her cheek gently with the hand that was oh-so-changed; he seemed to have control over its movement, at least. "I can do that myself, thanks. Comes with the territory." *If you'll wake me up,* his expression said, but there was no question in either of their minds that of course she would.

Once he was safely ensconced for the journey, she could concentrate on contacting Kost. His network of Marra contacts was something she needed desperately . . . a shame that she had to deal with him to get to it, but that was the way it stood. He alone knew how to contact the rest of their people.

When the other Marra heard what had happened on Meyaga—when they understood that loss of memory could cause them to suffer and die like the embodied— she was sure they would act. Somehow. Maybe in concert with the humans, maybe alone, but at any rate they had to do *something*. More than their culture was at stake, this time.

"Ready," he whispered, and she watched him change.

This time it went well. She knew just how well because he growled at her, as soon as the change was complete, and barely managed to refrain from going for her throat. Clearly, hatred of all other species was hard-wired into the hraas brain. She changed her own form quickly, watching him. His hostility evaporated, into something more like disgust; with a quick, agile motion he was gone from her side, loping toward the skimship with a graceful, steady stride. Which was appropriate action, for such a solitary species. The change had gone well.

Following behind him—but not too closely, lest the Tyr notice—she made her way toward the skimship ramp, to begin the first leg of their journey.

Whatever we may find there, she thought, *at least there is this: the Domes will be different.*

YUANG:
DOME FIVE

Everything would have been all right if the Raayat had just stayed quiet. Wouldn't it? Watched and stayed quiet, like it had done for the first week or so.

Well, maybe not all right (Yaan admitted sullenly). But certainly *better*.

He could no longer remember exactly when the Raayat first spoke. It was in his lab, he knew that. With Sung. They had almost become accustomed to its presence, were learning to ignore it, when suddenly the granite figure stirred to life and asked a question— some infantile, ridiculous question, he no longer remembered what it was—and the world altered ever so subtly, forever. That question! In one moment the Raayat ceased to be what it had been thus far, merely an observer, and became an integral if irritating part of their research process.

Now, everything must be explained. And explained as one explained things to a child, who had no formal education to support his comprehension. Sometimes the Raayat-Tyr would be quick to pounce upon a point, and devour it, as if its entire being was starved for information, and the humans had provided a feast. At such times Yaan was embarrassed at how simple they had made their explanation, for clearly the Raayat had an adult's understanding of how things worked. But at other times—and they came without warning, these moments of insufficiency, and followed no pattern that the humans could predict—the Raayat would be totally lost, and they would have to explain in simple words of limited meaning exactly what they meant. Explain it two and three times, and sometimes even more, while all the while their work was just left to sit, waiting until this last bit of blackmail had run its course and they could go back to what they'd been doing.

Yaan had promised himself that he would ignore the Raayat's presence. That had proven impossible, for more than one reason. In the beginning it was simply a question of constant observation, of those four bone-ringed eyes following his every movement about the lab, until his head was ringing with a need for privacy. Until the Raayat at last looked elsewhere, or decided to grace a different lab with its presence. But now? Now (he admitted grudgingly) he was intrigued. Now he found himself making empty gestures over his equipment, while his mind toyed with explanations for the Raayat's strange psyche. Now he no longer spent his meal breaks cursing the Raayat, but discussing its many strangenesses with his colleagues. Now he lay awake at night puzzling over what physiological truths might lie behind the Tyr's mental unity, and how they might be altered.

Now, when the Raayat greeted his answers with that disconcerting gaze, half confusion and half hostility, he wanted to scream at it, *What don't you understand? What? Why did it make sense to you yesterday, and today nothing makes sense to you at all?* But he knew that if he did, the Raayat would only stare at him in injured, angry silence, like a three-year-old who dared to ask *Daddy, why does the sky burn?* and was answered with *What? You should know that already!*

And he wasn't the only one. Tia had stated flat out that she wished she could try some word association exercises with the Raayat—the same words when it was "in its mood" and when it was normal. Asako was already visiting Yaan's lab at regular intervals, taking notes on what she called its "knowledge acquisition strategy." Tiro, who was doing a kinesthetic analysis of the beast, was quick to point out that changes in body language always accompanied changes in intellectual acuity.

Which got them nowhere, collectively. They were scientists enough to recognize a challenge when they saw it, and human enough to become fixated upon it. But they were also fearful enough that whatever courage it might take to openly approach the Raayat on the matter, they clearly lacked. How would the Tyr react to knowing that the humans were trying to analyze its weaknesses? Would it ever believe that a thirst for knowledge, and not military intent, was at the heart of their endeavors?

And was it, for that matter?

More than once he dreamed of the Tekk woman. She was due back now, any day, and he couldn't stop himself from dreaming the confrontation. She always asked him a question—one question—and he always gave her his answer. The questions were different, each dream, but his answer was always the same.

Daily I stand face to face with the information you want, he told her. *But how do we learn to interpret it?*

* * *

The alarm went off while he was asleep. He slept so rarely these days, and was plagued with so many nightmares when he did, that it took him a minute to place the sound—and then a good minute more to acknowledge that he was awake, that he knew what the siren signified, and that he had damned well better get moving. *Fast.*

One of the Domes had broken open.

He grabbed a robe and bolted from the sleeping cubicle. He dimly remembered that he should have done something safety oriented before opening the cubicle door, but couldn't remember what it was. Damn, what *were* those alarm codes? They had been drilled into him time and time again, on the longship that took him from Earth and the skimship that brought him to Yuang, and then in the Domes when he first arrived. Drilled into him so many times that he would have thought he could identify them in his sleep, and re-

spond in an appropriate manner without need for conscious thought. But that was when, fifteen years ago?
Twenty? He had never heard them since, although they
figured in his nightmares. Was it Dome Five's own
atmosphere that had been replaced by alien gases?
Outside his door or merely outside his dormitory? Was
the Tyr within range to help, or would the humans be
left to fend for themselves?

The corridor's air was still Earth-normal, which was
heartening. Maybe it wasn't Five after all that had suffered the damage. Most of the alarm codes were meant
to mobilize neighboring domes in the event of disaster; maybe that was all it was, a call for aid. He was
beginning to calm down, and remember things.

There should be a Honn at the dormitory's gateway,
to organize them. That was clearly the place to go. He
passed through the fire doors—now propped open—and
reached the cargo platform just as it was beginning to
drop toward the main floor. A dozen co-workers tried
to make room for him as he jumped down to join them,
but the crowding made it difficult.

"What is it?" he asked them, but no, nobody knew.

At the main gate was a Honn. It looked calm enough
(but when would one of those damned things look any
different?) and was clearly waiting for them all to as-
semble. A ragtag assortment of anxious humans, in
various stages of undress, was quickly assembling before it. While Yaan tightened his robe, he comforted
himself with the thought that surely they wouldn't have
been made to stand here like this, if the damage was
in their section. Would they?

*Unless Frederick betrayed us. Unless we're all meant
to die.*

Finally, the alarm died out. For one brief instant
Yaan imagined he could see the webwork of mental
contact that had caused that to happen, Honn linked
to Honn linked to Honn, and the whole of that webwork linked to all other Tyr, in all other domes. All
agreeing, in that instant, that the alarm had served its
purpose. Did that unity include Frederick? For the first

time Yaan wondered. Could any creature display such total ignorance of wordly affairs, when linked to an omniscient overmind?

Apparently the Tyr-whole was not content with their mobilization, for the Honn before them—and doubtless all the others—proceeded to explain the catastrophe that beset them.

Dome Eight. That was all Yaan absorbed, at first. Dome *Eight*. Not Five. Not his Dome. He felt like a drowning man, suddenly plucked from the water. Not his time, yet. He tried to absorb other details, found himself shaking as he did so. An explosion in lab 8-4A. A break in two dome seals. Partial pollution of the dome's western atmosphere before the seals were repaired, combined with the immediate results of the explosion . . . there were many fatalities. Many injuries. Many survivors to be rescued, although what their state of mind would be after partial exposure to the Yuang atmosphere was anyone's guess. And since one of the emergency outlets from Eight West led to here, the Tyr was asking them to mobilize. . . .

Once they understood, they were quick to move. Chemical filters were handed out, one for each to wear and several extra for each to carry. When reduced to a mere fraction of its normal concentration, the native atmosphere could thus be rendered uninjurious; in any greater concentration it was so deadly that no simple armor, for the lungs or for the body, could save them from its corrosive effects.

They took what vehicles they could; there weren't nearly enough for all of them, so the real doctors—the ones who knew how to work with live bodies, and how to keep them going—took the wheeled transport. The rest of them walked as quickly as they could, breaking into a jog at irregular intervals. Yaan was on a transport, a result of some five years' medical service on Earth, before he'd found his specialty. Sung was with him, and Ria and Asako. The rest of his crew were walking and the transport was filled with unknowns, laboratory technicians from some other division. The filters muffled their speech, making introduction next to impossible. Which was just as well. They were hardly in a mood for talking.

It might have been Five. It might have been them.

In the tunnel, overhead, the Yuang atmosphere was clearly visible. Light pulsed wildly about them as cloud after cloud ignited in flames, then extinguished; a storm just beginning. The thought of that substance contaminating his air supply was chilling enough, but even colder was his knowledge that it could do so without his being consciously aware of it. Could you smell the stuff, in that small a concentration? He seemed to remember that it wasn't possible. Either it burned out your lungs on the first breath, or was dilute enough to adopt a more insidious campaign; in either case, you never smelled it coming. A threshold poison, Sung had called it; a picturesque description.

He wondered what it was like, to have that deadly miasma suddenly leaking through the Dome, to have that corrosive fog filling the streets. . . .

"There!" Asako cried out and pointed. They had come a good three-quarters of the way to Eight's outer seal, and were the first rescue team to make contact. The transport quickly pulled over, making room for those due to follow. As they had drilled, a dozen times over. Yaan stepped down, and entered into nightmare. Of blood—radiation burns—open wounds that had made contact with Yuang's air and would have to be amputated—fit limbs that flailed with lunatic abandon as the more subtle poisons dissolved nerve cells and brain tissue before his eyes. (*And how much of that stuff is still in the tunnels?* he wondered. *How much will seep through the filters?*) They managed to pull the wounded far enough to one side of the tunnel so that the other transports could speed past them, and get chemical filters on the victims so that no further poison could reach them. They bandaged limbs, in a dimly lit nightmare sequence that reminded Yaan of the films he had once seen, of human medics who served during the Conquest. Hopeless, pointless aid.

The majority of these people would die. Of those who survived, a good number would succumb in mind if not in body; the Yuang air guaranteed that. Maybe one or two would live, at the most, out of the dozens that his crew were trying to save. But for those one or two, they had to keep fighting.

At last all the injuries were bound, all the precious lungs protected. No bones broken in this group, at least; that would make traveling easier on all of them. The more severely wounded who had managed to escape would still be far down the tunnel, no doubt writhing their broken limbs while in the grips of some hallucinatory nightmare. Yuang's air was a cruel victor. The whole of Dome Eight would have to be resupplied—gods of Earth, what a task! He wondered if they had gotten the internal seals up in time. Of if the whole Dome was gone.

Hear that, Tekk warrior? There goes our potential for nuclear power!

He settled himself into a corner of the transport, beside a man that Ria had bandaged. She was working on him now, and as the transport started to move—with a jerk that left Yaan's stomach behind—he imagined that he saw something in her eyes besides medical interest. Only a flicker . . . but why not? The man was attractive—a mixture of black and Oriental that combined the best features of both, dusky skin and almond eyes and a fine, strong body—exotic to say the least. If she could distract him from his recent loss effectively enough to start something between them, more power to her. She was attractive enough herself—although not of a type Yaan personally cared for—and had blatantly displayed a passionate nature, when last she had a lover. If Dome Eight was damaged badly enough, some of its inhabitants would have to be settled elsewhere; this man could wind up in Five for quite some time.

As she hopes, he thought, seeing the look in her eyes. He tried to read the man as well, but couldn't. Maybe it was the pain, or the confusion, or Yaan's own exhaustion, which made him unreadable. Or the Yuang gases. For it seemed for a moment that the man's face was alien, not human at all, and its expression had no analog in human experience.

Just for a moment. That was all. A fleeting, probably harmless illusion.

He doubted that Ria noticed.

* * *

In the morning, the real work started. Tissue samples from Eight began pouring in, routed through the Domes that had done salvage work. As always it was the Fivers who were most efficient, appending notes to each sample that explained exactly who and what the victims were, and detailing the exact symptoms of their decline. Usually madness. And for once, Yaan's groups might have enough material to figure out how the Yuang air worked, once it began to poison a human brain.

They spent the first shift sorting the samples, according to symptoms. Making calls to other labs, juxtaposing their data against a complete autopsy scenario. It was a busy day, and Yaan was glad for it. Bodily exhaustion was a small price to pay for getting his mind back down to earth again. He didn't even notice when the Raayat arrived, so intent was he upon the chemical puzzle that chance had laid before him. Which of Yuang's many gases was the culprit, here? What was the threshold limit for corrosion of brain tissue? Was an antidote possible—or even better, some manner of preventative treatment?

Suddenly he imagined insects (*bugs under glass!*) desperately trying to unravel the secrets of pesticide before being sprayed. The image made his stomach lurch.

"What is this?"

Coming as it did on the heels of such an image, the Raayat's rasping voice was triply unwelcome. Add to that a tone of voice that indicated Frederick was in one of its stupid phases, and Yaan came as close as he ever had to bodily throwing the Raayat out.

"We're working." he snapped. "Or trying to, anyway."

"Explain."

"I can't work and explain. —No! I simply can't. There's too much to do. These are parts of the brain that decay so quickly—*no,*" he said forcefully, cutting short the explanation. "I won't get trapped into it. We have too much to do."

"Real work," the Raayat observed.

Yaan looked up at it, shaken. *Easy to forget the hold it has over us. The power of life and death, over us all.*

"Real work," he answered quietly.

"You will explain."

No other choice.

So he tried. Gods of Terra, he tried. Tried to prepare his tissue samples while he talked, and then eventually put them down and merely talked, because his hands were shaking so badly he couldn't work. Tireza came over to spell him—with the samples or the Raayat, he wasn't sure which—but he waved her away. Let her stick to her own work. He had just received a forceful reminder that one word from the Raayat could have them all executed; no reason for her to share that revelation.

Gods of Terra, how long? How long before we crack, or make a mistake, or it just plain gets tired of us?

"And this," the Raayat was saying, "is like the Tyr brain?"

"How the hell should I know?" he asked irritably. "Do you think we've ever had a Tyrran body to study? Do you recall our getting anatomical charts for your species, that I could refer to? How the hell am I supposed to know how you function, much less compare it to a human brain!"

The Raayat stepped back, its upper eyes hooded. Yaan had the sinking sensation that he had gone too far.

"You cannot answer," it accused.

"No—it isn't—Terra, let me explain—"

"You do not have answers."

"It's a question of data. Frederick. Listen to me. It's not that I don't—"

But the Raayat turned away, and Yaan sensed with dread clarity that he had been tuned out. ". . . want to answer," he finished weakly, but the Raayat wasn't listening. It was walking, instead—and when it came to the doors it passed through them, without a word. And was gone.

"Frederick!"

"Jesus," Sung muttered.

Tireza shook her head. "It had to happen. Only a question of time."

"Do you think it's—"

"No," Yaan said firmly. "We don't think. We don't try to second-guess it. We've tried that before, and you know as well as I do, it just doesn't work. The damned thing's unstable on its better days, and worse than that the rest. . . ."

"It spared us once," Tirez said. "Maybe it will this time, too."

"It needed us then," Sung countered.

"Maybe it still does."

Maybe. The word hung in the air between them, a double-edged sword.

"If only we knew . . ." Yaan muttered.

"What it wants?"

He looked up at her. At Sung. Wondering whose face was palest, in the artificial light. Who looked most shaken.

"How it works," he said quietly.

Because then, my friends, all the rest would follow.

TIMEFUGUE

My sister leads me into the house. The tiled halls are silent and dark, and strangely discomforting. This isn't the house that I grew up in, filled with warmth and lamplight and the sounds of happily quarreling children, but rather the home of a stranger. Even the crickets seem quieter than usual, as if they, too, sense the wrongness. I start to talk, to question Yolanda—*what's wrong, what's happening?*—but she tells me only that father wants to see us, and will say nothing more.

He is waiting, in one of the smaller rooms. A single lamp—Palestinian, with a history as rich as his own—offers minimal light, but enough for our eyes. It edges the gilt carvings of his couch with fire, and picks up highlights along the edges of his features. A strong man with strong features, but now the whole of him is softened, somehow. Weakened. He takes us each by one hand, silently, and draws us onto the couch beside him. From this vantage point I can see the mural of my mother, a work he commissioned years ago. Her delicate limbs stretched forth in supplication to the gods, hair pouring down over her shoulders like molten gold, she seems more ghost than woman. The way I imagine an angel would look, when I hear the Christians speak of their heaven.

"Alexander. Yolanda." My father's voice is strained, as if speaking comes hard to him. "I have something very difficult to tell you—"

"Where's mother?" I interrupt, suddenly afraid.

My parents are always together, when they tell us things like this. My father picking the right words with care, explaining the ways of the world to us, and she, like a Roman goddess, guarding us with the mere fact of her presence. Where is she now?

His dark eyes, fixed on mine, hold them steady. "Your mother is gone," he says softly.

Gone? how can she be gone? I try to come to terms with what he's telling me, can only think of what the Christ's people would mean, if they said such a thing. "Dead?"

"No. Dear God! No. Simply . . . left us."

Simply. Is there any concept more terrible, more hopelessly complex? My young mind has no way to understand this, and as I glance at my sister, and see the tears in her eyes, I know that she feels the same. The rules by which we have always lived have suddenly changed, and this time there is no mother to help us deal with it.

"Not coming back?"

He shook his head slowly, sadly. "I don't think so."

"You don't *know*? She didn't tell you?"

I can see memory veil his eyes, briefly. "She told me," he said at last. "Not in words, as such . . . but I think she told me. I just wasn't listening." His arm about me tightens. "I thought she would stay until you were both grown. It's what I would have done, in her place. And it was easier to believe that than it was to listen to what she was trying to tell me."

"But why?" Yolanda demands. "Why did she go?"

My father sighs, a sound that I know all too well. It accompanies what he calls the Hard Truths—the things that he most hates to explain to us, and most needs to. Like, how the Hebrews wrote in their holy book that we were banned from worship. How the soldiers of the Christ burned the

Library, and what it will mean to us that they did. How the world is changing, and like it or not we must change with it.

But now his voice is gentle, filled not with warning so much as with sorrow. "Marriage isn't the same thing for us that it is for the daybound, Yolanda. We come together when we choose, take whatever vows the current culture imposes on us, and love in our own way. But when you have as many years as we do, you understand that things don't stay the same forever. Man changes, woman changes, and one day they don't want the same things that they did, so many years ago. Accepting that—and the loss it entails—goes hand in hand with accepting what we are."

"So she stopped loving us?" I whisper.

He squeezes me hard against him, until the growing wetness on my face is absorbed into the soft wool of his dalmatica. "She still loves you," he assures me. "She will always love you. But it wasn't right for her to live here, any more. She was a priestess, you know, back when this part of the world had such things. An oracle, when such were revered. To be degraded in the way that women are here, after having received the worship of thousands. . . ."

"Then why did she come here?" I demand. "Why did she stay at all, if she didn't like it here?"

He stares at the mural opposite us, and for a short while says nothing. Then, at last, his deep voice trembling, he begins to speak. Softly. "She came after the Library was burned. To see if they had really done this thing, which foreign rumor had hinted at. They had, of course. Their values are different than ours." His grip on both of us tightens, and I can hear the pain of the memories that possess him as he speaks. "I myself was . . . berserk. With anger. Beyond control. I killed. Not in this city, where I still had to live, but any place within a night's flight of here. I took them in their beds, or as they sat by their windows, or as they dared to walk abroad in the night. Christians every one of them, I made sure of it. Damn them all to their own miserable hell! Those that saw me as I struck wielded crosses and other symbols, and cried out prayers to their intolerant god—and I struck them down with that prayer still on their lips, drinking in their blood as though somehow it could slake the terrible hate within me. Or the fear, my children. I was very afraid. Because all about me I saw the old ways dying, and a new order taking shape. And it frightened me, more than anything ever had before, that I had no way to stop it from happening. That was what the Fire had taught me: my own helplessness, and the true vulnerability of our people.

"I met her then. She was trying to internalize what she had seen; I was desperate to forget it. She soothed me into wolven form, and gently coerced me into my first animal kill since the rage had claimed me. Slowly, I was weaned from murdering humans. That was her strength, knowing how to manipulate the souls of men. I came to love her for it. And she stayed with me, for reasons I only half understood. No daybound woman has ever been such a mystery to me as she was, you must know that. She bore you by choice, and nursed you in the way of our kind, on her own blood. Loved you, as dearly as I loved you. But that could never change the fact that she didn't belong here; this simply wasn't her world. Sooner or later, I realize now, it was inevitable that she leave. . . ."

"Then we should have gone with her!" Yolanda exclaims. "Why didn't she let us? We could have gone with her, couldn't we?"

Even I can see that he is choosing his words very carefully. "I think that your mother is searching for something. I believe that it doesn't exist

any more. But she's going to have to find that out
for herself. That's the kind of thing a person
needs to be alone to do. We have to learn to let
things go, Yolanda—things, and people. The
shortlived can pretend that nothing ever changes.
We, who have to face the centuries, know that
nothing ever lasts. She'll always love you, both
of you." He squeezes us, and I feel a new tear
course down my cheek. "It just wasn't right for
her to be here any more."

My sister's voice is an almost indiscernible
whisper, hoarse with tears. "She's never coming
back?"

My father lifts his head, stares at the mural on
the far wall. My mother's arms are spread wide,
in supplication. A man clad in fur and leather,
with the tight, short sleeves and red hair of a bar-
barian, kneels at her feet. His hands are raised
up in offering, and blood spills out from the crimson pool within his cupped palms.

I can feel him hesitate, torn between the lie that
would comfort us, and the truth that is part of our
heritage.

"No," he says gently, at last. "I don't think so."

YUANG:
DOME PRIME

They are fools! Ntaya thought, as she ran the new bio-chip through its final tests. *All of them—fools!*

How maddening it was, to have the fate of humanity in their hands. Sad little scientists, huddled in their turtle shells of plexiglass and solar foil, too timid to even *dream* of freedom—

A scream rent the air about her, so suddenly and with such violence that she nearly dropped the beaker in her hand. A terrible scream—tortured, unhuman—that ripped through the narrow corridors of the ang-datwa and set the glass tubes about her trembling as though an earthquake had begun.

Only years of discipline kept her from throwing down the chip as she left. The scream was followed by another, and then a third . . . but she put the precious bit where she knew it would be safe, and only then ran to the door of the workroom.

Snarls and hisses, set against a wailing that made her scalp tighten in dread. Not human, surely. She guessed at the direction of the source and ran, long stride consuming hallway after hallway, until she had to hold her ears to block out the pain of that anguished shrieking.

She skidded to a stop as the narrow corridor turned suddenly, and ploughed shoulder-first into another Tekk. A local. His eyes were wide and fearful, and as he pointed to the open place where four corridors crossed, she could see that his hand was shaking.

In that natural arena a fight to the death was taking place. On one side stood a hraas, its angular markings

livid against the black of its permanent stripes. Bright
red and orange, fading to gold over the haunches:
combat colors, a sexual display. There was blood on
one shoulder and across its face, and as it shook its
head wildly to clear its eyes, the deep purple fluid
splashed across the feet of some dozen Tekk onlook-
ers. Standing opposite it was a Raayat. The creature
had been slashed wide open in at least a dozen places,
and severed across the right lower arm so that one
hand hung useless, bound to it only by a single tendon
and a few shreds of skin. It was the Raayat who had
screamed—was screaming—a shrill, terrible sound that
made Ntaya's flesh want to crawl from her body and
sink into the stone itself.

They were circling each other, limping from blood
loss, hissing—or howling—their hostility. Neither
seemed to care that their confrontation was patently
impossible. That the hraas simply did not attack the
Tyr. *Ever.* That the Tyr, being unified, didn't indulge
in displays of vocal gymnastics; the Raayat could call
for help, or communicate need, or pain, or even detailed instructions, without ever using its voice. Why
would it even know how to scream, much less do so.

The hraas leapt. A fluid stream of amber lightening,
aimed at the Raayat's midsection. The Unstable One
brought down an upper arm, twisting it so that an armored spike would greet its opponent in midair. But
the spike had been snapped off short some time ago,
and the hrass thrust the stump aside and slammed into
the Raayat, knife-edged teeth seeking flesh. From behind the beast's shoulders talons arose, the last reminders that once, in the distance past, its ancestors had
flown. Thick ropes of corded muscle swung the fighting claws forward; Ntaya thought she could see the
echo of flight in the grace of their motion. Then they
struck, and were nothing but an extra set of claws,
razor-sharp.

The Raayat twisted, bringing up a knee into the
beast's abdomen. The knee was well armored and
beweaponed, with a bristling array of spikes and hooks

that were capable of shredding such an opponent, but luck was simply against it. The long spikes couldn't be angled properly in such close confines; the hooks, by chance, all curved in the wrong direction. Useless. Ntaya watched as the hrass ripped off whole segments of the Raayat's armor, thinking: *That was lucky, that the beast came in at just such an angle. Anything else, and it would have been impaled.*

Then she corrected herself: *Maybe not lucky at all.* What sort of calculations must the hraas have been capable of, to render the warrior-Tyr so helpless with a single blow? *More intelligence than we've given them credit for,* she thought. *Something to remember.*

The Raayat had no chance at all. It managed to score the hraas in at least a dozen places, but none of the wounds were deep enough to throw the killer off. The hrass' wing-claws held on, doggedly refusing to let go despite the Raayat's thrashing. Its other talons were therefore free to rip and tear, and all efforts were centered upon one area of the Raayat's body. Where the vital organs must be, Ntaya realized. The hraas knew.

Oh, we have underestimated you!

At last, the howling ceased. The Raayat was dead— or dying, but what did such distinctions matter to the hraas? It ripped out the throat of its opponent and threw the flesh bloodily against a far wall, glorying in its victory.

But its wing-claws didn't settle. Not yet. With hungry eyes it scanned its audience. Looking for something. Treading in the blood of its vanquished opponent as it turned to study them all, some dozen and a half Tekk from various backgrounds who had been drawn by the sound of the disturbance.

Suddenly it was off the ground again. Leaping directly toward her, it seemed, but she stood her ground. *I don't know what the Raayat did to inflame you,* she thought to it, *but our covenant is still in full force. I was Blooded for you in my youth, on the* Talguth; *I will not bleed for you again.*

The wing-claws snapped forward, so close that a

streak of blood was left on her face where one brushed
by. The Tekk next to her fell—and he, unarmored, had
little time to scream. The one who had pointed out the
battle to her, whose hands had betrayed his fear. Dead,
despite his Blooding. His covenant rent along with his
flesh, as the hraas made a quick end to his trembling.

Havoc reigned, in that instant, but she was calm. The
eye of the storm. A local Tekk pushed past her, running; the hraas brought her down in a single leap and
made short work of killing her. The beast was insane,
it was uncontrollable—so the Tekk cried out as they
ran—it had forgotten the message of the Blooding, the
bond between hraas and Tekk which had existed for as
long as the two had shared space. The Will was no
longer protection, for anyone.

So they screamed. Nine of them in all. Three escaped, into corridors or rooms whose entrances might
be blocked off. Ntaya wondered if they really thought
themselves safe, or were just buying time. Six fell to
the hraas' killing fury, and bits and pieces of them
joined the Raayat, littering the angdatwa's floor.

Ntaya remained. So did several others. She looked
them over as the hraas sniffed them, its teeth bared as
it hissed its hunger for new blood, new victims, new
flesh to rend. They stood tall, proudly, willing to die
if the Will so decreed it. Not afraid of death, or of the
beast who delivered it.

Not afraid. . . .

It came and sniffed at her, but she was hardly aware
of its presence. The man beside her was alive again in
her mind's eye and she watched him; saw the tremor
in his hands, heard the terror in his voice.

Fear.

She remembered her own Blooding, and all those
which she had witnessed. Remembered the hrass picking out those who would live and those who would die,
as the bloodstained children fought for courage in their
presence. And remembered the cry of the Raayat, recognizing its most terrible note: not pain, or anger.
Terror. That was the key. That simple. The Tyr had no

reason to fear death or injury; all minds were one, all parts equally expendable, and that which was wounded could simply be discarded. The Overmind endured. She had seen several Honn cut off with no warning, when the Tyr-whole decided they had been malfunctioning; there was no fear, no regret, no sense of mourning. Except in this one Raayat, whose unstable mental processes had somehow opened a floodgate of fear, drowning it in terror while the rest of the Tyr did nothing to help.

And the hraas had attacked. First the Raayat, and then those Tekk who had been unnerved by its combat. The Tekk who had come to *fear* it.

She looked to where the beast was nuzzling its kill—its wing-claws sheathed now, its colors fading—and then walked toward it, slowly. Until she came to its side. Until she stood so close that any normal predator would have moved to drive her back—or moved away itself, to reestablish its territory.

The hraas simply looked at her. Met her eyes. Hissed a token warning, and went back to eating.

A terrible beast, designed to be fearsome. The monarch of its planet's food chain, feared by all living creatures who saw it. How well could its instincts adapt to the Tyr, who were immune to terror? To the Tekk, who had followed the course of trial and error to perfect a ritual which weeded out the fearful?

We have indeed underestimated you, she thought to it. *And your importance, in the scheme of things.*

No more.

YUANG:
DOME PRIME

There were worse things than becoming a hraas, I assum. But not in my experience.

Taking on the form of an animal is normally a gradual process. The body change comes immediately, but the psyche seeps in slowly, gradually, as you use it. The longer you remain immersed, the more of it sticks with you afterward. So that for days after flying across the mountains with Kiri, I still dreamt of succulent worms and fought the urge to pick for parasites in my wing feathers. And a panther may recall being human, and want to regain its human stature, but who can say if an animal intelligence is capable of managing a shapechange?

If changing into animal form was a gradual immersion under normal circumstances, then taking on the form of a hraas was like being thrust suddenly into ice-cold water. I gasped for breath, and felt myself drowning. Not in fluid, but in sensation. Raw, primal, gut emotions. Storms of color. A tsunami of sounds and smells that crashed over me the moment my body changed shape, and threatened to drown my human self. I fought to adapt. I tried to shut out some of the onslaught—impossible—and then, in desperation, tried to accept it. Tried to submit to the change, as much as I was able, instead of struggling against it. That helped, marginally. The world settled down into an ordered—although by no means stable—state; the emotions and instincts which had so suddenly engulfed me were no less forceful, but more comprehensible. In the distance, some remaining shard of my

344

human soul attached names to the things I was feeling, and thus rendered them finite. Hatred. Fury. Frustration. I felt ready to claw out at the first thing that attracted my attention—and was well armed to do so—and it took all my self-control, human and otherwise, to redirect that hatred into a growl and a quick retreat.

The ground seemed to change beneath my paws, strange colors crawling across its surface; I had to shut my eyes to walk on it. Was this the hraas' normal state? I managed to get myself to the skimship somehow, and although the ground was marginally more stable, the smell of the Tyr nearly drove me to lose all vestige of control. It took all my strength to make legs walk that would much rather be leaping—pouncing—holding back claws that hungered to rend living flesh. Anyone's flesh. By the time I was inside, I was shaking all over, a trembling that must have been visible to anyone watching. Fortunately—for me, and for them—no one was.

Maybe Kiri was beside me. Maybe not. I was lost in the center of an alien body, fighting for my life. It was all I could do to locate Kiri when she arrived—to recognize her, and remember my mission—and then to leave the skimship when it opened and go where she led me, without turning on her in fury for displaying such dominance.

By the time we reached the lower tunnels I was exhausted, mentally and physically. It took us hours to find a safe place—I take it she judged it as such, I was beyond any such intellectual exercise—and nearly as long for me to master the hraas part of my soul so that she could alter my flesh again. When I regained my humanity, I fell gasping to the floor, and she held me for a long time until the fit finally passed. My face against the softness of her hair . . . it struck me for the first time how like a real woman she was, how easily one could forget that her body was no more than an organic envelope, artificially manipulated. I felt my body stirring in response to her, and quickly pulled away. That was animal instinct, still controlling my flesh. The man in me knew what she was, and—more important—what she was not. It would be small thanks to use her body for my release, when I had no equivalent pleasure to offer the creature that nested inside it.

The lower tunnels were naturally cavernous in nature, unlike the slime-smooth corridors of the Tyr; the jagged walls, floors and ceilings offered more than ample protection, for one who was willing to take the time to find a suitable crevice. Kiri chose the niche. She insisted on it. Looking deep into the rock, to see what was stable and what was not, what would be supplied with air, what was truly inaccessible from any other direction. When she had made her choice, I crawled inside, between layers of rock, and steeled myself for the death-trance. It was not unknown among my people for one to submit to it willingly; some chose to wait out the centuries that way, hoping for better times. But I, clinging to life, had never attempted it before.

She must have sensed my difficulty, for her hand, delicate as a butterfly, alighted on my arm. "I can help," she reminded me.

In answer I took her hand and squeezed it—so warm, so comforting—and bid the darkness come to me. Better that than hraas-form, I reflected; at least this was a human thing.

I can't do that form again, Kiri. Not for anything.
You will. You have to.
Sleep.

* * *

I stand with the sword in my hand, exhausted. Blood drips from it to the ground, staining the crushed grass beneath me crimson. A head lies by my feet, severed from its owner. The sword is his, and I cast it atop his torso so that steel rings on steel, and bright blood splatters on the outside of his mail shirt, to match that which seeps slowly forth from within.

Four of them. Not easily dispatched. It was suicide to take them on, especially when I could have slipped into shadow, or slipped into animal flesh, and never been seen at all. But this place has been a home to me, as much as any town ever was. Should I have left it to the whim of these drunken mercenaries, when I had the power to save it?

Only slowly do I become aware of the eyes fixed on me. Only slowly do I gain the strength to look up, and try to meet their gaze. Most turn away as I do so, muttering curses and psalms under their breath. A few are able to meet my eyes, but their expressions are so filled with horror that I cannot look at them for more than a moment, without feeling tears come to mine. Familiar faces have now become those of strangers: Marguerethe, whom I bedded; Peter, who taught me the art of training horses; Agatha, who let me lock the door of the room I boarded in through all the daylight hours, without ever a question to disturb my peace. Now made enemies in a single hour, by the very act that bought them safety. Because I made the mistake of defending them with the special skills at my disposal. I chose their lives over my secrecy, and now this is the cost. One holds a cross aloft, muttering imprecations. Another backs up warily—anxious to keep a safe distance between us, no longer certain just what a safe distance is. And Marguerethe . . . turns away and trembles, imagining what manner of unwholesome seed this demon's spawn might have left within her.

The loss is so absolute, so sudden, that for a moment I am rooted to the spot, without the strength to move. Shaking, like a leaf in the chill wind, trying to find some glimmer of acceptance among them. Dare I say gratitude? But that is like looking for love amongst corpses.

I curse myself for daring to hope and take to the air in a flurry of wings, anxious to be gone from this place. And curse them—and their stubbornness—and their damnable culture!—that makes it so impossible to negotiate any manner of truce between us.

The more fool I, to think it could ever be otherwise.

* * *

Yuang. Words fall short of describing it. How had I envisioned Hell, when early Christians first described it to me? Certainly not worse than this. The landscape seethed in a thousand hues of fire, all of them unnatural to my eyes. Great oily clouds greased the sky as they boiled across it, spitting out globs of some unwholesome fluid in their wake. Humanity in all its folly had never dreamed of settling on a world like this one; what madness had driven the Tyr to consider it?

I was shivering when I reclaimed my human body, and not wholly because of changing. Kiri looked at me curiously but waited, as if she knew that this was just some human thing I had to get out of my system.

Christ. To her it was probably just another planet.

"Do you know where he is?" I asked, when I felt I had control of my voice again. "This Kost of yours?"

"I'm not even sure he's here yet. Our voyage took long enough, it's possible . . . but how good is his network, really? He bragged to me about it, but that doesn't mean very much."

"A Marra braggart?"

"Afraid so."

"Sounds charming."

"I didn't say I liked him. I *never* said I liked him."

Something in her voice warned me off the subject. "So we have a whole planet to search."

"Twelve Domes. But it may be easier than that."

She seemed to hesitate. I raised an eyebrow, and waited.

"I presented his name to the local Tekk. They knew it. They thought it was one of their own codes. They gave me a location."

"That's excellent. Isn't it?" Her expression made me suddenly uncertain. "It means we know where to start, at least."

"The location they gave me was *eight*," she said quietly. "Dome Eight."

"And?"

She turned away. It occurred to me that she was debating whether or not to tell me something.

"There was an accident there," she said at last. "A terrible accident. The kind, I'm told, that every domer has nightmares about. An explosion in one of the labs damaged two dome seals. The native atmosphere seeped in. . . . There were many fatalities."

"You think he's dead?"

She turned back suddenly, and looked at me. The emotion in her eyes surprised me. Were the Marra capable of anger?

"No," she said evenly. "I think he's very much alive. I think—in fact, I *know*—that he's masquerading as a scientist from Dome Eight. Someone close to the source of the explosion, whose real body would have been destroyed."

"Is that so terrible? It's a way around the census computers, anyway. The Tyr would never question—"

I don't know what it was in her look that told me, but something did. The explosion was no accident. Kost's scientist had died for a purpose.

"Come on," she muttered. "They told me which domes did the salvage work. He'll be in one of them."

* * *

We found him in Five. We had no trouble getting there—well, little enough trouble—as we took advantage of the same disaster that had given Kost his dis-

guise. From my old days on Earth I knew how the
census computers worked, and could rig the programs
for my own ends; we called up the pictures and résu-
més of other fatalities, and designed ourselves bodies
to match. Myself in a body that was brown-haired and
bearded, but otherwise very much like my own. Kiri
in a red-headed body that suited her very well, fiery
eyes and freckles that emitted the same youthful charm
of her previous creation. If the Tyr saw us—and they
did, several times during our journey—they would
simply assume that their information was in error, that
humans *Aesim Kol Tagayrak No-Alym Hume* and *Kuell
Hunnaerag Summa Kan-Eslay Ti* were alive and well,
despite census programs to the contrary.

To say that the Domes were sterile would be an understatement. In Yuang's hostile environment, where
every square inch of building material must be lugged
across the vaccuum of space from some other source,
the noncreativity of the Tyr became hideously apparent. Corridors were white where good lighting was
required, gray-green or gray-blue otherwise. In def-
erence to human tastes, these hues were not mixed; at
least the inhabitants of the Domes system could take
their ugliness in small, uniform doses. But nowhere,
anywhere, was there ornament. I guessed that the Tyr,
seeing no need for visual diversity, was hardly about
to exert itself obtaining colored paint to humor a few
hundred captive humans.

Be grateful the colors are tolerable, I told myself,
remembering my cell on board the *Talguth.*

Long tunnels connected the Domes, and passage
along them was strictly controlled. As refugees from
Eight, however, we were permitted to pass. Homeless,
purposeless, the Tyr would let us wander until we
found ourselves a comfortable niche somewhere else.
Or until Eight West was repaired. I think it just simply
didn't want to be bothered with the creative job of
figuring out where to place all the refugees. How much
threat could we be, after all, wounded and scattered
and (the ultimate Yuang fear) labless?

I wondered what would become of human spirits in such a colorless place. Whether any mere exercise of scientific skills could compensate for the eternal, over-whelming drabness of their life outside the labs.

Until Five. There, for the first time, I saw a hint of life. Color about the doorframes, in measured doses. Heatset texturing, on the prefab plastic walls. I sniffed at a doorway in passing and detected a faint but rec-ognizable odor. So . . . Five's decorator had used chemistry's classic dyes, set in an opaque and presum-ably permanent base. Likewise the texturing could have been done with simple laboratory tools, altered for that purpose. I wondered at the personality of the man who would have dared such a thing, and at his determination. Or hers. Surely the Tyr would be less than pleased by this flagrant waste (as they would see it) of precious supplies. There was courage here, al-beit in measured doses. . . .

"This is the one." She stopped at an indigo door-frame, her hands lightly brushing the plastic. Within, I knew, the presence of a Marra was fully visible to her special senses. Hopefully the one we sought.

She knocked.

The sound of lightly running feet, probably bare-foot. A woman? "Moment!" a voice called. I was relieved to hear the use of English; not all Domes used it as a primary language. After a moment the plastic latch rattled, and the door itself swung open.

She was about thirty, with olive skin and dark fea-tures; in another time and place she would have been a stunning woman, but here, in a plain lab coat and severely functional hairstyle, her classic Hispanic fea-tures were compromised somewhat. I wondered what she looked like in her offtime. Wondered whether in this unique Dome someone hadn't managed to piece together more attractive clothing, from the waste prod-ucts of a biochem lab.

"We're here to see Kost," Kiri told her.

The woman nodded, and leaned down to pull at the heel of one shoe as she cried out "Kost! Some friends of yours." Her shoe now settled, she straightened up and smiled at us. "Eighters?" she guessed. I nodded, and Kiri offered our borrowed names. "I'm Ria," she answered, inviting us in. Not a number, I noted, but a real name. I considered it an excellent sign.

He came though an archway that was roughly cut into one of the room's plain white walls. I do not think it any monument to my Marra-sense that I knew him for what he was at first sight. The other Marra I'd met had all tried to be human, in one way or another. This one wore the body, but he wasn't playing the game. The arrogance in him was out of place in a land dominated by the Tyr's bland interiors; the intensity of the gaze which he fixed upon us—first Kiri, then me—was nothing he could have explained to Ria by any human motive.

"Old friends," he said quietly, and stepped forward to grasp my hand. A ritual of his disguise. He was more graceful than Paes', but not as comfortable in his body as Kiri herself. Something about him made me wary; I touched him no longer than I had to. He was grinning as he moved to Kiri, and something passed between them as they touched. Amusement, perhaps, at how easily humans panicked.

"Sorry to leave so soon," Ria apologized, taking up a heavy canvas bag and strapping it to one shoulder. When it was in place she hesitated a moment, and I saw the color leave her face. *Weaker than she looks,* I decided. *Or perhaps ill?* Instinctively I moved to help, but she shrugged me away, and smiled a smile that was just a little strained. "See you at dinner shift," she promised the Marra, and nodded a farewell to us.

The door closed behind her, sealing us in whiteness.

"Kiri," Kost mused. "An interesting name." Amusement was plain on his face. Meaning he had gone out of his way to put it there. "Who named you?

"And what does yours mean?" I snapped.

His piercing gaze fixed on me. "Well trained, isn't

he? It means *new beginning. That which challenges the old.* Appropriate?''

''I see.''

He was about to say something—but then his eyes narrowed suddenly and he stepped toward me, as if to make contact. I quickly made it clear, by reestablishing our distance, that that was unacceptable.

''What is it?'' he asked Kiri.

''A human male,'' she said quietly. ''And *his* name is Daetrin.''

''An embodied masschanger,'' I added, knowing the power of those words.

''It is possible? . . . I suppose so. You are here. And there's no denying the oddity of your existence, I could read that from a mile away. There's a lot I'd like you to explain . . . but later.'' His eyes fixed on Kiri. ''You called me here. To join me?''

She shook her head, and I thought I saw distaste in the gesture. ''But I do need your help.''

He waited.

''I have news that must be spread. Only you have the contacts—''

''I'm not a news service.''

''You're the closest thing we have. You told me you were in contact with many of the Marra. No one else is.''

''True . . . but does the situation merit my personal attention?''

''It does.''

He smiled. It was a distasteful expression. ''I'm listening.''

She told him. The whole story, from our arrival in Suyaag to Paes' death, deep within the tunnels of the Old Ones' city. And I watched him. Watched as the arrogance gave way to surprise, and then uncertainty. I wondered if there wasn't also fear, somewhere in there. An emotion he would never willingly display.

''You're saying a Marra died,'' he said at last. ''Not possible.''

''I'm telling you, I saw it! Held his life in my hands,

as it faded into nothingness. Searched the vicinity of expiration, on all levels . . . and found nothing. *Nothing!*"

"The implications are . . . unpleasant."

Talk about understatement.

"But it happened," she insisted. "Can happen to others, if they forget what they really are." *Might even happen to you,* she implied, but he played at not understanding.

"Killed by loss of memory," he mused. "What a fantastic concept! He believed he could die, so in fact he did. Rather frightful," he finally admitted.

"Terrifying," she agreed. I thought I heard a tremor in her voice.

"But it could be put to good use. Could unify us, against a common enemy." He laughed softly, an ominous sound. "Suits my purposes well enough. And I know you don't approve of me, or what I'm doing. So why, little-lost-Marra? Why put this in my hands, when you know I'll use it?

"You're the only one who can spread the word," she said quietly. "And unless more Marra know, more Marra may die."

"And no thought for your precious embodied folk? Such as this creature?" He indicated me. "No thought for the pets of yours that I might dominate, whom you would rather see free—"

"Stop it," I snapped. "She brought you information. Isn't that enough?"

"Ah, how protective! Have you replaced the Saudar-*kreda*, Kiri? Found a new master? I hope he treats you better than the old ones."

"I'm not—" I began, but a look from Kiri warned me to silence.

"That isn't an issue," she said.

"But he is *kreda*, yes?"

She hesitated, glanced at me. "The relationship has followed that pattern."

"Replaced one master with another, then. Well. The

habit was too strong in you, after all. I should have realized that, when first we talked.''

"At least I'm still following a Marra pattern," she snapped.

Kost was about to answer when the door flew open. Ria stood at the threshold, angry and frustrated.

"Fred's visiting," she said abruptly. "Niam sent some of us home. Didn't want Raayat germs on the tissue, I guess." She kicked off her shoes and grimaced. "This only happens when there's a lot to do. I'm going to—"

Then she saw my face, and stopped. "Are you all right?"

"Tell me about Fred," I said softly.

"Some Raayat from level three. Yaan's group. Gave its name as Frederick, when they asked. Harmless enough—until crazytime, that is, and then we're all dead anyway, so why waste time now, dreading it? *Tyr is as Tyr will be.*"

"From the *Talguth?*" I asked her. My throat was suddenly dry. It couldn't be my Frederick. Could it?

She shrugged. "How should I know? Yaan could probably tell you, or someone in his lab group. I think they talk to the thing." She was sliding her feet into soft-soled slippers, and unbuttoning her lab coat as she spoke. "Love, I'm off to rec." She yawned, and swayed for a moment as exhaustion overtook her. "They're meeting there . . . Terra, I feel awful."

"Have something to eat," he said mechanically. Something in his voice—and her condition—gave me a cold feeling inside. Because I suddenly recognized the pattern of their relationship. "You don't take care of yourself."

She wrinkled a kiss at him, and nodded good-bye to us. A moment later she was gone; the white door snicked shut behind her.

"You don't have to kill to feed, do you?" I spoke quietly, but even so, accusation gave my voice biting impact. "Or even leave a mark."

He smiled. Amused. "Fertile humans provide ex-

cellent nourishment. Or didn't you know that? Didn't
your Marra explain that, when it explained everything
else?''

"The *it* is a *she*," I pointed out. Kiri's hand was on
my arm—a warning—but I ignored it. "Understand?"

"The *she*, my dear human, is an unsexed biophen-
omenon that has no pronoun in your language. And if
it appears to be female, remember that the greatest
intensity of consumable life takes place during sexual—"

"Enough!" Kiri snapped.

"—involvement. Such as your own?"

I moved forward, obviously hostile. Her hand tightened on my arm, holding me back. He glared, but
there was laughter in his eyes.

"Does he supply you with food?" he asked Kiri.
"Or require it himself? Perhaps he feeds on you instead."

In answer she pulled me toward the door. "This
accomplishes nothing, Kost. We'll get settled. I'll
come back. And keep out of my interaction next
time," she warned.

His laughter accompanied us out.

In the hallway. I stood shaking, with rage and fear
both. He could kill me with a touch . . . but Christ,
how I longed to wring his neck! Just once. Even if it
wouldn't accomplish anything.

She watched me attempt to calm myself, hesitating
to touch me.

"He baited you, you know."

I nodded. "He sure did."

"He wants you to get angry."

"Then he must be very happy."

"Is that . . ." She hesitated. "Is that all this is?"

I knew what she meant. She was afraid that something between us might have been lost, when he revealed the truth. I looked up suddenly, pained that she
should doubt me. "Not you, Kiri. I knew all that. Not
about the sexual thing. . . . *No, not about that at all.
And I'm not sure how to take it.* "But that couldn't

have been why you chose a female body; you never
tried to—''

And then blind rage overwhelmed me and I had to
stop. "It isn't you," I repeated. "You never lied to
me about what you were. I understand that."

She paused, and I could see her thinking. Puzzling
over the complexity of human emotional response. "Is
it because he insulted me? A male protective response?"

It was, a little, and I nodded. Only later did I realize
that it was a kind of compliment to her, that I had
reacted in such a way. But that wasn't the whole of it.

I regarded the door before us, and thought of the
Marra who stood beyond it. And the woman he lived
with, her vitality gradually seeping out, drained by his
presence. A woman who was that much closer to
death, each time she affirmed life with her passion. I
wondered how to give a name to the hate that was
boiling up inside me. The revulsion.

And finally I found the word. The perfect word. An
Earth-word, that was properly chilling in all its connotations.

"It's just that I never met a vampire before," I told
her.

* * *

The master lab on the third floor of Five's science
complex was . . . well, a lab. A *real* lab. Not some
Tekk imitation, propped up with 1930's cabinetry and
real glass test tubes. Nor some Tyrran artifice, all
gleaming white and spotless chrome, where even a
germ wouldn't feel welcome.

I walked through the double doors and stood there,
breathless, trying to take it all in. It was cluttered.
Delightfully, deliciously cluttered. An enormous
room, and every inch of it was filled with marvelous
things; one couldn't have taken a step without tripping
over some vital instrument. Beakers of twenty-first
century plastel crowded together on shelves, turning

the bland artificial light into a rainbow symphony of spectral colors. Machines I had once used huddled close by machines I had only read about, and farther still were machines whose functions I couldn't even guess at. And on every table, notebooks and slides and calculators and magnetic clamps, and jars of half-empty pens and broken pencils, and even a sandwich . . . I blinked and realized tears were coming to my eyes.

"There was a part of Earth that I loved," I whispered to Kiri. "I thought it was gone. I was wrong. It came here."

There were several people at the far end of the room, crowded about a circular table. As they drew apart and turned to us, I saw a holograph rising from the table's center. Beautiful. Precise. How many years had it been, since Earth had seen that kind of technology?

"Can I help you?" The oldest of the group approached us. That he was their leader was clear from the way the others regarded him. His person was as cluttered as the lab itself, numberless items stuffed in every pocket. There was a brightness in his eyes, a restless curiosity, that I hadn't seen in anyone in too long a time. Maybe centuries.

"We're from Eight," I said, and I introduced us by our borrowed numbers. That explanation proved to be enough. He welcomed us with a warm handclasp, muttering words of reassurance. We were welcome. Please join them. There were others from Eight in this complex, did we know them? We listened to all the names and shook our heads, trying to look perplexed. We had learned that the accident in Eight had resulted in brain damage for many survivors, often affecting memory; we were safe in our lies, then, as long as we were vague enough for them to assume that was the reason.

He invited us in. I managed to make myself follow him. I would have preferred to stop and examine things, to sit myself down and try everything myself . . . my eyes were wandering over everything as we walked, trying to take it all in. And I hungered. God, I had forgotten what that hunger was like. Food is nothing to it. Blood is a mere distraction. The hunger to learn, the desire to *know,* is like nothing else in my experience. How had I managed to suppress it, for so very long?

Introductions. To a tall woman, lean features. Tireza. An Oriental man; Chinese ancestry, perhaps? Sung. Another man, features somewhat Amerindian. Tesla. Much to mv delight, all of them had hair.

And in the center of their table, a brain. They were peeling away its image, layer by layer, probing deep into its structure. The image's resolution was so fine that every cortical convolution was crisp and clear; it seemed that if one looked closely enough, one would be able to make out individual cells.

I forced myself to look away, to hear what they were saying. About us being welcome. And asking why we'd chosen to come to this particular lab, while assuring us, simultaneously, that travelers from Eight needed no specific reason.

"We heard about Frederick," I told them. "We were curious."

At that, the woman named Tireza laughed. "Terra, it gets more visitors than we do! Who was that man the other day—"

"Who? Tiro?"

"No. That new one . . . Ria's new boyfriend. You know."

"Kost," Tesla supplied.

"Yes, Kost. Came up here like he meant to interview the thing . . . good thing for all of us it hasn't been around lately. It might have pitched a fit if he'd gotten to it."

"He's left?" I asked.

"Who? Kost?"

"The Raayat."

Tesla grinned good-naturedly. "Yaan drove it off."

Yaan exhaled noisily; clearly he objected to that interpretation.

"Will he be back, do you think?" I was trying not to sound too anxious; God alone knew what they would make of that. But they took it fairly well.

"Soon enough, I expect. Who else will tolerate it?"

"There's more to it than that," Yaan said quietly. Something about what he said, or the way he said it, seemed to quiet them all. "One way or another, it'll be back. I promise you."

He followed my gaze to the flawless image at the table's center, and back again. "Have you done this kind of work?"

"Years ago," I said, choosing my words very carefully, "I studied the human brain."

There was a snort of approval from someone at the table, and the woman named Tireza pushed an unoccupied chair toward me. "Good enough!" she exclaimed. "We can always use an extra pair of hands around the place. Or two."

"You ought to ask them, first," Yaan pointed out.

I looked at Kiri. There was pride in her eyes—but a kind of sadness, too, that I had never seen there before.

I reached past the chair that was offered and pulled out a second, for her.

"We'd be honored," I told them.

* * *

You're healed, she said quietly, with that same vulnerable look that I remembered from the cave, outside Cantona. And I understood what she meant. What she was asking.

If I was healed, then the healer had no more duty.

I need you, I answered, and I took her hand. And for the time being, that was enough.

* * *

It was the lack of Eyes that made the difference. Or at least, the *perceived* lack of Eyes; Kiri and I had yet to see any evidence that the much-dreaded mechanism existed in the first place. But the Domes were guaranteed free of the visual bugs, and I believe this was part of the reason that we were welcomed into lab three's fold, strangers though we were. On the one hand, we were no threat: on the other hand, our unfamiliar mindsets—like any new stimulus—might inject something valuable into the charged creative atmosphere. And if we didn't quite know the nuts and bolts of domer science yet . . . there was the accident to blame for that, and plenty of time to learn. We were made welcome.

Frederick showed up on our third day. Yaan and Tireza and Sung and Kiri and I were in the lab, the usual firstshift crew. I was cleaning beakers. Kiri was cleaning beakers. The other three were dirtying them.

I heard a noise and turned around . . . and there he was. Twice as large and more festooned with aggressive hardware than I had ever seen him, but there was no mistaking the face.

"Frederick . . ." I whispered. For a moment I was too stunned by his sudden arrival to take in what it was he held in his arms. But I managed to remember that I was in a foreign body now, with no risk of discovery—and then I saw, without quite believing it, just what it was he was dropping on our main worktable, in the center of the room.

"This is trade," he announced.

It was another Raayat. A dead Raayat—Yaan made sure of that immediately—in excellent condition. Only one jagged gash marred the gray-black of its skin, a hole in its chest region the size of a man's fist.

I looked at Frederick. There was blood on one of his spikes.

"Is it good?" he asked.

It seemed that no one could answer.

"You need Tyr brain, to compare with human. Yes? I bring it. So you can answer questions. Understand?"

"We understand," Yaan managed hoarsely. "Thank you."

"It's . . . very helpful," Tireza offered.

"You can compare now?" Frederick demanded.

"Yes—with time to study it. Of course."

"Whatever you want," Sung offered.

"Good," the Raayat said. "I approve."

I moved forward. My heart was pounding wildly . . . but I had a hunch, and meant to test it.

"Does the Tyr know?" I asked Frederick. Aware that I was risking a lot, if my guess was wrong. "That you killed this one?" *That you gave it to us* was what I wanted to say, but it was enough if he answered the other question. More than enough, if his answer was *no*.

He looked at me for a long while, as though trying to place me. Or maybe that was my fear speaking; maybe he was simply contemplating the question.

"It is summer," he said finally, and turned and left the lab. Clearly, in his opinion, that was answer enough.

He left us stunned.

"Does he know," Tireza whispered, "that he just sold out his own people?"

" The question is not if he knows," I pointed out. Their eyes were upon me now, filled with questions. "The question is, if he *cares*."

YUANG:
DOME PRIME

Ntaya was actually working on the chip when the Honn came for her. As opposed to her usual state, which was that of pointedly *not* working on the chip. It was, after all, her only means of stalling, of giving the domers enough time to come to their senses. She had to make it last.

The Honn-Tyr entered silently, and waited for her to notice it. Without a word it handed her a thin sheet of plyex, with the mark of the Dome Five fax beside the date in the upper corner.

> We are severely handicapped in our work by our continuing lack of a functional synaptic scan. We appeal to the Tyr and the Tekk to see that this project is given priority, and hope that the repairs can be completed soon so that we may continue with our work.
>
> On behalf of Dome Five, and in service to the Will,
> Lab three project director
> Yangal Ho-ael Kasril Yed Saen

She somehow managed to keep a smile from her face as she looked up at the Honn, and nodded. Under the circumstances, it wasn't easy.

"I understand," she said solemnly. "I've had somep problems with the growth ratio, but it goes well now. I should be able to place the new chip within . . . say, forty-eight hours. Please inform them."

The Honn left without a word. Not till it was gone

did she dare to grin—but she did so then with gusto, a broad smile of exhilaration that said she knew exactly what the message was meant to communicate. The domers in Five were ready to talk. They wanted to know when she was coming, so they could make arrangements. They were ready, at last.

It was about time.

YUANG:
DOME FIVE

"All right. Fred's gone."

From his post at the double doors, Sung waved for us to start.

There were twelve of us about the table, two deep in places. All of us tense, fearful that the Raayat would walk in during this conference. Even though he was down in lab two, and seemed quite content there. Even though the lab two people had promised to let us know the minute he left. Even though there was a person at every entrance, here, ready to warn us to scatter the minute he showed his crests.

The Tekk woman was tense as well, but not fearful. Her bright, eager eyes fell on each of us in turn: memorizing our faces, assessing our value to her.

"You have information," she announced. A question. A demand.

Yaan nodded. But then he clarified, "We have *guesses.*"

She scowled her irritation.

"We received, as you now know, the body of a Raayat. One body only, from a species with three distinct subgroupings. We have no way of knowing how much its brain structure reflects that of the other types. Earth logic tells us they must be nearly identical," he said quickly, forestalling her objection, "but how can we know that applies here? So I make this disclaimer: we studied one brain, from one creature. And guessed at the overall pattern. That's all. Please bear it in mind." And he looked pointedly at the Tekk woman.

One body. One brain. But Christ, what we had seen in it. . . .

"First, down to basics. The creature had a brain. It was recognizable as such, and located approximately where we anticipated." Tireza had risen quietly and now she reached to where a projector was set up, turning it on. Holographic images—considerably better refined than any I had seen on Earth—floated above the center of the table. "Protected much better than our own, I should add." He shot a glance toward the Tekk woman, but her eyes were fixed on the image. "No easy access through the eyes, or any other organ. The skull is considerably thicker than our own, and stress analysis shows it to be a good bit more resilient in structure."

The Tekk woman muttered something, but I couldn't make it out.

"We found it analogous to the human brain in structure, but differing greatly on a biochemical level. In other words, Tyrran evolution used a similar blueprint to ours, but with different building materials. Lab one reports that the same is true of its body structure in general. Therefore," he said pointedly—and he looked directly at the Tekk woman as he spoke—"we must conclude that any *chemical* or *biological* offensive which is not specifically developed for and tested on the Tyr, will be doomed to failure. Or at best, give erratic results."

We had learned that, back in the Conquest. The hard way. The Tyr had left no bodies behind, for human science to investigate.

"Lab one can give you more details on that, if you want," he told her, and she nodded sharply. "Now: as to the rest." He took a deep breath. "The human brain is a triune structure. Its three components serve distinct purposes, and each has its own neural blueprint. An alien scientist with no knowledge of human anatomy, if he dissected the brain and studied it, would still be able to discern three distinct levels of neural organization, corresponding to levels of evolutionary development.''

He looked at the Tekk woman; the explanation was for her benefit. She nodded.

''We proceeded on the assumption that this would be true for the Raayat brain. And this is where the differences were most apparent. First, there were not *three* main divisions, but *eight*. Ranging from a simple, primitive structure—like our own brainstem—right up through a tight, columnar pattern, in an area analogous to our cortex. But in the Raayat's case, the progression wasn't nearly so neat. Several sections had neural patterns as complex as that of the cortex, but completely different. One was so primitive we questioned whether it could function. And one appeared entirely vestigial, as though evolution had discarded it somewhere along the line, and never assigned it any new purpose. Now—and we're guessing here, I want to stress that—this could be explained by a high degree of random mutation, and a survival process that selected for *something other than intelligence*.

''Such as linkage with the other Tyr,'' the Tekk suggested.

''Maybe. I want to stress that at this point we have found no organ or neural structure so unusual that we could assign it a role in the group-consciousness phenomenon. But that doesn't mean it isn't there.''

We need a live subject to study, I thought. And I probably wasn't the only one thinking it.

''But here's something interesting: within the more advanced sections of the brain, development was erratic. Unpredictable. We found areas where the brain was tremendously underdeveloped. Ganglionic density on a par with that of an idiot; neural development like that of a three-year-old child. I would say that those sections predominated, in fact.''

''Overall intelligence?'' the Tekk woman asked.

''That's a complex question. And impossible to judge. We simply need more data.''

''But you have . . . guesses?''

He looked at her for a long minute; wondering, perhaps, how such information could be misapplied. "We used an Earth model," he said at last. "It relates brain mass to body mass in adult mammals. The assumption is, that a given amount of living flesh requires a predictable amount of brain mass to keep it going. Any more than that—considerably more—implies what we would term 'greater intelligence.' A tremendous oversimplification," he warned. "But that's the gist of it."

"And?" she pressed.

"According to Earth norms—and we have no way of knowing if they apply, or to what degree—the Raayat Tyr fell into the range of what we would term *animal intelligence*."

I saw the exultation on her face. So did he, and he stiffened. "*However:* I was forced to question whether this assessment was accurate. We considered various factors that might have skewed the results, and came up with one that seemed significant. Unlike most Earth life, the Raayat carries a lot of dead weight. Its armoring is dense, and accounts for a good part of its overall body weight. And being mostly dead tissue, it requires little maintenance. When we took that into consideration, and allowed for it mathematically . . . Here, I'll show you."

The finished chart appeared on a screen behind him. A diagonal line cut through the field labeled *brain weight/body weight*. "This is what we can expect, among Earth mammals." Above it hovered a few dozen black points, some of them labeled. *Gorilla. Chimpanzee.* Farthest from the black diagonal, a lone point was labeled *Man*.

And beyond that, in red, was a point that he indicated as he announced grimly, "The Raayat-Tyr."

Several people cursed. I was among them.

"That's if the chart is even valid for its species—which I strongly question."

"You're saying that the Tyr is more intelligent than man." The Tekk woman's voice was openly hostile.

"I'm saying—*if* this test is even valid—that the

Raayat-Tyr we studied is *potentially* more intelligent than man. But how much of its brain is waste? How much is underdeveloped? If I were to attempt any single comparison between our two species, I would have to say this: evolution on our planet was reasonably efficient. Theirs seems to have been less so. Understand why that is, and we may understand the cause—and the nature—of the gestalt phenomenon.''

"It has intelligence," Tireza mused. "But it doesn't use it."

"Doesn't need to," Sung responded.

Yaan nodded. "Exactly. The gestalt mind does all its thinking for it."

"Most of the time," I corrected.

All eyes turned to me; the fivers, the Tekk, even Kiri. "I . . . knew a Raayat on board the *Talguth*." I had told them nothing before this point to indicate that my background was anything other than what was recorded, a lifetime serving Dome Eight. Even in childhood, according to the records. The fact that I had even been a longship at all gave lie to the whole of that identity, and I could see the questions in their eyes. The suspicion, in Yaan's. But I told them anyway, because the information had to be shared. About Frederick's "fit" on board the *Talguth*. I even timefugued back for an instant, to see that tortured face again, to understand suddenly that within the Raayat's brain, some vital element had temporarily ceased to function.

Others had stories to add, particularly the Tekk woman. Tales of Raayat madness, much of which ended in destruction. Tales of Raayat dysfunction, often not recognized as such . . . until now.

"We know that the Tyr-whole disavows any responsibility for Raayat madness," the Tekk woman said. "It has said, in so many words, *this I do not control*."

"Gods of Terra," A man from lab one whispered. "Divorced from the overmind? Even for an instant?"

"Suddenly on its own resources, without warning.

A child's brain, left to flounder; high intelligence suddenly shrunk to an idiot's capacity.''

"But why the aggressive response?" Sung challenged.

"Desperation."

"And the destruction?"

"Does a child understand all the consequences of his actions? I think what we're seeing is desperation. *Fear.*"

I saw the Tekk woman stiffen at that, but before she could speak someone broke in, "And the self-destruction? Mere stupidity?"

I spoke up. "On Earth, it was known that simple neurotransmitter inefficiency could cause a host of problems. Even a slight decline in brain effectiveness could trigger mood swings, antisocial behavior, depression . . . even suicide."

"And compulsive curiosity, without any regard for circumstances. The desperate desire to *know,* again." Yaan looked us all over. "It is unreasonable that under these circumstances a Raayat might kill? Or blow up a lab? We're talking about a phenomenon that has no analogy among our own species."

"If the Raayat isn't always connected to the gestalt—" Tireza said suddenly.

Yaan nodded. "Then the Tyr may not know," he whispered.

Before I could question him—*know what?*—the rear door to the lab slammed open. "On its way up!" a man gasped, leaning in the doorway.

We moved quickly. Our roles had been assigned in advance, and now that danger threatened we fell into them smoothly, immediately, as though we had done so a hundred times before. so that by the time Frederick arrived were were all working, just as we should be. And the Tekk woman was immersed in the bowels of the synaptic scan. Just as she should be.

He arrived, but said nothing. We said nothing. I took my cue from the fivers, who neither greeted him, nor commented on his arrival.

At last the Tekk woman stirred to life, and extricated herself from the scan. "Ploka! Not wholly good. I can make it function," she said to Yaan. "But it will not last. It will take another day to adjust—"

"Then do it," he said irritably. "And do it fast! We need the damned thing."

"A day," she repeated.

Yaan glanced at me. Only for an instant, but the moment was eloquent. *You are part of this now. An unmeasured variable. Ally or threat, you must be confronted.*

A day.

* * *

What does Raayat mean? I asked Frederick.
He answered without hesitation. *Gatherer.*
Of what?
Knowledge. Experience.
He paused, then added:
Options. . . .

* * *

Yaan came to where we were working, a library cubicle on the second level. And stood in the doorway, watching us. Kiri felt his presence immediately and pushed aside her screen, turning to face him. I saw her move, guessed at the reason, and did the same.

"We need to talk," Yaan said.

He entered the small room quietly, and closed the plastic door behind him. Kiri and I had discussed what we would do when he came. Many times. Arguing through all the hours we worked, my bad experiences balanced against her natural Marra optimism. And at last we had decided. Not an easy decision, but clearly a necessary one.

But now that the moment had come at last, I found myself unable to speak. There was simply too much at stake. I remembered how quickly Paes' humans had

condemned my nature, between one sentence and the
next, and the terrible sense of loss—of fury—which
had rendered me incapable of arguing with them. But
what had I really lost, on Meyaga? Merely one chance
to strike at the Tyr, and a badly organized one at that.
Here, on the domeworld, in a mere handful of days, I
had managed to make a home for myself. Like my
father, who translated ancient texts out of dead tongues
for the living, I had found a place where my years of
experience made me valuable. A place where the sun
neither rose nor set, and all my various handicaps were
no more than unpleasant memories. I could be useful
here for the rest of a lifetime, and maybe even longer.
Or I could lose it in a moment, as I had lost Suyaag.

*If this one reacts like all the others, where is there
left to go?*

He stood there facing us, his expression wary but
not yet openly hostile. "You're clearly not what you
seem," he challenged. He looked at us. At me. "What
are you?"

I had prepared an answer, but now it seemed too
cluttered, too inelegant. All the adjectives I might have
used had other meanings as well—too sterile, too mechanical, or else too steeped in superstitious legend to
be taken seriously by such a man. Earth languages
simply had no neutral words to describe my kind.

In answer to him, then, I changed form. Quickly,
and without fuss. Into the body I was born to, thin and
blond-haired—and now, tense as a hunted animal.

"Gods of Terra . . ." he muttered. He sat.

"Refugees," I assured him. "No more than that.
We took on local identities to get past the Tyr—nothing
more."

"We arrived just after the accident," Kiri added.
Thinking of something I had not—that he might suspect we were responsible for the accident in Eight, if
he thought we were here at that time.

He looked at me, and at her—she had changed back
also, into the body that had once nursed me to health—
and shook his head, in perplexed amazement. I could

almost hear his brain fighting to adjust, trying to take in the data we were offering without doubting its own sanity. Not an easy task. But if anyone was up to it, this man was. He had been standing up to the Tyr for years, he could certainly come to terms with us. And indeed, after a short while he nodded slightly, his expression tight, and I knew we had passed the first hurdle.

"Tell me," he said.

And we did. We had decided to explain about me, if we had to, but not about Kiri. Now, encouraged by his reaction, we explained both. A brief synopsis, but a thorough one. That I was human. That she was not. That within certain limitations, either of us could alter the body we wore. That it was a perfectly natural process. We avoided all the ancient words, with their myriad associations, but I saw awareness of them flicker in his eyes. *Werewolf. Shapechanger. Doppelganger.* How many legends were we responsible for, that hinted at but never fully explained our nature? How many Earth traditions reflected not only our presence throughout human history, but the secrecy we had embraced as a defense in this modern, destructive age? He listened. Silent. Thoughtful. Interjecting a question only when it was absolutely necessary, to clarify a point. And I explained more than I had ever dared to, with anyone save Kiri.

When we were done, he said nothing. Only looked at us, with narrowed eyes, while the mind behind those eyes tried to sort through all that we had said, and determine how much of it was plausible. How much of it was threatening. I held my breath, expecting the worst.

"You realize," he said at last, "that what you've told me is simply incredible."

I jumped as Kiri touched a hand to my arm; I was even more tense than I had realized.

"But I've seen stranger things, since they took me from Earth. The Tyr, for one." He looked at me, and I saw something in his eyes that was neither hostility nor fear. Curiosity? "You know our science. Better than anyone they brought us from Earth. Better than I did, when I got here." It was a question.

"We live a long time," I said, and managed to relax a bit. The tension in the room was slowly leaking out; I felt the muscles of my back unknot themselves, and a strange, unfamiliar warmth suffuse my limbs. I took Kiri's hand in mine, held it. "That part's a longer story."

He glanced at our hands—wondering, no doubt, what manner of relationship could exist between our different species. Hell, I wondered it myself.

"I can't help but question what you've shown me," he pointed out. "That's only rational. Human senses are fallible, after all, and ever since that business in Eight . . ." For a moment I saw the gray eyes flicker in fear, looking into the scientist's equivalent of Hell: just enough brain damage that the mind would appear to function, but be unreliable. Insanity, in undetectable doses. "You understand? Any of us would have to doubt. Would have to question."

The scientific formula. Familiar, and therefore comforting. "What can I do?"

My forthright manner seemed to reassure him; now his shoulders relaxed, and his posture eased slightly. *It must be a hard thing to deal with*, I thought. I had never considered that end of it before. "Are you willing to do that upstairs? In the lab?"

In front of his equipment. Shapechanging.

I looked into his eyes, and read his excitement there. Carefully controlled, for the moment—as it would be until my story was confirmed by his machines—but ready to burn like a newborn star, with the thrill of fresh discovery. So must the scholars of Alexandria have looked, when they found a man who read dead tongues, and could bring their ancient texts to life.

Slowly, I nodded. Wondering how my father had felt, when he committed himself to that partnership.

"Excellent." He stood, and smoothed his lab coat. "I'm grateful for your openness, at any rate. We could have theorized about you for days, without . . . well, we never would have guessed this. But I guess that goes without saying.''

He laughed then, softly, and shook his head, even as Kiri and I turned off our screens.

"Twenty years on this planet with nothing to do, and now this and the Raayat at once. God's answering my prayers with a vengeance.''

* * *

The PET scan/compiler, we learned, was not designed to accommodate wolves.

* * *

"Can you help me?"

He regards the vial in his hands and nods, slowly. The red of my blood is like crimson glass, filtering the gaslight. "I think so. But it will take time. Yours is no simple pathology, my friend. To find the cause will require much work. But can it be done? All things give way to science, in the end. That is the wonder of this modern age.''

He holds up the vial like a loving father, and for a moment I see it through his eyes: not a simple portion of translucent liquid, but a dance of named and unnamed particles which can be forced, in time, to render up its secrets.

I did right in coming here, I tell myself.

"I've had other patients with your need," he tells me. "They come here because of this new specialization." With his free hand he adjusts his spectacles, then smooths his black wool frock coat against his stomach. My blood is placed on a rack full of empty vials, and vials filled with clearer liquids: a ruby among diamonds. "None have had your particular array of symptoms, of course . . . but that is no guarantee of failure." He smiles at me, but the smile is wary; I sense some hidden meaning behind it. "You will, of course, stay on the grounds, while we proceed. I will instruct Louis to prepare a room."

"With all due respect, sir, I'd prefer to keep my own quarters, in the city. I can come here as often as you would like."

His eyes narrow, for a moment. "That would not be advisable."

"Nevertheless, I have my reasons."

"I must insist."

I can't even imagine the vulnerability that would result, were I to live out the daylight hours surrounded by this man's staff; the mere thought of it makes me shudder. "With all due apologies, Doctor, it simply isn't possible."

"May I know the reason?"

Because I will not make myself so vulnerable as to be in any man's power—and if you see me in the sunlight, I will be doing just that. "Those are personal, and mayn't be divulged. Suffice it to say that you won't be inconvenienced, in any way."

"That's not my major concern." He strokes his dark goatee thoughtfully, brown eyes taking my measure. "You understand, you come to me saying you must have blood to live. You're not the first to speak those words. This is a simple medical condition, given one of several causes, and is no reflection in and of itself on your behavior. But among those who suffer from such a need . . . must I point out how many are prey to—shall we say, the darker compulsions? How many are driven to seek out human blood, even when a butcher's produce would suffice?" He is tense now, all artifice gone from his manner. I feel myself trapped, without knowing exactly how or when it happened. "I'm not accusing you of criminal behavior, you understand; but it is in the nature of those who share your illness that criminality is at most a single step away. Therefore I must insist. You will remain on these grounds for the duration of treatment.''

I start to get up, see his glance flicker toward the door. God in heaven, why did I come here? What did I hope to accomplish? Just because human science was beginning to unravel the secrets of the bloodstream, did I think the daybound would be willing to share their knowledge? I acknowledge my mistake, and wonder just how much trouble I've gotten myself into. Is it too late to talk my way out of here?

But before I can speak, he claps his hands sharply in warning. Through the room's single door comes a pair of men, uniformed attendants who seem more than capable of taking on a single unruly patient. "Now, Mr. James, won't you spare us both the unpleasantness of further argument?" His voice is filled with the patronization so typical of this period, toward those who dare to be less than perfectly healthy. "You do no more than condemn yourself, when you so emphatically refuse our assistance."

I judge the distance between the two attendants, between the pair and myself, between myself and the window—and decide, in an instant, to risk their strength rather than give myself away by flying. Words will accomplish little, now; action is all. I lunge between them, hoping to take them by surprise. Strong hands grab my shoulders and arms, and they would surely pin me down if I let them. Instead I let my anger flow outward into my limbs, giving me strength. *You bastard!* I hear bone snap on my left, and a hand falls away. *Stupid, misguided bastard!* An arm is about my neck, and the pressure due to choke me—but I twist in its grip and slam myself backward, into the nearest wall. A rain of plaster and blood accompanies my assailant's groan of pain, and I have no trouble throwing him off.

I slam the door open, and run for my freedom.

I was a fool to come here!—to trust the day-bound in any way. Now it pains me to leave the sample of my blood behind—but how can they possibly use it against me? I catch sight of him staring at it, as I pass beyond the threshold, as if it will reveal some priceless secret. As he will stare at it for some time to come, I suspect, while more humane doctors bind up his wounded, and question him—in vain—as to exactly what happened. *The strength of a madman,* he will say. *The capacity of the damned.* As he stares into the depths of that precious fluid, and wonders which of the many particles suspended in it is responsible for criminal behavior, and whether a vaccine will be possible.

* * *

Endless work, without sleep. Tests overlapping tests; diagrams of my brain and body intermingled with reports on the Raayat, until only Yaan could make sense of it all. He was in his element now, maneuvering research teams through a morass of facts and equipment without pausing to take a breath. Studying me—and keeping my secret—while all about us the Raayat data continued to pour in, a million and one unassociated facts that must somehow be woven into a coherent—and useful—whole. Then that whole must be weighed, and sifted, and perhaps even rewoven from scratch, until it was suitable for presentation. For ultimately it was the Tekk women who must apply—or misapply—our findings.

As for myself, the mystery which had plagued me for centuries was starting to unravel at last, and I knew that another few months in this place might well answer most of my questions. As well as teaching me how to trust my fellow man . . . which is no small thing.

The second meeting had nearly twice as many people. The lab one team was there, with a general au-

topsy report. That meant Ria and Kost, among others.
She looked pale, and thinner than I remembered; he,
for a change, seemed surprisingly civil. All of us were
red-eyed, wrung out from lack of sleep; even Kost had
taken the time to redden his own orbs, since that was
clearly the most appropriate look.

"All right," Yaan said brusquely. "Let's assume
we're short on time—because we can't bring Ntaya
back again, not without looking damned suspicious.

"We had no time to sum up, yesterday. I'll do it
now. The most important thing that the Raayat brain
told us was that it *was* a brain—a whole brain, as well
as we can judge, and presumably capable of running
a body. Which isn't good news. If this Raayat is typical, then we have to conclude that even in the absence
of the gestalt Tyr-mind, the Raayat can function. Im-
perfectly, erratically, but function." He shook his head
grimly. "What that means, in plain English, is that
there is no magic kill. Even if there is a seat of consciousness, a Great Mother or Cloud of Knowing or
something like that—which I doubt—destroying it
won't provide an answer. All you'll do is confuse it,
a little. The parts will go on. That's a guess," he reminded us. "But an educated one.

"So: any attempt to defeat the Tyr must destroy all
the parts at once—and *all* the parts, because even one
Honn remaining means that the whole beast lives on—
or attack the gestalt mind itself."

"How?" Kost demanded.

"I have no idea. That's why we're here."

"But I do," the Tekk woman said. She was grinning. A warrior's grin, fierce and exultant. "There is
a weakness, in this creature. *It does not know fear.*"

"How is that weakness?" Sung asked.

She described for us the slaughter of a Raayat which
she had witnessed, in terms so vivid that we could
almost smell the blood, and our ears rang from its
shrieking. And told us what she had guessed.

"The hraas lives to hunt. We know this. We know
already that it will attack anything not Tyr, or Tekk.

But why? What do those two groups have in common?''

"The Tekk don't fear?'' a man asked sharply.

"The Tekk don't fear *the hraas*. Because those who do are killed in childhood. Dai? The early Tekk created . . . call it a religion. It works. It weeds out the fearful. I watched Tekk die that day,'' she said emphatically. "The beast killed them when it was finished with the Raayat. Everyone who feared it was slaughtered. The beast is filled with anger. With hate. I think it will kill *anything* that exhibits fear—even the Tyr.''

"But can we be sure?'' Ria protested. "What if that was one isolated hraas? Can we be sure that all of them have the same instincts, and will act on them?''

"Yes.'' I was remembering the hraas I had been, and all the things I had felt. And suddenly it all came together. "It has to do with their world-view. Creatures that don't fear it . . . don't fit into the whole, somehow. The hraas don't know how to deal with them.''

Several voices spoke out at once, demanding in a variety of heated phrases, *how do you know?* But Yaan only nodded slowly, understanding both what I said, and—even more—what was implied by the fact that I knew it.

And I met his eyes and nodded, to confirm it.

The Tekk woman looked around the table, at all of us. "Harosh! The hraas are an army. They go everywhere the Tyr go. Everywhere! An army, waiting to strike. And only one mind connected to the whole has to be affected, for them to attack!'' She turned to Yaan, with a look that was half accusation and half hope. "This is your work, your specialty. Tell us how to make it afraid.''

"It isn't that easy,'' Yaan muttered. "You say yourself that the Raayat was afraid; that didn't affect the Tyr-whole, did it? Who's to say if even a Honn or a Kuol can infect the gestalt with an emotion totally alien to it?''

"We, too, are an army," she retorted. "With one purpose only: the liberation of Earth. An army that's waited three hundred years for an opportunity to attack. You tell us what has to be done, and we'll do it. You tell us how to give the Tyr-whole fear, and I give you an army of hraas also, who have access to every place the Try might hide. We will wipe them out!—but you must give us the key."

"We have no time to argue," Yaan pointed out. "This path is dead-ending. Errol? Lab one?"

A red-headed man stood in response, and cleared his throat. "I have bad news . . . and bad news. Our subject did indeed have vulnerable points—arteries close to the surface of the body, vital organs that would rupture if struck properly—but, as you can see," and he touched the control that would bring up a new image before us, "little is accessible." He handed Yaan a pile of printouts, one for each of us: a detailed analysis of Tyrran anatomy. We studied them as he spoke, and I worked to commit the major points to memory. "Those armored plates don't grow at random. If Tyrran evolution did a poor job of designing the brain, it more than compensated in the armaments department. This creature is a fighting machine. There's no easy way to defeat it. You need a weapon that can pierce that armor, and then do major damage inside the body. A massive weapon, like the Raayat's own spikes. Or something that burns the whole of it, like the Tyr weapons do. Sorry for that news. On another front . . . we did find something interesting, although I don't know how useful it'll be. We found reproductive organs—rudimentary, underdeveloped, but potentially functional. Male *and* female," he stressed.

"So it's self-fertilizing?" someone asked.

"Or simply in a growth phase where sexual identity hasn't yet been decided. But there were a lot of eggs," he said, and shivered. "A *lot* of eggs."

"All right," said Yaan. "What do we know about their reproductive cycle?"

The Tekk woman shook her head. "There are no

young among their kind. Not for as long as we've served them.''

"Or you haven't seen them," someone challenged. She glared. "Do you doubt the Tekk?"

"Enough!" Yaan snapped. "There's no time to argue. We're all on the same side—aren't we? *Aren't we?*"

Everyone nodded. Even the Tekk woman looked slightly chastened.

"Rudimentary sexual organs might indicate that it's some other subgroup that does the actual reproducing. Even with eggs present," he said to the red-headed man. "We're used to a neat evolution, in which organs that aren't needed are usually discarded, or adapted to some other purpose. But the Tyr doesn't work like that." He turned to the Tekk woman. "You say there aren't young. But they do increase in number, we know that. How?"

"All we know is, periodically, all the longships leave their normal routes. They gather somewhere— not to say that I know the location, understand? We aren't told. Then most of the longships leave, to go back to their routes. Some will wait. Sometimes much time. When they leave . . . there's a new Kuol, and other Tyr attending him. A type of Tyr without armor, seen only at this time. We go to a new planet, and discover there are new Honn on the longship. These Honn and their Kuol make conquest, and leave the longship.''

"And the . . . the Tyr without armor?"

"I don't know," she said solemnly. "We never see them, after the beginning."

"How long between these gatherings?" I asked suddenly.

She looked at me, startled, and said, "I don't know. By your calendar. Time dilation makes it impossible to compare."

"What are you thinking?" Yaan asked quietly.

"Kiri and I were looking over the records of this . . . you call it a 'madness season.' The period when the Raayat are most unstable. The Domes have kept good records, number and dates and specific incidents . . . so tell me, if you can: what happens at the end of that season?''

I gave them a moment in which to realize that they didn't know, and then continued. ''I'll tell you. The Raayat disappear. They get on longships and leave Yuang—and are never heard from again.''

I gave that a moment to sink in, then pulled a wad of drawings from out of my pocket, and unfolded them. ''I first saw Frederick months ago. He looked very different, then. In size and armoring, mostly. I programmed the computer to calculate his recent changes, and figure out what he would look like in a month's time if that development continued. This is what I got.''

I held up the computer's rendering, turned it so all could see. It had the impact I had expected.

''God . . .'' one man muttered. ''A Kuol?''

''A Kuol,'' I agreed. ''When does the next gathering take place?''

''Soon,'' the Tekk said. ''Very soon.''

''According to Domes records, the Raayat are due to leave within a month. Frederick also, I assume.'' I looked toward the Tekk woman. ''I think your people have never seen the Tyr's young . . . because you never recognized them as such.''

''The Raayat?'' someone whispered. I nodded.

''They leave the conquered worlds . . . and mate?'' He shook his head. ''Terra, it's neat. Very neat. There's only one thing it doesn't explain. How does a creature who's only partly of the Tyr become a Kuol, who is wholly submerged in it?''

''There's the weak link,'' the Tekk woman hissed. ''Tell us how to break it!''

The door opened suddenly; given the level of tension in the room, it was almost like a blow in the face. ''Fred's coming,'' the lookout warned.

''Damn!'' Yaan looked at Ntaya, his eyes narrowed in quick thought. ''How much can you tell your people? If we find your answer, how well can you spread the news?''

''We have codes, and a way to send them. Short codes. We can send longer messages, enough details to organize the Tekk . . . but only once. You understand? The second time, the Tyr will suspect us.'' Her gaze was fierce. ''So make sure your answer is the right one.''

''I understand,'' he assured her.

As did I. All too well.

* * *

Sleep was promising to become a very rare commodity. And the last person I wanted to see in those few precious hours available for it was Kost. Which is probably why he showed up in my cubicle, and chose to do it when Kiri was absent.

''Busy?'' he asked.

''I was trying to sleep.''

''Yes. Humans do that, don't they?'' He pulled a chair panel from out of the wall, dropped it into position and sat. ''Kiri told me about you. Hard to believe . . . but here you are, aren't you?''

''Yes,'' I said. ''Here I am.''

''And you wish I would leave.''

''You're very perceptive.''

''I wanted to talk to you alone.''

''Try. I may fall asleep while you do it.''

His eyes flared angrily. ''You think playing *kreda* to a Marra gives you some kind of immunity from the rest of us?''

''I think you could kill me with a touch if you wanted to. And I'm very, very tired. So please, say your piece and go.''

''Ah, of course. Still performing like a trained animal in the laboratory till all hours of the night, are you?''

It amazed me that any being could have such a per-

fect handle on how to irritate me. But I refused to be
baited. "You obviously know, so why ask?"

"*Aaryeh!* How does she stand you?" He glared.
"But there's no denying what you are . . . which
makes us half-brothers, shapechanger."

I sat up and looked at him.

"Kiri encouraged your human side. That was appropriate; she needed your weaknesses. But now that
Identity's done with. She'll find another master—"

"I was never her master."

"—another *friend,* then." A contemptuous smirk
played about his lips. "However you two choose to
phrase it. Lovers, perhaps? No; I see by your face that
isn't the case. Pity."

"Get to the point."

He leaned forward; I could feel the intensity of his
presence reaching out toward me, a tendril of Marra-
ness without the flesh to mask it. Repellent. "The
point is this," he whispered. His voice was low, hypnotic. Seductive. "You are what we are, in all the
ways that matter. I accept that. It took time—but then,
you are an oddity. I accept you now. And I have plans
for the Marra. They can easily include you."

"Yes. Universal domination, isn't it? Kiri told me.
Funny, you know . . . I would have thought megalo-
mania was a chemical thing." I managed to shrug.
"Guess not."

He darkened. "Do you know what I'm offering? Do
you know what the alternative is? Go ahead and play
with them, like a human, play their games, and live
out your life in subservience. To the Tyr, or to us. It's
a fact of existence that one either rules, or is ruled.
You'll have to make that choice, soon; I'd rather see
it be the right one."

"And I thought your species had no altruism."

"You doubt my motives?"

"Oh, no. I think I understand them very well. Or
at least, I can guess at them. Would you like to hear?"
In the absence of any response, I continued. "What
all the Marra seem to need, more than anything else,

is interaction. It doesn't matter what kind of interaction, does it? As long as it gives you a framework for your Identity, and somewhere to hang up your memories so they don't get lost. You've got Ria right now, but that won't take you far. When it comes time to dominate other worlds, she'll have nothing to offer you. You need someone new to play off against in that context, some embodied being that will recognize your right to power and interact with your new despotic Identity . . . and I'm sorry, Kost, but I'm just not interested.''

He stared at me in frank hostility. Which told me I'd been right. No real surprise. The Marra, in their own chaotic way, were proving very predictable.

''You're a very foolish man,'' he warned me.

''And a very tired one. Is that all?''

He stood. ''You think because you travel with a Marra that it's all that easy, that all of us are soft. But only *your* Marra is like that. She's forgotten too much to be of any use to anyone, least of all you. And she'll bind you, you know; that's how the Nurturer works. She'll get you to need her, in whatever way she can—''

I swung my feet down to the floor and stood. And hesitated only an instant; then I grabbed him by the shirt front, as I would any embodied man, and forced him toward the door.

''What the hell do you think you're doing?''

''I'm throwing you out. No. Excuse me. I'm throwing your *body* out—you can stay or go, as you please.''

And I got him halfway to the door before he got over his surprise enough to stop me.

''You have spirit. But your attachment to her—''

''Leave my cubicle, *now*.''

''Ah, I understand. The male protective response. How embodied—''

I hit him. Hard. Thinking as I swung: *Strength is a function of form. If I can change my whole body at will, surely I can adjust a muscle or two.* So I did. And hit him with the strength of ten men, as the saying goes, square in the jaw. Bone shattered. His body went flying backward, through the doorway and into the far wall. Hard. There was blood all over, and the shape of his skull looked none too good.

"I happen to *be* embodied," I pointed out. "So this behavior is more than appropriate."

And I slammed the door as hard as I could—because that, too, seemed appropriate—and decided that I felt much better.

Ah, those primitive emotions.

* * *

Hours of sleep, blissfully dreamless. And then I woke to find her beside me. And for a moment, in the darkened room, it was almost possible to forget what she was and be lost in her warmth, in the bittersweet pleasure of wanting her.

"What happened with you and Kost?" she asked softly.

I managed to shrug. "He offered me power and glory. I called him an asshole."

"He's very angry."

"I said it well."

She touched a finger to my forehead, gently; I fought not to catch her hand in mine, to hold her there.

"Is he really necessary?" I asked her.

Her hand fell away. "He's necessary."

"It strikes me he'll do more damage than good."

"To your people, maybe. But to mine . . . The Marra are in a race against time, Daetrin. One they're not even aware of. And right now he's the only means I have of reaching them all. I have to use the tool that's available to me, or . . . you saw what happened to Paes'. It'll happen to others. And I can't just go and announce the truth to them; they won't believe it, any more than he did. The message has to come from someone who already has a place in their memory, someone who made contact before the delusion took hold. . . ."

I opened my eyes again and looked at her. "A *kreda?*"

"Certainly that, if it's available."

"Kost used the word for me. You've used it, too, I think. It means *master?*"

She hesitated. "Master. Keeper. Guardian. It was the title the Saudar had: *Kreda* of the Unity. And we used it for them, too, to describe their relationship with us. But not in a personal sense. They were the keepers of our memory, our history, our race . . . but there was nothing about individual dominance in it. That's an easy thing to forget, apparently."

She touched her hand to my forehead again, gently brushing back the few strands of hair that had fallen across it. "So, my *kreda,* how do you feel?"

"Tired. Weak."

"That nutrient contraption in the dining hall . . . it gives you what you need?"

"After I reprogrammed it."

"And the rest?"

I suddenly saw what she was driving at.

"You've been changing form for them. So they can run tests for you . . . and it's been getting harder. I've seen it."

"Yes," I whispered.

"You need life."

"There's none available. A few rats, all spoken for . . . not enough, Kiri."

"Let me help you."

She had reclaimed her old body. The one she had designed for me. The one I had reached for, in so many dreams.

"How?"

"As I did once before."

"How can I accept this? There's no life here for you, either."

"You're wrong. I can skim what I need off the froth of humanity's excess, and no one will notice. A fertile couple in a night's embrace supplies energy enough for a handful of changes . . . and Yaan has a collection of plants that need pruning, anyway. But you can't feed like that.''

I thought of holding her in my arms again, tasting her scent and her blood and all the heat of her life as though, even now, I drank in the wealth of what she offered. But there was more to my response than that, and the rest of it frightened me. I had never felt out of control like this, ever before. Never wanted a woman so much, when it was so wrong to have her. Wasn't it?

Would you find it flattering if you knew how I wanted you? Or simply inappropriate?

Then she touched her hand to my lips. Gently. I took it in my own, enfolding it within my fingers. As she had done to me, outside the Suyaag compound. My heart was pounding, and farther down there was a heat that grew steadily in my flesh, nearly painful in its intensity—but I focused myself upon the gift which she had offered, and let her flesh become a part of me. It was a kind of dominance I was unaccustomed to, but instinct proved enough of a tutor. Her hand was my hand, her flesh my flesh. Her blood, my blood. There was no distinction.

I kissed her palm, pressing my lips against the velvet softness of her skin. No longer remembering if one designed teeth for such a thing, or if merely human teeth would suffice. I could feel the beating of her heart as it echoed through the veins of her hand, a pulse so rich with life and warmth that I shook from the force of wanting her. And then her flesh parted beneath my lips, changing its form in response to my hunger. Blood flowed out, thick and sweet, and I drank deeply of her offering. It was delicious in a way that animal blood could never be, and doubly so because it was freely given; intoxicating, it sent shivers of pleasure coursing through me, body and soul. I lost all sense of my surroundings, knowing only that fragile bond between us, which allowed me to command her flesh as my own. A bond I dared not give a name to, because it was . . . inappropriate. Unfamiliar. Frightening.

And there were no teeth, nor any need for them. There never is, when blood is freely offered.

I had forgotten that.

* * *

If blackness can burn, then Bianca's eyes are pools of flame. Pupils distended by an infusion of belladonna, as is the fashion, but she doesn't suffer for it as the daybound do; her gaze is bright, her vision clear.

"I've hunted with you on four feet—now hunt with me on two." Her voice is liquid silver, sweetly cajoling. "I'll find you youths who deserve to die— useless bravos, long since disowned by their families, whom the law would execute if it could. Would that suit you? Would that satisfy your precious moral sense? We'll take them in the night, you and I—a feast of human blood that no one will ever avenge. Ah, Tonio . . . you can't know what human blood means, until you've tasted it regularly. You can't imagine, living off animals, what it means for us to feed as nature intended."

"And what about the bondage?" I demand. "Have you forgotten that? Do you simply ignore the bond that develops between us and the subjects of our hunger? Or is that what you want— to be emotionally bound to these street brawlers, as nature intended us to be bound to lovers?"

For an instant I see something flash in her eyes, that is neither hunger nor seduction. Pity?

"That's why I kill them," she purrs.

* * *

"There it is," Yaan said quietly. And he sat back to look at his handiwork.

Above the table before us, two images had been projected. Both were of brains. Both brains were going through the same set of mental exercises. And both brains had been indexed with a rich spectral assortment of colors, that showed us where and how each one was being used.

Two brains: one human, one canine. Both mine.

"They match, at first. Or very nearly. See. . . ." He ran them through the start of the test sequence again, and the holographic composites—thousands of paper-thin slices of data joined together in the bowels of the computer—obliged. Once more it was possible to see how closely related the two brains were, at the start. As though the dog-brain's owner, though clad in canine flesh, still processed his thoughts in a human pattern. But as time went on, the two patterns diverged. Soon there were deep violet sections in one brain, hardly used, that corresponded to amber in the other. Most of those were areas of activity in the human brain that had little or no analogy in the canine model. But after a short while, the opposite also occurred.

"There's when you reported distinct canine impulses." He looked at the project log before him, and shook his head in amazement. "It matches. Damn. It matches *exactly*."

I've never been one to worship gods, but I've known many people who did. And I suspect that the awe they experienced when contemplating the divine was very similar to mine at that moment, as the mysteries of my nature left the realm of magic forever, and firmly rooted themselves in the world of measurable things.

"I wish we had a real canine brain to compare it with," Yaan was saying. "Not that we could get a dog to do the math problems. But gods of Terra, if only!"

He looked at me. "It doesn't tell you very much that you didn't already know. Except for the timing. That's interesting."

"No." I whispered. "It tells me everything. Thank you."

"Your human patterns of cognition seem to last

longer when housed in a more sophisticated brain. Again, no surprise.'' He leaned back, pensive. ''There might be risk inherent in adopting a very primitive form—in trying to use a brain that couldn't support human thought, even for a while.''

He laughed softly. ''You realize what that means about flying, don't you''

Suddenly, I did. And I muttered, ''I hate bats.''

''But it is the best form for your purposes. Earth's only flying mammal. And a mammalian brain is clearly your best bet.'' He leaned forward over the controls, and keyed in another sequence. Two brains again, this time both human. One from before the shapechanging experiment, and one from after.

''Different,'' I whispered.

''You carry the effects back with you, for a time. That's *very* interesting.''

He looked at me, gray eyes playing at nonchalance when, in fact, I knew what he was thinking. Because I was thinking it, too.

The man who could become a wolf could become a Raayat, too. And just as his brain would absorb the persona of a wolf in time, and become a wolf in fact as well as image, it would presumably do the same with the Raayat.

The difference was that the Raayat was part of the Tyr. And in that brief time when the Raayat was acting independently—when it was no longer part of the Tyr-whole, but had partial access to it—such a man might gain guarded access to the gestalt mentality that had conquered Earth. And know, with the Tyr's own certainty, how it might be destroyed.

''It would be a suicide mission,'' I said softly.

''Yes,'' he agreed. ''Most likely it would be that.''

''And probably wouldn't accomplish anything. By the time there was contact with the overmind, I would no longer be wholly human. I might not even want to kill it.''

''Probably not,'' he agreed.

But underneath his pewter lashes, gray eyes argued,

*But if you did—and if you succeeded—Earth would
have a fighting chance.*

"I need time," I whispered.

He nodded, understanding. "If only we had it.

* * *

You know what your problem is, Alex?" Lu-
cille's eyes are dark, her manner fierce. "You
don't know how to give. I'm not talking about the
little things, all the easy gestures—you've got no
problem there, not with material generosity. But
you're afraid to *give* of yourself—don't you see?
You wall yourself up inside that head of yours
and won't let anybody near. We've been together—what, almost four years now?—and when
have you ever let me get a peek at what goes on
inside you? When have you ever opened up, even
for an instant—dared to be vulnerable, Alex!
That's the cost of it, yes! But that's what people
do when they have a relationship. Don't you understand that? Give of themselves, because
something else has finally become more important. . . ."

* * *

Two brains, projected above the table. One human,
one canine. Both involved in a test of cognitive skills.

Both Kiri's.

Yaan sat back in his chair and whistled softly. Tireza
and Sung, also present, were noticeably silent. Yaan
had insisted on explaining things to them, despite my
misgivings. Now I watched their faces anxiously, ready
to confront the grim specter of rejection the minute it
showed its ugly face.

"Is it all right?" Kiri asked.

Her voice brought me back to myself. "Fine," I
assured her. I took her hand, and noticed in some
distant part of my brain that it felt as human as my

own, now. That I was beginning to think of her as a
woman—and dream of her as such. What could have
changed so much between us? That I now relied on
her for sustenance? Or was it something more?

"The difference is . . ." Yaan fumbled for an ad-
jective.

"Incredible," Tireza whispered, leaning forward to
get a closer look. Sung muttered something in agreement.

The two brains were mostly violet, blue, and black.
Certain sections glowed brightly—motor skills, auto-
nomic functions, language processing—but for the
most part, there was simply no match between brain
and behavior. Kiri used the parts that she needed, as
she needed them, and no more. But to know that was
one thing; to see it hanging there in front of us,
mapped out in the PET compiler's eloquent colors,
was something else again.

Yaan shook his head, amazed, then looked at Kiri.
"If I said that I didn't really believe until now . . .
would you understand?"

I was sure she didn't, but she nodded anyway. Diplomacy.

We listened as Yaan summed up their findings: that
I, in changing form, subjected myself to the limitations of whatever brain I adopted. The longer I spent
using only a wolf's brain, the more like a wolf I would
become. For Kiri, no such process existed. She could
take on any body she wanted—dead, alive, or totally
inorganic—but it would never alter the way she
thought. I had always seen that as a weakness on my
part, but now Yaan phrased it as a strength: I could
become a wolf in fact. Kiri never could.

As for the implications . . . they were there, but still
unspoken. Yaan said it with his eyes, meeting mine
for an instant before he turned away. As for the others,
they were only now beginning to realize what was at
stake.

Only you, his eyes said.

Only me.

* * *

Tireza cornered me outside the dining hall. Touching a hand to my arm, a simple gesture that spoke
volumes for her acceptance of my nature.

"You were alive then, weren't you?" Her eyes were
shining. "Before the Conquest. Yaan told us." She
hesitated. "Was it like this, back then? On Earth?"

Child of the Domes: what was she asking? Was this
the flavor of Earth science, in the days when Earth
controlled its own future? This sense of plummeting
forward into the unknown with too little knowledge,
too little time, never enough preparation? Is this what
purpose tasted like, when Earth still had purpose?

"Yes," I told her. "For a few." *A lucky few.*

There was envy in her eyes.

* * *

We were in the lab when Frederick snapped. We had
known it would happen sometime; it was too much to
hope for that this one Raayat, out of all of them, would
be immune from the seasonal madness. But it took us
by surprise nonetheless, and when his body suddenly
spasmed, and his voice croaked out a command that
none of us could decipher, we froze where we stood,
to the last man, woman, and Marra among us.

Frederick rasped at us, and this time I thought I
could make out a single word: *Talk.*

I looked around the room. Sung and Yaan, Tireza
and Kiri and I. The fear was palpable.

"Talk," he said again, and there was an edge of
hysteria in his voice.

I caught Yaan's eyes for an instant, and knew he was
thinking along the same lines that I was. Trying to
apply what little we knew of Raayat madness fast
enough, and accurately enough, to fend off the storm
that was imminent.

But the Raayat moved first. Tireza was closest to
him. It was therefore Tireza that he reached out and

grabbed, powerful claws closing about her upper arm, as he demanded again, hoarsely, "Talk!"

"About what?" she stammered. I could hear the fear in her voice. "What is it you want?"

Tell me what you see, the Raayat commands. His tone of voice implies that I might well die if I fail to satisfy him. Not knowing what he wants, I dare the only answer I have. But his angry hiss tells me that it is not the right one, not what he wants to hear. . . .

The Raayat growled. His upper limbs were trembling, as if from suppressed violence, and his eyes were shot with red. He was angry, confused, possibly even terrified—but he lacked the ability to verbalize what it was he needed, and thus we were unable to help him. His hand tightened on Tireza's arm, and she cried out involuntarily as blood began to flow; any minute now the last of the Raayat's self-control might go, and God alone knew what the result would be.

"Talk!" he hissed. And because there was no real alternative, I hazarded a guess. The only one I had. Right or wrong, it would have to do.

"All right," I told him. Stepping forward, exhibiting a courage that I didn't feel. Important to get him away from Tireza, at any cost. "We'll talk to you. We don't know what you want, but we'll try." I saw Yaan out of the corner of one eye, nodding. "Get Asako," I said, and hoped he understood. Because now there was only Frederick, and Frederick's victim, and me. "Let me tell you about what we're doing here." *Talk.* Was there something he wanted to know, or did he just want input—any input? When the Tyr withdrew from him this time, had it left him bereft of vocabulary? Suddenly dysfunctional, unable to communicate, unable to even let us know the nature of his need?

Talk, he had commanded, and I did. Endlessly. Telling him stores; histories, fictions, anything. Eventually, his grip on Tireza loosened. Eventually, he released her.

"I can take over," a voice said from behind me.

Asako. I shook my head as I watched Tireza back off, and motioned for Asako to stay behind me. I wanted her there to watch what was happening, so that she with her linguist's skill could interpret it for us later. *Language acquisition during the madness season.* But as for dealing with Frederick's immediate need, soothing his all-too-rational fears and helping him stabilize himself again . . . that was my job. I had done it before, and knew how.

We're alike, the two of us. Far from home, and afraid. I understand. I'll help.

Slowly, he grew calmer. His upper eyes hooded. His posture relaxed. And at last I knew, without being able to say how, that we had passed the crisis point.

"You're among friends," I told him.

And the odd thing was, I meant it.

* * *

High above the floor of Five, supported by the struts of the dome's inner shell, a meter-wide circular track girdled the dome's circumference. God alone knows what moved the Tyr to build it, although it must have served some practical purpose; the Tyr built nothing for pleasure. But now it was a way of escaping the labs, the suffocating press of people and equipment, and finding a place to think.

I had been there a while when Yaan climbed up and found me. Staring out between the ranks of heat collectors, seeing nothing. His footfall on the plastel scaffolding was unfamiliar, but even so I knew who it was. Who it had to be.

He took up a position beside me, and stared out into the distance. I wondered what the landscape looked like to him, with all its implications of death and servitude.

"The *Kamugwa*'s made nexus," he told me. "Their skimship'll be on its way soon."

"And the Tekk woman will leave."

Out of the corner of my eye, I saw him nod. "And Frederick."

I looked at him, startled, but his gaze never wandered from the horizon. "Frederick's leaving?"

"Going home, he says."

Home. . . .

His strong gray eyes met mine, held them.

"We have some decisions to make," he said quietly.

I said nothing.

He turned away, to consider the landscape once more. "Sung asked what would happen if you succeeded. What would happen to the Domes, and all of us. Funny . . . I never brought it up because it seemed so obvious. I guess it wasn't."

I looked at the oily vista outside the Dome, and suddenly realized what he meant. The Domes depended on the Tyr for supplies; without food, water and oxygen, they stood no chance of surviving in the hostile Yuang environment.

If the gestalt mind was destroyed, or even injured, supplies would fail to come. Only Tyrran translation could bridge the galaxies and find this one needy point, to deliver such goods. And who's to say they would continue with their deliveries, even if I failed? An attempted revolt might be enough to earn their wrath and bestow a death sentence upon all the domers. Earth's elite, and the last bastion of her creative intelligence. The loss would be beyond measure.

"I didn't think," I said weakly. Insufficiently.

"Sung feels that we should contact the others. Gather all the domers together, and let them decide. It's their lives that are at stake, after all."

A thousand or more humans, trapped like insects in a jar. Suffocating slowly, or perhaps choosing a more dramatic end: exposure to the planet's ecosystem, and a quick but gruesome death.

I shuddered.

"I told him no," Yaan continued, softly. "Don't let them in on the decision. Because what happens if one of them—and it would only take one—lacks our courage, and warns the Tyr? Then everything would be gone. Us, our work, your freedom, countless lives, and all the years that the Tekk have invested in us. All gone. He said they have a right to know . . . but sometimes you have to play God, Daetrin. Sometimes the decision is placed in your hands and you just have to go with it, right or wrong, according to what you think is best.''

I drew in a deep breath, for courage. ''If I went—if I did this thing—where would it get us? What could I do?''

The gray eyes flickered back to me. ''Infect it with fear. Give it a dose of human emotion, something it wasn't designed to handle. Find out its weaknesses. Break its mating cycle. Gods of Terra, how can we know what will be possible? You're doing what no human being has ever done before; you'll have to make your decisions as you go, take advantage of whatever opportunities the situation effords you. We'll give you what support we can. The Tekk will be behind you. But ultimately, you're the explorer; you're the one who's going to find out just what we can do to this thing. We can't know before that.''

''Too vague,'' I whispered. ''Too vague.''

''There'll be the Marra, too. Kiri and Kost have committed themselves.'' I wondered when Kost came around to revealing his true nature. Wondered how Ria took it, when he did. ''They say their people will help, without question.''

''What can they do?'' I remembered Kiri telling me about her attempt to drain a Honn-Tyr; any direct offense seemed doomed to failure. ''They can't kill it.''

''No. But they can drive it mad.''

I looked at him, startled.

''Kiri pointed out that the Tyr excises any part of it that seems to be malfunctioning. If a Honn-Tyr sees something that simply can't exist . . . the part is killed. Immediately.''

''But that would only work a limited number of times. The Tyr-whole would see a pattern—''

"Not if you distracted it," he said quietly. "You see, that's all you really have to do. Keep the gestalt's attention occupied, while the Marra strike at key points. The Tekk will move in as soon as the structure weakens. And as for the hraas . . . don't you think that the Honn and the Kuol will learn fear, when the laws of nature appear to go haywire? Praise Terra the Marra are on our side," he said, smiling slightly. "Because I think they could drive any army mad, that didn't understand them."

"Do you?" I asked. Also smiling.

"No. And I suspect it's better that way."

But I do. Oh, I could imagine Kiri and her kind with the Tyr: playing, as with a brand new toy. Cavorting about the universe, designing nightmares to unseat the Tyr's chemical balance, and playing all the parts those nightmares required. And it could throw the Tyr off balance just enough to make a difference. For a creature unaccustomed to nightmares, it would be quite a blow.

Kiri . . . the mere thought of her awakened an aching need, a loneliness that was growing hourly. I would lose her soon. It was inevitable. But the fact that it would happen sooner rather than later, if I took on this mission, didn't make my decision any easier.

I stared at the yellow and mauve horizon in pensive silence. In the distance, with a thunderclap, a cloud ignited in spurts of flame. Black smoke bled across the landscape, enclosing the world in a poisonous shell. Memories bled into my consciousness, images not quite solid enough to be called timefugue, but almost as powerful, reminding me how much I hated the Tyr. How much I hungered to defeat it.

Reminding me, above all else, that I was human.

As from a distance, I heard the words come. "I'll need to take the place of an existing Raayat. Duplicate an existing body, so the Tyr thinks I belong to it."

"Well, fate has been kind enough to us in that regard—"

"Not Frederick," I said sharply. And because he

seemed about to argue the point, I said it again. *"Not Frederick."*

He stared at me in silence for a minute, then shrugged. "It'll be hard to find another one, and kill it when the Tyr's not looking."

"Then it'll be hard."

He sighed. "The risk is yours. I guess you can call the shots."

"When is the skimship due?"

"Between one and three days from now, is my guess."

"We'll need a written message for the Tekk. Something to explain what we're going to do, lay it all out for them. Kiri can smuggle it in." I looked out at the landscape again, and tried not cringe before the thousand and one details that would have to be hammered out before I left. Let them take care of that.

For me, there was only the changing. And that was more than enough.

*   *   *

She entered the dark cubicle in silence. Had it been anyone else making that entrance I might have missed it; I was too wrapped up in thought to hear a thing. But my body was attuned to her presence, to the sight and the scent and the feel of her, and so I stirred when she entered, and faced the door, that I might see her.

She closed the door behind her without turning on the light. Without asking me why I was sitting in the dark, or why I wasn't with the others, going over plans. With a healer's certain instinct, she knew.

I heard her walk quietly to where I was sitting; her clothing rustled softly as she knelt by my side, and the soft warmth of her body pressed against my leg. The contact was maddening, but I didn't pull away. I had no way to explain to her why my body ached for her with an intensity that was almost painful, my hands shook for wanting to touch her, I dreamed of her night after night; but now it was different, it had become something I couldn't control, and so I stayed as I was, my arousal hidden in the darkness. Because I couldn't bear to hurt her by moving away.

"You'll leave in the morning?"

I breathed it: "Yes."

"They're packing a baldric for you. From the Raayat Frederick killed. Lab one has isolated the proteins and amino acids you'll need."

"So you told them."

"Someone had to," she said softly.

That their savior drinks blood.

Her hand reached up and took mine, warm velvet fingers sliding between my own.

It took everything I had to keep my voice steady. To keep my hand from shaking. "What did they say?"

"Yaan said, whatever you needed, you should come to them. That you should have come to them earlier."

I closed my eyes and shook my head, but said nothing.

"Daetrin . . . I can follow you in body, go where you're going . . . but not in mind. No Marra can follow you there."

"You stay here," I told her.

Her hand tightened around mine. I could feel her blood pounding between our fingers . . . or maybe it was mine.

"You won't be able to change back without me," she said quietly.

I laughed softly, bitterly. "I doubt that will be an issue."

"You can't be sure."

"Kiri . . . when the Tekk turn against the Tyr, I'm going to be there. Inside it. When it knows that something betrayed it, and looks within itself to find out what . . . I'll be there. I'll be *part* of it, Kiri. Whatever happens, good or bad . . . I'm not coming back." I swallowed, hard, trying not to let the image shake me. I had committed myself to going. That was all that mattered. "You stay here, with Kost. He scares the hell out of me, Kiri. Get him under control, some-

how. Keep him . . . keep him from doing more damage to my people than the Tyr did, once the Tyr are
gone.'' *If the Tyr are ever gone,* I told myself.
Stop it. Be confident.

I heard her rise, felt the warmth of her breath on my
hair. Her free hand brushed a few stray strands back
from my forehead; the contact made me shiver with
wanting her.

"Kiri, don't. . . ."

"Shhh . . . It's all right."

"Kiri . . ."

"It's a normal reaction. Body-stuff, Daetrin. The
desire to spread one's genes about before dying. It's
all right."

"It's more than that," I whispered.

She released my hand. For a moment I thought she
would leave me. Then her voice came again, silk-soft
in the darkness.

"I know," she told me.

"You can't understand—"

"But I do. And it means more to me than you can
know." She touched both hands to my face, now,
stroking my temples in what should have been a soothing rhythm. Only where she touched there was fire,
and the rush of blood to my face—and elsewhere—left
me breathless. "The lower animals function automatically. Give them the right scent, dance the right dance,
and they'll do what nature intended. Not so with advanced intelligences. They sense when something isn't
right, and keep their distance. What you feel for me
. . . the intensity of it . . . is a very rare, and very
precious thing. A gift beyond measure."

She kissed me then, so perfectly human a gesture
that I reached out without thinking, and took her into
my arms. I could feel her heartbeat pounding against
my chest, its rapid daybound pace radiating heat from
her, through clothing and sin and into the heart of me.
Dimly I felt the shadow of a timefugue, Kost's voice
and its ominous warning: *She'll bind you to her, in
any way she can.* But the words meant nothing; all

that mattered now was that it was my last night as a
human being—that she was here, in my arms, and we
were agreed on a form and a purpose—and everything
was going to be all right, until morning. The time after
that could take care of itself.

* * *

We did the actual change in Dome Prime. I was
afraid to let the domers see me attempt it. The memory of my hraas-change was still very vivid, and
frightening; I feared a similar loss of control.

But though the Raayat body I took on was every bit
as surprising, it was for wholly different reasons. The
fit was alarmingly comfortable. Senses were altered,
coordination would be awkward at first, and the extra
eyes and arms had no analog in my human experience—but all those were minor things compared to the
eerie compatibility of the Raayat psyche with my own.
No alien instincts coursed through this brain, save
those required to maintain the body; no lack of adequate neural circuitry dampened my human intelligence, as it so often did in the bodies of Earth
mammals. A cold prickling spread through my body,
the Tyrran equivalent of excitement. I was treading
ground that no Terran shapechanger had even imagined possible, transferring my psyche into an alien
body that could fully support its human intelligence.
There was no earthly equivalent.

*Don't get carried away. The Raayat brain is little
more than a blank slate, a vehicle for the Tyr-whole to
use. When this brain starts to link up with the overmind, that's when the real change will start.*

My new vision scanned the entire Dome, three hundred and sixty degrees about my head and all the space
above me. A dizzying perspective. I managed to lid
over the two upper eyes, which was marginally better;
the frequency response was very different—the entire
dome seemed to blaze with chartreuse light—but that
was something I could deal with. There was no sense

of smell, at least in any form that I could understand; given the hygiene of my fellow Tyr, that was not an unwelcome development. The other senses were human-congruent, enough so that I got my bearings quickly. And practiced walking, until I was sure that the long, back-hinged legs wouldn't fail me.

Kiri helped me settle the baldric between my shoulder spikes, then checked to see that all its contents were secure. In addition to several hundred nutrient capsules, the thick plastic belting held notepads, writing implements, and medical supplies—all hidden. And two knives carved from the bony plates of Frederick's kill. *Never rely on metal,* my father had taught me.

Do you see me now, father? See how well I learned?

There were no good-byes. We had said them all the night before. And besides, human emotion might have compromised my new persona.

"I'll take care of Kost," she promised, and I nodded. That was it. She made me walk up and down a few times, making sure that my movement looked natural. Something bothered me as she did so, that went beyond the strangeness of my body. It took me a moment to realize what it was.

"Daetrin?" she asked quietly. Concerned, as always.

"No memories," I whispered. Always in my life before there had been memories, a constant subtext murmur of *what had been,* to accompany *what is.* The timefugue experience was its most extreme manifestation, but other, less extreme varieties existed. Now, for the first time, that murmur was gone. I felt strangely naked. And terribly alone.

"The skimship's loading," she reminded me.

I forced myself to move. Stiffness would be acceptable in a Raayat, half of them were suffering from mental disruption as it was. I would be all right. No one would notice me.

Convince yourself of that, if you can.

I, Raayat. Walked to the skimship. Stepped between

the lines of Honn and boarded. Strapped myself in, with unfamiliar hands, and avoided the eyes of my co-travelers.

Here I come, you son of a bitch. Let's see how well you fight, on your own home ground.

Liftoff.

DOME PRIME

The hraas anticipates.

The season of blood was coming. It was in the air, it coursed in the hraas' blood, it breathed from the stone itself: the madness that would make parts of the Tyr *right,* for an instant, the voice that would breathe, in tones the hraas alone could understand: *Come, come and kill—now is the time!* Already, once, the hraas had seen the mesh become whole enough beneath Raayat feet that the power which normally bound its limbs to servitude was severed like a knife—and it had leapt, and feasted, hot Raayat blood gone to slake its thirst for vengeance. But that was a mere appetizer for the season yet to come. There were years of imprisonment to drown out in blood, a symphony of species anguish that demanded death for a climax, a desire to rend and tear and—above all else—*avenge.* Soon, soon, the barrier that guarded the Tyr from harm would come down in that chosen few . . . and the hraas would be there. Talons bared. Wing-claws extended. Thirst, as always, burning like fire.

The hraas waits.

PART THREE:
TYR

LONGSHIP KAMUGWA

The Raayat named Frederick walked the corridors of the *Kamugwa*. Alone. No voices from other parts of the Tyr were inside him, even when he listened for them; no accumulated wisdom from ages before trickled down into this consciousness, even when he most needed it. There was still a pale ghost of what had been in him before, but no more than that; a distant echo, growing gradually fainter, that he might conjure into activity only with great effort. But the effort required was greater and greater, and he was less and less inclined to exert himself.

Nothing came easily, any more. All the sounds and gestures that should have come naturally to him felt foreign, and strangely uncomfortable. Sometimes even the ghosts left him, and then everything was so difficult as to be nearly impossible . . . but those times came only rarely, and besides, he was getting them under control. The humans had helped with that. Unknowing, perhaps unwilling, but they had helped.

How he had used them! As they had used him, no doubt. A true sharing, human-style.

Alone. He, the Frederick-part, the part that knew human secrets, was alone. Not absolutely, by any means. Nor permanently, yet. But that was coming. He could feel its imminence like a blast of heat across his back, the fires of summer just over his shoulder. The cruel light of the Tyrran sun, which he feared and longed for and barely, just barely remembered. But it had been different then, in his youth. For then the Tyr had still been within him. Then, he had belonged.

412   C.S. Friedman

He concentrated on what the humans had shown
him, as a way of not facing the uncertainty that lay
within. Concentrated on their brain-truths, on their
science-thoughts, on the way they reasoned and log-
icked their way through myriad mysteries, without ever
needing to be handed an answer. He envied them that.
He would emulate it, if he could. If for no other reason
than the exercise kept him from having to confront the
cold, dark feeling that was growing inside him, the
shadow that was slowly devouring him.

Because when he did confront it—those few times
he dared—it resembled what the humans called
"fear."

LONGSHIP KAMUGWA

If I said merely that the longship *Kamugwa* was different from the *Talguth*, I wouldn't be doing justice to either. The ship which I viewed through Raayat eyes was as distinct from that of my former prison as day from night—but how much of that was due to the ship and how much to the change in my eyesight, I had no way to judge.

Say simply that all things were different—the skimship, the longship, the Tyr themselves. Adorned in colors that I would not have imagined possible, so unlike my vision of the cold, dull-hued Tyr that for a moment I genuinely questioned my sanity. But the truth soon became clear. There *was* color in their world, as much as in ours, but human eyes were incapable of doing more than brush at the surface of it. And while we might have wondered about the color vision of a cat, or a butterfly, or even a hrass, the plodding, noncreative nature of the Tyr seemed to find its perfect expression in the dark and muddy hues we perceived about them, and so we never questioned their truth.

But now, seeing as one of them: among the Tyr themselves, I perceived distinct markings. Patterns of color that swirled about the armored plates, identical among Honn that shared the same background. Thus the Honn-Tyr that served us on Yuang were marked with a complex double whorl of carmine and gold, against a background of russet and ultramarine. The single Raayat who seemed to originate from the same angdatwa also wore those colors, and bands of the same hues guarded its many combat spikes. But the four other Raayat I saw on the skimship, from other backgrounds, were considerably different; and when we disembarked in the *Kamugwa*'s receiving hold, the group of Honn that saw to our needs there matched each other, but no others.

The walls themselves were streaked with a maddening display of intense, often clashing colors. My first impression was that a group of antisocial humans had been set loose there, with tabs of LSD and cans of spray paint. Later I realized that was too simple an explanation. The meandering rivers of chartreuse and orange and indigo had both destination and purpose, and as I watched my fellow Raayat follow them I realized that they were many things at once: maps, a gauge of distance, and instructions on how to work the many irregular doors of the longship. *Leyq*, then; I remembered Frederick's description. That they were there at all spoke much for the importance of the Raayat, and the allowances that the Tyr-whole was willing to make for their periodic madness. For no one but the Raayat would ever need such maps, all others having access to the omniscient gestalt. For them and them alone, the entire longship had been painted. And if it seemed to have been oddly executed . . . I considered the gait of the Honn and the Raayat, the juncture of their arms, and their balance. And yes—with a paintbrush in one hand and no other concern than that a line be painted from *here* to *there* . . . the result might look like that. Just like that. So much for LSD.

It didn't strike me until later what the leyq really meant, for me and for my co-conspirators in Dome Five. It meant that we had been right about the Raayat, right in all our guesses. For nothing else but total detachment from the Tyr could explain the need for such omnipresent mapping, or its obvious priority in the Tyrran scheme of things.

That was important. That was exciting.

I wished I had someone to share it with.

Into this world, this discordant symphony of color, I was set adrift. Cast ashore in the *Kamugwa*'s dock, and left to find my way as I saw fit. Five other Raayat were dispatched alongside me—the seasonal gathering was beginning already, with the collection of Yuang's future mating stock from the planet's surface—but they seemed as purposeless as I was, and wandered the dock in a state of random confusion until chance, or sudden inspiration, moved them to leave.

Well enough, I decided at last. If I was going to spend time on this unknown longship, I might as well learn my way around. And my sanity would thus be benefited, too; I could conceive of nothing worse for my morale than finding a corner to sit in, and simply waiting for the changing to grab hold of my psyche. No, far better to be busy. Useful, if possible—but at any rate, *busy*.

Thus it was that I began to follow the leyq. Each of them seemed to pass through miles of corridor, beginning as a band of color a mere handwidth, and ending as a broad, aggressive swath of pigment many corridors distant from its origin. The color vision of my new body was extrememly sensitive, and could distinguish between some thousand hues with little effort. Likewise I began to observe minute differences in the width of each band, until I could tell from practice how far a given section was from its leyq's point of termination. It took hours—but hell, I had hours. Might as well use them.

I had no idea, of course, what most of the colors meant. It would take years to learn them all. And that much time I *didn't* have, I told myself. Ignoring, of course, that if the Tyr truly absorbed me, if I lost my humanity in the process and became no more than another pawn in its galactic plans, I might have more than enough time—and a real need—to learn the whole of the system.

Don't think about that, I told myself sternly. *Ever.*
But I did.

* * *

    I was not fortunate enough, in my early hours, to find a source of food. Not that I knew what the Tyr ate, anyway, but even a human nutritive access would have been a welcome find. The capsules which Yaan's crew had tucked into my baldric were necessary for my survival, but alone they would not suffice as an energy source. God alone knew what the Tyr themselves ate, but I could certainly have guessed my way through a meal, maybe tried a few simple sugars to see how they went down. Maybe thrown them up again—but hell, I was used to that. Better than starving. It occurred to me that I might well have to prey on other members of my adopted species for sustenance . . . and the ramifications of that were frightening, too, so I tried very hard not to think about it.

    I was trying hard not to think about a lot.

    I had passed several Honn in my wanderings, all marked with the chromatic patterns of the longship's native crew. All going about their business as if I wasn't there, sparing one look—and one look only—to register my presence for the Tyr-whole, and then ignoring me from then on. Other Raayat did just about the same, although the look they shot me seemed more confused and frightened than anything. We were all doing pretty badly. But at last I decided to take my chances and stop one, and I did—a Honn-Tyr of formidable size who was engaged in probing the consistency of the black tentacular growths that clustered along the ceiling of one particularly dark hallway.

    When he went to move on, I blocked his way. Boldly, as I imagined a Raayat might do who was far gone into season. My human instincts cringed at the confrontation, but I tried not to let that affect my Raayat body.

    "Kiya!" he exclaimed—which meant, in Saudar, *What?*

    Food had been one of the first words Kiri had taught me. I turned it into a demand.

He looked at me for a moment—and I had the sickening sensation of being watched by something else, some much larger and far more alien creature that saw through its eyes—and then it gestured stiffly toward the far wall.

"Iyert," it rasped, and it tried to move past me.

I knew enough of the language to recognize that as a color name, but which of several dozen that existed on the far wall was beyond me; neither Kiri nor I had guessed that my life might depend upon communicating fine gradations of hue. So I put on my maddest look—and hitched up my nerve—and demanded, in a rising tone, *Food!*

With a twitch of the undereye that might have been its version of a sigh of resignation, the mighty warrior Honn turned away from its duties and led me, as one might lead a child, through the halls of the longship.

Promising myself that I would make myself an English/Saudar dictionary—*soon*—I followed.

* * *

One thing for certain, anyway: the Tyr would never win praise for its cuisine.

* * *

Phase one—*immediate survival*—was being taken care of. For the moment. Which meant that Phase two—*future survival*—was next on the list. As I saw it, that meant accumulating as much information about the Tyr as I could humanly (or otherwise) get my hands (or claws) on. As fast as I possibly could.

Which meant computer access.

On the surface, that was no problem. I had accessed the overmind's files back on Earth, seventeen times; I had done it again on Yuang, with reasonable success. The Tyr's system was symbolic rather than verbal for the most part, and thus transcended the boundaries of language. But finding it was another thing.

I tried searching, following random leyq to their termination points and then exploring. Using this system, I located a storage bay, two unoccupied prison cells, a greenhouselike chamber, and five empty rooms with a variety of shelving. And the mating chamber of a hraas, who warned me off with bared teeth and possibly would have moved to drive me more forcibly from the place, had he not been otherwise engaged.

At which point I was forced to remind myself that the longship was vast—far too vast for trial-and-error to prove a reliable locating system. Already I was wandering in areas so far from the human-appointed cells that I half expected to round the corner and come face to face with a member of another species. (Rumor said that the Tyr ruled five, and that the same longships served them all.) But instead I found only Honn-Tyr, and sometimes an occasional Raayat. I had been mapping as I explored, using the notepad and writing tools tucked into my baldric, but that, too, was a hopeless enterprise. The corridors were too long, and twisted too much along their length, for me to gain any coherent overview of the longship's internal layout.

At last I took my courage in my claws and dared to stop another of the warrior caste. It looked at me blankly, and I explained—in my best formal Saudar—what it was I wanted.

At which point it simply ignored me—as if I had never spoken—and went on its way.

I was so stunned that I didn't think to try to stop it. But when another one came my way, some two corridors farther down, I planted myself firmly in its path and demanded, with an aura of autocracy, to be taken to a library access chamber.

Once again, it simply ignored me. With a jerky move it sidestepped me, and made as if to pass. But I put myself in its way, and again made my demand.

This time it simply pulled the blaze from its harness, and pointed it at my midsection.

For a minute there was nothing but stillness, and

the dull thud of an alien heart pounding alien blood through my veins, too loudly for comfort.

At last—having no real alternative—I stepped aside to let it pass. The minute I did so it resheathed its weapon, and continued onward as if nothing had passed between us.

Christ. I was shaking. But I had to have that access. I waited until my limbs were steady—it took quite a while—then sought out another Honn and tried it again.

The results were the same. Exactly.

Evidently there were some areas we were simply not supposed to have access to. But whether that applied to all the Raayat, or simply those who were fully detached from the Tyr, I had no way to know.

At any rate, I couldn't afford to get nervous about it. The hraas prowled every hall, and occasionally one would cross my path. And as it sniffed the air in my direction I thought I could catch a gleam in its eyes, that had not been there before. Of hope? Anticipation? Hunger for the kill? I found myself looking away, unwilling to meet those eyes, afraid to be measured against the creature's alien standards.

Fear is death. Instantly. Remember that.

Great.

* * *

Attempt to sleep: like the attempt to find a library access, doomed to failure. The Tyr don't sleep. But humans do, and despite my physical form I was still mostly human in psyche. Hours of effort brought me only sleepless misery, and I longed for the Terran paraphernalia that one might apply in the search for slumber: alcohol, sleeping pills, boring novels, late night movies. I was exhausted, my mind was worn out from all that it had absorbed, I suspected that days had passed in the timeless corridors since I had first disembarked from the skimship . . . but the Tyrran body

I wore was not designed to sleep, and so, try as I might, I couldn't manage even a ten-minute snooze.

And that was scary. Really scary. Because while I might wear the body of a Raayat, and slowly become subject to its instincts, I was still mentally a human being. And human beings required sleep. No saying why, or exactly how much; science still hadn't worked that out, with all that it had been trying since the birth of modern science. But sleep was necessary. Without sleep—without dreaming— the mind gradually became unhinged. It lost its grip on what was real and what was not; there were mood swings in the early stages, hallucinations later on, and eventually madness—and death.

The thought of feigning madness in another species while falling victim to it in my human psyche was a chilling one. But like all such thoughts that plague men on their sleepness nights, it refused to go away.

* * *

You're fertile, Kiri had said. Whispering the words into the skin of my chest, her soft hair splayed across my shoulders.

I was fertile.

That hadn't been the case when we met. It hadn't been the case in most of our time together; the change had been recent, she knew that. Something in my body or my environment had triggered a change, and I had gone from a nonreproductive state to that of potential fatherhood. We hadn't had time to explore the issue; the night after she told me—the night after she noticed it—I left. But now, as I lay awake in an abandoned cell, on a longship hurtling toward *somewhere*, I considered what might have caused such a change, and what it said about the nature of my people.

* * *

When could I have stopped this from happening? I wondered. At what point exactly did I see where we were headed, Yaan's discoveries and the Tekk's disclosures and all the particular quirks of my nature . . . *could* I have stopped it? Could I have frozen our progress at a given moment, one particularly crucial moment, and simply said *no?* Or better yet, not revealed my nature to them at all?

I didn't dare think so. Because if I did, I invited regret . . . and regret, in the face of what was still to come, was a dangerous indulgence.

Say that it was fate.

* * *

I had no concept of how much time had passed, when I first saw Frederick. Long enough to test out most Tyrran foods, and vomit up those which were unacceptable. Long enough to work my way back to the longship's dock, aided by a Honn, so that what little sense of direction remaining to me might have some center of focus. Long enough that mental exhaustion was beginning to fray my nerves—although physical exhaustion was not an issue, the Raayat body renewing itself without need for sleep. All that time, and then some. There was no way of measuring it. The days passed, and also nights, and I was Raayat. Endlessly.

I met him in an upper hallway, close to the dock I had started from. He had changed considerably from the last time we'd met; he looked more like the computer's rendering now, the promise of eventual kuolhood plainly evident in his size and bearing.

I stopped a few yards distant from him, and he also stopped. Compared to the Raayat I had been seeing, he appeared a clearly superior specimen. There was brightness in his eyes, albeit worry also; readiness in his stance, to fight or parley or assess; madness in his personal aspect, but also a tight self-control that was markedly missing in his fellows.

Whatever we did for him, I thought, *it was good. It was right. He's adapting.*

It occurred to me then that if any of the Raayat knew where library access could be had, this one probably did. And unlike the Honn-Tyr, he might not be adverse to leading me there.

"I need some information," I told him. The words felt alien on my tongue, like the taste of some alien food that the body refused to absorb. "I'm looking for a library terminal."

His expression was strange; tense and perplexed and potentially hostile all at once. Had I risked too much, by addressing him? Did the Raayat not interact with others of their subgroup during this season? I was beginning to regret having spoken, and braced myself for possible combat, when he nodded—stiffly—and told me, "Come."

We were an odd couple, traversing those corridors. I could neither follow him nor walk by his side, but must be in some position both subservient and nonthreatening. He walked awkwardly for a while, breaking step and occasionally hissing, until at last we fell into the proper physical alignment. And I knew what it was, when we found it; exactly the proper distance to take, the proper position to be in, when one of the Unstable Ones chose to risk the presence of another.

Raayat instinct, beginning to function. The thought was chilling.

He brought me to where the wall sucked in the last splash of a teal leyq, and touched it at the point of termination. I found myself holding my breath as the door slid open, hoping a thousand things: that he had understood me, that he knew the way, that he had led me here correctly . . . but I shouldn't have feared. The vaulted chamber that opened to us was jammed with a collection of equipment that promised access to the data I required—some of it stacked in disused mountains, others obscured by a blanket of dust, but reasonably fresh wires laid along the the rough stone floor said that something here must function, I needed only to find it. And I did, soon enough.

A chest-high terminal was at last revealed, on which a Saudar touchpad sat. That was promising. I wondered how the Saudar would have reacted, if they knew that their technology would be swallowed up someday by a gestalt mind hungry for power. And wasted, because the Tyr comprehended so little. . . .

I contemplated the pad for a while, then touched up the power and gave the screen life. It was easier to work with the system now that I knew some Saudar, but most of the equipment was labeled in symbols that even an alien species could have guessed at. As had I, originally. I was halfway cleared to access the files I needed when I realized that Frederick was still behind me—and I turned, and saw his eyes leave the screen and fix upon me.

"It is knowledge," he stated simply. Meaning more. I had wanted something, and he had provided it. Now he had a need, and though he lacked the words to describe it properly, it, too, was part of our contract. A sharing.

Frederick, the Gatherer. I recalled his definition of that term, and nodded. Moved slightly to one side, so he could approach without touching me. It was harder to work the system from such an angle, but that was all relative anyway; the Tyr's four-digit hands, symmetrical about a center point, were hardly suited to touch typing.

"What will you know?" he asked me.

I looked at him, and hesitated only briefly. "The Tyr-home," I said at last. And turned back to the terminal, and started to feed it commands.

* * *

The purpose of death is life. The old generation makes way for its young, no longer competing with them for food, shelter, or mates. Simple asexual creatures do not die; the amoeba of today are minute fractions of that one, archetypal amoeba who first appeared in the amino-rich oceans of Earth. But bisexual creatures, who recombine their DNA in more and more complex patterns, must give way to their young in order for evolution to progress. And the balance of nature is perfect in this regard, its numbers carefully regulated. Thus the mayfly who lives but a single day provides the eggs for a thousand young; the elephant, with a lifespan of sixty years, must invest nearly two in carrying a single calf. Lifespan balanced against fertility, the unending perfection of evolution's dance.

You are fertile, she said to me.

Why?

* * *

The file I found was Saudar. They must have taken it in with all the rest, loading in a backlog of Saudar data along with the necessary programs. I found it because I recognized the heading, and from what Kiri had told me of Unity technology it appeared to be an early survey scan. Thank God we'd had the foresight to teach me a bit of the Masters' language. . . .

A planet was revealed to us. First from a distance—and it struck me at once, more than anything, how like Earth it was. Less land mass, perhaps. Few clouds. Bluer sky. But otherwise much the same, a vast globe that proclaimed, even from a distance, that it hosted fertile land and seas and a rich, complex biosphere of interactive life.

Our viewpoint moved closer. Past a few lazy clouds, and toward a carpet of lush azure plant life. Hard to distinguish land from sea, now, where they met; all things on the planet seemed to share the same color, stark mountains alone standing out like islands upon a vast azure landscape. Different shades of intense blue: the sky of a summer's day—an evening's twilight—the cool, clear color of early morning. A thousand such hues, all overlapping, that the human eye might not even be able to distinguish between. But Frederick and I could, and as I looked down upon the conqueror's homeworld, all I could think was, *Beautiful. Absolutely beautiful.*

We moved closer still, until our vantage point skimmed the surface. Now I could make out the leaves themselves, familiar spear shapes, serrated edges, teardrops of blue upon blue. Not unlike Earth, despite the color. And then a stirring, in one of the nearer trees. The camera stopped, hovered silently. Branches parted and a face peeked out—alien, to be sure, but still recognizably a face. This was a world not unlike our own.

I glanced at Frederick, whose gaze was still fixed upon the viewscreen. *Too* like Earth, I thought. Because if the planet was really that similar, the lifeforms it gave birth to probably would have been so as well. No planet this Earthlike would have given rise to the Tyr, that creature of a thousand bodies who defied every law of evolution that we and the Saudar held dear. No. There had to be more to it than that.

We watched the survey scan for hours. And studied most of the planet's surface, through a careful sampling of its various terrains; the Saudar were nothing if not thorough. And if I had to choose one word to describe the planet, it would have to be *fertile*. For although there was much less land than on Earth, almost none of it was wasted. We found no deserts, no desolate steppes, few mountains that rose above the timber line. The seas were shallow, and seemed to be teeming with life. The thousands of tiny islands that punctuated their waters, often smoking from the fires of recent volcanic activity, were blanketed in blue from coastline to pinnacle.

It might have been Eden. And that had to be wrong.

At last I turned off the display, and sat in silence considering the empty screen. Frederick stirred beside me.

"More?" he asked.

I indicated the control panel, and stepped aside. But he did not move. He might call up the pictures, as I had, but it took a fully developed brain to decide which pictures were important, and put them in a meaningful order. The Tyr had absorbed more data from the Saudar files than could be explored in a single lifetime, and Frederick needed me to sort it out for him.

"Later," I told him quietly. "I need to think."

* * *

What if we were wrong, all of us? What if this was how life was *meant* to be—all bodies linked together in a cosmic gestalt, sharing purpose, risk, and species progress in perfect unity—and only on other planets, with less hospitable environments, was that pattern disrupted? What if all our striving and restlessness and cultural frustrations were merely echoes of that greater loss: unconscious awareness of a state of mind we could never achieve, because the hardships of our planet had divided us?

And if so, what did that make of my mission?

* * *

Frederick was there when I returned; whether he had left or not during my absence. I had no way of knowing.

"There is danger," he said, as I entered.

I stopped walking, startled, and looked at him.

"There is danger," he repeated.

Maybe there was some kind of link beginning to operate between us—an echo of the Tyr-whole, meant to unite its Raayat in a single purpose. Or maybe I had simply learned to read him. But somehow I knew, with utter certainty, that this was not a simple warning; it was prompted by something in the gestalt itself, a bit of forbidden knowledge that he had glimpsed, as from a distance, and which he had decided to share with me.

"Here?" I asked.

He indicated the terminal. He looked confused.

"Do we stop?" I asked him.

"No," he said firmly. "We do not stop."

And then, brow furrowed, he added, "It is *there*."

Suddenly, I knew what he meant. The Tyr-home. The paradise.

Just great.

* * *

We use sleep to bracket our days. It is the punctuation of our existence, that breaks up our life into simple, comprehensible portions. The human mind can take in only so much information, before exhaustion propels it to sleep. And while it sleeps, it uses the symbols of dreaming to sort, and store, and comprehend.

A hell of a thing to lose.

* * *

I don't know how many hours we spent at that terminal, sorting through Saudar files. I do know how little of it made sense to me. Mostly because of lack of sleep; my senses were beginning to go haywire, and I had to constantly guard against the leading edge of mental instability.

Frederick and I watched as new scans were added to the survey log, each focusing on one type of lifeform, or one specific terrain. The Saudar clearly meant to collect as much information as they could, before they landed. Perhaps they felt as suspicious as I did; the place was too perfect, too welcoming. And far, far too peaceful. Carnivores ate their prey with relaxed, almost languid enjoyment. Herbivores cropped the deep blue grass with little concern for vulnerability, their young romping noisily in the open, exposed meadowlands. The winged species had enough food that they could fly for the mere pleasure of it, and often ignored what might have been prey as it scuttled across the bluelands far below them.

Too peaceful. Too easy. Too . . . wrong.

The survey showed the Tyr. No baldrics were on them, then, nor any kind of weapon. They hunted in groups, and I knew them well enough to see the gestalt patterning their actions. But to the Saudar, who had no reason to presuppose such a condition, they must have appeared wholly natural—primitive omnivores with a strong social sense, and a moderate dose of intelligence.

The Saudar landed.

They were ugly, Kiri's Masters, in every sense of

the word. Huge and pink and bulbous, with mottled gray markings that exuded clear slime, and faces full of tiny tentacles that writhed continuously about five bulging eyes. One might protest that beauty is in the eye of the beholder, but I believed that these creatures were archetypally ugly—that *any* species would have shied away, if it had any sense of aesthetics.

Little wonder they had given such priority to binding the Marra to their service! I considered the panic that would have ensued if these creatures had appeared on Earth, regardless of their intentions; far easier to send an ambassador who could wear a human body, to pave the way for tolerance.

I saw them interact with the Tyr. I read what I could of their notes on the planet, and although I was far from fluent in that tongue, I think I got the gist of it. The Tyr were intelligent, the survey said, but not very. Adaptable, to an extreme. *Not dangerous,* the survey insisted—and a chill ran through me as I read those words, and realized how much the Saudar had under-estimated them.

So had we all.

There was no record of the actual conflict, but I could guess what had happened. The Tyr had been learning, absorbing all it could through its many parts; the Saudar, who perceived the Honn as individuals—and *harmless* individuals, at that—could never have foreseen how much it would absorb, and how quickly.

It took their ships by force, I guessed, and used stolen knowledge to run them. Accessing the Saudar computer system—as it had seen its teachers do—it drew forth the data that it needed, and the maps that it required. Until, by studying Saudar mathematics, practical and theoretical, it learned that it could ride the whitewaters of nonspace as no other species could do, gaining access to all the galaxies.

The rest, as they say, is history.

I turned off the screen and looked at Frederick. Deep furrows about his eyes told me that he was thinking furiously, trying to apply his fledgling logic to draw some conclusions from the images he had just seen. I realized suddenly just how far beyond his fellows he had developed; another Raayat would have been totally lost, overwhelmed by the act of absorbing so much information, without an overmind to put it all in context.

I told him what I had deduced. And though he listened, though he hung on my every word as if it came from God himself—or the Tyr-whole, its nearest equivalent—though he nodded in the human fashion, yes, yes, he understood . . . there was also something in his eyes that I couldn't read. Some emotion, deep within that alien psyche, that I had never seen in a Tyr before.

Envy, perhaps?

* * *

Regular blood. Regular human blood, supplied by Kiri. Could that have triggered such a change in me, that fatherhood had suddenly become possible? Until Dome Five I had lived for the most part on animal fluids, or chemical sustenance; was it human blood, Kiri's blood in regular supply, that told my body it was time to reproduce? That the humans I lived with could support me—*would* support me—*would be willing* to support me, when the next generation came?

It was not the pattern of a predator, or a parasite.

But it could be the pattern of a symbiote.

* * *

We found what we were searching for during our fifth session together. Not that we recognized it as such, at first. On the screen was a map, of the Tyrran home system. Intense blue-white sun and seven planets; scattered remnants of what might once have been an asteroid belt. A system like any other, yes?

No.

I sat there staring at it, wondering what was bothering me. Wondering, *What is wrong with this picture?* Frederick couldn't possibly help. It required exactly the

skill that he lacked, that conceptual leap from fact to
speculation that we humans take so for granted.

"What is it?" he asked me, but I gestured for him
to wait. By now, we knew each other well enough for
him to indulge me with silence.

A system like any other. . . .

I put it on hold and went back into the files, until I
found other maps. Choosing one at random, I returned
to the Tyrran system. And superimposed the two, so
that I might compare them more easily.

And then I knew.

I banished the second map, so that only the Tyr-
home remained. And felt something cold and sharp
inside, that might have been fear. Or something worse.

"What is it?" he asked again.

I couldn't speak. For a moment, I couldn't even
move. Then I forced my Tyrran hands to the touchpad
again, and began to call up figures. Finding limited
solace in the knowledge that I had finally found what
I'd been seeking.

The orbit of the Tyrran home planet was a long and
narrow ellipse, far more extreme than any in the Sol
system. A cycle of sixty-nine Earth years plus some
brought it from an apogee far out in the reaches of
space, to a perigee that nearly brushed the sun. I called
up the Saudar's figures, and they agreed with mine.
The Tyr-home was too hot to support any water-based
life, in the summer; in the winter, it was little more
than a frozen wasteland.

It is summer, the Raayat had said.

The seas would boil.

And freeze.

And boil again.

And Nature had made her adaptation. . . .

* * *

I came upon my father in one of the inner corridors.

"Long way from home," he said pleasantly.

I was speechless.

"Don't care for that body at all. Liked the blond one much better."

"Father?" I could see the leyq through his foggy form, trembling slightly; otherwise, the fantastic image was wholly convincing.

"The four arms don't become you."

"What are you doing here?"

"Just visiting. Is there something wrong with visiting?"

Meanwhile he was growing fur, a thick silver-gray like my sister's.

"You're going to die," he said.

I felt my heart skip a beat.

"You hear me?"

"I heard you."

"You know it, don't you?"

I nodded. He had ears, now, stiff animal ears that covered his human ones. Gray.

"You had some illusions until that map showed up . . . don't lie to me, I can see the truth in you, clear as night. Kidding yourself, were you? Bad form, son." By now his fur had developed black stripes, like that of a Bengal tiger.

"Father," I whispered, "please go away."

"It's time someone said to you what you ought to be saying to yourself: go home. What can you do, go down there and let your blood boil? For what?"

"Please, father. You're a hallucination. Go away."

"It's going to be bad. You know it, son, deep inside, but you haven't faced it yet. It's in the parts of your brain that you're not used to using, the Raayat parts. That's why it hasn't gotten through. Yet."

"Father, please—"

"Don't do it, son. It's crazy."

"It has to be done," I answered grimly

"They said that when they burned the Library, you know? *You gotta do what you gotta do.* Different language, but the sentiment's the same. And look where it got them."

"Father!" I shut my eyes. "I haven't slept. I'm seeing things. You're not really here."

For a moment he said nothing. I cracked open an eye, to see if he was gone. He wasn't. His transformation complete, he stood before me—a silver hraas, with my father's eyes.

"All right," he said. "Go on. It won't matter, soon enough; the changing's already started. But don't say I didn't warn you."

He trotted ten feet from me, before he disappeared.

* * *

Something was happening. I could feel it.

Something alarming. It wasn't mere sleeplessness. Or mental exhaustion. It seemed to come from outside me, in waves—and when it came, coherent thinking was nearly impossible.

A hesitation in my thoughts. A sudden black cloud in my mind. A dense, sticky bog through which I must wade, simply to think. A veil of stupidity, which made me slow and careless and very, very frightened. Because I hadn't expected this, or anything like it.

I forgot things. Like the way to the library terminal. What foods I could eat. How the Tyrran weapons worked. That I had a pad, with notes on it.

We had been wrong. We had not only underestimated the Tyr . . . we had underestimated the changing itself. And the risk.

The problem wasn't the sleeplessness. I knew those symptoms well; this wasn't the first time in my life that fate had denied me sleep. This was different. More concrete. This was like someone—or some*thing*—was poking around in my brain, closing down certain crucial circuits. Thoughts no longer flowed smoothly through my brain, but jerked. And often jerked in the wrong direction. Or went nowhere at all; sometimes— like now—I would find myself staring, at a wall or a Honn or a viewscreen, with no knowledge of how I had come to that place, or what I had just been thinking.

We had assumed that the madness of the Raayat was wholly due to loss of Tyr-contact—given our data, a reasonable conclusion. But something else was going on. Something in the Tyr-whole didn't *want* the Raayat to think straight . . . and I was a Raayat now, enough that it was affecting me.

Their evolution selects for something other than intelligence. . . .

I took what precautions I could. I jotted down everything I discovered, no matter how trivial; God alone knew if I would even remember I had notes, or be able to read them, but at least it gave me the sense that I was doing *something*. I carried food with me constantly, slivers of a hard, digestible cake tucked in between my pad and baldric. And the day I found myself staring at a blaze, wondering what it was and about to throw it away, I forcibly cracked off the broadest of my combat spikes, shapechanged myself a hollow, and secreted the weapon within. The crack was barely visible once I had sealed the spike back in place. Maybe I was being paranoid, but that urge to disarm myself certainly hadn't come from within me. And for a high-tech species returning to a primitive world . . . say that I found it suspicious.

I prepared as best I could, considering that all I had were guesses.

Knowing, even as I did so, that it wasn't enough.

* * *

Mammals evolve quickly . . . and just as quickly become extinct. The price of their quick adaptation is overspecialization, a Darwinian dead end. A threat that all quickly evolving species have to live with, in order to exist.

Say that one species tried a different pattern. Used a fast turnover for most of its members, processing a generation each ten or twenty years, but reserved a few individuals, as a hedge against extinction. Individuals who preserved, in their genes and in their souls, the essence of the past; who must serve their fellow men because they were dependent upon them, who must have the gift of their blood in order to reproduce.

So that someday, if the rest of the human race failed, the past would still be there among them, in a form that could weather the ages. The DNA of past generations; fresh memory of man's worst mistakes. Teachers. Protectors. Servants.

Us.

* * *

I tried to find a Tekk. I wanted to give them what little I'd found out, in the hopes it could be put to use. I was becoming more and more afraid that I had gotten in over my head, that in a little while I would be of no use to anyone; it was important to hand over what information I had, before that happened.

But for once, the ubiquitous Tekk were absent. Try though I might, I couldn't find them anywhere. I even tried sabotaging a piece of equipment, in the hopes of getting one of them to repair it . . . but soon it became obvious to me that their absence was deliberate, and it would take more than a trick on my part to compromise it.

Politics of the season?

* * *

Don't say I didn't warn you, Dad said.
Thanks for nothing.

* * *

They came for me, some several days after Frederick had disappeared. Found me in front of the terminal, and flanked me there. Six Honn with *Kamugwa* patterns. One flicked the power switch into the *off* position . . . but that was all right. I was only staring at the same data once again, trying to find answers. They weren't there. Perhaps they would never be there.

"It's time," one of them announced. And inside my head, a voice that had never existed before agreed.

It's time.

I stood.

One of the Honn pressed a knife to my neck—but before I could even flinch, the plastic of my baldric parted and it fell to the floor, scattering bits of cake. They left it. A Honn grabbed each of my upper arms, and not so gently, they urged me forward. Into . . . summer. I saw it coming. Felt it waiting.

And feared.

With calm but wary detachment they brought me to the longship's dock. A skimship was waiting, far smaller than the one that had brought us from Yuang. The Honn and I were its only occupants.

Think, Daetrin, think. Don't give up your humanity now.

The fog was there in my brain again, and it was beckoning seductively: *Come, and submit. Do not think. Simply be.* I fought it with all my might, but evidently my might wasn't good enough; the edges of my mind were already lost in grayness, and the fog was seeping in. Slowly, inexorably. As it did with all the Raayat.

I am human, I told myself. *Human. Human!*

Only I wasn't, anymore. It was what I had wanted—what we all had wanted. And now, like it or not, the real changing had begun. The PET oceans of violet and amber in my brain had shifted, from a human pattern to one that was more Raayat. More like the Tyr. Second stage. The third stage would follow soon, in which the changes would become unalterable. In which true Raayat instinct would become my guiding force.

Father, you were right. I want to go home!

But home was beneath us, on the planet's surface. And even as I spoke—as I fought the fog to muster silent protest—the skimship lifted from its landing marks, and left to take us there.

MEYAGA: MOUNT SENGEY

The climb was steep, at times almost vertical. A set of Torginese suckerpads would have helped her immensely, or the foreclaws of a Kuate cliffclimber—but Kiri was determined to stay in human form, and thus had recourse to neither. One must always use the appropriate form, she reminded herself.

It was a long climb to the top. High above the timber line, where the last hint of life gave way to cold, naked granite, she finally rested. Not a hospitable place for a Marra, she thought. Still, he must have his reasons.

And then she found the lip of the cavern she sought and pulled herself over, away from the howling winds which swept across the peak and out into emptiness.

The cave itself was of modest size, more spacious in the rear than one would have guessed from the entrance. Certainly when she had reconnoitered it the day before, her feathered wings straining to tame the high, thin air, she had thought it a much smaller space. And there was little to suggest that the place was of any interest, beyond a wind barrier of dead brush and a single woolen blanket—the latter from Cantona, she noted—and of course, the man who sat on it.

He was old. Not by the standards of the human species in general, but by the harsh measure of Meyagan mortality. Fifty, perhaps, with a weathered face, and knuckles that glistened red in the fading sunlight. Fine lines fanned out from the corners of his eyes, fading into hair which age or stress had turned deep pewter, the last vestige of a black-haired inheritance. He nod-

436

ded sagely as she approached—his expression just a little too young, a bit too eager—and accepted her offering, a bundle of plant life, with a graciousness that was just a little too studied to seem natural.

"Sit, my child." He indicated a place by his side, on the blanket. She folded her legs to match his, in a strange backward pattern that was neither aesthetic nor functional, but which was—she assumed—appropriate. "Make yourself comfortable."

She nodded. "Thank you, priest-Marra."

He raised a hand to protest the title. "The high priest of Cantona was no more than a tool of the Evil One, sent to dominate and mislead the true sons and daughters of Earth. When his true nature was revealed his power base crumbled, and he was recalled to Hell in a flash of sulphurous fire that was the last Meyagan manifestation of his true malignant self."

"A good show, I thought."

"Thank you. Considering the need for a quick improvisation, I was reasonably pleased." He pulled a few weeds out of the bundle she had brought and breathed in their life as he spoke. "That burning bush of yours was an inspired move. What emotive depth! What symbolic resonance! It took all my self-control not to applaud on the spot. Magnificent execution! I haven't seen the like since . . . since . . ." He blinked. "No, that's gone. Sorry." He sighed. "Lost with all the rest."

"And now?"

"You mean this?" He indicated the cave, the windbreak, the distant horizon. "I am in a state of holy contemplation, my child. Trying to fathom the nature of the universe, the purpose of existence, the meaning of life. At least, that was the theory when I came up here. A human archetypal religious experience. It seemed appropriate, at the time."

"But now?"

"Boring as a hundati's neural patterns! What's to it? The nature of the universe is blatantly obvious. And as for the purpose of existence and the meaning of life, we Marra exist because we believe we exist, and when we cease to believe, then we don't—as recent affairs have more than aptly proven. It took all of ten seconds to figure that out. Then I thought maybe I'd work on contemplating why humans spend so much time trying to comprehend what they're not equipped to understand . . . but that's an exercise in futility, isn't it?''

''Absolutely,'' she agreed.

''To put it bluntly, I've run out of things to contemplate. And there doesn't seem to be much point in sitting up here without thinking. To be honest, I was reassessing my current Identity when you arrived.''

''You could try again with a different species.''

''No. I rather like the humans. Marvelously complex life-form, don't you think? Rich as the Saudar in potential, only much more obscure.'' He shook his head. ''Poor body design, though. The balance is atrocious.'' He snorted. ''A tail might improve it.''

''I've thought that.''

''I would hate to give up on them this soon. That last Identity was so satisfying . . . until countered by your own, of course. Perhaps I should look into alternative religious contexts,'' he mused. ''They have so many.''

She decided to uncurl her legs, into a position more appropriate to her physique. ''I gather you've heard the news.''

''About the Suyaag-Marra?'' He nodded. ''No surprise, there; he was never among the most stable of our kind. The key to satisfaction is a good Identity, after all, and he really lacked creativity in that regard. Still,'' he added solemnly, ''a bad omen for all of us. I do understand that.''

''And a good Identity is the only real defense. Is it not?''

That was the meat of her visit, and clearly he recognized it as such. His eyes blazed with interest.

''I take it you have something in mind?''

She shrugged. ''It came up. I thought you might be interested.

"With the humans?

"With the humans. Starting on a single world . . .
but the source of context would be mobile; ultimately,
it would require interaction on many worlds."

"Tell me more," he said hungrily.

She put her hands to the floor behind her, and leaned
back upon stiffened arms. "You already know that in
his last manifestation, a servant of the Evil One managed to dominate an entire human colony." She smiled
as she watched him, sharing the Marra humor of their
jointly created fiction. "Rumor has it he's come back.
Means to dominate on a galactic scale, using similar
means. Only this time he's a little more ruthless. A
lot more deadly. What do you think?"

He nodded thoughtfully, "Some sort of opposing
force is clearly called for."

She smiled slightly. "I thought so."

"An angel of the Lord, perhaps? Or a prophet?
There are precedents for both."

"It's your specialty, not mine."

"It really would require a complex Identity . . . he's
Marra, I take it?"

"In substance. But not in character."

"The Evil One always reveals himself, through the
flaws in His creations. There is always some crucial error,
to disrupt the verisimilitude . . . in this case, the personality. It's an interesting problem, Marra. God against
god? We haven't played at that since . . . since . . . oh,
hell, that memory's lost too."

"Might have been on Earth, you know. Their
mythology's a bit scrambled, but it hints at the possibility of early contact."

He chuckled. "Have you told them?"

"They haven't asked. I haven't offered."

"Don't," he advised. "Leave them their mysteries.
They value their faith more than most."

"All the more reason to preserve it."

He stood, a graceful motion that untangled his legs
and put them to use all in one fluid movement. It was
well done; he was more skilled than most. She watched

as he transformed himself, step by careful step. Into someone a bit younger, who stood a bit straighter. Someone tall and gaunt and dark-haired, loosely bearded, whose gaze fell upon her and fixed there, eyes glistening with the restless charisma of the fanatic. It was quite an impressive display, even for a Marra.

"Well? What do you think?"

"Magnetic," she assessed. "Arresting. The humans can't help but respond."

He spread his arms wide, and shut his eyes. After a moment he began to intone,

"After many long days atop an isolated mountain, cut off from all other life, and from material comforts—after a brief but merciless contemplation of my sins—I have decided to seek my redemption in the service of the Lord. Praise God! Who has sent a protector to walk among His people, and shelter them from the wiles of the Serpent . . ."

"His name is Kost."

". . . whose name is Kost, whose unholy mission is to dominate worlds. Yes, I like it. I like it very much. The human religious patterns are so intensely satisfying." He turned to her. "What do you think?"

"It suits you well." She got to her feet as she spoke, stroking a small branch to death as she did so. "But we need to get you to him as quickly as possible. Any minute now, the Tyrran transportation system may cease to exist." Which would mean that her *kreda* was dead at last. Or close to death, with next to no hope of survival.

We all adapt. We must adapt. Change is an inevitable part of life.

"And then the chaos starts," she murmured.

"Chaos?" he asked. Intrigued.

"I'll explain on the way," she promised.

TYRQA-ANGDATWA:
(HOME)

The Tyr's home planet was Hell. A baking, sterile domain that rivaled the nightmares of Dante—and even surpassed them, for while Dante's world supplied Christian tortures for Christian sins, this Hell was universal. Archetypal. Absolute.

And—for the moment—mine.

Clouds of steam and airborne particles obscured the planet's surface during much of our approach. I caught brief glimpses of a clogged, muddy sea, of land bleached of all its color, of bursts of orange fire and black smoke. Then we dropped beneath the particulate layer, and the Tyrqa-Angdatwa was laid out before me in all its dying, broiling glory.

Where there once had been grasslands, barren plains now stretched to the far horizon, riddled with cracks that ran in random, jagged patterns. Where there once had been trees, only black stumps remained, charred and split by successive fires, the last huddled vestiges of what had once been a rain forest. The earth had split wide in a hundred places, and lava spewed up through the cracks. One chain of mountains trembled even as we watched, and sent a torrent of rubble and boulders crashing down its sides, as whole mountaintops reshaped themselves in accordance with the dictates of Summer. The main island chain had exploded in fire, and pulsed with recurrent volcanic activity as we passed through its curtain of black smoke, debris, and airborne lava. Where molten rock touched water the two exploded, sending forth plumes of steam as each stuggled for dominance. Black ash clogged the

441

shallow ocean waters, turning them into thick gray sludge, and as we dropped even lower I could see that they were peppered with the bodies of sea creatures, choked and roasting.

It was geological madness, nature gone wild. Doing in a single handful of years what it had taken Earth several billions of years to accomplish: a complete re-structuring of land and sea, with the palette of life burned clean to boot. The result made the Valley of Fire look like a shady picnic ground, and Krakatoa a child's firecraker.

And on this ravaged, heat-blasted surface, the Honn meant to leave me. That took no words. As they dropped the skimship lower and lower, I felt their intention with a certainty that chilled me to the core. No human could survive it. No *Raayat* could survive it, for that matter. Even if one could escape the heat, and find stable ground to stand on, the level of radiation would wreak such damage that death would be swift to follow. Even in the early part of this season, the planet's limited ozone layer must have been hopelessly overburdened.

And yet, though it was convenient to imagine that the Tyr had found me out, and meant to abandon me here as punishment, that didn't seem to fit. Something about what was happening to me seemed too . . . too normal. As if all the Raayat, not only myself, were to be subjected to this. Flown here, and then abandoned.

A wonderful realization. And no help at all.

Suddenly, with jarring discontinuity, the skimship commenced its landing pattern. For once I didn't curse the conquerors of Earth for their lack of piloting skill; otherwise I might have been lost in thought until much closer to landing—and thus been that much closer to death.

I turned to where the Honn were standing—stiffly inanimate, *in storage* rather than *alive*—and an-nounced, with all the power I could muster, "We are not landing."

They looked at me. All of them. Even the pilot.

Considering that only one of them had to look for all of them to see me, it was clear a gesture was being made. *The Tyr,* it said, *is listening.*

"I will not be set down in the sunlight," I growled.

The pilot went back to its duties. The other Honn subsided into lifelessness. We continued our approach.

"No!" In Raayat rage I stepped forward, and swung the back of an upper arm into the face of the pilot. The spikes which nature had provided functioned very nicely, and I heard the bone of his skull crack open as I impaled him through a lower eye, forcing my way through a bone plate, and into his brain. I thrust him aside, flinging him violently off my spike, and quickly took his place. The controls were familiar to my fingers, if not my brain, and I quickly took us out of the approach pattern. Not until we had gained some height, and the passage of time had demonstrated that quick retaliation was not on the Tyr's list of priorities, did I stop to consider what I had done. Which was this: I, Daetrin didn't know how to fly this thing.

But I, Raayat, did.

I felt the eyes of the Honn fixed upon me, but refused to meet them. "We set down in darkness," I ordered harshly. Mind racing while I spoke. The fact that I had gotten away with this meant it was part of the Tyr's greater plan. To test the Raayat? To see if it could absorb enough of the Tyr-whole's knowledge to know where it was supposed to go, and get there?

If so, I was in real trouble. Because the only knowledge I had absorbed thus far was how to steer this skimship.

Think, Daetrin, think. Use your human brain!

I sat back in my pilot's chair as far as I could, although the spikes protruding from my back made the posture less than comfortable. And thought. Fought the fog back, the Tyr-spawned stupidity that seemed part of this awful game, and tried to think as a human would think. Reasoning it out. Seeing where it would give.

Think!

The Tyrran spring lasted less than twenty years; the Tyrran fall, the same. Little enough time for life to take hold again, much less erect shelters for itself. Some species would have to alter themselves into a form that could tolerate hard radiation; others might need to estivate, buried in sand or mud—or lava, perhaps?—to await the return of life-bringing coolness before venturing out to feed and mate again.

And the Tyr? I glanced back at my companions. Active creatures. Fully alert. Since the gestalt mind would contain individuals who were still on this planet, then a dormant phase was unlikely. It would have been reflected in all of them, right? Right?

Right, my human mind agreed reluctantly. But clearly it had its doubts.

There were no Tyr visible on the surface of the planet, nor any other life to support them there. That meant a change in domain was necessary. There were three options that I could think of, where the brutal heat would be mitigated: ocean, icecaps, and underground. I remembered that vast expanse of hot gray muck, speckled with dead fish, and shook my head. Scratch the oceans. Ice caps? It was remotely possible. . . .

And then I stiffened as I suddenly remembered. As the pieces came together.

Underground. The Tyr all lived underground, no matter where they went. Even when they settled on the surface of a planet they did so by building an artificial mountain—the angdatwa—and riddling it with tunnels. No windows, no outside light. Life-forms within that thrived on darkness, supplying illumination and oxygen and, presumably, food and water. The Tyr had simply reproduced the shelter it knew in its youth, and then added Saudar technology in such a way that it would not disturb the overall appearance.

Underground. The temperature underground was constant, I recalled, once one reached a certain depth. And volcanic rock was an exceptionally good insula-

tor. I remembered reading about ice that formed in
lava caves, mere yards beneath the surface of a desert.
Say perhaps that not only the Tyr, but all life on this
planet—all mobile life, anyway—followed such a
course. That for a decade or more the Tyr went be-
lowground, exchanging the heat above for the threat
of close confinement. . . .

With a start I noticed that we were approaching
nightside; the piercing blue-white disk had been cut in
half by a mountain range to the west, and deep shadows scored the ground. They wouldn't let me stall
much longer. We were on a schedule decreed by the
Tyr, and while it might let me choose my landing site,
with or without a site of my choosing, it would eventually put me down.

Where? I thought desperately. Not in the mountains;
too geologically unstable. Not near the shoreline; subject to deluge, as the ice caps melted. But that left
millions of mile of rock, and finding the single safe
cavern beneath them made the needle-in-a-haystack
cliché look like a pleasant afternoon's diversion.

Think. Use your human brain. Real Raayat would
be responding to the Tyr by now; getting their instructions from the overmind; I guessed that was what all
this was meant to accomplish, weeding out those few
who could hear the call clearly, leading them to safety.
I closed my eyes and concentrated, but all I could hear
was the pounding of my heart. If the Tyr was there, it
was being very quiet.

Think! The Saudar had come here in springtime.
They had made an exhaustive survey before even landing, knew the planet like the back of their hand before
they even considered setting up a base. And the Tyr
had clearly fascinated them. So: wouldn't they have
settled themselves near a center of Tyrran activity, if
such had existed?

I searched through the skimship's memory with
growing desperation; the files weren't there. At last I
turned to one of the Honn and demanded of it,

"Where was the main Saudar base located?"

446   C.S. Friedman

It looked at me for a long, silent moment, and again I had the eerie feeling of an alien *something* taking my measure. The Tyr-whole, deciding if it wanted to indulge me? At last it stirred, and waved me back. I hesitated only briefly, then realized what it wanted, and surrendered the pilot's chair to it.

It flew us the rest of the way.

Nightside. Far from the shoreline, and far from the mountains. I had been correct in that, at least. By the time I saw the glimmer of the skimship's searchlights reflected from something below us the heat was dropping, and the lakes were merely simmering as we flew over them.

Here there were bones. Thousands of them. Small ones, large ones . . . even Tyr. Most of the owners seemed to have been seeking shelter in the shadows of the Saudar base when the heat of the air roasted them to death; very few were in a condition that implied they had hunted, or been hunting, or had died of any other cause. Clearly not all creatures had the instinct or intelligence to save themselves, when summer came. *Not even all the Tyr,* I noted with interest. And misgiving.

The base was a bleached ruin, with silver sheets above that had been battered by centuries of hail and fire until they looked as though some giant hand had crushed them. Solar collectors, I guessed. Nonfunctional now, to be sure. We set down close by it, and dust obscured the viewscreens as the exhaust of the Tyrran jets blasted currents of additional heat at the ground beneath us.

Thinking furiously, I turned to my guards. Because that's what they were, without question; guards of the Tyr, meant to take me here and see that I disembarked, to undergo whatever trials a merciless Nature had arranged for my species. But within those limits, I suspected they might indulge me. Suspected the *Tyr* might indulge me, if it was intrigued enough by my behavior.

"You will wait here," I commanded, mustering all

the Raayat dominance at my disposal. "For a short while. It is *vital* that you not leave immediately. You understand?"

The lead Honn looked at me intensely, and something that might have been curiosity stirred in its eyes.

"We will not leave immediately," it agreed at last.

Bracing myself, I opened the door. If the Tyr had taken away my baldric, with its few meager supplies, it certainly wasn't going to permit me to improvise any form of protective covering before I left the skimship. Whatever I did to save myself would have to be done *out there*, beyond its sight. Thus, though the blast of heat almost knocked me off my feet, I forced myself to walk forward, into Hell's furnace, until I stood on the planet itself.

Now, I thought. *Close the door. And stay here a short while, all right?*

The door swung shut. And sealed itself, audibly. Inside, the ship would be rapidly cooling itself. Not a quiet process, as I recalled. I tipclawed across the burning ground, to the underside access of the skimship's storage bay.

Stay here, I crooned silently, prying the wide door open. A wave of cool air spilled over me, hot by Tyrran standards, but heaven itself compared to that which surrounded me. Quickly I worked—if the ship took off while I was inside it I would be dead—shapechanging claws to match my needs as I ran over the skimship's plans in my mind. Access to what I needed was not as difficult as I had feared, and within minutes I was out, vacuum tanks tucked under all four arms.

I ran.

They might have heard me, but if so they made no sign of it. The skimship blasted the ground beneath it and took off suddenly, but for once it left no circle of devastation behind it. With all its primitive engines, designed to vent their heat downward as they revved up to full power, they could do no worse to the planet's surface than time and the relentless sun had already managed.

I thought of what would happen to them when they tried to settle into atmospheric flight, and smiled grimly. Served them right for leaving me here. Serve the Tyr right, if they all fried in midair and crashed into a mountain.

Hefting the skimship's tanks of coolant into the most comfortable positions possible, I approached the remains of the Saudar base. One wall alone had stood the test of time, and survived; the rest of it varied, from heaps of whitened rubble to jagged sections of ex-wall, and most of the equipment that had once been inside had either rusted or melted or been crushed when the building collapsed.

But I found what I sought, a small room that still had most of its walls and a good part of roofing above. I set my burdens upon the ground, and turned one of the tanks toward the most complete corner of my shelter. Then, working its valve with the utmost care, I released a minute fraction of its contents. Liquid gas made contact with the air, and a tongue of cold gas shot out toward the walls. I let it go on until I could feel the chill of it on my face, then screwed the valve tightly shut. If I rationed it carefully, I told myself, I could probably keep this small space tolerable for at least a few hours.

I had bought myself time to think. Nothing more. But in a game where every moment counted, it might— it *had* to be—enough.

In short shifts, wary of the heat, I ventured outside my makeshift shelter and sought out whatever remains there might be of the Saudar's records of this place. I worked in shorter and shorter bursts, and as the heat began to settle inside me I found that simple immersion in cooler air was no longer enough to reenergize me. I was becoming hungrier and hungrier, and thirsty beyond bearing. And there was no food or drinkable water within sight, nor could I imagine any coming along. I had to find out where the main caves were, and quickly; there should be some form of sustenance there.

Hours later—too many to count—I finally found what I so desperately needed. They were fragments only, but fragments would have to do. I fervently blessed the Saudar in a dozen languages, including their own, for having such a thing here in hard copy. Ragged bits of plastic adorned with small bite marks; evidently their would-be devourer had decided they were unpalatable. To me they were beautiful. Because they were parts of a geological survey, combining surface photography and sonar and half a dozen systems whose names I couldn't even read, which provided a weathered but a clear-cut diagram of the land surrounding the base.

There. There it was. Caverns like worms, splayed out in a tangled octopus pattern. Put ridges of rock along the top of the caves, and it would look just like an angdatwa. Christ. The Tyr had copied it exactly, just duplicated its ancestral hiding place on a thousand other planets, without a change, even though it could have easily lived on open ground.

Dawn was coming. That was a deadine, real and absolute. I packed my remaining tank in a makeshift halter and left. The Saudar base had provided several tools, but none of them high tech; I had salvaged a spearlike shard for future use, but had left all else behind. Every pound would cost me dearly, when hiking in this heat. I didn't break out my hidden blaze yet, there being nothing alive to shoot at. And besides, I sensed that it was important for its presence to remain a secret—although from whom, I couldn't say. But I wouldn't forget that it was there, waiting for me.

I left the harts behind, for those unfortunates who might follow. Wondering, as I did so, if any true Raayat would have needed them.

LONGSHIP KAMUGWA

Ntaya was alert, and very cautious. She knew the risk of confronting a Raayat in this season—better than most, thanks to her time in Dome Five—and the Unstable Ones were everywhere. For which reason it was normally her custom, along with the rest of the Tekk, to limit her wanderings to the inner corridors during this season. The Tekk kept to their domain, and then hoped that the Raayat would keep to theirs. Usually, it worked.

But now Ntaya needed to brave the outer corridors. She needed to find a hraas. And while normally the great predators prowled the corridors indiscriminately, in this unstable time they would be keeping to the walkways of the Tyr, hounding the steps of the tormented Raayat as if in the hopes that their masters would suddenly become vulnerable.

As well they might, she reflected. And smiled, to herself.

She had already prepared one of the display chambers for this project. Now, standing outside its door, she swung her heavy burden to the floor and unknotted the rope that tied it shut. The sides of the plasticanvas bag heaved outward as its occupant furiously tried to tear through, to work its way free. When it was calm for a moment—or perhaps simply exhausted by its struggles—she quickly opened the bag's narrow neck and reached inside, to grab it by the scruff of the neck. It took all her strength to haul the creature up, half its squealing, squirming length still engulfed in the bag as it hung from her hands, convulsed with rage, trying to break free of her grip.

A Tahuus life-form, or so the records said. From the hraas' own homeworld. She twisted its short, hairy tail about her left hand and then let it fall, shoulder muscles braced to absorb the shock, until it was swinging upside down before her. A position of great vulnerability, for such an upright species. And therefore, a position of fear.

She had smeared its hide with the blood of another, to further signal her intentions. Now she waited, ears pricked to catch the slightest sound—of her intended contacts, whom she would welcome, or of the Tyr, whom she must flee. There would be no explaining this, she knew; she was taking a great chance in even trying such a thing.

But she had set forth her case before the elders of her new tribe—as well as she could, given the language barrier—and they had said *Yes. We must know. You may try.*

Or something like that. What did they speak anyway, some half-Hindi creole? Curse the Tyr, who sorted their servants by the color of their skin, and gave no thought to their cultural background!

Suddenly, she stiffened. The beast she was holding became suddenly silent, and its whole body started to tremble. It forelegs spasmed—in a running motion, Ntaya guessed. In its terror, it had forgotten everything but the blind instinct that said *Run! Run!*

Yes, it would know the smell of the hraas. And the silence of that great beast's approach. These things would be programmed into its genes, through the generations that ran and fought and managed to reproduce, in a land where those hunters ruled supreme.

It turned the corner now. A glorious beast indeed, whose breadth and patterning and aura of power filled Ntaya with a sense of awe. But she didn't forget her mission. With her right hand behind her she groped for the door's contact; then, as the door slid open, she backed up into the room behind her. Beckoning to the hraas, with words as well as gestures.

"Come," she whispered. "It's a gift. Come get it."

The hraas came forward to the threshold of the door. Slit sapphire eyes regarded her with suspicion, even as its wing-claws curled in anticipation.

"Come," she whispered again. And then she threw her burden to the far side of the room, and quickly stepped out of the way.

The hraas was a thunderbolt. A flash of fire. It was in the door one moment, and the next it was upon the beast, tearing its squealing throat out with one glorious, powerful move, ripping open its gut with another. She watched as colors rippled across the surface of its fur: combat colors, hunting camouflage, the deep red satisfaction of killing.

It turned to her when it was done, the blood of the beast dripping from its muzzle. But it did not eat. It waited.

She closed the door.

The only light in the room was that which came from the projector panel, a single luminous switch. By it she could see no more than the glitter of jeweled eyes, fixed upon her.

"I think you understand me," she said to it. "I think you understand a lot more than we've given you credit for. Maybe not my words, but my tone; maybe not language, as such, but gestures and gifts . . . and intentions. Dai, I think you understand a lot."

It licked its lips, cleaning one swath of the fur around its mouth. "Was it good?" she whispered. Noting with distant interest the seductive tone which had entered her voice. "The Tyr don't let you kill often, do they? Ploka, my friend. But we can change that. You and I, together"

She flipped the power switch up, and the screen came on. Then she keyed in the Saudar commands that would start the special sequence, and pictures came to life before them.

The hraas did not move. The jeweled eyes watched.

How to communicate, without language or common symbols? How to contact an intelligence so alien to that of humanity that hating the Tyr might well be their only common ground? An intelligence which just *might* be more than that of a simple animal; an intelligence that might be made an ally, if the right understanding was reached.

Pictures on the screen: Hraas, on their homeworld. Indigo grass. Carmine trees. Animals like the one she had offered it, squealing with terror in the high brush.

The hraas growled softly.

Pictures of the Tyr. Pictures from the Conquest of Tahuus, in which the hraas were netted and bound up and shipped off, into eternal slavery. Ntaya watched as Tyr died right and left, fighting to subdue the vicious beasts. But what did a hundred Honn deaths matter, or even a thousand, when the whole of the Tyr could never die?

Then the picture of Tahuus went dark, and in its place came the image of worm-holes. Tyr-caves. The hraas' current home.

The hraas growled again, this time not so softly.

Again the pictures changed. No longer moving, because Ntaya had lacked the time to create sophisticated fictions. Now the Tekk appeared, with the hraas by their side. Neither dominant, neither afraid. Now the two appeared in battle, the Tekk burning Tyr flesh to a crisp even as the hraas gleefully shredded their potential antagonists to bloody bits.

Now an open landscape, with the hraas set free. While the Tekk stood by their skimship—*their* skimship—and smiled in triumph.

The sequence ended. She turned on the room's overhead lights, adjusting them to their dimmest setting. The hraas' eyes had adjusted to partial darkness, and sapphire glinted dangerously, embedded in fields of blackest glass.

"You see," she whispered.

The hraas did not move. Its eyes did not blink.

''We can do it.'' She clasped her hands dramatically. ''Together.''

Slowly, the great beast rose to its feet. The bloodied muzzle swung down to its kill, and then opened; saberlike teeth hooked into the slaughtered offering, lifting it off the floor as the hraas walked slowly toward her.

It came to where she stood, and stopped. She could smell the blood on its breath, and the rancid odor of the smaller beast's fear.

It laid the body by her feet.

Slowly, heart pounding in excitement, she crouched down. Extended her hand until her fingers pressed into an open wound, coating them in blood. Then raised the fingers to her mouth and licked them, one by one.

The hraas snarled. It might have been laughter.

More likely—she thought—it was anticipation.

TYRQA-ANGDATWA
(REFUGE)

By the time I reached the place that I sought, the last of my strength was nearly gone. I had emptied the fourth tank of coolant long ago, and left its casing on the cracked plain behind me. Now, as I approached the pit that promised access to the Tyr's summer refuge, I had to force myself to take each breath, to push the burning air in and out of my lungs by sheer force of will, long after my body had ceased to desire such pain.

Only a short while longer, I promised myself. Wondering if it were true. *Soon, soon now, there will be shelter.*

The Tyrran caverns coursed beneath this very plain, obscured by miles of cracked, dry soil. Sometime in the distant past one section of ground had given way, collapsing into a burrow that ran too close beneath its surface. The resulting pit was long and narrow, with sloping walls formed by cascades of rubble and a dark, gaping mouth near one end.

For a moment I hesitated—and I sensed, with dread certainty, that something was watching me. Waiting. It had been with me all along, since the moment I left the skimship, but not until this moment had its presence been so clear. It was large, and dark, and burning. Hungry. It wanted very much for me to descend through the rock, into the heart of its lair—and because it wanted this, with such a dark passion that I cringed from the mere touch of it, I hesitated.

Come, it whispered. *Here is water. Here is food. Here is peace, at last.*

Despite the heat, I shivered. But a shaft of sunlight lancing over the horizon reminded me that dawn was about to break, and started me moving again. Fear of the sun was one thing, suicide quite another; when that blue-white disk cleared the eastern horizon and bathed this land in the full heat of day, no living thing would survive.

Exhausted, hungry, and full of misgivings, I entered the Tyr's dark warren.

It was like no cavern I had ever seen. Neither water nor air nor mere geological activity could have caused tunnels quite like these. The walls were utterly smooth, like polished glass, and crisscrossed with looping channels that made the whole of it look like an artist's conception of the inside of a twisted and knotted rope. I put out a hand to steady myself, and it came back from the wall slightly sticky. The walls and ceiling of the tunnel—designated only by their position as there was no real division between the parts—were lit intermittently by clumps of green moss, the same that I had seen in the longships. These were limp and dry, half-dead from the heat, but for Raayat eyes their light was more than sufficient. The bottom of the tunnel was carpeted in rubble, first pebbles and clumps of dry soil and later, as I progressed, rocks and bones. There were bones everywhere: large ones, small ones, most of them split open in several places so that the precious marrow could be sucked out. Bone chips stabbed through the soles of my feet as I walked, cutting through them so many times that soon I was trailing thin ribbons of blood behind me.

That was when I stopped, and shapechanged my feet into something a little more durable. What was the point in having such skills, if one died from blood loss while not using them?

It was then I heard a noise. I barely had time to turn toward it when something very large and very dark rushed me. For an instant it was silhouetted against the moss-light, and I saw the outline of a body as large as my own, and equally well armed. Perhaps if I were a true Raayat, accustomed to knowing where my spikes were and what they could accomplish, I would have met the attack head-on. As it was I was considerably less certain, and ducked to one side in an attempt to dodge the worst impact of the creature's lunge.

Something sharp gouged into my side, hard and cold and not at all like a claw. It ripped through the skin beneath one of my chest plates before grinding to a stop against bone. The pain awakened an animal fury, and suddenly my new Raayat instincts were at the fore. I backhanded the creature across what appeared to be its face. Three jagged spikes faced outward from my forearm, and they buried themselves in flesh and bone as I struck. By the force of their impact I knew that I had instinctively adjusted my muscles for strength, as I did in my confrontation with Kost. A dangerous move, but it had its desired effect. My attacker's combat spike was dislodged from my side, and my blow sent him reeling with sickening force against the nearby wall, ripping his face against my spikes as he hit, crushing the back of his skull.

Reason returned, and with it memory. With my other hand I hefted the spear-shard—muscles adjusting as I moved, tensing with augmented strength—and then drove it into the creature's chest, with all the force I could muster. Guessing where its heart must be, from its size and posture, and then just praying for luck. The Saudar metal screeched against bone as it pierced through, and blood sprayed my face as it sank deeper and deeper into the creature's torso. I leaned my weight onto it, panting, and barely avoided a spike that was thrust at my head. But the creature's movements were spasmodic, and as I waited, pinning it down, they became more and more uncontrolled. Finally its arms fell down by its side and a tremor shook its flesh; I watched as its silhouette jerked and twitched, until at last all motion subsided. Then, and only then, did I dare to step back and look at it.

It was Raayat.

I pulled its body into the light. A mere shell of bone

and dry, cracked skin, it had already been dying when
it jumped me. Starvation had taken its toll, and thirst;
the combat spikes, brittle, snapped when they struck
the floor.

I felt a deep satisfaction, an almost sexual content-
ment, as I regarded my battered adversary. And a very
real sickness, at the thought of taking such pleasure
from killing. Was this what it meant to be Raayat? I
felt sour bile rising in my throat, but managed to force
it back down. If Tyrran nature had decreed that a
primitive selection for strength and combat skill was
the way to choose its generations, I was hardly in a
position to argue. This fellow had failed to find himself food, but I had mine. And considering my physical condition, it had come not a moment too soon.

His blood was thin, but more than welcome. Like
most starving creatures, he had begun to digest his
own tissue for nourishment; his blood thus contained
what I needed, albeit in short supply.

For the first time in a very long while, I wondered
if I might not manage to survive after all.

* * *

Tunnels. Endless tunnels. I longed for a skein of
thread to reel out as I went, but had to settle for
scratching shallow marks into the stone walls with
bone chips, in the hope I could find them and remember their meaning when the time came to return. If
ever.

My vision was changing. Images came from all
around me, wove into a coherent whole somewhere in
my Raayat brain. Summer vision, from all four eyes
combined. It seemed natural. It was necessary. Danger was everywhere.

Sometimes, as I stumbled onward, I imagined I
heard a voice. Inside myself, or perhaps below; calling
to me in a tone that was repellently sensual, seductive
and cajoling and threatening all at once.

Come, it whispered. Thought without sound. *Come*.

The ultimate promise, with only a faint shadow of darkness about the edges.

I'm trying, damn you.

* * *

How many creatures crossed my path, crawling or leaping or slithering out of the greenglowing darkness to attempt to take my life, scoring my hide or tearing into my flesh with their teeth or their claws or their spikes before I managed to crush the life out of them, I cannot say. Dozens, perhaps. It seemed like hundreds. Some, like the Raayat, were dangerous. Others were merely pitiful, like the oversized lizard that accosted me at a fork in the corridor, lashing its tail in a frenzy of need even as its heart, overwhelmed by heat and hunger, succumbed to death before my eyes.

I staggered down endless corridors of night, and defended myself as best I could, with all four arms. My mind was elsewhere. I longed for the creature that waited below with all the passion that man reserves for woman. When an animal attacked me—it happened more and more often as I descended, and my adversaries were more and more desperate—my dominant emotion was that of irritation. That it had dared to stop me, that it might well wound me, that I must waste my precious time putting it to death, when I would rather be moving onward. That voice that came from below me, and its owner, had become my only concern.

Come, the voice beckoned. Electrical currents danced on my skin in response to the summons, sensations both painful and arousing. I saw Kiri before me, but she wore a Raayat tail. *For balance,* she told me. *Do you like it?*

I remembered the weight of her body on mine, and shivered with longing.

"No," I whispered. "Yes. Anything you are. Anything you want to be."

A creature attacked me, and she vanished. I fought.

I won. I descended. Foot by foot, a path strewn with
bones and blood and Raayat sweat. I was blind to time,
deaf to danger, unresponsive to all but the call of the
creature that crouched somewhere beneath my feet,
and an occasional vision of pleasures past.

Come, it whispered. The voice was in my head. My
own voice.

I had no desire, other than to obey.

Tentacles. Overhead. I remembered them, vaguely.
Remembered I didn't trust them, for some reason.
Why? All I could recall was that they supplied the
caves with oxygen, a vital link in the underground
summer ecology. Why did I give them such a wide
berth, sliding against the far wall so that I need not
even step beneath them, much less come in contact
with their vegetative flesh? What memory had I lost
that was vital to my survival—what memory had been
taken from me, as part of the game that the Tyr was
playing?

I couldn't remember for the life of me. Nor did I
know when I had lost my weapon, whether I had left
it in the flesh of a kill or simply dropped it as I stumbled onward. That, too, was part of the game. *Its*
game.

The only game in town.

Leyq. I had found them. Swaths of dried slime that
streaked the walls in shades of gray, pale imitations of
their longship counterparts. I reached out to touch one,
and my hand trembled slightly. I was close. Very close.
The landscape was more and more familiar to me, an
ancestral memory reinforced by the longships' inten-
tional mimicry. As the leyq grew wider, the tunnel
would progress.

I ran.

The leyq grew wider. So did the tunnels. The two
were interconnected, I understood now. And when I
saw the first leyq-maker, I wasn't surprised. Jellyfish-

like, it clung to the wall near a fork in the tunnel, digesting the rock beneath it with mindless patience and leaving, in its place, a trail of adhesive excrement. It and its brothers must have carved these tunnels eons ago, while the Tyr still huddled in geological caverns and trembled at the thought of earthquakes. Surely no life on this planet could have developed the continuity that the Tyr had, much less its intelligence, without a summer shelter that would last through generations.

The voice from below had become far more, now. It was a rumbling that vibrated through the rock—wordless promises that made my flesh tremble with longing—an ecstacy of knowledge injected directly into my brain. Where that voice was, there was an *end*—to running, to fighting, to killing. And more than that. Somewhere in the part of me that still clung to a human identity, I recognized that at last I was headed toward where I needed to be. And the Tyr itself was urging me onward.

I turned a sharp corner, and suddenly found myself in a fair-sized chamber.

Facing a Raayat.

He came at me with a roar, and I barely had time to note that he was in excellent physical health before he struck. This was no weakened animal, driven half mad by starvation. He hit me full on, driving one of his shoulder spikes full length into my arm; I heard my own plates split as I tried to pull free, and blood ran down both our bodies. Mine. He knocked me down to the floor and pinned me there; the shock of impact cracked off most of my rear defense spikes. I barely had the wherewithal to see where we were, to take stock of my options—very few, and all of dismal outlook—before he struck at me again. I managed to turn him aside, trying to adjust for greater strength as I did so. But I had worked too many changes on too little life; the change did not happen quickly enough, and as he brought one arm down across my throat, cutting off my air, I knew that I was fighting against more than I could handle.

The thought of dying here, so close to my objective, was infuriating. Anger bought me a moment's new strength, and I somehow managed to angle my foot against his torso. Over his shoulder I could see a tangle of black tentacles, that hung down almost to chest level. I levered up and pushed, with all my might. And broke him loose. He fell backward, caught himself on a jagged edge of rock—and then lost hold of that, and went sprawling into the slimy black tangle at which I had aimed him.

It is only carnivorous in summer, Frederick had assured me.

I watched only long enough to see the tentacles close tightly about him, and to hear the screaming start. I had no strength left to witness his suffering. Turning away, I lay my head on the hard stone floor and shut my eyes, mimicking sleep. And perhaps I was wounded enough, or simply tired enough, for I drifted into something that might be its equivalent. It was darkness, anyway. For now, that was enough.

A food chain without beginning. Noah's ark without a pantry. Thousands of animals trapped in near-darkness, with only each other for food, for a decade or more. Is it any wonder that Nature experimented with other modes of life, and found individualism wanting?

Darkness. Parting slowly. Fog drifting back. Thoughts coming clear, for the first time in God knew how long. Jesus Christ . . . how long had I been out?

I opened my eyes. They were sticky with blood, and offered little vision. I lifted a hand to wipe them clean—and pain shot through that arm, so sudden and so intense that I cried out and let it fall. And tears came, which was good enough. Those, too, could wash away the blood.

I was not where I had been.

I stared at the ceiling. Few tentacles growing here, and no naked stone; the whole vault above me was lined in moss, a rich glowing green that filled the cavern with surreal light. Could so much have grown since I fell unconscious? The mind demanded a simpler explanation. I had been moved. But to where?

I used a good arm to raise myself up, until I could lock that one elbow behind me.

And I saw.

Bathed in rich green light, it stood in the midst of a forest of columns. It might have been Raayat once, or Kuol; the form was similar, although few spikes remained. It was hard for me to see where its body began or ended; bits of it seemed to extend to the columns, where they merged into the pale, gleaming rock without visible boundary. Its chromatic pattern— a sunburst of gold and cerulean, with secondary spirals of half a dozen other bright hues—extended out onto these bands of connective tissue, making the creature look as though it sat at the heart of a rainbow. Or perhaps at the center of a web. The latter seemed more fitting as I realized who—and what—it was.

"Tyr," I whispered.

Yes.

The voice was like a vacuum, sucking me forward. If my body had been whole, I would have moved toward it, despite myself; thank God for the wounds that made that impossible, buying me time to think. For the first time in days my mind seemed clear, Yaan's instructions as precise as if he were standing before me. *Infect it with fear. Overwhelm it with human emotions. Break the mating cycle. Distract it.*

Or kill it. That, too, was an option. Whatever it was, it seemed to serve as the focus of the Tyr's gestalt consciousness. Killing it might not hurt the other parts, but it was bound to confuse them.

And with the Marra and Tekk out there, waiting to take advantage of any weakness, confusion just might prove to be good enough.

I pushed myself up farther on one sound arm, while forcing another toward my thigh. There, inside its bony shell, a Tyrran weapon lay dormant. If I could get to it before this thing got to me, I might yet accomplish what I came here to do.

It stirred. Ripples coursed outward along its flesh, colored strands trembling against their columnar anchors. To look at it was to be drawn into a whirlpool, to feel one's mind and soul sucked out of one's body, drawn into an infinite hunger.

You fought well, the voice whispered. Smoothly, seductively, placing each word in my brain so close to the centers of pleasure and mating that I shivered each time it spoke.

It is not necessary for you to be alone anymore.

A flood of sensations swept over me, memories from my human life and promises of my Raayat flesh, combined. Kiri's softness and entering a woman and being one with the All and successful combat and thrusting eggs deep into the Giver . . . I shook my head and tried to fight it off, tried to calm my pounding heart and concentrate on the motion of my questing hand, which would be armed the moment it snapped that one spike free.

Come, it whispered. To my horror, I felt myself struggling to my feet. The urge was too powerful to resist; I fought vainly to remember that I had a weapon, to focus what little shapechanging was left to me upon the fault in that bony chamber. Knowing that I lacked the strength to defy its will for more than a moment longer, and must kill it quickly if I meant to fulfill my mission.

And then I stumbled on a rock and fell, and the rock came into my hand as I tried to right myself. Its sharp edge cut into my flesh, provocatively; with sudden inspiration I grasped it in my upper hand and struck it against the stubborn spike, with all the force that remained to me.

Bone snapped. I dropped the rock in time to grab the blaze before it fell, and braced my knees against the cavern floor as I took aim. The creature's power was hypnotic; I dared not look in its eyes as I fired, nor give it a moment to speak to me. My Raayat claw felt for the trigger, and—

—*thousands teeming beneath the surface, Raayat killing and growing and killing and feeding on blood, again and again, the blood of Honn and beast and fellow competitors, until it comes at last to the birthing chamber—*

—*here where the sun never enters, where the radiation that mutates each new generation is powerless to reach, where the Giver of Life can assess Its mates, and take their eggs, and fertilize—*

—*It sits in the cavern of life and waits, as It has waited for thousands of years. Knowing that Its presence keeps the race stable, that calling each generation back to this one place to mate with it serves to weed out those mutations which are too extreme, Raayat-seed so damaged by summer's radiation that any union must prove sterile—*

Knowing also that there will come a time when the race must change, when It, too, must give way to that which follows. When a Raayat will kill It as It once killed its predecessor, and take Its place in the heart of all life, to mate with the next generation—

My finger trembled on the trigger. I didn't fire.

Taking the Giver's place! It exulted. *Becoming the new Giver of Life! Serving the Tyr, forever!*

My hand was shaking. I felt it drop slightly. *Fire, damn you, fire!*

Kill me, It crooned, *and you will take my place. An even exchange, is it not?*

I couldn't.

Part of the Tyr. . . .

God help me, I couldn't.

Forever. . . .

If I fired, I would become what it was. Forever. I couldn't bring myself to do it.

There is no magic kill, Yean had warned.

Hell.

I would have been willing to die, I thought. I would have given my life for Earth, even to buy her the

slightest chance of freedom . . . but not this. Even if
I wanted to, I couldn't bring myself to do it. Become
the enemy, mate with the enemy, be the focus of its
intelligence for the rest of God knows how long . . .
I couldn't do it. I tried; sent the message down my
arm that told the fingers to move, lift, close . . . but
the flesh would not respond.

All I ever asked, I thought, was the right to die in
my own body.

The whirlwind absorbed me. I was lost in a gust of
burning color, gold and crimson and cerulean winds,
and all there was was the Voice. And memory. Human
memory, squeezed out of me by the Giver, poured into
that great pool of knowledge which served its species.
Secrets. Emotions. Aspirations. The truth about the
Marra. The plots of the Domes. I tried to stop the
knowledge from leaving me, but it was like trying to
stand before a flood. Human mathematics, and all their
implications. The Age of Imagination. Religion. Phi-
losophy. Speculation. Libraries of human thought,
squeezed from me cell by cell. History, as I had lived
it. The pain of rejection. The fear. Running . . . Timefugues overlapping. I was lost in a whirlpool of Tyrran
hunger, sinking deeper and deeper . . . and at the heart
of it was something which mere human learning could
not satisfy.

It reached into the core of me, to the seat of my
huddled humanity. Reached in and pulled, until the
walls that bounded my creativity collapsed, and a
nightmare progression of images poured forth. All
right, I thought, you alien bastard, look: look at humanity, in all its glory; the nightmares and the insecurities, the restlessness and the hunger for beauty and
above all else Mortality, that merciless master whom
we cannot escape. See the counting of days and hours,
the endless sorrow and the tears and above all else the
fear that it's all of it wasted, every bit of striving and
blood and sweat that we pour into the world, for we
have but a finite number of years and then what are
we? This is what our gods are made of, this is our

beginning and our end, the constant awareness of death which all other creatures on Earth have been spared, all but us! The great Fear that drives us to create, madly and endlessly, in the hope of leaving *something* behind when the darkness closes in and takes us at last. . . .

And in answer, I saw the Tyr. It had taken me in and now I was part of It. I shared the hunger that had burned in It for generations, since aliens first set foot on Its planet. Since the Saudar had taught It that It lacked something vital, that Its consciousness did not contain that quality which had allowed other species the freedom of the stars. For many long generations It had sought to isolate that quality, and to understand it. It hungered for knowledge of what It lacked, burned with a drive to compensate for what Nature had refused It. And I had provided the answer. Now It contained my human motivations, and all the facets of individuality that made true creative thought possible. Now, for the first time, it understood us—and itself.

Feed it human emotions, Yaan had suggested. How the hell were we supposed to know that was just what it wanted?

It released me. In body only, for now I was part of It. But a human kernel still remained within, for which reason the flesh must be dispatched. It was not yet confident that It could simply order my body dead, as It did with Its own children. And so It searched through my memory for a way to make my dissolution complete.

And I opened up. Gave it all the patterns of death that I knew, fixed in images which the Age of Imagination had impressed upon my brain, over and over again, as the truths of my kind. One stood out, so much so that it could make no other choice.

There was a bundle of branches in a corner of the cavern, tentacular growths that had fallen to the ground and then dried there, hardening. The Giver picked up one of the straighter pieces and struck it against a column, snapping off one end to create a jagged point.

I summoned up all of my strength in anticipation, knowing I would have just an instant to save myself. Wondering if I had the strength to do it.

And then It drew back, and cast Its homemade lance. Across a bare four yards of open space, at a body that could not flee. The sharpened stake struck with enough force to drive me back, even as it pierced between two broken plates; I felt it bite into flesh, pierce a lung, and then accomplish its appointed goal: a clean thrust through my Raayat heart, transfixing it with wood.

I reflected, as I died, that it was the first thing that had gone right all day.

Tension. Fear. My father's grasp on my wrist, tight as steel. His eyes upon me, dark and loving. "Ready?"

I try to reassure myself that this is, as he says, necessary. And nod, tensely. His hand squeezes tighter for a moment, a gesture of encouragement. Then his other hand stabs suddenly downward, and drives the sharpened wooden shaft through the palm of my hand.

The pain is like fire, and tears squeeze forth from my eyes. I try to remember what he's taught me, try to accept that this wooden object is now part of me, as much as the flesh I was born with. Try to get my body to accept it, so that it will correct the wrongness and heal what is injured, using the skills that are natural to us.

After a short time, the pain passes. The shaft has been sliced through cleanly where it met my skin, and it breaks into three separate segments. Two—from above my hand and below it—fall to the floor, clattering on tile. The third is now flesh and blood, and resides within me.

I look at my father, hopefully. Failure is part of the process, he's told me. Such skills can only be learned with much practice. Indeed, he nods and tells me, "Better. But not good enough. If you're struck in an extremity, it will do. But what if a weapon seeks out some vital organ? If less than a second is left to you, before fatal damage is done? You must take the weapon in as it enters you, my son—make it part of you as soon as it passes through the body's outer boundary— accept it as such and you can change its shape, as quickly and as surely as you change your own." He releases my hand for a moment and tousles my hair; his loving strength almost knocks me from my chair.

"Iron and steel you must always fear," he warned me, "as well as most stone. But the things which come from living creatures have no power to hurt us, provided we are prepared. . . ."

I do understand, father. I do. I do.

Darkness. Pain. Blood pounding loud in my veins . . . but that was good, that it was still in my veins. That anything was left there at all. The wound would have emptied me, had I not healed it.

Proud of me, father?

. . . and voices. The sound of claws on stone. Raayat ecstacy, and the Giver claiming seed.

It thought I was dead, I realized.

Was I?

I heard a footstep. Familiar.

I forced my eyes to open. Stared at the ceiling.

And heard a familiar voice.

"Yes," it hissed. In a voice filled with pain and pleasure both, and I could imagine why. "I come."

Frederick.

It took everything I had for me to turn myself, lift up my head so that my blurred vision could register his presence. Hoping that the Giver was too preoccupied to notice me.

It was.

Frederick's colors were the same as before, as was

his pattern of cresting, but he was now as large and every bit as powerful as the portrait the computer had conjured for me. A Kuol-Tyr, in almost every sense of the phrase. There was only one thing left for him now, and that was total absorption. And as he stepped forward like a man entranced, his attention wholly fixed upon mating, it occurred to me that I had one last chance to do what I came for. To throw a wrench into the works at last, and hope that my allies could make use of it.

First, carefully, I worked a changing. It took all my remaining strength—but what would I need it for, after this? My flesh had altered during my descent, from a pure Raayat pattern into one more suitable for mating. Now I changed it back, knowing that the Tyr would have a hard time reabsorbing me when I wore a brain not suited to such things.

At last I was done. "Frederick!" I yelled. And I held my breath, waiting.

He turned.

My hand on my weapon tightened. Thank God I hadn't dropped it.

"Don't do it," I warned. "You will *die.*"

Nonsense! the voice cajoled. But Frederick kept on staring at me. In recognition, perhaps?

"Listen," I said desperately. My voice was ragged and hoarse; it took effort to speak. "Everything you've worked to have . . . all the human knowledge you've been collecting . . . you'll lose it, Frederick. All that individuality, that you so desperately value. Everything you've learned. This thing will suck you dry of knowledge and eggs and leave you no more than an empty shell. Cannon fodder for some new Conquest. You will be *gone,* Frederick, *gone.* The Tyr will exist, but the part that is Frederick won't. *That's what death is.*"

It looked at the Giver and back again, a quick look, but one rich with meaning. I had him doubting. Afraid. That was good. I needed for him to be afraid.

If I been wholly absorbed into the Tyr, my human

fear would have been lost—wasted—diluted by a species' worth of stolid Tyrran emotion. If Frederick was
absorbed now, it would be much the same. But (I reasoned) if the Giver died, and the Tyr accepted Frederick as a substitute—if Frederick *became* the core of
his species—might he not then infect them all? Might
they not become lost in his emotions, instead of the
other way around?

*Forgive me, my friend. In war we must use the
weapons that fate puts in our hands. Forgive me that
it had to be you.*

"Is it true?" the Raayat whispered. There was terror in his voice now, as he contemplated the implications of what I had told him. The death of one's self
is a terrible thing to contemplate, and this was his first
exposure to it. I watched his eyes lid over as he tried
to cope with it, watched him shake his head violently
as the Tyr tried to draw him in, as he fearfully fought
its growing influence in his mind—

Now!

I fired. Into the heart of the rainbow's web, where
the Giver's body stood. Strands of flesh curled free
from their columns as the blaze shot raw heat into their
center. I heard the scream of flesh turning to ash, the
sizzle of bodily fluids boiling free of their contain-
ment. My body spasmed, but I did not stop firing; It
could have no control over the form I now wore, I
refused to let it move me. My hand gripped the blaze
so tightly that I could feel blood pounding beneath my
fingers, trapped there by the pressure. And still I fired.
Until the Giver was burned to a crisp, and whatever
thoughts Its brain had housed were scattered across the
whole of Its race.

Kill me and you will become like me, It had said.
But now It was gone and I no longer wore the body
that would respond to Its needs. The Tyr-whole must
compensate, by claiming another. A Raayat who had
proven its worth by reaching this place, whose body
could be molded to a new sex and purpose.

Frederick, I'm sorry. Forgive me.

I shut my eyes, and wished I could shut out the knowledge of what I had done. Wished I could shut out the terrible fear, that resounded through the Tyr-whole and echoed in my body. Frederick's fear, which I had inspired. No longer the simple, finite emotion of one individual, but the dominant mindset of an entire species.

I wondered how the hraas would react, when the masters they despised were suddenly overcome with terror. Frederick's terror. I was suddenly glad I wouldn't be there to see it.

"I'm sorry," I whispered. To all of them.—

We do what we must.

LONGSHIP KAMUGWA

There is no other pleasure, Ntaya exulted, *equal to that of killing one's enemies.*

Her brisk pace took her quickly through the outer corridors. The hraas at her side matched her speed exactly, its wing claws twitching as it ran. *Hungry for more battle*, she thought. *As are we all.*

There were bodies in the corridor. The *Kamugwa*'s crew—no, its *former* crew—cut down wherever the hraas found them. Those few Honn who had managed to run to shelter later fell to the Tekk, whose eyes blazed bright with the indignation of three centuries of slavery as they took their revenge on those miserable creatures who had dared to become Earth's masters. It was a battle to make their warrior ancestors proud—and on the planets themselves, where the Marra were, it must have been even more glorious. God alone knew what the shapechanger human had done to make it possible, but surely if there was a Heaven somewhere out there, he would be part of the angelic elite.

Now, the worst of the fighting was over. Tekk casualties had been collected and consigned to chemical dissolution. Honn bodies were cast into space. They hadn't found the *Kamugwa*'s Kuol yet, but she had no doubt that when they did that would be the last of them. The last of the Tyr on the longship—*her* longship—and the final blood to be shed in this long and highly invigorating war.

She stopped to make sure that a body was dead— she thought she saw it still twitching—but the hraas

nudged her calf and growled, as a way of saying *don't
bother.* She trusted its judgment. They were bloodthirsty allies, her four-footed brethren, but bloodthirst
was what battle called for. All the shapechangers'
games in the world couldn't have given them victory,
if the Tekk's meager ranks hadn't been supplemented
by the claws and teeth of those chameleon killers.

The receiver in her ear buzzed faintly, a prelude to
transmission. She touched it lightly, aligning it with
her ear channel. They had never needed such things
before, having always relied on the Tyr for communication; now, separated by miles of rock, needing to
act in unison, they had applied their knowledge of
technology toward forging a more solid link.

"... *skimship coming in* ..." the receiver buzzed.
She cursed softly and adjusted it. Her grasp of their
creole still wasn't good, but she had prepared herself
by memorizing key phrases. She hoped they remembered to use them.

"... *report from landing bay two. Repeat, landing
bay two. Last skimship coming in from planet's surface.
Suspect Honn contigent. Intentions unknown. All available Tekk, report immediately to landing bay two* ...

"Battle," she whispered, and the hraas' ears pricked
forward hungrily.

They ran. It was a good bet that no other Tekk were
closer, that she and her companion would be the first
to reach the bay. And if it was indeed the missing
Honn contingent, that raised questions no Tekk could
answer. A dozen Honn had been sent from the ship on
the eve of battle, with a full set of armaments and
supplies. The Tekk had assumed they'd been called
back to the home planet, and would not be returning.
Why would they come back now?—and even more intriguing, and possibly threatening, what might they
have brought back with them?

Or who, she thought, and her heart pounded wildly.
Might they have brought back reinforcements, some
last desperate troops, sent out from the Tyr-home to
save the longship? Or worse—to destroy it?

There was only one way to find out. She gave all her strength to running, the hraas loping easily by her side. Bay two was in her section, a mere quarter-mile down the main tunnel. She checked her blaze as she ran, making sure it was still fully charged. They had lost several Tekk already, by not anticipating that their power would fade; she had no desire to add to that list.

And then the doors were before her and she hit them at a run, slamming her palm into the contact point and thinking *Open, open damn you!* Because if she could make it inside and take up a position before the skimship opened up, her chance of success would be multiplied a thousandfold.

Sure enough, the battered hull was just pulling itself into position as she entered. No other Tekk were there yet, it seemed. But they should be coming soon. If she could just manage to contain the Honn, limit their movement to the bay, victory was almost guaranteed.

"Hide," she hissed. The hraas understood her tone if not her words, and its fur rippled to packing crate gray even as it slipped behind a stack of storage boxes that matched. She found a similar niche in the opposite corner, and slid her lean body into the narrow space. From here, they could not be seen. Now, let the bastards disembark . . .

The seconds it took for the skimship to secure itself seemed like an eternity to Ntaya. But fighting beside the hraas had taught her many things, among them boundless patience. *The hunter does not frighten its prey,* she thought, *before he has it where he wants it.*

And then the skimship opened, and a ramp slid forth. She held her breath, and her finger tightened on the blaze's trigger. One Honn, then two, descended the ramp. Then a third, more slowly. Then . . .

She caught her breath as she saw it exit the skimship. A Kuol . . . but surely not the *Kamugwa*'s Kuol. It didn't look the same. . . .

It stood in the middle of the landing bay as the rest of the Honn disembarked. Eight in all. Which didn't mean that they weren't part of the dozen who left, merely spoke of some outside threat that had thinned their ranks by a third.

Then the Kuol did something she would never have imagined possible. It slid its baldric over its head—the blaze still holstered to it—and dropped it to the floor. Then went from Honn to Honn, and disarmed each one in turn.

"It's over," the Kuol announced. To anyone who was listening. To her. "You've won." Then it took a deep breath and announced, just as steadily, "I need to speak to the Tekk."

She noted that its armor was cracked, and that less than half its combat spikes were intact. Wherever it had been, it had come through a lot.

She decided to chance it.

She stepped out. After a minute, so did the hraas.

The Kuol regarded her for a moment, then whispered something under its breath. Her name?

Something clicked. It seemed impossible . . . but was any other explanation more plausible?

"You're the one they sent," she challenged.

An odd expression crossed its face, as it looked from her to the hraas. It might have been a smile. "Under the circumstances, am I likely to say no?"

She exhaled noisily, in frank disbelief. "Then you are back from the dead."

"In many ways . . . yes."

"It just let you go?"

The four eyes fixed on her. There was a depth to the scrutiny that made her skin crawl.

"No. I would say . . . no." The next words seemed to come only with difficulty, and it winced as it spoke them. "It is a trade."

"You bargained with it?"

"It made me an offer," the false Kuol said softly. It was hard to hear past the rasping of its speech mechanism, but she thought there was pain in its voice. "I now make one to you. It does you no good to remain at this nexus. There are no other habitable planets here, besides the Tyr's own. You will—''

"The Tyr is still alive?" she demanded.

"The Tyr will live on until its last body dies. That is irrelevant. I offer to take you out of here. There's work still to be done, if your species is to be salvaged.'' It paused. "Or would you rather try to colonize the Tyr's home world? If so, I assure you you'll regret it."

"But if the Tyr—"

"The Tyr has changed. It's not a threat to you—but nor is it helpless. Land on its planet, and you'll be the ones to suffer. It has no fear of you there."

She heard running feet, and held up a hand in warning. The two armed Tekk who arrived seconds later looked dubious, but backed off.

"We can't translate space without the Tyr," she countered.

The false Kuol made a sound that might have been laughter. Or pain.

"I *am* the Tyr," it told her.

It began to walk away from the skimship, toward the main entrance behind her. The Honn made way for it. So did she.

It stopped when it was beside her. And looked at the two other Tekk, and at her. "Prepare for translation to Yuang nexus," it told them. "And to any other point that will allow you to evacuate the longship, so that all species currently trapped on it may live."

"Why is it letting you do this?" she demanded. "What does it stand to gain?"

It looked at her with all four eyes, and something in its expression—or perhaps something missing from it— caused her to take a step backward, chilled.

"That," it said quietly, "is not for you to ask."

LONGSHIP KAMUGWA

We were many days past the Yuang nexus, before I could bring myself to go down to the planet. I left the Honn behind. As for the Tekk, they and I had a neat arrangement: I didn't go near them, and they didn't go near me.

I had stayed in a Raayat body, which kept me out of contact with my newly adopted species. The result was isolation, a dark balm to my soul's wounds. I left the control center only when required, to pass a message along to the Tekk, or to check on some aspect of the longship's maintenance. The Honn could have done that just as well, but the Tekk didn't trust them. They hadn't trusted me either, until Frederick had made a gesture of surrender, giving them the *Kamugwa*'s Kuol. Now they would deal with me if they had to, but hostility was plain as sunlight in their eyes, and I had no doubt that if an alternative to my presence presented itself—*any* alternative—they would quickly adopt it. *The feeling's mutual*, I thought grimly. Human company had become acutely painful. I had no regrets that they would be leaving me, before the last leg of my journey.

The skimship trip to Yuang was uneventful. Frederick knew how to work the vessel, therefore I did also. Radio contact between the fourth and sixth planets alerted me to the fact that the evacuation of the Domes was well underway, to a cold and dismal but infinitely preferable terrain, in the same solar system. The *Kamugwa*-Tekk would disembark here as well, although whether they chose to remain was another issue. They would have all the skimships, and all their stored fuel, so I supposed that if they chose to take a chance and look for a planet of their own, they might possibly succeed in finding one.

The other Subjugated species on board the longship had been settled long ago. We had found them all suitable terrains, and in several cases had been able to reunite them with one of their own colonies. It had required three nexes, in all. Three translations. Three descents into a memory that even now cast its shadows across my soul.

When I'm human, I promised myself. *When all this is over. Then I can forget.*

I wondered if that time would ever come.

* * *

I should have anticipated that Yaan's group would have computerized their records. The man was impressively organized, even in exodus. From the landing bay at Dome Prime I was able to access his data, which told me who was where, and what was where, and who was doing what, and how functional everything was, wherever it had been set up.

I found what I wanted. Kiri's name. It frightened me that I felt so empty, reading it. I think I had hoped that the prospect of seeing her would heal . . . something. I couldn't put a name on it. Some part of my soul that I left behind, when I withdrew from the Giver to start my journey. Some wound I had carried inside me, in all my subsequent days.

She kept the name I gave her, I reflected as I walked. For some reason, that was comforting.

* * *

I found her down in lab one, using her Marra skills to put the lab animals to sleep, so that they could be packed. And for a moment I couldn't say anything, but merely watched her.

Finally she turned. And I'll give her credit, she didn't drop what she was holding. She managed to put it to one side—white rodents bundled up for a snooze in their black plastic traveling frame—even as her face lit up with something that might have been amazement, or joy.

"You're alive?"

I nodded.

"You look hurt—" she stepped toward me, but I backed away. Instinctively. I immediately regretted it, but that couldn't change my response. Physical contact of any kind had been almost unbearable, since my bargain with Frederick in the caverns. Only now did I feel the full pain of that loss, as confusion and incomprehension clouded a face that I would never willingly have brought a moment's anguish to.

"It's all right," I managed. "Raayat reflex. It's . . . it has nothing to do with you." It was a stupid thing to say, but I had no better words.

Precious Marra . . . I would rather die than hurt you.

"You've been injured." She whispered it.

I had never bothered to eradicate my wounds; I did so now, exchanging them for healthy flesh.

"Inside," she said gently.

I wanted to tell her a thousand things. I wanted to explain . . . but there were no words for it. Partly because I didn't understand half of it myself.

"It'll heal," I assured her lamely. "In time."

Only as the words left my mouth did I realize what I had said. In the Time Before, she had been my healer. Now, in essence, I had rejected her.

How could I tell her what had happened? How could I communicate that standing before her, now, and feeling no echo of desire—no last fragment of what had been between us—was in some ways more terrifying than all the rest of what I had experienced?

"I lost something out there." I heard myself whisper. "A part of myself. I can feel the hole where it was, but I still don't know just what's missing. Or if it will ever come back again." A human emotion came welling up from the depths, strangely alien to my current mindset. "I'm afraid . . ."

"You need to be human again," she said quietly. "You can't heal yourself in this body." She approached me slowly, as one might a frightened animal. Which is perhaps what I was, deep inside. A frightened animal cowering in the hollows of a Raayat body, overwhelmed by what it had seen, and done, and been.

She took my hand gently, and this time I didn't draw back. She tranformed one small patch of skin, as before. This time it was effortless. If my Raayat self understood nothing else, it knew how to submit its flesh to another's dominance.

When she was done, she let go of my hand and stepped back. It shamed me that I was relieved.

"Kiri, I—"

The door flung open. A man I didn't recognize strode into the lab, a glass vial in his hands and triumph in his eyes. He wore long robes that seemed more suited to the biblical period than this one, and I can't say whether it was that or his slightly maniacal manner—or perhaps the two in combination—that told me he was Marra.

"The Evil One hatches new plots even as we speak," he announced. His dark eyes flashed with fanatical excitement. "He's altered a Yuang germ to disable the intestines of its victims—a truly demonic design. He means to release it on our new Earth, and let it eat its way through the domers' new colony . . . then save them himself, to earn their loyalty." He presented the vial to her with a flourish, his aura radiating pride. "But *I* have anticipated him. You hold my inoculant. Instructions on the bottle. If you'll see that the domers get it—"

"I will," she said gently. Clearly torn between the desire to reinforce his behavior with praise, and a desire to have him leave. She settled for looking toward me as she spoke, and hoping he caught the hint. "The domers will be grateful to you. Without your help, they'd be at his mercy."

He grinned, an expression strangely at odds with the rest of his character. Then finally realized what she was trying to communicate, and bowed out of the room as gracefully as he could. Which was not very.

"Problems with Kost?" I asked.

She looked at the vial and grimaced. "It'll pass. All things pass, with us." She shook her head sadly. "For now . . . it seems to be under control."

Then she looked up at me, with cinnamon eyes so painfully familiar that they sent a pang of lost humanity echoing deep in my soul. But the response that should have been in me wasn't. That part had died. Most of me had died.

"I'm going on to Earth," I said quietly. "I can't change till I get there. Otherwise the translation . . ."

Then the words caught in my throat, and I couldn't say anything. I shut my eyes, and struggled to explain. "Kiri . . . I've done many things in my life. Crazy things, to survive. But never . . . Jesus, I don't know how to explain it. . . ."

"You're still Raayat," she said gently. "This will heal, in time. It'll take time, but it will heal."

"Will it? We didn't test me for that long, you know. Only hours. We should have run tests for days. Should have left me in another form for a week or so, then checked the scans. . . ." I let the words flow quickly, so that fear wouldn't stop them from coming. "What if there's a point beyond which the change is permanent? What if my body can change back, but not my soul? Do you realize how long I've been out of human form?"

She shook her head. I found the courage somewhere to take her hands. They felt strange to me, but the contact was comforting.

"I'm going home," I whispered. "Frederick'll send me there; that was part of our bargain. Not all of it, you understand, I never would have allowed . . . not for that alone—" I took a deep breath and tried again.

"I need my people. I need to be human. I need to surround myself with human beings and nothing else. Maybe it'll work, Kiri." I dropped her hands. "I don't know what I'll do if it doesn't."

She nodded, and I knew by the look in her eyes that she understood. That I was saying good-bye.

"The domers need you," I told her. "Your people need you. You're a sane voice in a species full of . . ." I looked at the door the Marra had passed through, and wondered what I dared say. *Lunacy?* I decided to say nothing. "You belong with them, Kiri. They need you. They need healing. That's your strength."

I was almost afraid to meet her eyes. There were depths in them that I couldn't respond to. Things that called out to the human in me, when that human was dead and buried. And had to remain dead and buried, if I was ever to get home.

"I understand," she assured me. Then she leaned forward—moving slowly, so that I might not back away—and kissed me gently, on the side of my face. A human gesture. It pained me that I lacked the capacity to respond.

"Thank you," I whispered. Then found I had nothing else to say.

But that was all right. Because she understood silence, too.

* * *

One last time, I told myself. *Then you'll be home. You can make it.*

But I shivered as I entered the longship.

The Honn-Frederick were waiting for me in the control center. Eight disarmed warriors, all that remained of those who had come down into the tunnels to get me. Eight bodies that had shed their blood to give me strength and then brought me back, half dead from shock, to the world of men. Eight Honn-Frederick who would die when this was over, because that was the way of the Tyr. Even when it wasn't the Tyr any more.

I sat down in the pilot's chair and tried to stop myself from shaking. Three times now I had taken us through translation, and it hadn't gotten any easier. But now all six captive races were settled on planets that could support them; the longship was deserted except for my small company. This was the last time I would have to die, in order to get us through nonspace.

But what of the other longships, and their prisoners? How will they survive? Have you given so many their freedom, only to turn their longships into floating timbs?

I touched the back of one hand with another, feeling the skin which Kiri had transformed. It was hot, and seemed to be swollen. A problem we hadn't foreseen. If something went wrong—Nothing would go wrong. I had to believe that.

I leaned back into the chair, as far as my rear armaments permitted. And shut my eyes—all of them— and let the voice speak to me.

Brother. Teacher. Lover. Why do you hesitate?

I want to be human again, I answered. I want my *soul back.*

You knew the price when you bargained with me.

My eyes squeezed tightly shut, and I felt my hands shaking.

I didn't understand.

And if you did, the voice persisted, *would you have chosen any differently?*

I thought of the winds on Yuang, beating on fragile glass domes. Of the thousands of people who might have been trapped inside, suffocating slowly when the Tyr failed to come. Starving to death even as they did so.

"No," I whispered. "No."

Then let go of your boundaries. Give yourself to me now, as you did then. The bargain cannot be fulfilled if you remain apart.

Submit myself . . .

Yes.

I had no other choice.

Carefully, I changed my body into that of a Kuol. I could feel my mind slide within the overmind's grasp as I did so, my brain adopting the proper configuration for full Tyrran contact. Then I reached inside myself, as It had taught me to do, and voluntarily stripped myself of all that made me human. Tore down the walls that had protected me, and let the Giver in. Into my body. Into my soul. I felt myself dying, sucked down into darkness . . . but that was all part of it. So was the pain. Personal death was a prerequisite of Tyr. Frederick had learned that the hard way.

At last, there was only flesh. A handful of cells in Kuol formation, no more meaningful than any other such arrangement. And something beyond, that spanned the galaxies. Something that had drawn me in, and would not let me go.

Now, I/we whispered.

Translate.

* * *

I lie in pain, waiting to die. Dreaming, perhaps. Of a voice that comes to me, whispering promises. It can't be real. Can it?

"You have something I want."

I open one eye, and see a misty form leaning over me. Frederick . . . or what once was Frederick, that now is something else. Something more.

"Take it," I breathe weakly. "Take what you want, and let me die." My eyes are wet, and not with blood. "I can't stop you."

"Ah, but you have stopped me." The creature's voice is seductive, caressing, but without the repellent undertone of its predecessor. Perhaps because it has become more human? "You have already, by changing your form. Even if I wanted to take you by force, it would be futile to try while you wear this young a body."

I stare at it in horror, not wanting to comprehend.

"Your intelligence is bound by the flesh it wears," the new Giver of Life explains to me. "Therefore, as much as possible, I assume you must design yourself a body that can support a human identity. Your wolf brain is therefore capable of more intelligence than the average of its kind, although still within that species' natural limits. Your Kuol form, likewise, must maximize the potential for creative thought—"

"No." I suddenly see where its reasoning is headed. "No!"

"That potential must exist in every cell of your body, from the structure of your brain tissue to the pattern of your DNA. To the eggs that were in you, when you first came down here."

"Christ," I whisper, and shut my eyes at the thought of what it wants. "I can't. . . ."

"You can," it corrects me, "and will. You see, I know your price." A hand grasps my shoulder, the familiar claws of Frederick the Raayat on a not-so-familiar armor plate. "The Domes," it tells me. "Now is your chance to save them. Once you belong to me I can translate you through to any nexus. Do those thousands of lives mean so little to you? I would have thought you'd jump at the chance to save them."

"And the war?" I ask it.

"Your people are winning, a tribute to their planning. Now that I contain your memories, I can appreciate so much . . . But now they could lose, just as easily. So much depends on how quickly the Tyr recoups. Which depends, in turn, upon my state of mind. Upon my priorities." He paused, meaningfully "I think you understand me."

"Frederick . . ." I whisper. Visions of Tyrran couplings swim before my eyes—and my altered flesh betrays me, by warming in response. No. No!

"I know your limits," the ex-Raayat tells me. It releases my shoulder, and stands over me. It is no longer the Frederick that I knew, but the core identity of a new Tyr. And it is arguing for the future of its species. "I know your priorities. I know *you*. I contain all of that, along with your memories. And I tell you, you can have your victory, and save the lives you value. And go home. For one simple act, Daetrin Ungashak To-Alym Haal. One last shapechange. To give full creative potential to my children." It pauses dramatically, then adds, "Our children."

Then it steps back, and says simply, "Choose."

* * *

I brought the skimship down in Australia. Near Sydney, where the angdatwa had once stood.

It was rubble, now. The stone spider was dead. Blackened brickwork and half-filled pits revealed where the Tyr's lair once had been, but the war that had taken place in its tunnels had ripped the place asunder. There was no more left of it than there had been of Sydney, when the Tyr were done Subjugating it.

I chose an open stretch of ground well outside the city, and brought the skimship to earth. And limped out, into the hot summer night.

Then I stood there, breathing in the clear Terran air, not quite believing where I was. Still in shock from all I had been through, burdened with a shame over events that now seemed incredible. Perhaps I had dreamed it. Death's proximity could bring on strange visions.

A stabbing pain in my arm convinced me otherwise. The entire limb was a mass of tumors, distended flesh stretched taut across misshapen bones. This from the flesh that Kiri had changed for me, which my Tyrran body would not accept. I had lain in fevered agony for most of our journey to this system, not daring to heal myself because that would mean giving up the human DNA, and remaining Tyr forever. Kiri was galaxies away now, and while mankind might yet attain the nearer stars, such travel as the Tyr had known would always be beyond us. That fevered flesh was precious to me, both as a link to my native species and as a memory of her. And as for the pain . . . it had been there for so long that I was used to it. My only concern had been that the cancer would let me live long enough to get back to Earth. And it had, though barely.

Carefully, I reclaimed my human form.

It hurt; the flesh was unfamiliar. I looked at my hands, and counted the fingers like a nervous mother. Five. Human. Arms where they should be, jointed like a man's. I fell to my knees on the hot, dry ground, remembering. And ran my hands over the blessed soil, like a child discovering earth. I caught up a handful of dirt and squeezed it tightly—real Terran soil!—and then I lowered my face until I could feel its gritty substance against my skin, my whole body shaking as I let the earth cleanse me, as I used it to drive out the memories that were alien and fill my soul with a human past again.

Time would heal even this. That was the wonder of my kind, that kept us sane through the centuries. Time would hide the memories away, and keep them hidden unless I needed them. Time would bring forgetfulness, and thus restore my humanity.

Still shaking, I wept shamelessly into the dust of my native planet.

I had come home.

EARTH

The hraas runs.

Glorying in the feel of this alien world, in the rich, taut mesh beneath its feet. Glorying in sensations it had nearly forgotten, in a tapestry of sounds and feelings that urged it to hunt, to rend, to kill. It could have anything it wanted, on this new and wonderful world, but it did not stop to take stock of its new domain. There was time enough later to listen to the alien mesh-songs, to feel the tremor of life beneath its paws and learn to interpret each shiver, until it could read the beasts of this world as easily as it had once read the beasts of its own. For now, it was enough simply to run—glorying in the vast acres before it, in the knowledge that it could go anywhere—anywhere!—and the mesh would still be whole beneath it.

The hraas celebrates.

Freedom: a heady concept. It hadn't known this joy since its cub-time, a hazy memory of warmth and open spaces too long buried under miles of Tyrran rock. Now, remembering, it gloried in the concept. Its shining coat rippled in a rainbow cascade, over and over again, tasting all the colors of this strange new world. It could hunt, if it wanted to, or choose not to hunt. Kill, if it felt like it, or simply run. The choices were almost too many to contemplate; the joy, almost too much to bear.

The hraas stops.

From the great shattered cities on the eastern coast, to the plains and ravines of the inlands, the hraas had avoided all human settlements. But now, at last, it saw

a man—an Earth-man, native to the hraas' new world—
and it stopped, to look at it. And cautiously approached.

The man seemed to be a primitive, as the humans
measured such things. His coverings were of animal
hide, still scented with the rich perfume of killing. The
merciless southern sun had burned his skin a rich, dark
brown; the Tyr would have given him to the Tekk, had
they taken him. But his ancestors had fled the cities, or
perhaps had never settled there in the first place. The
smell of wilderness was on his skin, a look of wonder
in his eyes.

And sufficient fear to make the mesh tremble with
meaning.

The hraas considered killing him. It considered not
killing him. And it decided that having the freedom to
choose was pleasure enough, for now. There was certainly enough room on this planet for two species of
intelligent hunters, provided they respected each other's territory. And should the humans fail in that regard, the mesh of Earth was sound enough to support
a sufficiently bloody territorial conflict, in the finest
tradition of the hraas' home planet.

With a token growl of warning, the hraas turned
toward the western horizon and continued on its way.

EPILOGUE

EARTH

Humankind changes quickly, which is both the blessing and the bane of daybound existence. Speed means adaptation, potential overadaptation, species deadending, and extinction. It also means rapid recovery. The Earth I returned to was wounded and desolate, a land out of sync with my memories. But now that the Tyr was gone, the healing could begin. I could see the seeds of it already, and I did what I could to nurture the change. I was only one man . . . but hadn't nature designed us to do just this? Hadn't it given us the ability to inspire change, by permitting us to take on whatever form might spark mankind's imagination?

My own people were slower to heal. When I thought I knew who and what I was again, I sought them out. Like the Marra, they lived fearfully, cringing from shadows long after the Tyr had disappeared from their lives. There were few of them left, now, and most were at least marginally unstable. A few had gone back to the old ways with a vengeance, and had hopelessly confused myth and reality in doing so. One of them, an older-bodied fellow haunting the Carpathians, had even talked himself into a garlic allergy.

It was hard to remember that once I had lived that way. Harder still to accept the fact that there was little I could do for them, other than explain that the Tyr was gone—*forever*—and then wait for time to do its healing work.

Then one day she came to me. Without warning, like a summer storm. Sylphlike, drawing her substance from the shadows themselves. For a moment,

493

all I could do was stare at her. And wonder if I were dreaming.

"Kiri?"

She said nothing, just stood there. Young. She looked so young. I had forgotten that.

"What are you doing here?" I stammered.

"Visiting. Just visiting. That's all right, isn't it?"

I was speechless.

"It sounded like an interesting planet. I thought I'd see it for myself. Are you all right? You look a bit—"

"Shock," I muttered. "I'm in shock, that's all."

I wanted to hold her. I wanted to take her in my arms and bury my face in the softness of her hair, and tell her how wrong I was, how I should never have left her behind. How once I had recovered and tried to mend the fragments of my life, I found it could never be the same. Not with her missing. But now she was here. And all I could manage was, "How?"

"On your longship."

"Mine?"

"The *Kamugwa*. It was the only way to get here."

"But that was *years* ago!"

She nodded, and her expression softened. There was a tenderness in her eyes that said healer, and Marra, and woman, all at once.

"You looked like you needed some time," she explained. Then added, "*Kreda* often do."

The implications of what she was saying were only slowly seeping in. "You can't go back."

"Not in this time frame," she agreed.

"But your people—"

"They'll take care of themselves. Personally, I can't think of anything more tedious than watching Kost trying to get one up on the domers. They're infinitely more intelligent than he is. I thought I'd come and see what Earth was all about, hang around for a lifetime or two . . . someday I'll change, and want to do something else. In the meantime, if you don't want me around, it's a very large planet—"

"I want you," I told her, my voice shaking. "But God, I thought I'd lost you . . ."

"Well," she said brightly, "you were wrong."

What could you say to such a creature?

"Look," she told me. "A good *kreda* is very hard to find. I invested a lot of time and memory in you. I had no intention of giving all that up, just because you were going to be in a bad mood for a decade or two."

"You're incredible," I whispered. Loving her, in the way that only a *kreda* can.

"Possibly," she agreed. "And by human standards, certainly. So . . ." She stepped back. "How about showing me around? I haven't been to this part of the world before."

And before I could speak a word, she changed. Put on wings and took to the air—and then hovered above me, waiting.

Then I realized what form she was in, and I tensed.

"Kiri," I began. "I don't do—"

And then I thought, *Cliché be damned. It's only a body, right? So it hasn't got feathers. Don't think of it as a bat. Think of it as . . . a leather bird.*

What the hell.

I made myself the body of a leather bird, and joined her.

DAW

**THEY WERE THE ULTIMATE ENEMIES,
GENERALS OF STAR EMPIRES FOREVER OPPOSED—
AND WORLDS WOULD FALL
BEFORE THEIR PRIVATE WAR...**

IN CONQUEST BORN
C.S. FRIEDMAN

Braxi and Azea, two super-races fighting an endless campaign over a long forgotten cause. The Braxaná—created to become the ultimate warriors. The Azeans, raised to master the powers of the mind, using telepathy to penetrate where mere weapons cannot. Now the final phase of their war is approaching, when whole worlds will be set ablaze by the force of ancient hatred. Now Zatar and Anzha, the master generals, who have made this battle a personal vendetta, will use every power of body and mind to claim the vengeance of total conquest.

☐ **IN CONQUEST BORN**   (UE2198—$3.95)